CHILD OF VANRIS

THE WARDEN'S SON
BOOK ONE

NIKKI McCORMACK

ISBN: 978-1-7367938-8-6
First Edition 2024

Published by
Elysium Books
Bellevue, WA

Written by Nikki McCormack (https://nikkimccormack.com/) Cover Design by Robert Crescenzio (https://robertcrescenzio.artstation.com/) Typesetting and Design by Brian C. Short Editing by Alexander Lockwood

To my excellent D&D storyteller, Kai, without whom I might not have come up with the idea that led me to this character. And to Kasiel, for taking over my life so completely with your story at a time when I desperately needed an adventure.

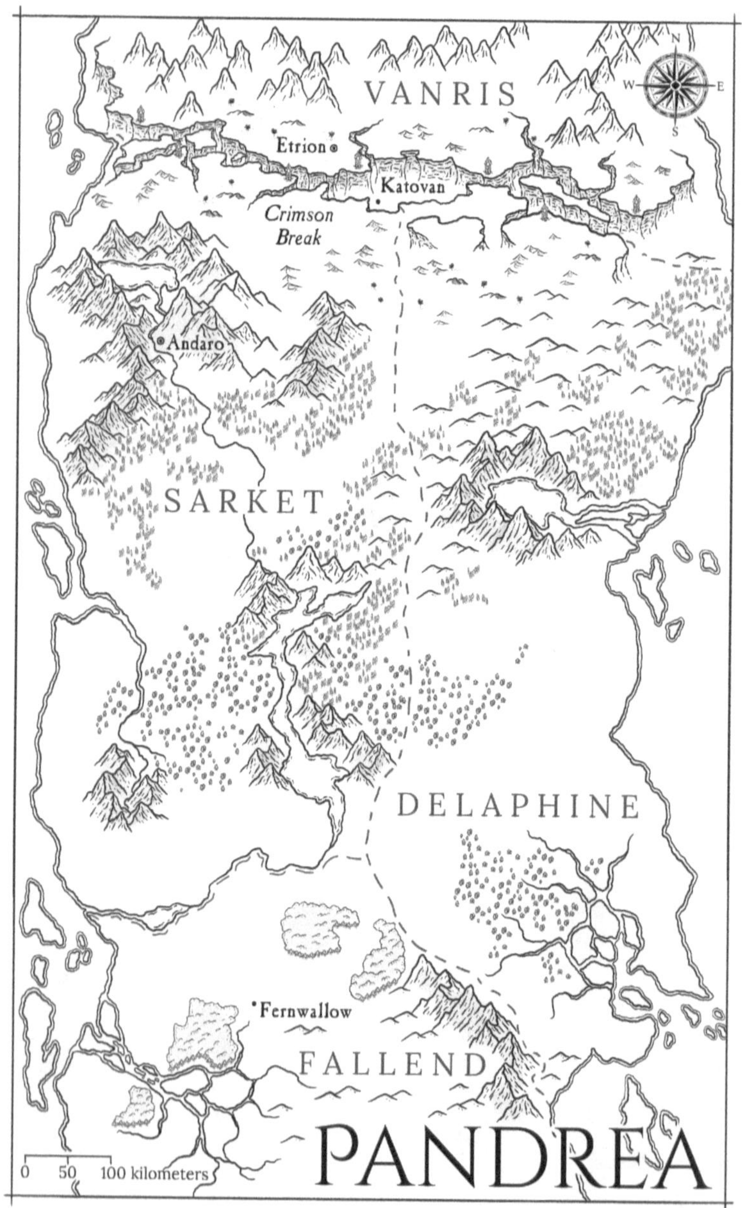

N
W
E
S
VANRIS
Etrion
Katovan
Crimson
Break
Andaro
SARKET
DELAPHINE
Fernwallow
FALLEND
0   50   100 kilometers
PANDREA

Kasiel glanced at the scroll as he picked it up. Notes about telepathy. Or no, this one was mind control. All theoretical, of course. It belonged in the Psychic Disciplines section either way, not on the floor of the study.

Was that a tiny smear of anso nut butter on the corner?

Kasiel chuckled to himself as he wiped at the smudge with a cloth before adding it to the stack of books and scrolls he was carrying. Most he had found strewn haphazardly across the tables in Professor Edmund Danovan's cluttered study. A few, like this one, had migrated to the floor. He wandered through and collected them occasionally. It helped to keep him busy and assuaged his fear that one of the untended candles Edmund left burning might catch a page and set the entire building ablaze.

To Kasiel's right, the door to Edmund's laboratory opened enough for the professor to pop his head out. Dark hair hung unkempt around a face that had acquired a webwork of faint age lines in recent years. Despite the shadows under his hazel eyes that attested to a lack of sleep, an inexhaustible determination shone through in his intense regard.

"I thought I heard my careful organization being disrupted again." A hint of a smile tugged at his lips, mostly hidden by a mustache that needed trimming.

Kasiel grinned as he flipped another book closed and picked it up from the table. "You caught me."

"Well, lad, if you can tear away from this no doubt enthralling task you've assigned yourself, there are some things I'd like you to go get for me."

Someday, Edmund would cease referring to him as "lad." At least Kasiel hoped he would. He would be seventeen in a matter of days, after all. Although, since Edmund had raised him from the age of five, he should probably count himself lucky that he had graduated up from "child" to "lad" somewhere along the way.

Kasiel shifted the load of books to his left arm. "Village or forest?"

Edmund poked an arm out through the opening, a scrawled list in his hand. "Village this time."

Kasiel skimmed the items. A package from the leatherworker's shop. Another from the blacksmith. Ingredients for Edmund's favorite tea from the herbalist. Something from the bakery. Not the usual stops, aside from the herbalist, which was an almost weekly trip. Still, anything that gave him an excuse to visit with the smith's daughter, Danica, was worth the excursion by itself.

He met Edmund's eyes. "What is all—"

"Oh, and could you spare me a few drops of your blood before you go? Leave it on the table there." He turned his hand so Kasiel could see the small vial he was holding behind the list. "The knife over there should do. I cleaned it this morning."

Kasiel took the list and the vial. "Consider it done."

"You're a good lad, Kasiel," Edmund said in his typical, faintly mystified tone before vanishing behind the door again.

The professor said that often. Exactly that way.

"You're a good lad, Kasiel."

He always sounded mildly surprised, as if there were a reason Kasiel should not be a good lad. Kasiel assumed it was due to his lineage. He was Vanrian. A child of the enemy in a war being waged nearly a thousand miles to the north. So far away that the people of Fernwallow rarely gave it a thought. Some days, he could shrug it off. Today it left him with a nagging unease as he hastily stored the books and scrolls he had gathered in their proper places on overcrowded shelves. When he finished, he pricked a finger with the dagger and squeezed several drops of blood into the vial. After sealing it and setting it on the table nearest the laboratory door, he left the workshop and sauntered out along a stone path through the garden.

The garden was well-maintained despite the unceasing efforts of the forest to reclaim that patch of land. Kasiel had trained some persistent vines up and over one section of the arbor. They now cast shade on a selection of plants that preferred a darker, cooler environment. Elsewhere, a consistent regimen of trimming and redirection kept wild vegetation from overshadowing the more sun-loving herbs and vegetables.

Pausing next to a collection of nightshades, he plucked two ripe peppers, then entered the main house through the side door into the kitchen. He dropped the peppers by the sink and snatched a bag of coins from a table in the next room before heading down the hall to his bedroom. It was the tidiest room in the house, even though such cleanliness didn't come naturally to him. His obsession with trying to achieve it was a defensive response to living with Edmund, whose idea of organization was setting anything literally anywhere and later asking Kasiel to find it for him.

He reached for a dark gray cowl folded on a table by his bed. His hand stopped a few inches from it. A drop of ruby blood had gathered on his fingertip where he pricked it with the knife. He brought the finger up before his eyes, staring at the glistening drop.

Research.

For as long as he could remember, Edmund had been collecting occasional samples of his blood for research. The professor never allowed Kasiel in his laboratory and had never fully explained what he was researching. The best he got was some mumbled justification involving trying to understand and prevent an illness Kasiel might be susceptible to because of his race. Edmund had found him one rainy night on the outskirts of Daco, almost a hundred miles south of the Vanrian border. A five-year-old child lying in the muddy water at the bottom of a ditch, near dead from exposure. Though most would have killed Kasiel simply for being what he was, the professor had taken him in.

Kasiel turned to the mirror hung on one wall, sliding jaw-length straight red hair behind one ear. He traced a finger over the scar that formed the upper edge of his ear.

Vanrians were easy to identify on sight, so Edmund told him, because of their slightly elongated ears that tapered to a fine point. When Edmund found him, someone had recently cut the pointed tops of Kasiel's ears off. The mutilation left them shaped more like the ears of any southerner, except the upper edges didn't curl over. Instead, they ended abruptly in ugly, white scars.

Because of the war, the three southern kingdoms that made up the Pandrean Alliance banned the Vanrian people from entering their territories. But in Fernwallow, no one paid much attention. The village was a quaint melting pot of Alliance races. That was why Edmund raised him here. But no matter how different the people here might look from one another, they all had those naturally rounded ears. Kasiel might pass for being southern born at a glance, but his scarred ears wouldn't fool anyone under closer scrutiny. He would never be the same as them.

With a sinking sensation in his chest, he brought his hair forward to cover his ear again and absently sucked the drop of blood from his finger. When the wound appeared disinclined to continue bleeding, he pulled on the cowl and left the house.

Edmund warned him repeatedly over the years to keep his lineage secret. His hair was long enough to hide his shortened ears, but the hood of the cowl made certain of it.

What would the villagers do if they knew he was Vanrian?

Kasiel preferred to think they wouldn't do anything at this point. He grew up here. This was his home. But Edmund apparently believed otherwise, and that made him reluctant to get too close to anyone. These people would never be his family. Except for Danica. One day, he would tell her. She was the one person he knew would never reject him.

Fernwallow was a fifteen-minute walk from their house. The dense evergreen forest that embraced their home dwindled and gave way to an open field bordering the village. His boots slipped and squelched along the wagon tracks, made muddy by spring rains. A few modest houses, one with a pigsty alongside it, and a communal storage barn marked the edge of the village.

A couple of locals called out greetings as he passed.

"Hey, Kas!"

"Afternoon, Kas!"

He waved politely in return, all the while searching for a particular face, his unfortunate ears tuned to the sound of a particular voice.

The leatherworker was across from the smithy. Kasiel went there first, pausing out front to glance at the building on the other side of the street. Someone ducked out of the window of the smith's shop. He cracked a knowing smile, a thrill of anticipation surging through him as he turned and entered the leather shop.

"If it isn't Kas Danovan. I was expecting your father today."

Kasiel shifted his hood back a fraction and offered a nod to the leatherworker standing on the other side of the counter. "Afternoon, Barden. Edmund's busy with his research."

"No surprises there, I suppose." Barden stepped back from the counter, bending over to dig around for something behind it.

Barden was one of the original founders of Fernwallow. His darkly tanned skin matched much of the leather hanging on the walls. Kasiel liked the way his eyes crinkled when he smiled. Within those deep lines was etched the story of a happy life. He was one of a handful who referred to Edmund as Kasiel's father, even though they looked nothing alike. Edmund never corrected them, so Kasiel didn't either. In fact, he rather liked it. Edmund was the only father figure he had ever known. It was nice to imagine it was real now and then. That he could be a young man like any other, rather than the product of a hated race whose people he didn't remember. That he could go about each day without worrying that his ears might expose his shameful truth.

"I've got a special package for you today." Barden lifted a parcel wrapped in woven hemp and set it on the counter. He held up a hand when Kasiel opened his pouch of coins. "No need for that. Edmund paid for this in advance."

Kasiel pulled the string to close the bag. He gestured to the package. "What is it?"

Barden's grin had a distinct edge of conspiracy to it. "You'll have to ask Edmund when you get home, won't you?" He leaned to one side, peering past Kasiel, and pushed the package across the counter. "I'd love to catch up, but it looks like someone's waiting for you."

Another jolt of eager anticipation shot through Kasiel. He glanced over his shoulder in time to see someone stepping away from the leather shop window. A flash of dark skin and darker hair. Grabbing the package, he blurted a quick thank you, glancing at his reflection in the window on the way out. Thin. Pale. Not the most impressive specimen, but maybe that didn't matter.

Kasiel shoved open the door. When he closed it behind him, he found the blacksmith's daughter, Danica, standing alongside the shop. A sheen of sweat drying on the mahogany skin of her face and muscular arms told him she had been working the forge with her father moments ago. She wore her long black hair woven into myriad small braids, all pulled together into a thick mass that she tied back to keep it away from the fires.

She held a wrapped bundle up between them. "Father said you'd be coming for this."

Kasiel struggled not to stare at her lips.

She had kissed him unexpectedly a few weeks ago. His first kiss. Most likely hers as well. He had expected her lips to feel soft and warm. What he hadn't expected was the way it affected all of him, waking up every nerve from the top of his head to his fingers and toes. They had been friends most of his life. A companionship born of necessity, as the only two around their age in the village, which developed into a genuine bond over time. The kiss hadn't really changed their friendship in theory, but it had left him with an awkward craving to explore beyond that.

What if she didn't want to kiss him again? Had it merely been a moment of curiosity for her, now satisfied? He had yet to muster up the courage to ask.

"I..." His gaze dropped to the long, thin bundle she

held, skipping intentionally past her lips and the curves of her chest. With the kiss fresh in his mind again, he couldn't think of anything to say to her. "Thanks."

"Don't be like that." She stomped one foot in a manner that reminded him distinctly of an impatient foal.

The gesture made a crack in the shell of his insecurity. He breathed a soft laugh, making himself meet her dark, warm eyes. "Like what?"

"You're usually so easygoing, but you've been distant around me ever since…" She paused, biting at her lower lip. "Well, you know."

The uneasy shifting of her feet told him she felt at least as awkward about it as he did. A realization that emboldened him enough to ignore the giddy flutter in his stomach and take a step closer. "Since?"

She arched a brow, lips pressing together as though he had annoyed her, but a smile tugged at the corners of her mouth. She copied his step forward, lowering the bundle to her side, and stared into his eyes.

"I see I'm going to have to jog your memory." Her gaze sank to his lips.

Danica once told him how much she loved the rich red of his hair. This felt like the right moment to remind her of that, especially since there was no breeze to potentially expose his ears. He pulled back his hood and leaned a little closer, captivated by the hopeful sparkle in her eyes. Were they going to kiss? Here in the street where anyone, her father included, might see them?

Someone shoved Kasiel's shoulder, spinning him away from Danica, then grabbed the front of his shirt and slammed him back into the wall of the leather shop. The impact knocked the breath out of him. His head bounced painfully against the wood siding.

"What do we have here?" The stocky stranger brought his nose close to Kasiel's, his breath coming out hot and foul from somewhere within his overgrown beard and mustache.

Straining to get his breath back, Kasiel turned to the side to escape that awful stink. Blackness started closing in around the edges of his vision. It wasn't the creeping black of approaching unconsciousness, but more like the threat of something dangerous—something powerful—moving through him.

A blond woman with a thick scar running down one cheek grabbed a handful of Kasiel's hair and yanked it back, peering at the side of his head.

"His ears are round," she snapped.

The man holding him shifted back a few inches, using his free hand to press Kasiel's head against the wall as he peered at the exposed ear. "Nah. Look." He grabbed Kasiel's ear, yanking painfully at it with calloused fingers. "It's been cut. Long time ago, looks like."

The pain of the initial impact gradually abated, but the tightness in Kasiel's throat and chest made it so he still couldn't draw a full breath. Resisting the threatening blackness, he attempted to twist free of the stocky man's grip. The man tightened his hold and slammed him into the wall again.

"Let him go!" Danica grabbed the stocky man's arm, trying to pull him away from Kasiel.

Years of working the forge with her father made her strong enough that she almost succeeded before another man, this one tall and thickly muscled, engulfed her in a bear hug from behind, lifting her off her feet. "This don't concern you, kitten."

The stocky man leaned in, assaulting Kasiel with his rank breath again. "How old are you, boy?"

Kasiel glanced around at the three strangers, searching for anything that might offer insight into what they were after. He wanted to believe they were nothing more than miscreants looking to make trouble, but their interest in his ears and age suggested a more targeted purpose. They were well-armed and dressed in pieced-together chain mail and leather armor. Danica, despite her considerable strength, still hung in the air, struggling to break free of her captor. If she couldn't fight one of them, he would only get hurt trying to do so. Recognizing that he was useless to help either of them brought a burning to his cheeks.

"Get your blasted hands off my daughter before I cleave your skull in two!" Garrick stormed out of the smithy with a heavy battle-axe in hand, looking more than ready to put it to good use.

The brute holding Danica set her feet on the ground and let go, backing away from the fierce figure of her enraged father. The blond woman stepped around to Kasiel's left side. Her strong fingers dug into his shoulder. The stocky man turned and moved to his right, clamping a vice-like grip on his biceps, reinforcing the message to stay put. Kasiel's package from the leather worker and the one from the smith that Danica had been carrying both lay in the mud.

The blond woman made a subtle beckoning gesture to the towering, black-haired man who had been holding Danica. He strode over and traded places with her on Kasiel's left, his large hand engulfing Kasiel's shoulder. The woman took a few slow steps toward the armed smith. Danica moved close to her father, her wide-eyed gaze homing in on Kasiel.

"What's this about?" Garrick demanded, his arms thick and muscular enough to swing the heavy axe with deadly force, whether or not he had any actual skill with it.

"You have my apologies." The blond woman took another step toward Garrick, holding her hands up in a gesture of peace that Kasiel considered far too late in coming. "We didn't mean to get your daughter involved in this. Our business is with the young man."

As she spoke, Barden came out through the door next to them. He moved around to stand beside Garrick, a short sword ready in one hand. Several other villagers were emerging from nearby buildings or stopping in the street, many armed with weapons or tools that would serve as such in a pinch. In a remote place like Fernwallow, the people had to stick together to survive, and they appeared ready to do so now.

"Kas is a resident of Fernwallow." Garrick's deep voice rang out, loud and resolute, the conviction in it eliciting nods from several villagers. "If you have business with him, you have business with all of us."

Danica, looking calmer now and dangerously determined, drew a dagger from her belt.

The woman raised her hands a fraction higher. "I can see we've got your hackles up. Let's cool things down a bit. My companions and I have been on the road a long time." She turned to Kasiel then. "Kas, is it? Why don't you join us at the tavern? We can talk this out in a civilized fashion?"

Kasiel raised his head and lifted his lip in a slight sneer, emboldened by the villagers gathering around them. No one needed to know that he was shaking apart on the inside. "You attacked me. I think we're past the point where I might have been willing to speak with you."

"Go home, Kas."

Meeting Garrick's eyes, he found the courage to move away. The two men holding him tightened their grips for a second, then let go at a nod from the blond woman. Kasiel grabbed his packages out of the mud and walked over to Garrick. His legs were trembling stalks of mush, but they supported him somehow.

"Edmund needed a few more things in town." He spoke in a low voice, pulling the list from his pocket.

Garrick's gaze didn't move from the three strangers. "Give the list to Dani. She can pick up the rest for you and bring it out to the house. Go home. Tell Edmund what happened here."

A chill swept down Kasiel's spine at the grim expression on the smith's face. Garrick was one of Edmund's closest confidants. The only other person in Fernwallow who knew Kasiel was Vanrian. Had he seen the strangers looking at his ear?

Kasiel handed the list to Danica before turning to scrutinize the three mercenaries—at least that's what he suspected they were—who had attacked him. He wanted to remember them, not only so he could try to avoid this trio going forward, but so he might recognize their kind in the future. They were a fierce-looking bunch, decked out in mismatched leather and mail armor, with no shortage of lethal weapons at hand. If they had intended to kill him, it would have been easy enough to accomplish.

What did they want with him, then?

His gaze moved up from their gear and he met their eyes, realizing with a sudden chill that they were taking measure of him too. Remembering him, perhaps so they could have an easier time finding him again. The interest they showed in his cut ears couldn't be a positive thing, though he honestly didn't know enough about it to fully understand the reasons why. He understood Vanrians weren't allowed in the southern kingdoms because of the war, but why would anyone come hunting for them in a village so far from the front? And why did it matter how old he was?

He wrenched his gaze away, a shiver sweeping through him as he pulled his hood up, turned his back on the trio and the villagers, and started toward home. It was difficult keeping a steady stride when he wanted to run. It was also hard not to cast a last glance at Danica. Was she disappointed by how easily the strangers had overcome him?

He resisted the urge. It might be a mistake to emphasize his interest in her any more than he already had in front of them. He would see her, for better or worse, when she came to drop off the rest of Edmund's items.

He didn't head straight toward home. Instead, he cut up to the next road, hoping to throw off the strangers if they were watching him. Once he was out of their sight, he turned for the house. None of the villagers, all of whom knew where he lived, questioned the choice. That struck him as confirmation that it was the right one. He broke into a jog, trying not to slip in the mud as he passed the last house at the edge of the field, eager for the calm logic he knew the professor could bring to the chaos spinning in his head.

•

A short time later, Kasiel knocked on the door to the laboratory with one trembling hand.

"A moment," Edmund called from within.

Kasiel shifted from one foot to the other, staring at the door and willing it to open. He had made himself take a few minutes to catch his breath and drink some water after his run to the house. Now he waited what felt like years for Edmund to appear, though he suspected only a matter of seconds passed before the professor opened the door enough to peek out.

"You're back earlier than I…" He trailed off, his gaze lingering for several heartbeats on the two packages covered in dried mud. Then he looked up, and whatever he saw in Kasiel's face drew him from the room. He shut the door behind him and placed a hand on Kasiel's shoulder. "What's happened, lad?"

Kasiel blurted out everything. As much as he wanted to be something more than a lad to Edmund, he knew he sounded like a frightened child. Tears streamed silently down his cheeks by the time he finished.

Edmund took the packages from him, set them on a table, and returned his hand to Kasiel's shoulder. Deep lines furrowed his brow. "You said they pulled your hair back to see your ear and commented on it being cut?"

Kasiel nodded, afraid to speak lest his silent tears scale up into full, infantile sobs.

"And one of them asked your age?"

Kasiel nodded again.

Edmund pulled Kasiel into his arms and hugged him. Such gestures of affection from the professor were rare, especially now that he was no longer a child. Kasiel gritted his teeth, struggling not to cry harder. It felt safe here in Edmund's arms, safe enough to let everything go, which made it remarkably difficult not to.

"I am sorry, my boy. I was a fool to believe that they might never discover you here."

With his nose pressed close to Edmund's shoulder, Kasiel could smell the acrid tang of the experimental alchemical components the man had been working with. He breathed deep, letting it sting his nostrils and distract him from the emotion of the moment. After several seconds, Edmund pulled back and gently turned him with a hand on his arm to face the table.

"Your birthday may still be a couple of days away, but perhaps it would be wise to let you open your gifts a little early."

Kasiel eyed the packages. He wanted nothing to do with them. Looking at them brought back that horrifying flash of panic and pain from being slammed into the building by the stocky mercenary. "I don't—"

"Trust me," Edmund said, a hint of command in his voice.

Kasiel took a deep breath, wincing at the flare of pain in his back when he did so. Reaching forward to take hold of a package hurt, too. His muscles seized, resisting the motion.

"I'll make you some tea when we're done here. A brew that will ease the pain and help you sleep."

Kasiel answered with a small nod.

The package on top was the one from the smith's shop. He pulled away the hemp wrapping to reveal two blades, one a short sword, the other a dagger. They were simple and functional. Beautiful in their practicality. He lifted the sword, ignoring the protest in his back, to appreciate the precise balance between hilt and blade. He was not a skilled swordsman. Not even a particularly good one really, but he had been joining Danica at her lessons with some regularity of late. The weapon would not be entirely useless in his hands, and that despised sense of helplessness faded while he held it.

"The other." A hint of a smile lifted Edmund's tone.

Kasiel placed the sword on the table and opened the next package. Within, he found a full set of sturdy leather armor, as functional and simple as the blades.

He turned to Edmund. "This is… It's amazing. Thank you." The threat of more tears stung his eyes. He willed them back with marginal success, wiping away the one that escaped.

"You are a son to me, Kasiel, though I may not show it much of the time. You are also becoming a man now, and, while I wish I could always keep you safe by myself, I know I cannot keep you hidden away forever. These items will give you confidence and the ability to protect yourself better, especially if you should choose to continue your lessons with Danica."

Something twisted in Kasiel's gut. He had been a fool to believe he might hide his activities from the professor. "You know about that?"

Edmund chuckled. "Of course, I do. I have no objection to you learning to defend yourself, though I would prefer you to be honest with me about the time you spend with Garrick's daughter." He took Kasiel's hand and gave it a firm squeeze. "Now, there's something I must do to make these ready for you, but they will be yours to use by morning. First, however, I'll prepare you that tea."

Kasiel found he could muster a smile now. It was tremulous, but still an improvement. "No need. I'm familiar with the brew."

"I imagine you are." Edmund kissed his forehead. "I'll leave you to it then and start preparing these items."

Kasiel watched him disappear through the door with the weapons and armor in his arms. As it closed, a barrage of questions popped into his head about what had happened during the day that only Edmund was going to have the answers to. He would have to ask them later. For now, he would prepare the mixture, but he wouldn't brew the tea yet. No matter how his back and head hurt from being slammed into the building, he wanted to be awake and clear-headed when Danica came by with the remaining items on the list. He needed to see if she looked at him differently now.

For a few minutes, he searched the shelves for a book about Vanris. He had never found one in the professor's collection before, so it didn't come as a surprise when his efforts now yielded the same results. Finally, he pulled down a tome on local flora and carried it into the house with him, determined to look for new ways to deal with the forest encroaching on their garden.

Kasiel startled awake sometime later at a knock on the door. His sudden movement sent a streak of pain through muscles in his back that had stiffened during his brief sojourn. The book on local flora lay open in his lap. He set it on a side table and lifted himself from the chair with a low groan.

At the door, he hesitated with a hand resting on the latch, a tickle of dread making the hair stand up on his neck. He was probably being paranoid, but he held off opening it yet. "Who is it?"

"It's me, Dani, and my father."

Her bright voice chased away his fears. He popped

the bolt and opened the door.

Garrick's eyes scanned the room before settling on Kasiel. "Glad you're being cautious, boy."

Kasiel's cheeks colored. Did the smith have to call him a boy in front of Danica? He did his best to ignore her nearly inaudible giggle as he stepped to one side to let them in. Garrick strode into the house like he owned it. Something he did everywhere he went from what Kasiel had observed. Danica stopped next to Kasiel and offered him two bundles, a small one that smelled of herbs and a large one that smelled of sugar and cream.

"The little one is Edmund's tea. The other one's from the bakery. It smells delicious. My mouth has been watering all the way here."

His eyes met hers as he reached out to take them, searching for any indication of her feelings toward him now. Her smile faltered. Was she worried for him, or was it something else?

Then the weight sank into his arms, and he grimaced.

"Oh." She snatched the parcels back from him. "I'm so sorry. I forgot. Let me carry these to the kitchen for you."

"I can handle…" Before he could finish objecting, she was on her way to the next room. "Uh, thank you."

"Where's Edmund?" Garrick flipped open the book Kasiel had left on the table, scowling at the pages.

Edmund strode into the room before Kasiel could answer.

"I'm here. I understand we have important things to discuss."

Without so much as a glance his way, Edmund bustled through the living area and herded Garrick into the private sitting room. The door closed behind them. Kasiel nearly jumped out of his boots when Danica spoke next to his ear.

"Well, are we going to eavesdrop?"

He hesitated. Under other circumstances, he would rush to engage in mischief with her. Unfortunately, this time the two men were discussing events that involved him and might say something he didn't want her to hear. She was already taking up a position near the edge of the sitting-room door, however, where the crack would allow more sound to come through. With a soft sigh, he shuffled over to join her, scuffing his feet across the floor all the way.

Would his aching back slow him down if they had to move away in haste? Did it matter?

Danica smiled as he crouched next to her and placed a hand on his arm. A warm, calloused hand. Regardless of what Edmund and Garrick said in that room, he was suddenly more than willing for her to hear it if it meant she would maintain that gentle contact a little longer.

Closing his eyes, he focused on the warmth of her touch radiating through him and the voices beginning to speak beyond the door.

"I assume Kas told you what happened in town," Garrick began.

Kasiel could imagine a slow nod from Edmund in the moment of silence.

Garrick continued. "Something's changed, Edmund. Those mercenaries had Pandrean Alliance insignias on their armor. The Alliance found out about the boy somehow. They must suspect who he is. What he is. They wouldn't go to this much trouble if they didn't." A solid thud shook the wall as if the smith had punched it. "But how, by Havaad's fires, did they figure out he's here?"

Kasiel could feel Danica's eyes on him, perhaps questioning why anyone would come searching for a random, unremarkable boy from Fernwallow. Or maybe she wondered, like he did, who and what he was that the Alliance would even give him a second thought. Their words implied the uncomfortable possibility that

Edmund knew far more about his past than he had ever let on.

Kasiel kept his eyes closed.

Edmund exhaled heavily. "This is my fault. Twelve perfect, peaceful years made me complacent. I should have been more careful."

"You know what needs to be done, Edmund. If the Alliance suspects who he is and Vanris gets word of it…" Garrick trailed off.

Something in his tone sent a shiver through Kasiel. Danica's hand tightened on his arm.

"It's not that simple anymore." Edmund's words sounded heavy, as though he struggled to carry them past his lips. "Kas is like a son to me."

"But he isn't your son," Garrick stated forcefully, then his tone softened. "I understand how you feel. We've all grown to like him. The whole blasted town cares about him. You should have seen them coming out to defend him from those bastards. But we knew this day might come when we brought him here."

"Yes," Edmund drew the word out with audible reluctance. His voice gained conviction when he continued. "Yes, but I'm not willing to give up that easily. These mercenaries who accosted him, are they still in the village? We need to know who hired them, why they're looking for him, and what led them to Fernwallow."

"It won't change anything," Garrick's voice was as hard as the hammers he used to shape metal. "We agreed on this before we came to Fernwallow. That agreement was made for a reason. We can't afford to ignore it now."

"We don't yet know why this is happening." Edmund's tone was equally firm. "It gains us nothing to panic and rush blindly ahead. The lad's life is at stake, not to mention everything we've been working toward. I was close to a breakthrough, I'm sure of it."

At Edmund's words, Danica wrapped an arm around Kasiel, pulling closer to him and resting her head on his shoulder. If the circumstances were different, he would be flying high at that moment, but apparently his life was at stake. That was something of a mood dampener.

"You're right." Garrick sounded exhausted now. "I'll find them and bring them out here tomorrow. I doubt they'll wander far now that they believe they're within reach of their target. We won't decide what to do until we have more information."

Kasiel and Danica separated when they heard footsteps approaching the door and hurried to sit in two chairs near the kitchen. Garrick emerged, his steps heavier now than they had been going in. He avoided looking at Kasiel as he gathered his daughter and ushered her from the house. Danica cast one worried glance back at Kasiel before Edmund closed the door behind them.

The professor vanished into the kitchen for a few seconds. When he returned, he gave Kasiel's shoulder a squeeze. "Brew your tea."

Kasiel said nothing. He stared at the front entrance a moment longer, aware of Edmund wandering back into the kitchen. The side door off of the kitchen opened and closed. The professor no doubt returning to his laboratory. All those unanswered questions would have to wait again. For now, his heart heavy with the weight of uncertainty, Kasiel would do as he had been told and brew his tea.

limbing up from sleep was like wading through hip-deep water. It barely seemed worth the effort. Then Kasiel rolled onto his back and the tenderness from his forced collision with the leather shop wrenched him free of the clinging murk. He opened his eyes, squinting at the brightness that stabbed between the cracks in his shutters. The crisp light of a new morning. He had slept clear through the night.

For a few minutes, he lay there, staring at the ceiling. Everything about the attack in the village played back in his mind, followed by eavesdropping on Garrick and Edmund later, the distress from what he overheard colliding with the pleasure of Danica's touch. He even remembered brewing his tea. He just didn't remember it being this potent the last time he used that blend. How had he gotten to his bedroom? The one thing he didn't recall was ever leaving the chair in the front room after he sat down to drink the tea and read.

For now, all that mattered was dragging himself out of bed to face a new day. One different from all those that came before. Today, he knew Edmund was keeping secrets about his past that were a lot more significant than he could have ever imagined. The assault in town wasn't a random act of aggression by a group of bored mercenaries. It had been a targeted attack by people hunting for him specifically. At least, that was what Garrick appeared to believe. Edmund had sounded less certain. Either way, the professor had to tell him the truth now, didn't he? As he had said himself while talking to Garrick, Kasiel's life was at stake.

He threw off the covers and sat on the edge of the bed, taking a few deep breaths to stretch the aching muscles in his back. It wasn't as sore this morning as he expected it to be. He could probably thank the tea for that. Edmund knew many such medicinal brews.

After washing up at the basin on his dresser and throwing on trousers and a shirt from the folded stack of passably clean clothes on a chair in the corner, he stepped out into the hall. A pile of weapons leaning against the wall in the entry stopped Kasiel in his tracks. That sword came from a sheath on the blond woman's back. The axe next to it belonged to the large mercenary who had grabbed Danica. Each weapon took its proper place on the person who carried it in his memory. It surprised him that he could recall those details so distinctly. The encounter had left quite an impression.

He ducked out of sight alongside a bookshelf in the hall when he heard the sitting-room door open.

"Thank you for your time. You may return to the village for now." The icy edge to Edmund's voice undermined his polite words.

"We're not done here." Kasiel recognized the voice of the stocky man who had slammed him into the wall, his tone heavy with threat.

"Go on." Garrick's voice and words were carefully neutral. "I'll find you later, after the professor and I have had a chance to talk this through."

The mercenaries said nothing more. Kasiel peeked briefly around the bookshelf to see them gathering their weapons. He pressed back against the wall, his heartbeat thumping in his ears as though a herd of horses galloped through his head. He stayed there after the front door closed, hoping Edmund and Garrick might reveal more of what had transpired while he was sleeping.

"It's late for Kasiel to still be in bed, isn't it?" Garrick asked in the lengthening silence.

"I added something to his tea last night to help him sleep. I imagine he'll wake up soon." Edmund sounded distant, distracted.

An itch of unfamiliar anger rose in Kasiel toward the man who had raised him. Not the usual annoyance at not getting his way, but a more potent sense of fury. Knowing that Edmund had withheld knowledge of his past from him made the fact that the man had drugged his tea into a dire betrayal. He steadied himself, fighting the urge to storm out and demand answers. Anger rarely led to anything productive. Edmund taught him that. A realization that only fed his growing resentment.

"This is worse than we expected," Garrick said, worry weighing down his words. "Vanris will have gotten word of this by now. I don't think we have a choice. Letting the boy live could put all of us in danger."

The smith's words sent a chill through Kasiel. He couldn't have heard that right. Garrick couldn't be suggesting that he needed to die, could he?

Edmund's voice picked up a slight shake when he spoke again. "I don't know if I can do it. I raised him, Garrick. It wasn't supposed to turn out this way, but Vanrian or not, he has been like a son to me for twelve years."

"Don't do it then." Sympathy took the edge off Garrick's naturally gruff voice. "Perhaps we could pay the mercenaries to take care of the problem. They'd rather do that than drag him all the way north anyhow. Far less hassle. We can ask them to make it as quick and painless as possible."

"No." Edmund's prompt rejection pulled a soft sigh

of relief from Kasiel, but the feeling didn't last. "They might prefer to kill him, but they're being paid to present him to the Pandrean Alliance council alive. Those fools haven't considered the risk of taking him so close to Vanris. It falls on us to make certain the Vanrians have no reason to come hunting for him. I'll add something stronger to his tea tonight. He deserves a peaceful and painless death, at the very least. Once the mercenaries report back that he's dead, Vanris will have no reason to get involved."

Kasiel could barely breathe. Blackness crept in at the edges of his vision, the way it had when the mercenaries attacked him. He struggled to push it back.

"For what it's worth, I'm deeply sorry, Edmund. It's a shame you couldn't complete your research, but we'll find another way. I dread breaking the news to Dani, though. She's grown quite fond of the lad." Heavy footsteps moved toward the front door. "I'll make sure the mercenaries don't come around again today. I can give you that much."

"Thank you, my friend."

Kasiel dared to peek out again. Garrick stood by the door, casting a mournful gaze at Edmund as if he were the one in imminent danger of losing his life. He remained that way for several seconds, looking as though he wanted to say something more, before giving a nod and trudging out. The moment the smith was gone, Kasiel darted across the hall to his bedroom, easing the door shut. He stripped down to his undergarments and crawled into bed, trying to slow his breathing and think. An effort made more difficult by the threat of that ominous darkness.

Edmund couldn't truly mean to kill him. How could the professor, the only father he had ever known, consider poisoning him the night before his birthday? A peaceful and painless death was as final as any other.

Not much of a gift.

There was a knock on his door. "Kasiel?"

He curled on his side and stayed silent.

"Kasiel?" A firmer knock.

This time he groaned something that might have been a groggy yes.

The door opened and Edmund entered. He sat on the edge of the bed as Kasiel rolled onto his back, wincing with genuine discomfort.

A hint of sympathy softened Edmund's regard. "How do you feel?"

Kasiel rubbed his eyes and blinked at the light as if adjusting to it for the first time that morning. "Hurts. Not too bad, though."

"Good." Edmund nodded thoughtfully. "I need to go to town for a few supplies. I want you to keep the doors bolted and stay inside until I return. Those mercenaries are still around, and I don't trust them."

Kasiel almost perked up at that and had to remind himself that he had supposedly just woken up. Maintaining his drowsy ruse, he muttered, "What do they want with me?"

Edmund gave him a reassuring smile. A lie. Not the first, apparently. "Nothing. It was merely a case of mistaken identity. They're looking for a particular Vanrian fugitive, but we both know you're not the one. They've been stubborn about letting you go, given that Vanrians aren't permitted south of the Break, but they'll move on soon enough."

Lies. All lies. Kasiel furrowed his brow. "Are you sure?"

Affection warmed Edmund's smile. He brushed Kasiel's hair back from his face with gentle fingers, something he had stopped doing a few years ago. "I'm certain."

That warmth resonated in Kasiel. It gave him hope.

Edmund couldn't look at him that way if he wanted him dead. Perhaps, if they talked through the problem, they could find another solution for whatever was happening here.

"This is all because I'm Vanrian," Kasiel began tentatively. "You told me once that you would explain the research you've been doing with my blood when I was older. Does this have something to do with that?"

Edmund tilted his head, a hint of moisture giving a shine to his eyes. Then his gaze shifted to the cut ear he had exposed by moving Kasiel's hair and his expression closed up. He stood and walked to the door. "Perhaps it is time to tell you more about these things. I've been working on a new tea blend. We can try it out this evening while I explain what my research is all about."

Panic swept through Kasiel as Edmund set up the perfect opportunity to poison him, and his hope disappeared. He felt sick. Somehow, he summoned forth a drowsy smile. "I'd like that."

Edmund glanced back at him again. His smile looked forced this time. "You're a good lad, Kasiel," he said in a soft voice.

He was glad the professor left then. Those last words broke something inside Kasiel. A lifetime of mentoring, of kindness and gentle instruction. It couldn't end like this, could it? It had to mean more than this to Edmund. He knew it did because the man said as much. What was so dangerous about the possibility of Vanris learning he was here that made the need for his death eclipse the twelve years Edmund spent raising him as a son?

He clenched his teeth and sat up on the edge of the bed. Hot, silent tears slipped from his eyes. Anger burned in his chest, fighting for dominance with that intense heartache.

He had to leave. But where could he go? His whole

life was here in Fernwallow with Edmund and the people of this place. He had exactly zero experience in the world outside the village and surrounding woods. It was never that important. Edmund always made it feel as if nothing beyond this quiet, simple life mattered. Had the professor had an ulterior motive in discouraging curiosity and wanderlust in him? Or was he simply becoming suspicious of everything now that his world was falling apart?

Kasiel got up and dressed again. He picked up a backpack he used when hunting in the woods for various ingredients for cooking or brewing teas. After tucking a change of clothes into it, he went about the house, gathering other necessities. Bandages and salves for wounds, herbs for medicinal teas, a few cooking supplies, and snares for catching small game. He also grabbed flint and steel from on top of the hearth. Surviving in the wild would be a lot easier with a fast way to start a fire.

A satchel Edmund used for transporting books between the house and study lay in one corner of the front room. He threw that over his shoulder and filled it with bread, dried meat, and fresh vegetables from the garden. The two packs weighed a little more than he liked, but he had no experience with surviving on his own. Anything that could help him stay alive long enough to find someplace new was a good thing, especially since he had no notion where that might be.

He stood in the garden, staring at the house, trying hard to focus on immediate needs and not the overall situation. What else should he have?

Slowly, he turned toward the building that contained Edmund's study and laboratory.

Weapons and armor. Edmund had taken the blades and leather armor out to the laboratory to do something with them. He knew where the professor hid the laboratory key. He had known for years. Retaining Edmund's trust always struck him as more important than indulging his burning curiosity to see what was in that room. Trust was no longer a factor.

Fresh determination lengthening his strides, Kasiel approached the building and pulled the key to the front door out from under a loose stone at the edge of the path. He unlocked the door and entered, tossing the key to the floor in a small show of defiance. He paused, fighting the urge to pick it back up as he looked around the study. A room full of books that he always found warm and welcoming. It had an unfamiliar gloom about it now. A sense of hostility.

Swallowing against the knot in his throat, he strode to a bookshelf in the far-left corner and slid out a fat blue tome. Third in from the right on the fourth shelf from the top. The laboratory key rested in a notch carved into the shelf beneath the book.

He placed the book on a table and set the backpack and shoulder satchel on the floor. His hand shook as he picked up the key. Such a simple object. To consider using it would have been an unforgivable act of deception and defiance only yesterday. Now it was a desperate effort to save his own life.

He went to the door and slid the key into the lock. It clicked over easily. Leaving the key there, he entered the large, dark room. There were no windows, but a narrow skylight at the peak of the arched roof let in a band of morning light filtered through the boughs of evergreens. He walked out and lit one of the many candles in the study, then carried it in with him, his index finger tucked through the loop on the side of the candleholder.

The light jittered, dancing with the tremble of his hands. Flasks, books, scrolls, and an array of tools, both strange and familiar, lay strewn about the room. Journals and parchments littered the tables, covered in hastily scrawled notes. Papers full of diagrams and symbols were tacked up on every bare patch of wall. Maps too, of unfamiliar places. The Crimson Break was noted on the corner of one map. Another two, hanging side-by-side on one wall, were labeled Eastern Vanris and Western Vanris. A glance at the books revealed several volumes about Vanris, the Pandrean Alliance, and the war. Books on subjects Kasiel had asked about often over the years only to be told repeatedly that the Professor didn't have any such volumes in his collection.

His sword and dagger lay on a long table next to the armor set. The hilts of both weapons now had a set of strange symbols upon them. Markings that looked as though someone had burned them into the material that wrapped the grips. Those same symbols appeared scrawled on notes and diagrams around the room.

At first glance, the armor looked untouched, but a more careful examination revealed more symbols burned into the inside of the various pieces. What were the markings and why had Edmund put them there? Another mystery that would have to remain unsolved. Every minute wasted was a minute closer to Edmund returning before he made his escape.

Kasiel set the candle on the table and put on the armor. It took far too long for his liking. He had worn similar armor in practice with Danica, but his hands hadn't been shaking like this when he fastened the pieces on.

Danica.

He couldn't think about her. Everyone here was part of his past now. His future was…

His future was empty, the road ahead a solitary, bleak one.

Clenching his teeth, he finished donning the armor and slid the sword and dagger into the sheaths on the belt he had found sitting next to them. With those things done, he reached for the candle and froze. Spread out on the other side of the candle from where the armor had lain was a section of pale hide, tattooed with symbols like those on the armor and weapons. Kasiel picked up the hide and brought it closer to the light. It was soft and supple. Familiar somehow.

It was human.

He dropped it on the table and took a step back. With his eyes adjusting to the dim light, he could now see a rack in the corner that had more tattooed sections of skin hanging on it. Human skin. Vanrian skin.

That was one of the few things he had learned about Vanrians, though not because Edmund had taught him. He had overheard talk in the tavern once about their tattoos. The conversation stuck with him mostly because of the curiosity and unease it stirred in him when the two travelers took a brief interest in him.

"Lad over there looks a bit like a Vanrian whelp, don't ya think?"

The speaker's companion eyed Kasiel severely and nodded. "Does a bit. Not like to find one of them bastards this far south though, eh?" He turned back to his drink. "Ever wonder what all them tattoos they have mean?"

The first man took a long swallow from his mug and clapped it down on the table empty. "There's one I seen on a lot of the male corpses. Two lines curving hard to the right from a kind of star at the base. You've seen it, right? Always figured it meant they couldn't get it up."

The two men had laughed heartily at that, though Kasiel hadn't understood the joke back then. He had been thirteen, and a sheltered thirteen at that. When he asked Edmund about the tattoos they mentioned, the professor diverted him to another subject. He never pursued it again after that.

Kasiel lifted the candle and looked around the room with a more critical eye this time. Vanrian symbols.

Books on Vanris. Maps of Vanris and the Crimson Break. Vanrian skin.

He glanced down at the finger he had pricked for Edmund the previous morning like so many times before.

Vanrian blood.

He abruptly threw up alongside the table. Then he turned and hurried from the building, pausing long enough to grab his packs from the floor in the study. Once he was outside, he ran. Away from his home. Away from Fernwallow. Any direction would do.

Kas!"

Kasiel woke up shivering in the dim light of early morning. It wasn't that cold out, but the damp ground made for a miserable bed. He had been dreaming of Danica. About that day she caught him by surprise with a kiss after sword practice. Only, in the dream, when she leaned close to him, the three mercenaries had appeared. They pushed her away, then threw him down and started kicking him, shouting that they would skin him alive and bleed him dry. Danica had screamed his name in the dream, the desperation in her voice snapping him awake.

"Kas!"

He bolted upright and peered around. Lying on the lumpy ground had made his back stiff and sore, but he couldn't let it slow him down. That was Danica's voice, and he was confident that he wasn't dreaming it this time.

He almost called out to her, but rustling from another direction warned him she wasn't the only one out searching for him. Crouching low, he crept up close to the tree he had slept under and snuck a quick look around the trunk. As he scanned the woods, he adjusted the sword belt at his waist. He had kept it on all night despite how uncomfortable it made his already less than pleasant sleeping arrangements.

"Kasiel!"

That was Barden, the leatherworker. How many villagers were out searching? They had caught up with him fast. Edmund must have raised the alarm almost immediately after he got back from the village. Kasiel had dared hope it would take the professor more time to determine that he had run and get a search organized. He had also slept longer than he meant to. When he curled up on the cold, damp ground last night after traveling much of the day, he honestly hadn't expected to fall asleep at all.

He needed to get away from here, and quickly.

Kasiel started to turn, and someone slapped a meaty palm over his mouth. A thick arm wrapped around his chest, pulling him back into a wall of solid flesh. He flailed, struggling to free himself, until the stocky mercenary who had slammed him into the leather shop wall the day before came in from the side and slugged him in the gut, knocking the wind out of him. He sagged in the large man's arms, wheezing through the hand covering his mouth.

The blond woman came into view and glanced up at the man holding him. "Bring him. Keep him quiet." She looked at the one who had punched him. "Grab his things. We need to get out of here."

She took a step away, then stopped and met Kasiel's eyes, now teared up from the blow to the gut. Her smile made him hate her, drawing that unnerving blackness in at the edges of his vision. Part of him wanted to let that unknown darkness have him.

She tapped the end of his nose with one finger. "Nice of you to make this so easy."

Smirking to herself, she walked off in the opposite direction of the searching villagers. The man who had punched him stepped in again. The one holding him moved his hand away from Kasiel's mouth. Before he could scream, the stocky man shoved a twisted cloth in his mouth and tied it tight behind his head. They made quick work of binding his hands, too. Then the stocky man removed Kasiel's sword belt and followed in the direction the woman had gone. The big man threw Kasiel over one shoulder with a grunt and went after the others.

It was like being laid over a brick wall. Kasiel wasn't short by any measure, though he had a way to go before his muscles filled out. Even so, it was humiliating, being tossed over someone's shoulder like a sack. The greatest insult was to his already brutalized gut. He struggled, doing his best to make carrying him difficult as they moved away from the calls of the searching villagers. The big man grumbled complaints under his breath, but he continued onward, resolutely ignoring Kasiel's efforts to break free.

Though Kasiel was still thrashing about, he was already wearing down when they reached a group of four tied horses waiting among the trees. The big man tossed him off, watching with a hint of amusement as he hit the ground on his already sore back, grunting through the gag.

Kasiel glanced at the blond woman, hoping for a glimpse of maternal kindness.

She caught his look and answered it with a wicked grin. "We're supposed to deliver you to the Alliance council alive. Don't mean we have to do it gently." Her grin vanished and she spat at him. "Vanrian scum."

"Tie him over the saddle on the spare horse, Nix?" the big man asked.

"Blazes, I don't give a shit," the woman, Nix, snapped back.

"Don't want him to ride with you, hips grinding together in the saddle?" The stocky man smirked at her, gyrating his hips crudely.

Nix raised one side of her lip in a snarl. "You think that's so funny, don't you, Loak?" Her hand sank to her sword hilt. "You'd better drop it, or I'll show you how funny it isn't."

Loak bared his incomplete array of teeth in a broad grin.

Kasiel yearned to contribute to the conversation. If only to express his desire not to be tied over the horse's saddle, but they appeared uninterested in any opinions he might have on the matter. They wanted him alive, though. In a desperate way, he could consider that an improvement over his situation in Fernwallow.

The big man heaved Kasiel up again, carrying him to one of the horses.

"Better let him sit upright in the saddle," Loak said. "I've seen a man asphyxiate tied over the saddle for too long. Didn't matter so much that time, but we don't get paid if this little bastard dies on us."

The big man set him down beside the horse and gestured to the stirrup. Kasiel cast a wistful look at the surrounding trees. A snort brought his attention back to the man.

"Try it."

The eagerness in his eyes convinced Kasiel to abandon any notion of running for now. He put his foot in the stirrup, grabbing hold of the pommel awkwardly with his bound hands, and pulled himself up into the seat. The animal wore only a halter and lead rope. Nix maneuvered her mount close enough to take the lead. As soon as the two men joined them, she kicked her horse up to a trot. Kasiel's focus turned from coming up with ideas for escape to trying to maintain his balance. He had minimal riding experience, and his aching back protested the rough gait. Since he wasn't going to get a say in the situation, he bit down on the gag and held on.

They kept going throughout the day, not letting him off the horse again until the sky grew dim with the onset of evening. A few breaks along the way allowed the horses to recover or gave his captors an opportunity to relieve themselves. The three mercenaries ate and drank while they rode. Kasiel, who hadn't eaten since the sparse meal he'd had the night before, listened to his stomach growling, hoping one of them might hear it too and take pity on him. By the end of the day, thirst had grown more insistent than hunger, especially with the gag making him salivate. Pain had also become an overwhelming presence. His legs, back, and rear hurt from unaccustomed long hours on horseback.

Despite not drinking, his bladder ached with need by the time they finally stopped for the night. He hesitated in the saddle as the other three dismounted, afraid he might lose control of that insistent pressure in his groin if he moved. A hand grabbed his shirt and yanked him off the horse, letting him fall to the ground. He hit face first, the skin of his cheek splitting on a sharp rock. By some miracle, his bladder didn't let go.

Dazed, he looked up to see Loak standing over him, hands on his hips.

"Ha! I'm impressed. Figured that'd make you piss yourself. Guess you've earned a chance to do it in a more dignified manner." He turned toward the larger man. "Lorin, take him out to piss."

The big man, Lorin, quietly obliged, lifting Kasiel to his feet. Warm blood trickled unchecked from the painful wound on his cheek. Once he had relieved himself, a process made more difficult than necessary by his bound hands, Lorin escorted him back to where the other two already had a fire burning. Nix was pulling food out of her saddlebags. Loak sat digging through Kasiel's pack, tossing the food he had brought over to Nix.

Lorin stopped Kasiel near the fire and pointed to the ground. Kasiel sat, though he might have been better off walking the stiffness out of his muscles. He didn't have the energy left for much activity or the will to defy them while the pain in his cheek was sharp and fresh. Now that his bladder no longer ached, he trembled with hunger and that desperate need for water.

Lorin sat next to him and took off the gag.

"You don't have to—"

Lorin cut him off with a knife to his throat, the blade's edge pressing hard against his skin.

Nix cast Kasiel an icy look. "You want to eat, you keep quiet. Otherwise, the gag goes back in, and you go hungry. Got it?"

Kasiel nodded as best he could with the blade against his throat.

"Good." Nix inclined her head to Lorin, who returned the dagger to its sheath.

"Not so impressive for the alleged son of The Warden," Loak commented, tossing Kasiel's change of clothes out in the dirt.

"Who's—"

Kasiel cut himself off this time when Lorin grabbed for the dagger. He held up bound hands in a gesture of surrender and let his curiosity burn. The mercenaries ate in silence, far more interested in the meal than any conversation. They made Kasiel feed himself with his hands still bound, giving him less than a quarter of the food they took for themselves. The blood coming from the wound in his cheek eventually stopped on its own, though the stinging remained on top of a deeper ache from the impact.

For the next several days, Kasiel's situation changed little beyond a deepening misery. The mercenaries split the contents of his bags between them, abandoning his extra clothes in the mud when they left that first camp. They let him wear his leather armor, something he appreciated less on the two days it rained all day, but his belt with the sword and dagger they tied to Nix's saddlebags. Most days, if he behaved himself, they provided a scant meal in the morning, deliberately weakening him to keep him compliant. An unfortunately effective tactic. He longed to know what the Pandrean Alliance wanted him for but gave up trying to talk to them after the third night, when his efforts earned him a bloody stripe across the throat.

He tried to dismount immediately when they stopped each night to avoid being yanked out of the saddle and dropped again. Nix preferred to loathe him from a distance, but Loak appeared to enjoy inflicting pain on him and looked for opportunities to do so.

Fortunately, Lorin handled him most of the time, taking him to and from his horse to the fire or to relieve himself. The big man spoke little and rarely went out of his way to harm Kasiel. Nor did he make any effort to keep him from getting hurt. The Alliance council apparently wanted him alive. But alive covered a broad range of conditions. It looked like he would arrive at the low end of that range. The Pandrean Alliance had headquarters in the capitals of Delaphine and Sarket, the two northern kingdoms. The closest one was still a few weeks' travel north of Fernwallow. He wasn't sure he could endure another few days of this.

By the evening of the eighth day, Kasiel could barely think. Weakness from lack of nourishment and little sleep, given the many discomforts that kept him awake, sank him into a semiconscious fog. They hadn't allowed him to move much when he was out of the saddle, keeping his muscles perpetually stiff and sore from riding. The binds on his wrists had rubbed his skin raw in places, but that was only another pain within the haze. He was becoming so accustomed to being in the saddle that, by the end of the first week, his body learned to stay upright while he drifted somewhere between sleep and waking.

He was in this semi-awake state when they stopped at the end of that day. Hands slammed into his side, shoving him from the saddle. He hit the ground with bone-jarring force. Burning fury burst from some hidden reserve, driving him up to his knees, but he didn't have the strength to take it farther. Instead, he knelt there, wavering in the dirt, yearning for the flash of rage to return.

"Does that piss you off? Make you want to hit me?" Loak was in the mood to torment him, leaning down to stick his nose in Kasiel's face. "I'd love to see you try, you piece of Vanrian shit. Want me to free your hands? You can give it a go."

Now, when he was weak as a day-old kitten, the bastard finally offered to take his bonds off. Coward.

Kasiel stared up at him, loathing sweeping through him. He longed to spit in his bearded face, but the gag prevented it. All he could do was glare.

Loak barked a laugh. "Finally growing a spine, you Vanrian mongrel?" He punctuated his words with a punch to the gut.

Kasiel curled over, struggling not to vomit with the gag in his mouth. Though the mere thought made it more likely. He squeezed his eyes shut, tears forming in the corners as he fought for control. A soft, whooshing sound reached his ears, followed by a meaty thwack in front of him. Kasiel opened his eyes to see Loak lying there with a spear through his neck, his eyes popped wide in almost comical surprise.

"Shit! Lorin, don't let them take the boy!"

Nix sprinted toward Kasiel, weapons drawn, a lethal fury in her eyes. She looked as if she meant to kill him. He almost welcomed the idea.

Kasiel struggled to his feet, hoping to at least die

standing, as several hooded, well-armed figures charged into the camp. Three of them ran at Lorin. Someone lunged into Nix before she reached Kasiel, ramming her into the side of his horse. The animal panicked, spinning its powerful hindquarters into Kasiel, and slamming him back into a tree. It felt as if he hit the tree and the ground simultaneously, though he knew that wasn't possible. A different blackness closed in around him, the noise of fighting fading into the background.

ushed voices tugged Kasiel back to awareness. He was lying on something soft. His head hurt from the impact with the tree, but not any more than the rest of him. He would be hard-pressed to pick one spot on his body at this point and say it was the worst.

The voices were both male and unfamiliar, speaking Pandrean Common with thick accents.

"He needs to rest. Tell the others to crack a stone and settle in for the night."

"With pleasure, Ahninveth." There was a hint of friendly teasing in that last word followed by the sound of a door closing. Someone's name, perhaps?

The image of Loak with a spear in his neck surfaced in Kasiel's mind. He snapped his eyes open and came up on one elbow. The pain in his head flared and his arm gave out with an agonizing protest.

"Easy, tehnaak. You've been through a lot." A young man around his own age stepped into view, his pale features lit by the flickering light of a lantern. "I'll help you sit up."

Kasiel stared in dumbfounded silence as the youth leaned in to arrange pillows behind him and helped him shift into a sitting position. The young man had slender features and light brown hair that hung down below his cheekbone on one side. On the other, three tight braids ran along the side of his head, exposing an ear that tapered to a fine point. The top of a symbol tattooed on his neck in deep green peeked out above the collar of his shirt. He wore simple leather armor and carried no weapons that Kasiel could see.

Once Kasiel was upright, the stranger sank into a chair next to the bed, resting one ankle across the other knee.

Kasiel stopped staring at him long enough to take inventory of their surroundings. They were inside a tiny cabin that looked abandoned. A pile of well-used blankets made for a soft bed on the worn wooden frame underneath him. Darkness beyond the window told him it was night, but offered no insight into whether it was still the same day. Several voices drifted in from outside, though not clearly enough for him to make out what they were saying. The gag and wrist bindings were gone, and, for the moment, no one appeared intent on trying to kill, maim, or restrain him. Someone had also cleaned the wounds on his wrists.

He looked at the youth again. "You're Vanrian."

The young man grinned. It was a disarmingly open and friendly expression. "You're quick," he teased with a wink. "I'm Jethan."

"I'm—"

"Hahren Cavenos," Jethan stated with disconcerting certainty.

Kasiel shook his head slowly. "Kasiel Da..." He almost gave Edmund's last name. Little more than a week ago, he would have done so when introducing himself to someone new. Now? He lowered his gaze, fighting the twist of sorrow in his chest. "Just Kasiel."

"Ah. I suppose they would have given you a new name. Kasiel works for now then." He picked up a metal cup full of steaming liquid from the rickety table beside the bed and offered it to Kasiel. "Tath found herbs among the mercenaries' things that she said would make a good restorative brew."

Kasiel tentatively took the cup. "The herbs were mine." He sniffed at it. "Smells a little off."

"Sharp nose." Jethan said, as if praising a student. "She added something to ease your stomach so we could get a decent meal into you without making you sick."

Fear twisted Kasiel's gut, but he had already been unconscious and at their mercy. They could have easily killed him before now if that were their goal. He took a few sips. It tasted like Edmund's brew, with a hint of something else that left a pleasant aftertaste.

Someone knocked on the door and opened it a crack. "I've got the food you asked for. Is he awake?"

The feminine voice triggered a disjointed memory of waking up in pain at some point prior to this. Someone had placed a flask to his lips, and that voice had told him to drink. He remembered nothing after that.

"He is. Come on in, Tath. We were appreciating the excellent tea you prepared."

A woman entered. She looked a little older than Jethan, with long red-blond hair braided back, and finely pointed ears like his. As she approached, she inclined her head to Kasiel.

"My lord, I hope the tea is acceptable."

It took Kasiel a second to realize she was addressing him and not Jethan, who sat watching him expectantly. "Oh. Yes, it's fine. Thank you."

The aroma of cooked meat and vegetables reached his nose from a curved metal plate she carried, making his mouth water. His stomach took control of the conversation, growling enthusiastically. Kasiel's cheeks grew hot. Jethan sputtered out a laugh that he hastily transformed into a fake cough.

Tath colored as well, her lips pressing together to hold back a grin. She handed Kasiel the plate and stepped back. Before he could thank her or taste the food, the door flew open, swinging wide enough to strike the wall with a thud, dislodging an old bird's nest from a corner of the room. It landed on the floor with a damp splat. A man with long blond hair stormed in, holding a familiar belt up before him with Kasiel's sword and dagger in it.

Jethan hopped to his feet, intercepting him a few strides from the door. "What's going on?"

The man's accusatory gaze jumped to Kasiel. "These weapons have Vanrian symbols on the hilts." He held them up for Jethan to see.

Even from the side, Kasiel could see a slight souring of Jethan's friendly expression. "Give them to me."

The blond man handed over the belt. On each cheek, running parallel to the line of his jaw, he had two stacked lines of small dark blue symbols tattooed in a blocky style. Faint age lines around his eyes suggested he was a fair bit older than Jethan, though the youth appeared to be the one in charge.

Jethan gestured toward the door. "Go. I'll handle this."

The man stood his ground. They switched to a language Kasiel didn't recognize for a brief, heated exchange. Then Jethan flipped back to the familiar Pandrean Common tongue.

"That's an order." A compelling power of command strengthened his voice this time.

Tath strode to the exit, taking the other man's arm as she passed and ushering him out. She shut the door behind them. Jethan stood facing partly away from Kasiel, inspecting the weapon hilts for several seconds. Kasiel's stomach grumbled into the silence.

"Eat," Jethan encouraged, coming back to sit in the chair again.

He did. Some demands required little persuasion. This was by far the best thing he had eaten since his last meal at home in Fernwallow. Or maybe he was just that hungry. Jethan continued to inspect the markings for a few minutes and Kasiel got the sense that the other youth was delaying to let him get some food in his stomach. When he began shoving food into his face a little less aggressively, Jethan looked up from the weapons, regarding him thoughtfully.

"Who did this?" he asked, holding the dagger hilt up in the light.

"The man who raised me. The weapons were a gift for my seventeenth birthday. There are similar markings inside the leather armor." He nodded toward the armor currently piled on a chair in one corner, trying not to think about how thoroughly he must have been out for them to have removed it without waking him.

"Interesting execution." Jethan set the weapons aside. "He was researching us." It was less of a question than a conjecture. "Trying to figure out if there's a connection between our tattoos and our abilities. Although he has a long way to go, given his usage here." His eyes narrowed as he considered Kasiel. "Maybe he was trying to awaken you."

"To what?"

"Nothing. We can't do anything about this right now. Our mission has to be our priority."

Kasiel sniffed, catching the smell of mold from the cabin now that his plate was clean. "And that mission is?"

"I thought that would be obvious." Jethan's smile returned. "To bring you home."

The word "home" sent a wave of nostalgia coursing through Kasiel. Longing for the home he had known most of his life. For the simplicity and peace of the life he had there until the day the mercenaries arrived. The room blurred around him as tears stung his eyes. He pressed the heels of his hands to his temples, trying to stop the memories and a surge of pain that wasn't physical this time.

Jethan stood. His tone, when he spoke, was gentle. "Why don't I go get us a bottle, tehnaak? When you're ready, we can crack a stone together and talk some more."

Afraid to try speaking past the lump in his throat, Kasiel answered with a slight nod. Once the door closed behind Jethan, he pulled his knees to his chest and wept. A flood fueled by emotion, exhaustion, and pain that he feared would never stop. Despite how long it took him to wrestle his emotions back under control, the Vanrian youth hadn't yet returned. He leaned his head against the wall and dozed until the sound of the door opening woke him.

Jethan entered, closing the door behind him. He held up a lumpy round object that looked like a rock but had a tapered top with a cork in it. He also carried two mugs that he set on the table, smiling at Kasiel conspiratorially.

"You've never lived until you had Vanrian Black Mead." He sat in the chair by the bed and worked the cork free with the edge of a dagger. "I've waited a very long time to crack a stone with you, tehnaak."

"You carried mead all the way from Vanris?"

Jethan stopped short of pouring the liquid and handed the bottle to Kasiel. To his surprise, while the weight of the contents was about what he expected, the container itself added almost nothing to it. Oddly, it had the texture of rock too. He now understood where the phrase "crack a stone" came from.

"It's stoneglass. A type of alloy that preserves the flavor like glass yet has the durability of steel and the weight of a feather. But the best part is what they put inside." Jethan took the bottle back and poured some in each mug. He put less in the mug he handed to Kasiel. "You're not in top shape, tehnaak. Best not to overindulge."

Kasiel accepted the mug and sniffed the contents. Edmund always discouraged him from partaking in alcohol. That seemed as good a reason as any to try it. This had a powerful scent to it. He took a sip. The flavor attacked his tongue, offensive in its boldness, and burned in his throat. A silky, sweet aftertaste followed it down, as if apologizing for the initial assault. What he quickly came to appreciate about it, however, was the way that, after a few drinks, he felt warmer and calmer.

"What does tehnaak mean? You've called me that several times now."

Jethan chuckled. "You look like you're bracing for an attack."

The warmth spread up Kasiel's neck into his cheeks. "Honestly, I figured it was some kind of insult toward non-Vanrians."

Jethan smiled, though he averted his gaze now, a hint of color rising in his face. "Ah. No. Quite the opposite. We have a practice in Vanris known as spirit bonding. As soon as possible, after a child is born, they're paired with another child born at or near the same time through a ceremony that creates a powerful connection between them. From that point forward, the two are considered spirit siblings, or tehnaak. They're raised and educated together. It's done to ensure that everyone has someone there to support them throughout their life. A partner with whom they can share struggles and victories. It's especially useful in military families. When the parents of one child are called to fight, the family of their tehnaak will care for both children. If one child should lose their parents, they are automatically taken in by the other child's family."

Jethan met his eyes then, a hint of sorrow stealing away some of his brightness. "You and I are each other's tehnaak."

"But..." Kasiel tried to think around the confusing

fog of exhaustion and mead. He had a brother, sort of. He wanted to be excited about that. Mostly, it made him feel even more lost. "I was five when Edmund found me south of the Break."

"Found?" A flicker of anger shadowed Jethan's expression. He nodded to himself and said, "You weren't quite five. But I've recovered you now. Our connection is why I'm in charge of this mission."

Kasiel dodged the jumble of emotions wrapped up in this revelation and grasped at something he had been desperate to ask about since Loak first mentioned it. "You must know who my actual parents are, then. The mercenaries said I was the son of *The Warden.*"

Jethan poured more mead into their mugs, giving himself a much larger serving this time. "The Pandrean Alliance has a lot of names for your father. The Bane, The Waking Nightmare, Beast of the Break, Warden of Vanris. Vanrians know him as High Lord Arhk Cavenos, Dhomvalen of Vanris and Right Hand to Khevarin Seylin Markanis."

That was a lot to take in. "What's a khevarin?"

"Khevarin would be like a queen or king in the southern kingdoms. And, before you ask, dhomvalen translates as warden or protector." Jethan took a swallow of his mead.

How was he supposed to feel about all that? Whoever Arhk Cavenos was, he sounded impressive. Kasiel didn't feel like the son of someone so remarkable. Then again, if this was all true, it might help explain why so many people had suddenly taken an interest in him.

A spark of anger flared in him. "Why now?"

"Good question." Jethan took a longer drink of his mead this time and set it down on the side table before answering. "When you were taken, those in power felt there was too much risk in sending Vanrian soldiers beyond the Break. They didn't know where to find you or whether you were even alive. They couldn't justify sending a unit wandering aimlessly around the southern kingdoms without something more to go on. Over the last year, our spies in the Alliance territories started catching wind of rumors about a Vanrian fugitive living in a remote part of the kingdom of Fallend. A youth about the right age to be the dhomvalen's missing son. When the Alliance started taking an interest in the same rumors, your father wanted to send a unit to investigate and extract you if the rumors turned out to be true. He convinced the khevarin it was necessary, so here we are."

Jethan's use of the word "taken" by itself was enough to shake Kasiel. Edmund always framed it as if he had been abandoned. Cast away by his people. His parents. But, like many things the professor told him, that appeared to be untrue.

Kasiel shook his head and downed the rest of his drink in one swallow. He wasn't sure how much of the room's spinning was the drink and how much was an overload of information, but he was having trouble focusing. He rubbed at his temples, trying to ease the sensation.

Jethan winced apologetically. "A little too much for one sitting, huh? I can't imagine what it's like learning who you really are for the first time this way." He took Kasiel's mug from him and set it on the table, then leaned in closer, his brow furrowing. A hint of anger flashed in his eyes. "That cut on your cheek could have used a few stitches when it was fresh, but it should heal all right." His gaze flickered back to Kasiel's hair, and he reached out. "May I?"

Understanding, Kasiel moved his hair back on that side, showing the cut ear. For a second, Jethan's hand closed into a fist, his jaw tightening. Every hint of kindness in his expression vanished. He looked like he could hurt someone. Anyone. The anger in his dark gaze sucked the warmth from the room. Then the youth's demeanor shifted again. Sorrow swept in with something else. Guilt, perhaps, judging from the way he averted his eyes when he leaned back.

"You should get some rest, tehnaak. You look like you've been camping on death's doorstep. I'll be outside if you need anything. Anything at all." He picked up the two mugs and the half-empty bottle before trudging out.

The voices continued beyond the door, still low enough that Kasiel couldn't make out their words, though he got the impression from the sounds he could hear that they were speaking Vanrian. Loneliness folded itself around him like a dark blanket that gave no warmth. He ached for the comfort of a familiar face now more than he had even when he was bound on the back of a horse with the mercenaries. Perhaps that had to do with spending the last hour looking into the eyes of someone who should have been a dear friend, had he grown up in his birth home.

What had Jethan said? Something about learning who he really was for the first time. He had less idea who he was now than he'd had that morning. Until recently, he would have called himself the son, in every way that mattered, of Edmund Danovan. But Edmund had, for reasons he still didn't understand, been prepared to kill him rather than let the Alliance or Vanris have him. And yet, he didn't feel like the son of this High Lord Arhk Cavenos. The name meant nothing to him. He might as well have never met the man at all.

He shifted down in the bed, lying back to stare up at the dark roof. The murmur of voices outside became strangely soothing.

Why now?

Jethan had answered the question, but it still didn't make sense. Why risk this group of people going after a son he hadn't seen in twelve years? Perhaps he should find it flattering that the man wanted him back this badly. And what of his mother? Jethan hadn't mentioned her. What did it say about him that he hadn't thought to ask?

Could a father still yearn for a son who was unlikely to remember him? Jethan came across as genuinely pleased over being reunited with him, even though he couldn't possibly remember their supposed childhood together any better than Kasiel could.

Maybe that meant there was something to this spirit sibling connection. He had felt curiously safe in the other youth's company, considering he didn't know him. If he wanted to find out, this was his chance. They apparently intended to take him all the way to Vanris. Back to his birth father. Did he want to go there? Where else could he go?

When it came down to it, he was now a Vanrian fugitive in a hostile land. At least with this group, no one appeared to mean him harm, for now.

The first rays of early dawn light crept in through abundant holes in the rotting thatch roofing. Kasiel stared at them for a time, watching the dim glow gradually brighten. He desperately had to pee, but a fierce anxiety had set in at the idea of stepping out of the house into a group of strangers. And they weren't your usual strangers. After talking to Jethan, he got the impression these people knew more about his origins and who he should have been than he did. For a time, he considered peeing in a corner, but the stench of urine would undoubtedly overpower even the mold in this place.

Finally, he pushed back the blankets and got up, doing his best to move normally despite the weakness and pain. After a few seconds wasted pondering his armor and ultimately deciding it was too much work to put on, he eased open the front door. The deceitful thing wanted no part of his attempted stealth. Its hinges squealed loudly enough that the four individuals sitting around a campfire in front of the house stopped talking and looked at him. One he recognized as Tath, and another was the tall blond who had stormed into the house during his chat with Jethan.

All four inclined their heads.

A young man with white hair greeted him with, "Good morning, Lord Hahren."

"Don't... I'm not..." Kasiel took a deep breath and reconsidered his approach. "Please, call me Kasiel."

Almost as one, they looked to Kasiel's left, and he turned to see Jethan striding up alongside him. The youth glanced around at them and gave a slight nod, giving his support to Kasiel's choice of names.

Four more people were still sleeping, two of them women, all bunched close together for warmth. They had nothing covering them. Kasiel turned back to the tiny house behind him, recalling the cozy nest of blankets he had slept in.

"Your blankets," he murmured.

"Don't make a big thing of it," Jethan said as he stepped past. "We unanimously agreed that you needed them more than we did. I don't know if you've looked in a mirror lately, but there's not much left to keep you warm." He gestured toward a log set near the fire. "Have a seat. We were about to cook up something to get us going for the day."

Kasiel glanced toward the trees. "I just need to..."

The tall blond got up as if he meant to escort Kasiel, but Jethan put out a hand to stop him. "He'll be fine." He nodded to Kasiel. "Be careful. The footing's rough in the bushes there. And if you go too far, you might run into a deposit Kince left earlier that could probably knock most creatures unconscious with a single sniff," he added with a teasing smirk.

The blond settled back down, casting a scowl at Jethan. Kince, Kasiel suspected.

He nodded and walked away from the camp, picking his footing with care given his weakened physical state. Jethan didn't appear concerned that he might try to bolt, but was that a matter of trust, or because he knew Kasiel wouldn't get far if he did try to run? Either way, in his current state, he had little choice but to put his faith in the Vanrian youth and his companions.

He almost regretted not asking for help as he stumbled through the rougher footing, nearly faceplanting in the bushes twice. His legs weren't only weak from lack of nourishment, but also stiff and awkward from the mercenaries refusing to let him walk around much when he wasn't on horseback. Still, the best way to gain his strength and mobility back was to eat and to use his body. Better to begin working on that right away in case he needed to make a run for it at some point. Besides, he'd had more than enough of someone watching his every move over the last eight or so days. He would manage on his own.

Kince was watching for him when Kasiel emerged from the trees again. The rest of the group was awake now, two of them cooking while others picked up the camp and checked on their horses. They had the four mercenary animals tied to the line among the Vanrian mounts. The mercenaries had no need for them now.

All the Vanrians had shoulder-length or longer hair except Jethan, whose jaw-length hair was the shortest among them. Tath and another woman who had long white-blond hair wore theirs pulled back into a couple of loose braids. The rest wore their hair in styles like Jethan's, with multiple braids worked tight along the scalp on one or both sides. Every one of them showed off those distinctive pointed ears. For all the years he had spent hiding his cut ears, he had never been more horrified by the idea of someone seeing them than he was now.

Tath noticed him watching and gestured to an empty spot on a log near the fire. "Have a seat, Lord… Sorry, Kasiel."

He sank down on the designated log, happy to get off his feet. "Thanks. I'm not *lord* anybody."

She didn't argue the point, but a hint of sympathy showed in her smile as she sat beside him, holding a small carved wood container in her hand. She twisted off the lid. "This will help the wounds on your wrists. And it should make the cut on your cheek finish healing a little better." She lifted his head with her fingers under his chin to peer at the healing cut across his throat, her touch at once gentle and professional. "This one's beyond the point that I can do much for it." She stared at it a moment longer. "I'd like to kill those bastards again," she muttered after a few seconds, releasing his chin.

It was unexpectedly comforting to hear that moment of hatred for the mercenaries in her voice. Jethan and Tath displayed a protectiveness toward him he never would have expected from strangers. It made him feel marginally safer in their company. As safe as he could, given that he still barely understood how all of this had happened to him.

As she took his arm in one hand and dipped the fingers of the other in the yellowish salve, he noticed the tattooed symbols on her wrists that peeked out of her sleeves. Looking around at the others, he caught glimpses of more tattoos showing at the edges of collars or sleeves, or sometimes in plain sight on someone's face or hands. In fact, Tath had a symbol tattooed in light bronze under her right eye that he had missed in the dim cabin. The symbols must have significance, though he wasn't yet comfortable enough to pry.

Whatever the salve was, it stung enough to draw his attention back to the wounds. The pain faded quickly, replaced by a pleasant cooling sensation. When she had slathered it over the injuries on both sides, she grabbed a strip of clean cloth and brought it toward one wrist.

Kasiel jerked his arm away so fast it made Tath jump.

She placed a gentle hand on his arm. "This is to cover the wounds."

Of course, it was. Feeling foolish, Kasiel gave her

his arm back and glanced up to find Jethan watching them, his jaw clenched. The other youth managed a strained smile when he noticed Kasiel looking his way. The rest of the party was making a pointed effort not to watch. What did they think of him? Weak and wounded. Flinching away from a simple bandage. Probably not what they expected from the alleged offspring of a man who had earned names like the Beast of the Break and Warden of Vanris.

The memory of having his wrists bound by the mercenaries was so stark and fresh he could still feel the ropes pulling tight. A moment that put him at their mercy, of which it turned out they had none. His shoulders ached from long days and nights with his hands tied in front of him. He wouldn't let anyone do that to him again. Not if he could do anything to stop it.

Something in Jethan's troubled regard and Tath's gentle manner told him they suspected what had caused his violent reaction. But what about the others? Then again, why did he care so much about what they thought?

A curved metal plate full of something that looked like porridge appeared in his line of sight. He glanced up to see Kince standing there. The man's lips pressed tightly together, but he gave a slight nod of encouragement. Kasiel took the offering with an answering nod and set it on the log beside him to let Tath finish her work.

"What happens now?" he asked as she bandaged his other wrist.

"Now we take you back where you belong, which is a lot easier to say than it is to do." She moved his hair back enough to show the cut on his cheek and dabbed a little of the salve on it. "For now, you're welcome to take one of the mercenary horses or, if you're not feeling that strong yet, you can ride double with someone."

Too weak to ride by himself? That would impress them.

Tath leaned her elbow on her knee and gave him a stern look, as if he had spoken his thoughts aloud. "There's no shame in needing help. It's obvious those mercenaries nearly starved you to keep you from giving them trouble. Their kind does that a lot. It makes bringing in bounties considerably easier, but it doesn't do the captive any favors. No one here expects you to jump up and run a race after what you've been through."

Her words rang true. Still, he had no desire to be pressed together on the back of a horse with a stranger. "I'll try to ride alone."

Her expression hardened, as if she wanted to argue. Instead, she put the lid on the salve and stood. "You'll need your strength, then." She nodded toward the plate before walking away.

They put less on his plate than he had seen on others, but he wasn't about to complain. They were probably trying to avoid overfeeding him after his eight-day starvation diet. Besides, it was still more of a breakfast than he had eaten since leaving Fernwallow. Despite not being the most attractive substance, it turned out to be edible and filling. When he finished, he had to talk himself out of licking the plate clean. Not wanting to appear useless, he got up to rinse it as he had seen others doing. Jethan intercepted him, taking it from him and sending him back to his seat.

When he finished cleaning, Jethan beckoned Kasiel to follow him into the little shack. Kasiel hurried after him, realizing as he did so that he was being obliging and obedient because that was how Edmund raised him. Maybe now wasn't the right time to resist that conditioning, but it was something to ponder later.

Inside, Jethan looked him over with a critical eye. "How many days did those mercenaries have you?"

"Eight, I think."

"Bound and gagged most of the time?"

Kasiel nodded.

"I wish we had caught up to them sooner, but wishing won't change it now." He gestured to Kasiel's armor. "You're going to need help to put this back on. Are you all right with me being that help?"

He glanced at the armor. Jethan wasn't wrong. Between the injury to his wrists and their lack of use while bound, his hands didn't want to work quite right. They would recover, at least he hoped they would, but he was going to have a hard time dealing with all the fastenings on his armor. Of everyone there, Tath was the only other person he might consider letting help him, but the alleged spirit sibling connection made Jethan the obvious choice.

"If you're game to dress me up, I'll play along," he answered with a hint of weary humor.

Jethan grinned. "Glad to hear it. Let's get this done then. We've got a long, rough road ahead and daylight's wasting."

A short time later, they were ready to depart. Lorin had been lifting Kasiel into the saddle for the last several days because he was too weak to climb up on his own. Before he could figure out how to admit that without dying of shame, Jethan came to give him a leg up, not allowing him the chance to fail on his own. They put him on Nix's bay gelding. It had the best fitness and temperament of the four mercenary mounts. The other three animals they led along with them in case they needed them later. In addition to giving him his own horse, they also returned his weapons to him. Another sign that they didn't consider him their prisoner.

Before starting their journey, Jethan gave a round of introductions, presenting the others in their spirit pairings. Tath's partner was Ahrin, the slender young man with white hair. Kince was paired with Darro, another tall man around the same age who had light brown hair like Jethan's and a scar on his chin. The woman with the white-blond hair and a line of white tattooed symbols climbing her throat was Merrin. Her spirit sibling was Avris, a redhead with pale green eyes and black symbols tattooed in a series of nested half circles on her left cheek. The final two were Wedro, another redhead with striking light blue eyes, and Chander, whose brown hair was the darkest among them. Those two wore matching smirks that whispered of mischief. All eight inclined their heads to him in gestures of respect. Ahrin and Merrin even addressed him as "my lord" upon their introductions. He was getting the impression that his father's status might have as much to do with their reserved manners as his being a stranger did.

They maintained a moderate pace through the day, not pushing the horses or their riders too hard. Tath and Jethan took turns riding next to Kasiel, never leaving him on his own. Initially, he thought it might be to keep him from bolting, but the way they constantly checked in on his comfort and energy convinced him it was a genuine concern for his well-being and ability to stay in the saddle. The bay gelding was more spirited than the horse he had been riding, given to periodic attempts at racing past other horses if he got complacent. After Tath took a few minutes to show him how to correct the animal, he could get it to settle for a time before it tried again.

Kasiel noticed the others stayed in their pairings most of the time, including Tath, who had Ahrin close by even when she was riding with him. After a noon break that was longer than he suspected any of the others needed, he mustered up the courage to ask about spirit siblings. Now was as good a time as any to start learning who these people were, especially if he was honestly considering letting them take him to Vanris. He was in no shape to object to it now, but Vanris was a long way off yet. There would be opportunities to reconsider his course, not that he had anywhere else to go.

Tath rode beside him when they struck out again, putting her on the spot to field his questions. He preferred that. Jethan being his pairing made him a little hesitant to ask the other youth about it. Somehow, not understanding the bond they supposedly shared felt like an insult to Jethan.

"How are you doing?" Tath asked as they urged their mounts along with the group.

"Sore and tired, but I'm not tied up or gagged. That does a lot for a person's outlook."

Her answering smile was the most genuine one she had given him yet. She came across as intimidatingly strong and competent, but the warm expression balanced that. She reminded him a little of Danica at that moment. Capable and kind. Fierce and caring. The association helped to relax him.

Encouraged, he tried to ease into the subject. "Everyone rides in their pairings. Is that typical for tah… ten…" His cheeks warmed as he fumbled the Vanrian word. "Spirit siblings?"

She breathed a soft laugh and nodded. "Tehnaak. Yes. Spirit siblings look out for one another. That means we're almost always sent on assignments together and we try to look out for each other in potentially hostile situations."

"That's why there's an odd number of you. Because Jethan has no spirit sibling."

She put pressure on the bit when her mount broke into a trot, bringing him back in line with Kasiel's horse. "Jethan does have a spirit sibling. He's always had one. You just weren't around for a while."

"Twelve years is a long while."

"Mm-hmm."

He glanced toward the front where Jethan rode, constantly scanning the trees ahead to pick the best route. "Can't someone get a new spirit sibling if something happens to theirs?"

"Sometimes, if there is someone else of a close age also in need. Jethan never considered it though. Most people assumed you were dead, but your father insisted they would find you someday. Every time Jethan's parents brought up the possibility of searching for a new match for him, Arhk convinced them to wait one more year. By the time he turned nine, Jethan had fully embraced the belief that you would come back one day."

They moved apart to pass around a tree in the path, the horses gravitating together again naturally once they were clear of the obstacle.

All those years, his father and Jethan hoped to be reunited with him. He had never known enough to wish for the same. "You said my father believed they would find me. What of my mother?"

Her expression closed, and she faced forward as she spoke. "The ones who took you killed your mother that night. A small strike team made it across the Break and into our territory while most of the attention was on a larger battle to the west of where you and your mother were. They don't think it was random, though it's still unclear how they knew where to strike and who to take."

"Why me?"

"The only child of one of the most powerful mind-crafters ever to live?" She glanced over at him. "Mind-crafting runs in bloodlines. Whether their goal was a mind-crafter to experiment on or merely to eliminate a potential future threat, you were an excellent choice."

"I don't understand what that means. What's a mind-crafter?"

Her eyebrows popped up. "Wow. They *were* keeping you in the dark. A mind—"

"Tath." Jethan interrupted, riding up on Kasiel's other side. "Why don't you take point for a while?"

The healer lowered her gaze, looking chastised, though Kasiel couldn't imagine why. Without another word, she kicked her horse up to a trot and moved to the front.

"How are you holding up?" Jethan asked as if nothing out of the ordinary had occurred.

Kasiel frowned after Tath. "I'm managing. Why did—"

"Good. We need to find a better place to set up camp. The trees are too sparse here. Can you handle more speed?"

Kasiel fought the dreadful sinking in his gut. Jethan's timing hadn't been accidental. The other youth was keeping something from him. He forced a nod. "I think so."

"Let me know if you have trouble." With that, Jethan called on the party to speed up. They urged their mounts to a canter that required Kasiel to turn his full focus to staying upright and in control of his horse.

By the time they stopped in a cozy clearing amid a denser stand of trees, Kasiel could barely keep his seat in the saddle. He nearly fell dismounting, but Chander, who was walking past at that moment, caught his arm and steadied him. As soon as he was solidly on his feet, Chander continued on his way with a slight bob of his head and a muttered "my lord."

Jethan hurried over to him. "I apologize. I should have expected that."

"It isn't your job to take care of me at all times," Kasiel grumbled.

"That's where you're wrong, but we can sort that out later. Tath and Ahrin are setting up a spot for you to rest while we arrange camp. You look ready to pass out."

Kasiel lowered his gaze, gripping the edges of the saddle hard enough to make his wrists ache in protest. He had spent his whole life being sidetracked and lied to by Edmund, the person he thought he could trust most in the world. That revelation had come recently enough that the wounds were still raw. As a result, his anger with Jethan's interruption when he asked Tath about mind-crafters had blossomed in the hours since.

Jethan leaned closer, lowering his voice. "You'll get plenty of opportunities to pull your weight, tehnaak," he said, misunderstanding Kasiel's dark look. "Be patient with yourself while you heal."

Kasiel faced him. "And when I'm recovered, then will you tell me about the secrets you're keeping, *tehnaak?*" He growled the last word under his breath.

He half-expected the other youth to get angry with him at that, but Jethan's expression softened instead, and he placed a hand on Kasiel's shoulder. "I will tell you everything in time. I promise you that. Right now, I'm trying to keep my unit alive and get you safely back to Vanris. I'm also trying to adjust to the fact that, for the first time since I was a small child, I have my tehnaak with me." He blinked back a hint of moisture in his eyes as he spoke those words. "Please, be patient with me."

Guilt twisted in Kasiel's chest. He drew a deep breath to ease that hurt. "I'm sor—"

"No." Jethan squeezed his shoulder gently. "Don't apologize. We're both dealing with unusual circumstances. We're going to make mistakes along the way. I'm not foolish enough to expect you to trust me yet. I will earn that. Until then, I promise I will try to do my best by you, if you promise to tell me when I fail."

Kasiel nodded, at a loss for what to say. Jethan was a stranger. One who treated him like a long-lost friend. It was confusing, and yet he found the youth's presence unexpectedly comforting.

Jethan took a step back, his gaze sinking to Kasiel's sword belt. "Can you use those weapons?"

Kasiel let out a bitter laugh. "Not very well. And certainly not right now." He held up his bandaged wrists to emphasize the problem.

"I expect you to heal and get your strength back so we can start working on that, then." Jethan gestured toward the developing camp with a jerk of his head. "Go. Rest."

Kasiel did exactly as directed. He was exhausted, and the brief exchange made him more aware of the toll that was taking on him emotionally as well as physically. Jethan woke him sometime later to eat. After that, he tried to stay awake to listen to the conversations around the fire, hoping to learn more about his new companions, though they often slipped back into Vanrian when speaking amongst themselves. Fatigue dragged him down again before he heard much of anything at all.

The next day, they kept to a more aggressive pace. The sense of urgency about the group had intensified. They hurried along as if they were being chased rather than simply eager to return home. Several times throughout the day, a pairing would drop behind and disappear for a while, then come galloping back later to engage Jethan in hushed conversation without breaking pace.

As the day wore toward evening, Kasiel found it increasingly difficult to keep his seat in the saddle. The growing ache in his wrists also made it hard for him to control his horse over the long hours. Both Tath and Jethan kept a close watch over him as they rode along. Jethan finally called a halt, glancing behind them as if he expected to see a pack of wolves swarming out of the woods.

"We need to rest the horses and ourselves." He led them out into a meadow with a creek flowing along one edge of it. "Merrin. Avris. Scout the area. Make sure we're alone. The rest of you, fill your water skins while we've got the chance and eat something."

Merrin and Avris dismounted and jogged into the woods back the way they had come. Jethan reached Kasiel's side before he could half-fall from his saddle again. His supporting grip was reassuringly steady.

"We're being followed," he said when Kasiel's feet touched the ground, striking an immediate spike of alarm in him. "We need the rest, but we may have to leave in a hurry. Be ready to move if it comes to that. I'll be here to help you."

Kasiel scanned the meadow as if he might spot the threat, then silently chided himself for being foolish and turned to Jethan. "Who is it?"

"I'm not positive. Could be more mercenaries or someone from your village, given what little Chander and Wedro could figure out earlier. They aren't Alliance troops at least, but still a potential problem." He offered a determined smile. "Don't worry, I won't let anything happen to you. I've worked too hard to get you back."

The words weren't as reassuring as Jethan undoubtedly wanted them to be. What if their pursuers were from Fernwallow? What would happen then? Kasiel gave a slight nod as the youth took his mount to tie to the line with the other horses.

The forest here was different. Large numbers of deciduous trees, thickening with new spring foliage, grew amidst a sparse sprinkling of the evergreens he was familiar with. More grass covered the ground as well, with less of the ferns and snagging underbrush he had grown up around. The weather had been kind enough, only dampening them once with a light misting rain. Nothing like the two soaking days of rain during his stint with the mercenaries. Perhaps it wasn't as wet in this part of the country. He didn't know if they were even still in the kingdom of Fallend or if they had crossed the border into Sarket.

Tense silence hung over the group. They ate without building a fire, dining on root vegetables and dried meat that didn't require cooking or plates. Nor was it as filling. They left their saddlebags on the horses, pulling out only the items they needed and returning them to the bags when they finished.

Kasiel's eyelids were heavy with the demand for rest. He felt a fraction less tired and weak than he had the previous day, but still lacking in strength and energy. He yearned for a repeat of the brief nap he had gotten before dinner the prior evening.

The glow of an orange sunset was moving across the sky when a strange bird call rang out from the trees. The Vanrian unit was on their feet in an instant, heading for the horses. Jethan stayed with him as promised, giving him a hand up and guiding him to the edge of the meadow with the others.

As they were mounting, Merrin and Avris came sprinting from the trees. Chander and Wedro galloped out to intercept them, leading the two women's mounts. The group waited, horses stomping and tossing their heads in response to the stress of their riders. Once the two women swung up into their saddles, kicking the animals into action, the rest of the group urged their horses to run.

"Kas!"

Kasiel pulled his mount to a stop almost before it began moving and spun it around. Behind him, several of the others dropped sharp exclamations as they wheeled their horses around as well. Vanrian curses, he suspected. The voice that had called out to him, though, was Danica. Hers was a voice he shouldn't be hearing out here, and one he couldn't ignore.

Twelve riders emerged from the trees on the opposite side of the clearing. The majority were strangers, armed and armored in mail and leather like the mercenaries who captured him had been. The three in the lead he recognized instantly. Edmund, Garrick, and Danica. Edmund signaled the group to stop, motioning Danica forward with him as he rode out a little more into the open. Danica managed her mount with a natural ease, her long black braids pulled back in a band, dark skin picking up a bronze gleam in the light of sunset. In that moment, she was one of the most beautiful things Kasiel had ever seen.

Their eyes met across the clearing, and she brought

a hand to her lips, her expression turning to one of horror. "Oh, Kas! What have they done to you?"

In his periphery, he could see the Vanrian group moving up around him. Jethan stopped at his side.

"They didn't do this," he called back, determined, for some reason, to defend these relative strangers. "The mercenaries did this."

"Kas." Her tone turned desperate, pleading. "Please, come home."

How he wanted to go to her and erase the worry that cast a shadow over her features. To return home and have everything back the way it was before the mercenaries came to Fernwallow.

"Kasiel, you've had us all quite worried." Edmund's imploring tone struck a chord of anger in Kasiel. "You shouldn't be with these people. Come back to Fernwallow where you belong."

"These *are* my people. They always have been," he countered, though the sentiment wasn't sincere. He didn't feel like he belonged with any of them. Not the people from Fernwallow. Not the group from Vanris. He was adrift. Lost somewhere between.

"These people don't care about you," Edmund asserted. "They only want to use you."

Kasiel gripped the pommel of the saddle to hide the trembling of his hands. A tremble born of anger, but also of longing for something he could never have back. "Use me? You mean like you did? Experimenting on me like I was some kind of animal."

"Now, Kasiel, you willingly gave your blood for my research. You have enabled—even assisted—my studies all these years. We make a great team, you and I." Edmund's gaze swept over the Vanrian unit as he spoke.

Kasiel caught a slight tensing in several members of the group alongside him and a few glanced his way. The implication that he had helped Edmund research their people didn't appear to sit well with them, which wasn't much of a surprise.

A few of the mercenaries in the opposing group slowly repositioned themselves out to the sides, as if they hoped to work their way around the Vanrians. To Kasiel's left and right, two of the spirit pairings shifted their mounts to face those riders, making it obvious that they had noticed the movement.

Kasiel stared at Danica, aching to move closer to her. To talk to her without the others there. Had she volunteered to come? Insisted maybe? Or had they simply brought her along to manipulate him? "Dani, did they tell you they were planning to kill me before they dragged you out here to lure me back?"

"That's not true, Kas. It can't be." Looking confused, she turned to Edmund, who ignored her. She glanced back at her father, seeking reassurance that didn't come.

Kasiel knew Edmund well enough to see the strain behind his smile when he spoke again. "Danica's right. You've clearly been through a lot, lad. Your mind is playing tricks on you. Or perhaps your companions are playing tricks with your mind. Either way, you know I would never hurt you. I raised you. I love you like a son."

Kasiel hesitated. The last ten days had held him in their grip like a nightmare he couldn't wake up from. Could he have somehow misunderstood the conversation between Garrick and Edmund? Could he be remembering events wrong after everything he had been through? Still, it was hard to misconstrue the intent behind the words he recalled overhearing. The meaning had been clear enough that he believed running away was the best answer at the time. That wasn't a conclusion he would have come to easily. They had planned to kill him.

Jethan urged his mount a few steps forward. "It's obvious that you all have considerable history together. Perhaps we could sit down and talk this through peacefully."

"Not another step, mind-crafter." A mercenary flanking Garrick raised his crossbow to aim at Jethan.

Kasiel couldn't have said what drove him, but he moved instantly, kicking his mount forward to bring it in between Jethan and the threat. Edmund scowled at that and signaled the crossbowman to lower his weapon.

"You see," Jethan said in a low voice, "your heart knows where you belong, Kas."

Kasiel glanced back at him.

"Kas." Tears gave a raw edge to Danica's voice now.

He turned to look at her, feeling the same heartbreak he saw in her eyes stabbing through his chest. They had grown up in the same town. Shared grand adventures together. Trained together. His relationship with her was the closest thing he had to the spirit pairing his new companions practiced. Only with her it was different because he cared about her romantically, too. That development hadn't been intentional, it just happened. He didn't want to leave her behind when he had barely discovered what she meant to him.

"Kasiel." A hint of a sterner, paternal edge crept into Edmund's tone this time. He was growing impatient.

Kasiel turned his attention to Edmund. He didn't trust the man anymore. It hurt, but he'd had over a week bound and gagged to come to terms with that sorrow in silence. The time hadn't made him feel better about it, but it had given him a chance to consider all the things Edmund must have been keeping from him. Enough that he would never trust the man again.

All of that aside, he also didn't want to see anyone hurt. Certainly not Danica, and, despite everything, not Edmund either. More surprisingly, he genuinely hated the thought of seeing any of his new companions come to harm, Jethan in particular. And someone would get hurt if he let Edmund take him. The Vanrians would fight for him. They had traveled all the way from beyond the Break to find him. They weren't going to sit back and watch the professor ride away with him.

Kasiel turned again and met Jethan's eyes, a great chasm tearing open inside him. He didn't say anything. He didn't have to. Jethan lifted his reins and, moving almost as one, the Vanrian group wheeled about and kicked their mounts hard, driving them to a gallop.

A sharp pain cut across the outside of Kasiel's arm at the elbow, where the armor didn't cover. He clenched his teeth and leaned forward, encouraging his horse for once to give into its more competitive urges. The animal took charge, galloping close on the heels of the others as they dodged through the trees. Kasiel focused on staying on. His grip strength, undermined by the injuries to his wrists, wasn't enough to slow the gelding down now, even if he wanted to. His legs, also weaker than they should be, struggled to keep him in the seat.

He couldn't tell if someone was choosing their path or if they were sprinting blindly through the darkening forest with the sole purpose of getting away. Branches whipped around them, lashing and grabbing at them as if to stop them. Part of him wanted to turn around even now. Maybe Edmund and Garrick had changed their minds and decided to let him live. Maybe they could give him back the quiet life he had before. They wouldn't have brought Danica along if they still meant to kill him, would they?

Questioning his choice soon became too much of an effort. All Kasiel could do was cling desperately to the saddle and will his hands and legs to hold on a little longer. He was losing the battle when two horses closed in on either side of him. Jethan grabbed his reins while the other rider reached over to take his arm, stabilizing him. They pulled all three horses down to a rough trot for several strides before the animals dropped into a weary walk. A few more stumbling steps, and they stuttered to a stop together.

Jethan swung off on the left side of Kasiel's mount, not letting go of his reins.

"He got grazed on the arm," the person on Kasiel's right said, still holding him upright. "It's bleeding pretty good, but I don't think it's too deep."

Wedro appeared alongside Jethan. Together, they helped Kasiel dismount. A flurry of activity commenced around him. People grabbed horses and took them to be tied. Jethan and Wedro began walking him somewhere. It was dark, but a little moonlight broke in between the trees, making it possible to avoid tripping over bushes and branches.

"How long do you think we have?" Wedro asked.

"I don't know," Jethan answered. "They were reluctant to engage in a full-speed chase. They may plan to rely on trackers to hunt us down later. I'm hoping our turning down the middle of the river for that stretch will throw them off."

River? Had they ridden through a river? His pant legs were damp, so maybe they had.

Someone took hold of his right arm near the elbow and pain flared. He jerked away in surprise.

"Tath!" Jethan called.

Barely a second passed before she jogged over to them. "What?"

"Looks like a bolt caught his arm. Glancing strike, but can you see if it needs stitching?"

They sat Kasiel down on a stump, and he sagged there, exhaustion beating in his head like a slow drum, discouraging all thought or action. Tath knelt next to him, poking painfully around at the wound on his arm.

"Anyone else hurt?" Jethan called.

"Kince took a bolt in the shoulder," Merrin replied from somewhere to the left, "but it looks like it wounded more armor than flesh."

"I'll check it," Ahrin said.

"One horse has an arrow in his hip," someone else called. Darro, Kasiel thought, though he wasn't entirely sure he had their voices all matched up with their faces accurately in his head.

"How bad?" Jethan asked.

"The animal won't be able to keep up," Darro answered after several seconds.

"Move its packs to one of the mercenary horses and leave it," Jethan ordered. "We don't have much choice." He turned to Tath, putting a hand on Kasiel's shoulder. "How does it look?"

The prodding finally stopped and Kasiel, realizing he had been holding his breath, sucked in crisp night air.

Tath rambled off something that made no sense at all, and Kasiel furrowed his brow at her. Had she spoken in Vanrian or had his language faculties given out?

She offered him a tense smile. "Sorry. I said it's hard to tell in this shit light, but I think a tight wrap should be sufficient for now."

Jethan gave his shoulder a squeeze. "Do it. We'll check it again when we have better lighting. See if Ahrin needs help with Kince when you're done."

Tath and Jethan both disappeared then. Kasiel stared at the dark ground in front of him. His eyes drifted closed. They snapped open when fresh pain shot out from the cut. Tath had come back and was kneeling in the dirt, snugly wrapping the wound. Kasiel clenched his teeth and bore the discomfort in silence. When she finished, she hurried away before he could thank her.

Seconds later, Jethan returned.

"We need to move again. I want you to ride with me. You're in no shape to handle your own mount right now."

"No shape to stay in the saddle," he muttered.

Jethan chuckled, though the sound wasn't as easy as usual. He held a hand down to Kasiel. "Come on, tehnaak. I'll keep you on the horse."

Kasiel eyed the hand for a second. What would they do if he told them to leave him? Did he really want to know?

With a weary exhale, he took the hand and let Jethan help him up.

haring a saddle required some squishing. But Jethan was slender like Kasiel, who was thinner than usual now himself, so it wasn't as uncomfortable as he had dreaded it might be. It wasn't as awkward either. Or maybe he was too exhausted to care. Jethan was a skilled rider, directing the animal primarily with subtle leg movements that left his hands free to help support Kasiel when necessary.

Exhausted, Kasiel drifted in and out of awareness as they rode, much as he had the last few days riding with the mercenaries. This time at least, he was neither bound nor gagged, and Jethan's periodic adjustments to help him stay upright were helpful and oddly comforting. They didn't travel fast, they simply kept moving relentlessly on through the darkness.

Despite not getting anything resembling normal sleep, Kasiel began waking up some as the first hints of morning light crept through the trees. His stinging arm pulled his thoughts back to the encounter with Edmund's group.

"Jeth?"

Several seconds passed before the other youth responded. "You know, only my family and close friends call me that."

Kasiel tensed, that previously absent awkwardness

sweeping in. "Sorry. I'm not sure why I did that."

"Oh, I don't mind. You're my tehnaak. You merely caught me by surprise. What do you need?" He shifted a leg, adjusting the horse's direction to move around the stump of a fallen tree.

Unease twisted in Kasiel's gut, but he pushed past it. "That mercenary back there, or whatever he was, he called you a mind-crafter."

"He was guessing."

"Was he right?"

A weighted silence hung between them, followed by a heavy sigh from the other youth. "Chander. Wedro. Ride ahead and see if you can find a place to stop," Jethan called out. "We could all use some rest." In a lower voice, he said, "I'll explain it to you after we stop. Promise."

"All right," Kasiel agreed, anxiety rising in him. Did he really want this? How would he feel about whatever he was about to learn?

From that point forward, he peered ahead, conflicted about the coming rest. A chance to get some proper sleep sounded fantastic, but finally getting answers about mind-crafters could be good or bad, or both. Still, he wanted to know, as much because he hated feeling like they were keeping things from him as because he was simply curious. Edmund had kept this knowledge and more from him. A simple thing to do in the very isolated town of Fernwallow. If he were ever to become comfortable with Jethan, he needed to believe the youth wouldn't treat him the way his former father figure had.

Wedro came riding back sometime later, when early morning light brightened the sky enough that they could pick out details of the surrounding woods. The evergreens had disappeared. Left behind with everything else familiar.

"We found a small homestead ahead," Wedro

reported. "Looks like it's been deserted for a while. We can all rest inside for once."

"Well done." Jethan's praise coaxed a smile from Wedro, who, like most of them, looked about ready to collapse. "Lead the way."

They arrived at the homestead, which included two small houses and a barn, all slowly being reclaimed by the forest. Jethan led Kasiel into one building then immediately left again. Tath came in and sat him on a bench by an old dining table. She removed the bandage on his arm and silently cleaned the wound. Then she stared at it for several long seconds, her lips pressed tightly together before wiping salve on it and wrapping it with a fresh bandage.

"Pay attention to this," she advised. "We don't want it becoming infected out here. It should heal all right, though." She stared at the bandage a little longer and shook her head.

A worrying thought dug its fingers into him. What if she was upset with him? "Did I do something wrong?"

"I can't believe they tried to get you to go with them, then turned around and shot you." She looked into his eyes, her gaze searching. Jethan entered carrying a satchel. He stopped behind her, but her attention stayed on Kasiel. "Did you really help that man research our people?"

"I guess I did. He never explained what he was doing." Kasiel lowered his gaze, shame and anger rising hot in his cheeks. "I trusted him."

Jethan tapped Tath's shoulder.

She took another few seconds to check under the bandages on Kasiel's wrists, then stood up. "He's all yours," she said to Jethan as she walked out, leaving them alone in the building.

"Where are the others?"

"They're in the bigger house. I thought we could

use a little privacy to talk." Jethan looked around then wandered into the next room.

After a few seconds, Kasiel followed, finding him perched cross-legged at the foot of a bed that was in relatively good repair. He sat down near the head of the bed, mirroring the other youth's position.

Jethan pulled two mugs, a stoneglass bottle, and a smaller flask out of the satchel. He poured himself a drink from the bottle, then poured something into Kasiel's mug from the flask. "This is just water with some herbs mixed in to help with the various pains. It should let you sleep a bit more soundly."

Kasiel took the mug, eyeing it uneasily. "Do we have time to sleep?"

"We've seen no signs of pursuit so far, and we'll start losing horses if we don't give them a break. More importantly, we don't want to lose you, so you will rest. I have the others alternating shifts. We'll try to get everyone at least a little sleep before we head out again." He nodded to Kasiel's mug and took a drink of the mead he had served himself.

Kasiel sniffed the liquid, then drank half of it down. It had a slight sweetness to it with a faint, bitter aftertaste.

"Good. Keep at it." Jethan took another swallow of his mead, gesturing for Kasiel to take another drink too before speaking again. "You wanted to know about mind-crafters. They're individuals gifted with a natural ability to influence the minds of others in different ways. For example, a Dampener can interfere with the mind's perception of senses. They can make a person, or group of people, unable to see, hear, taste, touch, or smell for a short time."

Something tightened in Kasiel's chest in response to this revelation, but he held his silence, giving Jethan a chance to explain more.

"A Frightener can inflict a sense of terror on a person, or group of people, drawing on their fear. Your father is a Frightener, actually. An impressive one. An Enkindler can inspire people, helping them feel more courageous or confident than they might otherwise be. There are many abilities."

Kasiel forced down another swallow of the drink, finding that he could only taste the bitter now. His stomach twisted as he recalled all of Edmund's scrolls about "theoretical" psychic disciplines. "There are really people in your country who can control the minds of others?"

Jethan turned to fully face him, legs still crossed. "*Our* country. And yes, that's what I was trying to explain."

"And what are you?" He fought to keep his sudden unease from his voice, but exhaustion undermined him. The question came out sounding somewhere between accusatory and fearful.

Jethan considered him for a long moment. His expression guarded. The distant sound of someone laughing reached them. He finished the rest of the mead in his cup in one big swallow.

"I'm what we call a Charmer. I can manipulate a person's thoughts to get them to do things, such as go along with a plan or give me a better deal on a trade. I can only influence one person at a time, though, and their attention must be on me for it to work."

Kasiel narrowed his eyes, fighting the urge to get up and leave. In his current condition, and with the deep drowsiness that was dragging him down, the gesture wouldn't amount to much. "Have you ever *charmed* me?"

Jethan took a deep breath and shook his head. A shadow fell across his features as he stared into his mug. "There's no way for me to prove to you that I haven't, but I haven't." He looked up then, staring intently into Kasiel's eyes. "I would never use it on you, tehnaak. Never."

Kasiel looked down into his own mug. Jethan was right. Nothing he could do would prove that he had never manipulated him. Kasiel wanted to believe him, though. He wanted to believe that this individual with whom he supposedly shared a special bond wouldn't abuse his trust in such a way. He couldn't though. Not after Edmund's betrayal. Trust of that magnitude was too much to ask for just now.

He drew a deep breath and raised his gaze, fighting that feeling of shame. "Edmund was collecting information on mental powers like the ones you mentioned. He insisted it was all theoretical, though."

Jethan's eyes narrowed. "And you believed him?"

Kasiel couldn't stop a yawn. His eyelids were becoming impossibly heavy. He leaned against the wall alongside the bed. "I had no reason not to. All I knew of Vanris before now was that I was born there and that, because of a war happening nearly a thousand miles away," he added with a pointed look, "the Vanrian people weren't allowed in the southern kingdoms, so I should avoid letting people know I was one."

Jethan absently rotated his empty cup in his hand. "You never asked him about your people or the war?"

Kasiel tried to suppress another yawn and failed. He shook his head in a futile attempt to clear away the deepening fog. "I did, when I was younger, but Edmund avoided those subjects. He made it all sound so irrelevant. Life in Fernwallow was simple. I guess it all seemed too far away to matter."

His eyes wanted to drift shut, so he let them for a moment.

When someone shook him awake sometime later, he lay stretched out on the bed. He opened his eyes to

Avris's pale green ones staring down at him. For a second, he could see nothing else.

"You have incredible eyes," he blurted, wondering distantly if he had said that out loud. That wasn't something you said to a person the very first time you spoke to them.

Avris laughed softly. "Oh. I hope I didn't put too much kenis seed in that water." She slipped an arm under him and lifted. "Come on. We've got to get back on the road. There are signs of movement in the forest to the south."

He struggled upright with her help, trying to give the news she presented the gravity it deserved, but finding it hard to do so. "What signs?"

"Well…" She paused, her brows pinching together as she glanced down at the bandage on his arm. "Um, there are birds clearing out of the trees to the south of here as if something startled them." She wiggled her fingers while lifting her hand as if to illustrate the birds taking flight.

He contemplated lying back down while she took hold of his less injured arm and started pulling him up from the bed. "How could you see that?"

"*I* didn't." She groaned when he sat back on the bed again. "Wedro saw it from up near the top of a tree." She let go of him, watching with her lips pressed together in a thin line of disapproval as he lay down. "Jethan's going to kill me." With a shake of her head, she reached into a pouch hanging at her waist, pulling out a pinch of something. She held it under his nose. "Sniff."

He did as instructed. A stinging sensation raced violently up his nostrils, snapping him awake. He jolted upright, rubbing his nose and sneezing several times.

"Sorry. It'll pass in a second, but we've got to go now."

She took his arm again and led him from the room, still rubbing his stinging nose. By the time they reached the front door, the stinging had subsided. He was still wide awake, though. Whatever she had subjected him to, it was effective.

"What was that?"

"It's a spice. Don't worry. It has no lasting effects, but it's great for waking people up. I've put it in candles before." She pushed open the front door. "It's fun to light one and stick it under people's noses after they've been up drinking all night."

Kasiel gave her a sideways glance, and she shrugged. She pointed to where Jethan was waiting with their horses alongside the barn and gave him a light shove in that direction. Kasiel staggered the first step, then continued with a bit more control toward Jethan. He felt perhaps a fraction stronger. Sleep had helped, but he was hungry enough to eat a meal fit for an entire family by himself. The thought of more hours in the saddle before he could finally get something to eat was a discouraging one.

"Sorry. I hoped we would have time to eat too," Jethan said, uncannily perceptive to the cause of his frown. He held Kasiel's gelding's reins along with his own. "We'll probably be moving fast again. Do you feel well enough to ride solo?"

"Yes." He wasn't going to slow them down this time.

Jethan handed him the reins and gave him a leg up. When Kasiel had settled in the saddle, Jethan swung up on his own mount and turned to face him. "Stay close to me. If you need help, don't hesitate to say something."

Kasiel nodded and followed him out to join the others.

They rode as fast as they safely could through the rougher woods for a time until the group burst out of the trees onto a roadway. They pulled up, halting abruptly enough that Kasiel fell partway forward onto the gelding's neck before he could catch himself. He hastily straightened and shifted back into the saddle, hoping no one had noticed. The stinging in his arm had jumped in intensity over the last few hours. A quick inspection revealed that the wound had bled through the bandage.

The sky above them was turning ominously dark. Darker by far than was appropriate for the hour, at least as close as he could figure it. Jethan cast a sour glance up at the looming storm clouds. Kasiel followed his gaze, and a fat drop of rain struck his nose. Avris, who had stopped alongside him, snorted a laugh, and covered her grin with one hand.

Jethan turned to Darro, a hint of deference in his manner that Kasiel hadn't noticed before. "With this storm moving in, we might get away with sticking to the road for a short time, don't you think?"

Darro nodded his agreement. "There shouldn't be many people about and it'll let us keep a faster pace."

Darro looked at Kince, who gave a gruff nod. Watching them, Kasiel realized that the pairing was probably the most senior in the group, not that either appeared much older than thirty. This might be Jethan's mission, but he was young. It made sense that a few more experienced soldiers were there to offer guidance when needed.

Jethan beckoned Kasiel over. "The road will allow us to gallop the horses for a short time. How are you...?" He trailed off, scowling at Kasiel's bleeding arm.

"I'll be fine. Let's go." The more distance they put between themselves and Danica, the less tempted he would be to go back and find her, he hoped.

Rain began falling in earnest then. Big soaking drops. They turned the horses north beneath a clap of thunder and urged them up to a gallop. The bay gelding flattened its ears and kicked up his heels once, sending Kasiel's heart into his throat as he struggled to keep his seat. After expressing its annoyance, the animal settled into a run, allowing him to focus on staying mounted. The pain in his wrists and his weakness, while progressing in the right direction, hadn't improved enough yet to make another ride like this pleasant.

They sprinted along for a time before Jethan drew the pace back to a controlled canter. The rain had soaked them through, and the occasional crash of thunder or flare of lightning across the sky kept the horses on edge. Kasiel's thoughts were consumed by three things: hunger, pain, and the intense desire to stop running.

When would it end? Would Edmund give up eventually? If he did, would they be any better off? For the Vanrians, Kasiel included now, this was enemy territory. They wouldn't be safe from the threat of attack until they crossed to the other side of the Crimson Break.

Maybe he should have gone with Edmund. They had brought Danica with them. He still couldn't believe they would involve her in their efforts to get him back if they meant to kill him. Would he be resting at a campfire right now, laughing with her and delighting in her humor? He could almost hear Edmund and Garrick apologizing for the terrible misunderstanding that led to all of this.

The world jolted around him, and suddenly he was diving forward and down. He and his mount plunged toward the ground together. In the instant before he hit, he heard a strange snarling and a cry of alarm from Jethan. Then everything turned to pain and chaos as he slammed into the hard-packed roadway. He tumbled briefly until something heavy pinned his leg and he skidded to a stop on his back, the taste of blood on his tongue.

A few yards away, Jethan, also off his horse, was getting to his feet, pulling his sword free as he rose. Shouts came from the others amidst panicked whinnies from several of their horses. The motionless weight of Kasiel's fallen mount had his leg trapped, and a massive wildcat now stood with its front paws on the dead animal's ribs, staring down at him. Broad swaths of charcoal fur tipped in white puffed out around its face and tufts of white rose from the top of its ears, giving it an owl-like appearance. It might have been cute, if it wasn't half the size of the horse it was standing on, and currently baring its fangs at him in a fierce snarl.

Jethan shouted at it. "Come on! Come for me!"

The cat ignored him until he threw a rock that hit the side of its head. Then it obliged, leaping in Jethan's direction, driving him toward the trees along that edge of the road.

"Someone help Kas," Jethan shouted toward the chaos of panicked horses as he faced the massive predator.

Another cat burst from the bushes, plowing into Jethan from behind. It sent him slamming to the ground face first. His sword flew from his grasp. The beast caught its claws in his shoulder, flipping him onto his back, and lunged in.

"No!" As Kasiel screamed, that odd blackness swept in around the edges of his vision, crashing to the center. Though his eyes were open, everything went dark for an instant. When his sight returned, the two cats were standing there, neither moving. Their sides heaved with the effort of their attack, but they were no longer on the offensive. They stared at him as if waiting for something.

"Go! Get out of here!" Kasiel shouted.

The wildcats loped off into the trees.

Jethan struggled to his knees and sat back on his heels. He had a scrape across one cheekbone and blood trickled between the fingers of the hand he had gripped tightly over his shoulder.

"By the Break, Kas, you're a Feral." He took a second to spit blood to one side, then said, "That's brilliant."

Kasiel dropped his head back on the wet ground, staring up into the pummeling rain. His heart was trying to hammer its way free of his chest and, if any part of his body didn't hurt, he had yet to identify it.

Darro appeared, standing over him. "Kince. Ahrin. See if you can lift the horse enough for me to pull him out."

Groaning with effort, the three worked to free him from his organic prison. Off to the side, Tath was helping Jethan to his feet, pressing a folded cloth to his injured shoulder.

Then the weight lifted, and Darro dragged him clear of the horse. "Anything broken?"

A heavy fog of pain clouded Kasiel's thoughts. So much hurt that he could hardly focus enough to be certain, but he did his best to assess the damage. "I don't think so."

Darro breathed a laugh. "You sure can take a beating, Cavenos."

Kince joined him, and they reached under Kasiel's

arms, lifting him to his feet together. The skid along the road had shredded his trousers on the recently pinned leg from the knee down, the side of the leg scraped and bleeding, but it bore his weight without too much protest. He spat blood and searched his mouth with his tongue, finding the offending cut on the inside of his lip. At least he still had all his teeth.

"Ahrin," Darro barked, "get the packs off this horse and move them to another one. Kince, remove his tack and throw it out into the trees. The werdyn cats will come back when we're gone to claim the carcass."

Darro scanned the group, still supporting Kasiel with a hand under his arm. "Tath, Jethan will ride with you. Avris, you get Kasiel. Chander. Wedro. You two scout ahead. We need someplace to get out of the storm. A house or something. Preferably back from the road. Do whatever's necessary to make it secure."

As everyone moved to do as directed, Jethan walked over, one hand holding pressure to his shoulder. A trickle of blood ran from the scrape on his cheek, mixing with the rain. "You woke your ability to save my life, tehnaak."

Kasiel stared at the dead horse, trying to wrap his head around what had happened. "Did I?"

Jethan smiled, winced, then nodded. "How badly are you hurt?"

"I'll tell you in about twenty minutes," he answered, his body still vibrating with panic that hadn't yet faded.

Jethan chuckled, the sound cut short by another wince. A spot of blood was soaking through the cloth pressed to his shoulder. Tath and Avris hurried over with their horses.

"Is my horse sound?" Jethan asked.

Tath shrugged. "He's got a scrape down his shoulder from hitting the road. Seems sound enough now, but we may not want to put anyone on him until we're sure."

Jethan nodded.

Kince, done tossing the dead horse's tack out into the trees, came over to help them mount. In minutes, they were moving again, the road behind them cleared of everything except Kasiel's dead, stripped-down mount, its head thrown back at an unnatural angle.

Kasiel lost himself in a cloud of pain on the ride that followed, coming up from his misery occasionally to look over and see how Jethan was faring. The Vanrian youth sat in front of Tath in the saddle, eyes closed, mouth twisted in a grimace. The cloth on his shoulder had soaked completely through with blood now. A problem the heavy rain wasn't helping with.

Eventually, Chander intercepted them on the road and led them off on a side path into the trees. The path ended at a well-kept house with a large barn and enclosures for livestock. Ahrin and Tath escorted Kasiel and Jethan inside, hurrying them into a comfortable front room warmed by a blazing fire in the hearth. Kasiel noticed a strange couple sitting at the dining table with two children. The woman, eyes wide and brimming with tears, had her small daughter pulled close to her, and one hand on the shoulder of her son, who glared at them defiantly. The father sat glowering at them, a bruise rising around his left eye. Wedro stood in the corner behind the family, one hand resting on his sword hilt.

They took Kasiel and Jethan to what appeared to be the children's room, with two narrow beds pushed against opposite walls. They placed Jethan on one with his injured arm toward the center of the room. Ahrin sat on the other next to Kasiel, shoving a tattered doll off the pillow before presenting him with a flask. Kasiel ignored it, watching as Jethan took a swallow from the flask Tath had given him.

"It'll put you to sleep, Lord Ha... Kasiel, so we can assess and tend to your injuries." Ahrin brushed a lock of white hair away from his face, exposing an elaborate blue symbol tattooed next to his eye.

Kasiel recognized it as the same one he had seen under Tath's eye.

"The symbol of the healers," Ahrin stated, apparently noticing his scrutiny. "It means you should do as I say and drink some of this."

"Will Jethan be all right?"

A pleased smile curved Ahrin's lips. "Your tehnaak is in excellent hands. Tath will get him stitched up. We'll probably put a few stitches in that cut on your arm too since it appears to want to keep bleeding." He offered the flask again.

This time, Kasiel accepted it and took a swig before handing it back.

Ahrin nodded his approval. "It might make you feel sick when you wake up—dangers of using it on an empty stomach—but there's a bedpan on the floor here that looks clean if you need it." Sympathy warmed his pale eyes. "After that fall, I don't envy how you're going to feel when you wake up."

"Neither do I." Kasiel cast another glance at Jethan. Tath had him lying back on the bed and was peeling away the cloth over his injury. Not eager to see how much damage the wildcat's claws could do, Kasiel rested back on the bed and stared up at the ceiling until the drug pulled him under.

He woke to someone poking him in the shoulder, which hurt far more than it should. When he opened his eyes, the little girl he had seen with her family on the way in was standing there, her long, dark hair in disarray. At a guess, she looked to be around six years old. She chewed on a fingernail while staring intently at him.

"I can't sleep." She pointed toward the corner.

Kasiel slowly turned his head, wary of the faint nausea now making itself known. The doll Ahrin had pushed aside lay in the corner. Gritting his teeth against the pain of moving, he picked it up and handed it to her.

"Thanks for letting me borrow her," he said.

She nodded solemnly, as if the borrowing of her doll were a grave business.

"Gabbie!" a frantic woman's voice called from the next room.

Seconds later, the door pushed open and Wedro leaned in. He gave the girl a stern look. "Remember how the big, mean guy said you were supposed to stay with your parents at all times?"

After a muttered "thank you" to Kasiel, the girl darted out the door, dodging past Wedro as if she feared he might bite her. Wedro leaned out to watch her for a second, probably to make sure she went in the right direction, then stuck his head back in the room. His gaze wandered to where Jethan lay with his eyes still closed, then over to Kasiel.

"Need something to eat?" he asked.

"Um, yes. I'm starving, and my stomach hates me."

Jethan opened his eyes. "Make that service for two."

"Of course." Relief brought a hint of lightness to Wedro's voice. "How are pain levels? Need me to send Tath or Ahrin back in?"

"I'll be all right." Truthfully, everything hurt, but Kasiel didn't want to risk being put to sleep again, though he suspected he might regret the choice later.

"I'm fine," Jethan answered.

Wedro arched a doubtful brow at each of them, but he didn't argue. "I'll see what I can find to eat." He ducked out, shutting the door behind him.

Kasiel struggled upright, every move bringing pain to fresh places. They had cut away his trousers at the knee and wrapped his leg. As shredded as the material had been, he wasn't surprised to see that they had gotten rid of it. His arm where the crossbow bolt grazed it also sported a fresh wrap of clean bandages. If he undressed, he suspected he would find bruises on top of bruises over much of his body.

Jethan's shoulder had a thick bandage around it, the arm now in a sling. Undoubtedly to keep him from overusing it and pulling the stitches. With one arm, he began shifting himself upright.

"Need help?" Kasiel asked, swinging a leg off the bed.

"Stay put. I'll manage." After several more seconds of awkward wriggling and shifting, he did exactly that, moving a pillow behind his back to lean on.

"Stubborn is fine, but keep in mind that Tath will probably kill me if I let you pull those stitches." Kasiel gave him a sideways glance, catching his wry smirk.

"And your father will kill me if I don't bring you back in one piece, so let's agree to avoid anything that ends in one of us accruing any more injuries."

Would his father literally kill Jethan if he failed? Beast of the Break and The Waking Nightmare both sounded ominous enough that he couldn't help wondering. He was reluctant to ask, though. Instead, he settled for a pained smile. "Agreed."

They were both silent as Kasiel adjusted himself, trying to find a halfway comfortable position. The bed was decent, but his current condition yearned for something better than decent. He finally gave up and looked over to see Jethan regarding him pensively.

"You went down hard, tehnaak. I'm glad you weren't hurt any worse."

"Same here," Kasiel replied, uncomfortable with the emotion in Jethan's voice. "I've never seen a wildcat like that."

Jethan rolled with the change of subject. "Werdyn cats. I've never seen one in the flesh before, but I read about them when I was doing research for this mission." His voice caught when he shifted his arm. He paused for a second, leaning his head against the wall, then took a deep breath and continued. "The species is unusual in that they're more active when it's raining. Their coats are waterproof with a layer of scales along their backs that sheets away moisture if any gets through the fur. They're essentially designed for inclement weather.

"I never would have expected a beast to attack us on the road, though. People, sure, but not something like that. Two months in Pandrean Alliance territory and our worst animal encounter before today was a hawk that stole the meat off Merrin's plate while she was eating."

Kasiel chuckled at that, but the humor faded quickly. He had questions he wanted to ask, but the answers would change even more about who he once thought he was. "What is a Feral?"

"I wondered when we'd get to that." Jethan regarded him with an instructor's patience. "A Feral is a mind-crafter who can control animals with their thoughts. I'm amazed your ability awakened to save my ass." Despite his flippant tone, genuine pleasure shone through in his sudden smile. "Early trauma can awaken abilities in rare cases, but for most mind-crafters, they have to wait until they turn thirteen for the Trial to awaken their ability."

Kasiel moved the pillow against the side wall, turning so he could face Jethan. "The Trial? What's that?"

Jethan shifted around to mirror his position. It took him longer with one usable arm, but he managed. "Well, you prepare by going on a restricted diet for three days. Then, before dawn on the fourth day, you're taken into an isolation room and given a special tincture. The mixture takes away muscle control and causes disorientation. Then your tehnaak is brought in. If you don't have one, as in my case at the time, a family member or someone else close to you is used. While you sit helplessly watching, your tehnaak faces some threat they can't possibly survive. At least, that's how it's staged to appear. For most people, the drive to protect their spirit sibling triggers the dark snap and their ability awakens."

"The dark snap?"

"Your vision went dark for an instant before you stopped the wildcats, right?"

Kasiel remembered the moment with a shudder and nodded.

"It's the same for all of us. They call it the dark snap."

"But how does the Trial work if you know going in that the threat's staged?"

Jethan shrugged. "The tincture takes care of that. It causes paranoia along with its other effects, and drives the emotional mind to expect the worst, stifling logic and reason. A lot of youths preparing for the Trial place bets on whether they'll be able to resist the effects. We all want our ability awakened, but resisting would be an impressive feat of will."

Kasiel was quiet for a few minutes, thinking back on everything that had led to that moment on the road. The mercenaries starving him and his resulting weakness. The emotional and physical toll of events leading to that point. Being trapped under the horse and rendered helpless when Jethan's life was in danger. His spirit sibling.

He looked at Jethan, who sat watching him with a slow, tired grin creeping across his lips.

Kasiel grinned back.

"Happy Trial Day, tehnaak," Jethan said.

Kasiel breathed a weary laugh. "Happy Trial Day, indeed."

They remained in the house through that night and the next day. The plan was to head out the following morning if the weather let up. They couldn't risk lingering for too long, but for now, the storm continued to rage outside. Darro and Jethan agreed that the severe weather would have forced the party from Fernwallow to seek shelter as well. Meanwhile, the heavy rain would wash away their trail, making tracking more difficult. It was an informed gamble. One that gave Tath and Ahrin a chance to tend to injuries in a controlled environment.

Kasiel appreciated the break. He took the opportunity during the day to force himself to walk around, getting more of his leg strength back and working out the stiffness. In the afternoon, he went to pace the interior of the barn, so he wouldn't have to look at the family they were holding hostage. Aside from an initial altercation between Wedro and the father, the Vanrians treated the couple and their children as graciously as possible. Still, they had to ensure no one snuck off to alert authorities to their presence. That meant keeping them under constant supervision. It made Kasiel uncomfortable.

When he went to the barn, Jethan accompanied him. Chander and Wedro also came along, climbing up into the hayloft to enjoy a game of dice away from the curious children and their distraught parents.

While Kasiel paced, the wound on the outside of his lower leg giving him a slight limp, he pondered the challenges they faced now. Jethan's mount had gone down along with his, but it struck the ground less violently. With a superficial injury to its shoulder, the animal was still sound for riding. The fall left Jethan stiff and bruised, though much less so than the full-body collision with the roadway that Kasiel had experienced. Jethan's arm was a problem. The claws sank in deep enough for there to be a considerable risk of infection and re-injury if the wounds didn't have adequate time to heal. That meant that, ideally, he wouldn't use it much until the stitches were ready to come out.

Jethan currently sat on top of a stall door watching Kasiel pace up and down the aisle.

"I'd be all right riding double for a while," Kasiel suggested on his way past. "Or maybe someone could lead your horse while you ride. Then you wouldn't have to use that arm to control it."

"I have a better idea."

Something in Jethan's tone caught his attention, and he turned to find the other youth analyzing him shrewdly.

"Oh, that's a fantastic idea," Wedro said, swinging over the edge of the loft, his bright red hair struck through with bits of straw from leaning on the hay bales. He grinned at them and let go, dropping to the floor.

Chander climbed down the ladder, rolling his eyes at his spirit sibling.

Kasiel looked around at them, clueless as to what idea they thought so clever.

Chander took pity on him. "You're a Feral, Cavenos. You could control Jethan's horse without touching it. Though you haven't had any practice, so it could be a little risky."

A few of them had adopted Darro's new habit of referring to Kasiel by his birth father's last name. It seemed a silly thing to worry about the first few times it happened, but it appeared to be spreading. Perhaps he should say something. Although, he had far more important things to try discouraging now.

"I haven't the first clue how to go about controlling an animal with my mind. What if I did something wrong and Jethan got injured even worse?"

Jethan eased down from the stall door, using his uninjured arm to control the movement, then strode over to join them. "I think you can do it. Besides, you'll have to start practicing sometime. Horses will be easier than the other mounts you could end up working with in Vanris."

"I don't..." He trailed off as Jethan's words sank in. "You have mounts other than horses?"

Wedro grinned. "They're called kanodraks. We brought them here from our old homeland. You'll need a lot of practice before you can even consider working with one of those bastards. Only the most skilled Ferals can ride them."

"Are Ferals common?" A confusing surge of apprehension accompanied Kasiel's question. Did he need to be something special? Since leaving Fernwallow he found out he was the son of the Dhomvalen of Vanris, Right Hand to Khevarin what's-her-name, and now he was a mind-crafter too. That should be exceptional enough for anyone, shouldn't it?

"Ferals aren't as rare as certain types of mind-crafters, though they're far from the most common," Jethan said. "Those skilled enough to work with kanodraks are scarce. Given that you pushed those two werdyn cats away without knowing the first thing about what you were doing, I'd say your ability is already showing promise. You simply need to put in the effort. You're getting a late start. A domesticated horse ought to be easy enough to practice with." Jethan started toward the front of the barn. "Come on. Let's try it."

He stopped at the gate, looking out at the paddocks they had put their horses in. The animals huddled up under two shelters, trying to stay out of the pummeling rain. Kasiel walked up on one side of Jethan. Wedro and Chander stopped on his other side, both absently resting a foot on the bottom rung of the fence in perfect mirror poses.

"There's the dun mare Tath rides," Jethan pointed at the animal where she stood in the middle of one shelter, fully protected from the weather. "See if you can get her to push her way out into the rain."

"I don't know what I'm doing," Kasiel protested.

"Focus on the mare and on what you want her to do. I mean, *really* focus on her. You're trying to get in her head."

Kasiel looked at the mare. She was a lovely bay dun with a black mane and tail and a distinct dorsal strip down her spine. Her ears twitched in irritation at another horse who kept nipping her hindquarters, but she refused to relinquish her cozy, dry spot in the middle. Her big brown eyes were soft and warm. Gentler than he had expected.

He focused deeper, wondering at her thoughts. Was she hungry? Was she content to be off the road and resting? Might she be debating kicking that nippy gelding behind her in the teeth?

"Think about what you want her to do. Make her want it," Jethan said in a low voice.

"Is that how your ability works?" Kasiel asked, only partially listening for the answer.

"It's similar. Now focus."

Of course. He didn't need to know the mare's thoughts. He needed to give them to her. What would accomplish his goal? That she wanted to get out of that stuffy shelter. She wanted space. She wanted to feel the cooling rain on her back.

The mare lifted her head, ears pricking forward. She started making her way out of the middle of the group. When she had cleared a path, pushing and biting her way past the others, she stepped out into the rain and stopped, turning in Kasiel's direction as if waiting for additional guidance.

Chander let out a low whistle.

Wedro muttered a Vanrian curse under his breath.

"Well done, tehnaak," Jethan praised. "You're a natural."

The compliment compelled Kasiel to stand a little straighter. Succeeding at something felt good. Not physically. Physically, he still felt like shit. But something about what he had accomplished left him feeling like more than he had been before. More than a simple-minded village youth. Jethan's approval significantly boosted that.

A giddy pleasure bubbled up in his chest. "Did I really do that?"

Wedro gestured to the animals with his chin. "Given her sudden desire to get back out of the rain, I'd submit that leaving the shelter isn't an idea she would have come up with."

Now that he was no longer influencing her, the mare was attempting to get under the shelter again, but the other four horses in that paddock had spread out, filling in the covered space. An ache built in Kasiel's chest as he watched her, the pouring rain soaking through her coat. It was his fault she was out there, after all. He turned his attention to the animals still under the shelter, observing each for a few seconds before focusing on all of them at once. On how warm they were before, huddled around the mare in the center. On how they wanted to let her back in and restore that pleasant environment.

The four horses lifted their heads the same way the dun had, ears swiveling forward as if they had heard something. All at once, they walked out of the shelter, opening the way for the mare to reclaim her place in the middle.

Chander barked a laugh. "Showing off already? You *are* your father's son, Cavenos."

"*Very* well done." There was a hint of pride in Jethan's soft voice.

The front door of the house opened and Merrin leaned out. "Stop messing around and come eat. We only get a few more good meals before we're on the road again."

Wedro and Chander hopped the fence, cutting across the paddock toward the house. Jethan lingered, and Kasiel hung back with him, sensing that he had more to say.

"Are you starting to feel like you belong with us yet?" Jethan asked after the other two had disappeared through the front door.

Something began closing up protectively inside Kasiel, but he fought it, trying not to let his fear of this strange new life limit the possibilities it offered. "In some ways. This certainly helps."

Jethan glanced over at him. "I'll admit, it surprised me when you chose to stay with us instead of trying to return to your old home. Though, honestly, what really shocked me was the way you put yourself between me and that crossbow."

Kasiel stared at the horses. The fact that he had controlled them with his mind was surreal. He wanted to explore that more, but he pushed it aside for now. "If we're being honest, I can't imagine not wanting to defend you. Since the moment I woke up in that hut, you've treated me like a long-lost friend. I never had a lot of friends in Fernwallow. There weren't many people around my age in the village. Mostly just…" Her face appeared in his mind, tears in her eyes. Tears he could have stopped, if he had gone to her.

"Danica. That was her name, wasn't it?"

He looked at Jethan and nodded. "We grew up together. Our relationship was turning into more than friendship." A hollow feeling expanded in his chest. He picked a few slivers of wood from the edge of the gate, inclining his head, so his hair would fall forward to hide his sorrow from Jethan.

"For what it's worth, I'm sorry. I wish you hadn't had to make that choice."

The person next to him was supposed to be his closest confidant and friend. Kasiel drew in a deep breath and lifted his head, tossing his hair back. He blinked away the moisture in his eyes. "I could have been happy in Fernwallow if all this hadn't happened. Edmund raised me to not want much. To be content with simple things. Looking at it now, I suspect he had an ulterior motive for instilling that in me, but I don't suppose it's a terrible trait to have."

He considered the fresh bandages on his wrists. Tath had changed them that morning. His hands were feeling more limber. Healing. "And yet, the more I discover about who I was supposed to have been, the harder I find it to imagine going back. There have been plenty of times out here that I wanted nothing more than to have my simple life back, but not because I'd be content with it. Just because it sounds better than always running or watching my…" He glanced at Jethan and smiled. "Watching my tehnaak get eaten by a wildcat half the size of my horse."

Jethan's pleased grin filled up a corner of that hollow space.

The door to the house opened again. It was Avris

who leaned out this time. "Hey! Kids! Get a move on."

"We better go before she puts something awful in our food." Jethan stepped back from the gate and started toward the path to the house.

"You know," Kasiel said as they strode through the rain, "I get the occasional 'my lord' or 'Cavenos' from the others and I feel like I'm more important than I'm ready to be. Then Avris shows up and I feel like a twelve-year-old boy about to get swatted for something stupid, like forgetting to dump the bedpan."

Jethan chuckled. "She has that effect on most people."

The stormy weather broke by midmorning the next day. Before they left, Jethan spent time alone in a room with each member of the family. When Kasiel asked Tath what he was doing, she said he was using his Charmer ability to convince them their experience with the unit hadn't been all bad. He couldn't change their memories, but by having a conversation with them while skillfully manipulating their reactions, he could leave them with an overall positive impression. The hope was that it would also lead them to question whether they had been complicit in harboring the Vanrians illegally and discourage them from alerting local guards.

While that was underway, Kasiel selected another horse. When they lost a mount to the crossbow bolt, its rider had taken over Lorin's horse, and the werdyn cats had killed Nix's. Given a choice between Loak's horse and the one he rode during his captivity, he chose Loak's. They now had only one spare animal left of the four they had taken from the mercenaries.

For the first few days back on the road, Jethan rode the extra horse, letting his usual mount heal before asking it to carry someone again. Kasiel tried out his Feral mindcraft on the horse Jethan rode, directing it as necessary. Most of the time, it was content to follow the others, requiring little intervention, but Jethan encouraged him to practice, regardless. His ability let him move the animal along when it tried to stop for grass and keep it calm when they increased the pace. At first, he got distracted easily and would lose his mental link to the animal. By the sixth day, maintaining a connection with the horse was becoming enough of a habit that he could stay in control without having to apply all his attention to the task.

For Kasiel and Jethan, long days in the saddle were painful, but they had little choice. Safety was a long way away. Discomfort left them both exhausted by the end of the day. One of the two healers gave them each a swallow of the sleep-inducing painkiller in the evenings, ensuring they could get the healing rest they needed. It meant Kasiel had limited chances to engage in conversation with his new companions, but recovery had to be the priority.

They saw no sign of Edmund's group, almost as if the heavy rain had washed them away. Kasiel quietly hoped nothing unfortunate had befallen them even as relief eased some of the tension in his gut. With the awakening of his Feral ability, staying with the Vanrians became more than the right choice. It was the only choice. They could teach him how to use it now that it was active. Around anyone from the Alliance kingdoms, it would be one more thing he needed to hide. He also hated to think what experiments Edmund might run on an awakened mind-crafter, especially given Jethan's suspicion that the symbols on Kasiel's weapons and armor were an attempt by the professor to trigger that awakening.

As his health improved and controlling Jethan's horse got easier, Kasiel had more energy for taking in the unfamiliar terrain and observing his companions. With both him and Jethan getting better, the group pushed a faster pace and longer hours in the saddle.

They were traveling through increasingly populous territory, with a greater risk of encountering locals. As a result, they kept their hoods up and stayed more alert to their surroundings.

That changed dynamic showed a deeper side to the connection between them. The entire unit communicated efficiently with gestures and looks. They were always acutely aware of each other, noticing immediately if anyone appeared uncomfortable or fell behind.

This silent rapport was most profound between the pairings. On the trail, the spirit siblings moved together like birds in flight, uncannily aware of their proximity to each other without ever looking to check. Wherever they were, in the saddle or at camp, they finished one another's sentences or handed one another things they needed before the other asked.

Would he and Jethan ever have that? They were getting a much later start than the other pairings, who had spent their entire lives together. It seemed unlikely, but then, several things had happened in his life of late that he would have thought impossible mere weeks ago.

The morning of the seventh day, Jethan called the group together while Tath changed the bandages on his wound. Kasiel watched her work, doing his best not to cringe at the set of four stitched slices across his teh-naak's shoulder. They were healing well, and Tath said the stitches could come out in another week. That was encouraging, but it didn't stop the moment of the attack from playing back in Kasiel's mind. The cat's strike. The pain and terror Jethan must have experienced as the beast flipped him like a doll and lunged for his throat.

Jethan caught him staring and a faint smirk drew up the corner of his mouth. He glanced around at the others. "Did I tell you all that I felt the werdyn cat's whiskers on my throat when it closed its mouth and backed away? It was that close." He held his thumb and finger up almost touching to emphasize the point. "A heartbeat later, and you all would have been short one exceptionally charming Charmer."

Chander slapped a hand on Kasiel's shoulder. "That's what we picked this guy up for. I knew he'd come in handy, eventually."

A round of laughter followed the comment, though Kasiel might have been happier not knowing that detail. A heartbeat. That left little room for error. He had never held someone's life in his hands before. Good thing he hadn't realized he was doing so at the time, or he might have choked on the pressure.

He answered Jethan's grin with one of his own, though he could tell by the slight sobering of the other youth's expression that his discomfort showed through.

"Right. Back to business." Jethan unrolled a map with Ahrin's help. "We're about here." He pointed to a forested region that looked exactly like every other forest on the map to Kasiel. "This mountain range gets impassably steep through here and here." He moved his finger to indicate the problem areas. "The only good crossing that won't add weeks to our journey is in this river valley, but that means coming out next to Andaro, the capital of Sarket. There will be local and Alliance patrols around there. We'll need to be invisible. That said, we're also getting shy on healing supplies and other necessities. There's a trading outpost higher in the valley. I propose we stop there to replenish our supplies."

Jethan's gaze moved up from the map. He met Kasiel's eyes. "Kas can pass as a local better than the rest of us with his accent. We can't send him in alone, though."

Kasiel nearly argued that he was the one without an accent, then it dawned on him that, to them, the opposite was true, so he held his silence.

"I can go," Tath offered. "I'll make sure he gets the right supplies."

Jethan nodded. "And I'll go. I can use my ability to make sure we get good deals without too many questions."

Darro, who sat cleaning his fingernails with the tip of his dagger, leaned forward, resting his elbow on his knee. "I'm not comfortable with this. We'd be risking the team leader, one of our healers, and our mission objective all at once."

"We won't be going into the city," Jethan countered.

"There will still be patrols out there, and probably Alliance presence," Darro said, holding to his objection.

Jethan leaned back. "What do you propose, then? Should we forge ahead and hope no one else gets hurt? We need someone who can talk to the merchants. Kasiel's the only one with an accent that won't draw too much attention. I can use my ability to help things go smoothly. We could leave Tath back if she gives us a list of what she needs."

Tath's lips twisted in a disappointed frown.

Darro glanced over at her. "She's the one I was least worried about losing."

She grabbed a twig off the ground and tossed it at him. "Thanks, calloch."

Kasiel had no clue what a calloch was, but he got the impression it wasn't polite from the cringing laughter of the others.

Darro caught the twig and snapped it between his fingers and thumb, winking at Tath. "Anytime."

Jethan shook his head at them and continued as if they had come to an agreement. "We'll plan on Kas and I going in with the possibility of adjusting our approach when we're close enough to scout the area."

"I still don't like it," Darro muttered.

"Noted." Jethan handed the map to Ahrin to roll up and tuck away. "Let's get moving."

It took the better part of two more days to reach the

market, avoiding major roadways. When they stopped late in the afternoon of the second day, Kasiel joined Jethan, Darro, and Kince on foot at the edge of the tree line on a hill overlooking their target.

For a trading outpost, it was busier than Kasiel expected, not that he had ever seen one before. A large circle of rough-built shops faced inward from the outer perimeter, with a smaller circle of stalls facing out from the inner edge set around three large central buildings. The smallest of the three in the middle appeared to be a tavern. The two larger structures were multi-story storage buildings, judging from goods being carried in and out.

Brightly colored flags and streamers hung between the shops and stalls, and crowds of people strolled about, bartering energetically back and forth with shopkeepers. A group of musicians on a stage near the tavern played a festive tune. At least seven riders wearing plate armor displayed the red and gold colors of the Pandrean Alliance on their surcoats. Five more well-armed individuals wore green and silver over their armor. Local guards moving through the crowd.

"Looks like some kind of festival," Kince said in a low voice.

"So much for that idea." Darro started turning away.

Jethan caught him with a hand on his arm. "No. This is perfect. The crowd will make it easier to blend in."

Darro shook his head. While the two switched to Vanrian to debate the situation, Kasiel scanned the market, spotting something that made his blood run cold.

"That's Garrick."

The others fell silent, turning to look at him.

He met their eyes, stomach turning as if he had eaten spoiled food, and pointed toward the market. "The dark-skinned man talking to an Alliance soldier alongside the tavern. That's Garrick, the smith from Fernwallow. Danica's father."

Jethan's gaze followed the direction Kasiel was pointing. He cursed under his breath. "The others are also here, then. They must have pushed on through the storm. They must have noticed we were trying to avoid roads and figured they could get ahead of us by using them."

Darro nodded. "It would have been easy to guess which way we were heading. There are only so many routes to Vanris in this region, and most are too difficult to be practical options." He met Jethan's eyes. "You know what this means."

Jethan brought a hand up to rub at his temple as if his head pained him. "It means the patrols will be watching for us, if not actively hunting us."

Kasiel's skin prickled. "What do we do now?"

"We give this place as wide a berth as we can and get in position to move past the city after nightfall."

At Jethan's words, the three headed back toward where the rest of the group waited. Kasiel lingered a moment, peering at the bustle of people. Was Danica down there somewhere?

He shook his head and followed the others. It didn't matter. It couldn't matter anymore.

They made their way around the outpost, staying deep in the trees on the side of the mountain. The terrain was rocky, forcing them to lead the animals so they could pick the best footing. As they moved along the edge of the mountain, the massive city of Andaro came into view.

Kasiel had never seen such a large city outside of drawings in books. It was strikingly white, built from the pale stone that lay exposed throughout the landscape. Huge, both in sprawl and in height, it had several towering, multi-level buildings, some of which had spires atop them, giving them even greater reach. A vast white wall surrounded much of the city, butting up against the cliffs on the far side of the valley. That left them one way to get past.

The river ran through the near side of the city, sweeping under the wall. The main road split at the city gate. One branch went through the gate and the other crossed the river, swinging around through a wide swath of forest that nestled between the wall and the steeper parts of the mountainside.

As soon as they were in position to make a run through that swath of forest after dark, they stopped and tied up the horses. They would take advantage of the remaining daylight to eat and rest before their nocturnal sprint. Tath took a few minutes to pull the stitches from Kasiel's arm. With the healers' care, the wound was closing nicely, and no longer needed them.

After she left them, he and Jethan laid back on the rough ground to try getting some rest. Tension bounced through Kasiel like a bolt of lightning, leaving him wide awake, staring at the darkening sky above the canopy of the trees.

After a few minutes, he glanced at the youth lying next to him with his eyes closed. "Jeth?"

"Mm-hmm." Jethan didn't open his eyes.

"You asleep?"

Jethan breathed a laugh.

"Sorry. Stupid question." Kasiel hesitated. Maybe this wasn't the time to worry about such things, but a question had become stuck in his head. If he asked, perhaps having the answer would allow him to rest a little. "How were you so sure it was me? I mean, that I was, what was the name? Hahren Cavenos?"

Jethan looked at him, a flicker of amusement in his smirk. "You have two tattoos. One with the symbol for your bloodline, kind of like a family crest," he added when Kasiel furrowed his brow, "and one with the symbol for my bloodline as your tehnaak. Tath checked for them when you were unconscious."

Kasiel shifted onto his side. "I don't have any tattoos."

Jethan's arched brow and deepening smirk begged to differ. "They're small. On the back of your head under your hair. Every child gets them."

"You're saying I have tattoos on my head I never knew about?"

Jethan looked up at the tree canopy. "I am. You were a month old when you got the spirit bonding one. They gave you the other right after your first birthday."

Kasiel rubbed the back of his head as if he might feel these alleged markings. "You're sure I have tattoos?"

Jethan chuckled. "Try to get some rest. We'll probably have to ride through the night. We can talk about these things more when we're away from this place."

Kasiel closed his eyes. He lay there chewing at the inside of his lip for a few seconds, fingers still feeling the back of his head. His hand brushed the cut edge of one ear, and he opened his eyes again. "Was it Tath who told you my ears had been cut? She must have seen them when she looked for the tattoos."

Jethan swallowed hard as he lay staring up at the treetops. "Rest, tehnaak," he murmured and squeezed his eyes shut.

When Avris woke them after midnight, the moonlit darkness that greeted Kasiel had a dreamlike quality to it. The group prepared in relative silence, communicating mostly with looks and gestures. They had left the horses saddled and ready to go. As a result, it took little time to get everyone pulled together and mounted up. Before they lined up to head out, Jethan moved his horse beside Kasiel's.

"Try to stay with me, but if anything happens to me, stick with any of us you can see still pushing north. Whatever you do, keep going north. Even if we all fall, we will have succeeded in our mission if you make it home."

Kasiel wanted to argue that he was no more important than the rest of them, but this wasn't the place or time for such debates. He would hope nothing bad happened, so he didn't have to make that call.

They moved through the woods single file. The moon was bright, but in the cover of the trees, darkness prevailed. They had to be cautious of rocks, fallen branches, and other obstacles that could injure the horses. If they stayed in a line, only the lead rider had to worry about picking their route. For now, that was Merrin, who apparently was quite skilled in the art of pathfinding at night. Avris followed her. Then Jethan and Kasiel followed by the rest. Darro brought up the rear, in place to defend against an attack from behind if necessary.

Kasiel flinched at every sound not made by their horses as they progressed slowly onward. They stayed off the road, assuming that would be under surveillance, especially alongside the city where guards on the wall would see anyone passing. He peered into the surrounding forest, looking for lights that could be torches, or for movement in shadows that might suggest a waiting soldier.

The white wall, barely visible beyond the trees, appeared to stretch on forever. Once or twice, they came close enough to hear the distant sound of soldiers on the wall talking. Unrelenting tension balled up into a series of knots in Kasiel's stomach. It wasn't until the wall started curving away from them that he felt like he could contemplate breathing normally again.

The group slowed, and he noticed a few deeper shadows in the dark with suspicious shapes. While he peered at one, it moved. He started raising his arm, intending to point it out to anyone paying attention. Kince rode up on his opposite side and placed a hand on his arm, pushing it back down. When Kasiel looked at him, Kince lifted a crossbow and fired into that shifting darkness. An unmistakably human grunt accompanied the thwack of the bolt striking home.

A whistle sounded through the trees, and several shadows moved at once. The Vanrian group instantly sped up, their horses falling out of line as they kicked them up to a canter and angled toward the road. Stealth had failed. Now they had to make a run for it. Kasiel heard the crack as his mount's hoof struck a rock. The animal stumbled but righted itself quickly. Something skimmed past his shoulder. He didn't look, focusing instead on Jethan, who had fallen back beside him as they leaned low over their horses to avoid the branches.

When they broke out onto the roadway, another rider burst from the trees on the opposite side, raising his mace. Jethan ignored him, turning up the road and kicking his mount to a full gallop. Kasiel followed his example. Darro plunged out of the woods and charged at the soldier, shoving his sword through an opening beneath the man's upraised arm with unerring precision. The rider dropped his weapon, tumbling forward. Darro yanked his blade free and rejoined the group, driving his mount up alongside Kasiel.

At the speed they were now moving, it took all Kasiel's riding skill to stay centered in the saddle, ensuring that he didn't disrupt his horse's balance. He yearned to check that everyone was still with them, but he could at least see Merrin and Avris ahead, and Kince and Darro now on either side of him and Jethan.

The wall curved away on their right and the forest thinned out, giving way to an open rocky hillside that sloped gradually downhill alongside the river. The road clung close to the water, bending with the flow of the riverbank. Their group cut tight around the bends, barely staying on the solid footing of the roadway.

It sounded like more than their eleven horses pounding down the roadway to Kasiel, but he didn't turn to look. Two arrows whistled past, both missing their marks, assuming the opposition intended them as more than threats. That at least confirmed that they had enemies in pursuit. A horn blared somewhere further back, calling for additional soldiers.

"Ahrin!"

Tath's shriek rang out at the same moment a horse's head disappeared from off his left flank. Based on what Jethan had told him as they were leaving, he should keep going, but then Darro and Kince also dropped away. Kasiel pulled his horse back, noticing that Jethan and the two ahead of them were now doing the same.

When he spun his mount, he saw Tath kicking her horse back in the other direction to engage a city soldier. A few feet away, Ahrin sat in the road looking stunned, his white hair aglow in the moonlight. An arrow shaft protruded from his back and one arm twisted at an odd angle, broken by the fall from his mount. The soldier was forcing Tath on the defensive as the rest of their pursuers skidded to a stop behind Ahrin. There were twelve of them, six Alliance soldiers, five city guards, and Garrick.

"Stand down!" Garrick bellowed, his deep voice booming over them.

Darro kicked his mount up beside Tath and grabbed her reins, pulling her horse back along with his own. The soldier she had engaged with retreated to his side. For a second, the only sound other than the heavy breathing of the horses was that of Ahrin groaning and wheezing for air.

Garrick maneuvered his mount to the front of the opposing group. "Return Kasiel to us and we will allow you to take your wounded friend and go."

A few of the Alliance and city guards looked sharply at him as if surprised by the offer, but they held their silence.

"Tath." Ahrin coughed. Blood trickled from the corner of his mouth and streamed from a laceration above one eye.

Tath let out an animalistic groan. She tried to jerk away from the grip Darro now had on her arm, but he held on. Tears ran unchecked down her cheeks.

Unwilling to watch her suffer, Kasiel urged his mount forward a step.

"Don't," Jethan growled under his breath.

The distant sound of horses galloping from the city reached them. In the moonlight, Kasiel could see a large group coming through the gates, leaving a cloud of dust in their wake. He looked from Garrick to Ahrin and back again.

"You can fix this, Kasiel." Garrick's voice was softer now, his gaze locked on Kasiel.

He could. If he let them have him, he could get Tath her tehnaak back. From where he was sitting, it looked like a reasonable trade to save Ahrin and make sure the others escaped.

He urged his mount forward another couple of steps. A victorious gleam lit Garrick's dark eyes.

Ahrin coughed again, his breath coming in strained gasps. He looked at Tath. "You'll be... all right... tehnaak." Then his gaze moved to something behind Kasiel, and he nodded.

A crossbow bolt flew past Kasiel's shoulder from somewhere behind him, sinking deep in the side of Ahrin's neck. The young healer fell back with an awful choking sound, the arrow in his back snapping against the ground. Blood spurted out around the shaft of the bolt in his neck. Tath let out a broken wail. Anguish and rage flooded Kasiel. He drove the storm of emotion into the horses across from them, making them want to escape. To cast off and hurt the people riding them.

The opposing horses broke into a frenzy. They fought their riders, rearing, bucking, and twisting to break away. Caught by surprise, one Alliance soldier and two of the city watchmen fell. The Alliance soldier's helmet took a strike from the hoof of another animal, and he dropped back the way Ahrin had, either dead or unconscious.

The rest of the soldiers and Garrick were jumping clear of their mounts, letting the animals go and drawing weapons.

"Kas," Jethan shouted, "bring Darro and Ahrin's horses."

He glanced around. Darro had jumped into the saddle behind Tath, one arm wrapped firmly about her waist as he steered her horse with the other. His mount, now loose, started running away from the conflict. A little closer, Ahrin's gelding stood trembling as if it expected to be the next to fall. The Vanrian group wheeled their horses, ready to run. Kasiel took control of the two animals, pulling them over to join the rest as they bolted from the scene. Behind them, the opposing soldiers were rushing to collect their mounts now that Kasiel's concentration was elsewhere.

They rode hard from there. The pursuing group gave up almost immediately. Perhaps the realization that they were up against at least one mind-crafter had shaken them. It was a good thing they didn't realize it was him, or they would know how inexperienced he was with his ability. They only knew someone in the Vanrian unit could control their mounts. Having no way to identify who it was or if they had other mind-crafters with them was apparently enough to crack their resolve.

Were there more mind-crafters in the group? Aside from Jethan, of course. It struck him as odd now that he had never asked. Had Ahrin been a mind-crafter?

Kasiel was distantly aware of moisture trailing down his cheeks. When the group finally slowed their pace, he looked around and noticed tear tracks in the dust on the faces of all his companions. He barely knew the young healer and his chest ached with the loss. The others had to feel it much more intensely than he did. Ahrin was one of them. And yet, someone among them had fired that bolt, denying Kasiel the chance to save him.

His gaze shifted to the crossbow fastened to Kince's saddle. He wasn't the only one with such a weapon at hand, but something made Kasiel suspect either Kince or Darro would have had the resolve to take that shot. Darro had been busy with Tath. That left Kince. He glared his fury at Kince's back for the rest of the ride, struggling to resist the urge to send the man's mount into revolt.

They stopped shortly after dawn in a clearing at the center of a dense patch of trees. The sun was rising above their now diminished group, oblivious to the sorrow that weighed them down. They all climbed wearily from their horses, except for Kasiel. Fueled by an inner fury he could barely contain, he leapt off and stormed over to Kince.

"You killed Ahrin!"

Kince wheeled on him, and Kasiel fell back a few steps, shocked by the anguish and fury that twisted the man's tear-dampened face.

"Yes! I killed my friend! I killed one of our healers." His hands clenched into fists. "Tath's tehnaak." His voice cracked as he said the last.

To Kasiel's left, Tath broke out in heart-wrenching sobs. Wedro strode over and pulled her into a firm embrace, a few tears slipping from his eyes as he held her.

Kince took another step closer, glaring at Kasiel. "I killed him because he told me to. You know why he told me to? Because he knew he would die from his injuries anyway, and he saw—we all saw—that you were considering giving yourself to them. None of us wanted to lose Ahrin. But we *can't* lose you. Don't you get that! You're the reason we've been here, risking our lives for the last three months. You're the only one who absolutely must make it back or we did all of this for nothing. You don't get to judge me for doing what they sent me here to do. I would never have had to make that choice if it weren't for you!"

"Enough, Kince," Jethan snapped, stepping up alongside Kasiel.

Kince's glare moved to Jethan. Then he spun and stormed off into the trees.

"I've got this," Darro said, jogging past them in pursuit of his spirit sibling.

Kasiel turned in the opposite direction, avoiding looking at any of the others. He followed Kince's example and strode out into the trees, desperate to get away from them all. These people who somehow believed he was more important than any of them. He wasn't. He never would be. Nor did he ever want to be.

He kept going for several minutes, his body humming with adrenaline and a directionless fury. With no goal in mind and no clue where he was heading, he continued until he came to the edge of a large pond. A pair of ducks at the edge startled at his approach, flying up from the surface only to land again toward the middle. He put his hand on a tree, seeking stable support in a moment when everything was in upheaval. The bark was thin and papery, nothing like the rough evergreen bark in the forests around Fernwallow. Still, he found something soothing in the soft crackle as he rubbed off a flake with his thumb.

Footsteps approached behind him. He didn't have to turn to know who it was. The other youth's presence was like a warm blanket on a chilly night, bringing comfort he didn't want or deserve right now.

"You did well back there," Jethan said, his tone careful, as if he feared startling him like an easily spooked deer.

"Really?" Kasiel snapped, staring out over the pond. "How do you figure that?"

Jethan came up beside him, unfazed by his temper. He looked out at the water too, its surface like glass now that the ripples from the ducks had settled. "If you hadn't thrown their horses into a frenzy when you did, we might not have gotten away. You bought us time, and I believe you scared them. I don't think they were expecting us to have mind-crafters this far south of the Break."

Kasiel glanced over at him, squinting his eyes against a glare of sunlight from the pond's surface. "Are there others in the group?"

"Mind-crafters? No. Just you and me. Vanris rarely sends awakened mind-crafters beyond the Break. The southern kingdoms are far too eager to kill us all. They agreed to risk sending me because we're paired."

Kasiel snorted derisively and faced forward again. "You mean because you were the only person they could send who might not hate me when this is over?"

"It's not your fault, tehnaak. They informed us of the mission's goals and risks going into this. We're just all hurting right now."

Something about the tightness in his voice caught Kasiel's attention. He looked over to see a silent tear sliding down Jethan's cheek. The other youth made no move to wipe it away.

Kasiel lowered his gaze. "Will Tath be all right?"

Jethan drew a shaky breath. "Not anytime soon," he answered honestly. "Losing your tehnaak is like losing part of everything you are. We'll have to keep an eye on her."

They stood there in silence for a few minutes, feeling the warmth of the morning sun, watching insects move among the plants at the edge of the pond. Kasiel noticed the buzzing of those insects and the occasional whisper of a breeze drifting through the trees and grasses. The peacefulness of the spot presented a stark contrast to the chaos and pain that brought them here.

"Kince was right, you know," Jethan said. "That arrow was deep, and in an awful spot. If you had let them have you in trade for Ahrin, it would have only given Tath the chance to watch him die slowly without being able to do anything to save him. Ahrin was a healer. He knew what he was doing when he gave Kince that nod."

Kasiel ground his teeth, fighting the tightening in

his throat. "I don't want anyone to die for me. Not ever again."

He didn't like the flicker of pity he saw in Jethan's gaze. "It won't be the last time, Kas. Not given who and what you are. But, for what it's worth, I'm here to help you face what's ahead."

Kasiel gave him a hard look. "I'm going to hold you to that. Today, and every day after this."

Jethan lowered his gaze, kicking a pebble into the water. He blew out a puff of air, sending the front of his hair flipping briefly up, then nodded. "Fair enough, tehnaak."

Kasiel noticed a blossom of red in the middle of the bandages on Jethan's shoulder. "Your shoulder's bleeding."

"Yes. I may have pulled a stitch or two."

Kasiel turned around, gesturing for Jethan to join him. "Let's get it taken care of, then."

Jethan peered out over the pond for a few seconds, brushing away another tear that crept down one cheek, then he fell into step alongside Kasiel.

CHAPTER THIRTEEN

The dynamic of the group changed after that. The comfortable rapport the Vanrians shared remained, but their manner was more subdued. Unfortunately, the camaraderie that had been developing between Kasiel and some of them suffered as well. He got the sense Kince wasn't the only one who held Ahrin's death against him, and he didn't blame them for it. He probably would have felt the same. They might have come into the mission informed of the risks, but how could being told that they might lose someone adequately prepare them for the moment someone dear died for the sake of a relative stranger?

Tath barely spoke at all to anyone. In the evenings, she sat staring off into the distance, often with tears tracking silently down her cheeks. If not for the gentle prodding of the others, she wouldn't bother to eat. No one pressed her to engage. Nor did they let her out of their sight. Even when she went off to relieve herself, Avris or Merrin would coincidentally need to go as well and join her.

They had less cover as mountains gave way to open plains and they left the forests behind, but the one patrol they encountered rapidly retreated after Kasiel panicked their mounts. They would undoubtedly report the incident, but the Vanrian group was clear of the area long before anyone could come to investigate. Large stretches of open ground let them keep an aggressive pace, riding long hours under pleasant skies that did nothing to chase away the storm cloud hanging over them.

After a few days of travel, they stopped outside a remote village not much larger than Fernwallow. Kasiel and Jethan ventured in to sell the remaining mercenary horse and purchase supplies. With Jethan's Charmer ability, the process went smoothly. The people they dealt with directly succumbed easily to his manipulations. A few villagers who eyed them suspiciously from afar appeared unwilling to venture close enough to investigate.

Three days after that, they arrived on the southern edge of the Crimson Break. They made their approach through one of the derelict border towns under the cover of dark, wary of being spotted by patrols or one of the Pandrean Alliance watchtowers that dotted the horizon. After another long day in the saddle, they holed up in a mostly intact barn on the edge of town, giving themselves and their mounts a rest before making the final push across the Break. It was a hideout the Vanrian group had discovered on their way south. The barn was spacious enough to bring the horses inside and the empty hayloft provided a place for the weary riders to stretch out.

Looking out a window in the loft, even in the dark, Kasiel could see the change in the land beyond the watchtowers. The ground here supported sparse plant life and was scorched black in places. According to Darro, the scorching was mostly the Alliance's doing. They had a variety of alchemical bombs they favored both for offensive attacks and as cover to let them fall back when certain types of mind-crafters accompanied the Vanrian troops. That scarred desert landscape stretched out for miles north of the border and ran east and west all the way to the coastlines.

Jethan stepped up next to him, placing a hand on his shoulder. "You should eat and try to get a little rest. We'll be pushing to get across the Break in a hurry."

Kasiel faced him. "Will your arm be good for it?"

"It should be. Tath pulled the stitches." He lifted his sleeve to show the four healing scars. "Come on."

Kasiel followed him over to join the others. They all looked wide awake, perhaps excited to be on friendly soil again. He touched the back of his head absently as he sat down next to Jethan.

"Isn't it kind of cruel to tattoo infants?"

He kept his voice low, intending only Jethan to hear, but a few soft chuckles rose around the group. Wedro opened his mouth as if to say something, but it was Tath who spoke first, brushing away one of a seemingly endless supply of rogue tears as she looked at him.

"It's not that bad. The tattoos are small, and we give them something to put them to sleep first. By the time they wake up, it's done. We use a salve that helps them heal quickly and with little pain."

"That doesn't sound so awful." He touched the back of his head once more, then shrugged and met her eyes before she could disengage again. "You've got more effective healing elixirs and salves than anything I've ever used or read about."

Tath picked up a piece of dried meat, staring at it as if it were a problem to solve rather than something to eat. "A lot of the plants we use we brought with us from our homeland. It took a long time to replicate the proper growing conditions when we got here. If things hadn't gone bad with the southern kingdoms when they did, we probably would have shared or at least traded some of our resources and knowledge with them."

Kasiel glanced around at his companions. He knew so little about Vanrian culture. Now that they were close to their destination, he found he had a million questions. It was hard to pick one. "How did the war start?"

Darro and Chander began speaking at the same time. Both fell silent, looking at one another.

Darro inclined his head to Chander. "You're our resident history enthusiast."

The group passed more food around and settled in to listen.

Chander sat up straighter, grinning. "You really were cut off from the world, weren't you? It's rare I get an audience who doesn't already know most of this stuff. I guess I should start with how our people ended up here. Our original homeland was a large island to the northeast of Pandrea. About 150 years ago, give or take a few, a chain of volcanic eruptions gradually rendered much of the island uninhabitable. We had to abandon our homeland using fleets of fishing boats, along with some larger vessels we constructed to carry plants and animals that were integral to our society. About a third of our population died in the early eruptions. Even more died during the crossing. The survivors landed on the northern end of Pandrea. There were no previous inhabitants in the region, so we set to work making a new home for ourselves. After we established a few coastal settlements, we gradually spread east, west, and south until, a little over 100 years after our arrival on Pandrea, we ventured into the desert and ran up against the northernmost edge of the Sarket and Delaphine kingdoms."

He paused, taking a long swig from a stoneglass bottle of Vanrian Black Mead someone had dug out of their pack. "The encounters in the border settlements were peaceful at first until a young Charmer—"

"Always the Charmers making trouble," Avris said, winking at Jethan.

"As I was saying," Chander continued, "a young Charmer started showing off his ability to impress a local girl he fancied."

"Love makes fools of us all," Wedro chimed in before taking a swallow of the mead and passing the bottle along.

Chander nodded. "Indeed, it does. When the southern kingdoms learned that some of us could manipulate people's minds, that budding trust started breaking down. Anytime something didn't go the way they wanted—trade negotiations, card or dice games, friendly competitions—they accused us of using Vanrian mindcraft to influence the outcomes. Even when the people involved weren't mind-crafters. Fights started breaking out in the border towns almost daily."

Kasiel accepted the bottle from Jethan. He took a drink, pleased to be part of the circle cracking a stone together. It felt like a step toward healing the rift between them.

Chander went on. "A brawl broke out one night in a tavern in a little border town called Crimsondale, named for the vibrant red blooms produced by a type of cactus that grew there in abundance. The fighting spilled into the streets. One of the Vanrians involved was a potent Frightener. He used his ability on the entire town. People got trampled to death trying to flee. A few even killed themselves to escape the terror.

"Word spread fast after that, and soon the Vanrian people were being banned from more and more towns south of the border. Within a year, relations deteriorated enough that the Pandrean Trade Ministry halted all imports of Vanrian goods. Vanris returned the favor, putting an end to imports from the southern kingdoms. Crimsondale was the first town to fall to full scale battle. Within five years, the entire border was a wide swath of destruction. They started calling it the Crimson Break after the first town to fall."

Darro picked up the tale when Chander paused.

"The southern kingdoms formed the Pandrean Alliance to keep us from crossing the border, which wasn't such a tragic thing. We had everything we needed in the north. After a couple of years of uneasy quiet, however, some southern groups started running strike missions across the Break specifically aimed at killing mind-crafters. That didn't go over well, so war broke out again. Fighting has continued ever since. It fluctuates, ebbing and flowing, sometimes with the seasons, sometimes simply because things work that way. It's never fully stopped, though. Both sides maintain active military bases and watchtowers along the border now."

Darro took a swig of the mead that had made its way around to him. Then he cocked his head to one side, considering Kasiel. "Does that answer your question satisfactorily?"

"It does." He chewed his lip for a second. "I just feel like I don't…" He hesitated, finding it hard to speak candidly with all of them looking at him, a few with more reserve than others.

Kince took the bottle from Darro as he spoke. "No one is going to expect you to be versed in our culture overnight, danro. Your life is about to be transformed. Give it time." With that, he tossed back his head and started taking a long drink.

Wedro popped Kince in the shoulder. "Save some for the rest of us, calloch."

As if his life hadn't already gone through dramatic transformations. Kasiel looked at Jethan while the other two tussled briefly over the bottle. "What's danro mean?"

His tehnaak leaned closer, speaking in a low voice. "There's not a precise translation, but danro is essentially someone who has trouble fitting in or doesn't belong. Don't let the language issue worry you. We all learn Pandrean Common alongside Vanrian in school.

You won't run into anyone who can't understand or talk to you."

Somehow, that wasn't especially comforting. Knowing they had all apparently had an organized education while he grew up learning what little Edmund or the villagers in Fernwallow had time to teach him was intimidating enough. That the Vanrians would always know what he was saying, while he would only know what they were saying if they wanted him to, made it worse. He truly would be a danro in Vanris.

Avris leaned across Jethan. "Hey Kas, if you want, I could do a few braids for you? Help you fit in."

She was clearly trying to make him feel better, but the thought of having his hair braided back, revealing his cut ears, made his throat squeeze tight.

Jethan leaned forward and whispered something in her ear.

Her cheeks colored. "Sorry." She averted her gaze. "I forgot."

The mead came back around and Kasiel took a swig. He brought it up to take a second one, hoping to calm his nerves, but Jethan caught his arm.

"Easy, tehnaak. I need you sober for this ride."

Kasiel lowered the bottle and corked it, passing it on reluctantly. "I take it we expect trouble."

"A chase is likely, at the very least. We made it across unnoticed coming south, but there are more patrols moving between the watchtowers this time. Might have been an incident since last time we came through. Regardless, we'll try to time our run so that we're starting out when the patrols are at their farthest points from here, but it would be a miracle if none of them spotted us."

"How long will the crossing take?"

"It's about two miles to our border from here," Wedro said. "It's also nice and flat, so the horses should be able to keep up good speed. We ought to be within sight of our watchtower before any pursuit can catch us. The Vanrian patrols in this area are watching for our return and will come to our aid if we get into trouble."

"We have to get close enough for them to spot us first," Chander muttered.

"We will." Jethan's tone was encouraging and confident, a leader reassuring his soldiers. Or maybe he was trying to reassure Kasiel.

They stayed for another hour, a few of them managing to get a brief nap in. Kasiel wasn't one of those. The crossing itself made him nervous, but not as much as what waited on the other side. An entire country full of people he had grown up believing were bad because, on the rare occasion someone in Fernwallow mentioned the war, they framed Vanris as the aggressor. The tale they had shared presented a far more complicated reality. Soon, he would come into that culture as an outsider. A stranger who knew next to nothing about them and had grown up thinking of them as the enemy.

When the hour was up, Jethan rallied them, and they climbed down from the loft to collect their horses. They would ride out the back entrance that opened onto the Break. Kasiel, standing near the front of the building, was about to mount up when the door behind him slid open about a foot. An Alliance soldier stepped into the opening. His eyes went wide as they adjusted to the darkness within. Panic froze Kasiel in place. He opened his mouth to shout a warning, but fear strangled his voice.

Darro appeared from out of the deeper shadows and grabbed the soldier, yanking him inside. He swung around behind the man in a smooth, dance-like motion. With one hand, he lifted the man's chin while the other drove a dagger into his throat. Even in the dark, Kasiel could see the pain and horror in the man's eyes before his life drained away. Darro let him fall in the dirt.

"Roland?" another voice called from outside.

Darro signaled them to move with one hand, waiting until Kasiel had mounted alongside Jethan to hurry to his own horse. They shoved the door at the back open and burst out into the night, plunging full speed ahead before they were even clear of the barn. A horn rang out and Jethan cursed.

"Stay with me," he shouted at Kasiel.

Kasiel kicked his horse hard as the rest of the group slowed to drop behind him and Jethan before urging their mounts up to speed up again. He knew what they were doing. They were putting themselves in danger to protect him again, and he hated it. The best way to keep them safe, however, was to make it across the Break. He leaned low over his horse's neck and slipped into its head, encouraging it to run as fast as it could. The animal stretched long, pushing for greater speed. The ground swept past beneath them.

More horns blared from the two nearest Alliance watchtowers. He had no way to know how close their pursuers might be, since the guard's arrival had thrown off the timing of their departure. They were well into the battle-scarred land when a few arrows flew past. He heard a grunt close behind him, but absent the sound of anyone falling, he held to his course, focusing on keeping his mount moving ahead. Jethan's horse stumbled a few strides later and started fighting his rider. Kasiel slipped into its head as well. The animal was in pain, but he had to force it onward if Jethan was going to make it to the other side.

The terrain was relatively flat. That, along with the shorter distance, would be why they chose this crossing. He could see a massive watchtower looming in the darkness far ahead of them. If he could see the black monstrosity in the moonlight, maybe the people manning the tower could see them.

An arrow flew past, skimming the side of Kasiel's leg armor. He heard another pained grunt behind him, but all the riders and horses kept moving. How many times could they get that lucky, though? One of them wasn't going to make it. They would lose someone else, and they would hate him even more because of it.

Anger and frustration welled up in him. He could turn back and face the Alliance soldiers pursuing them, panic their mounts like he had done before. If someone had to die, why couldn't he be the one to decide who took that risk?

His horse's speed faltered in response to his thoughts.

Then that sense of looming despair vanished, an overwhelming confidence taking its place. Without a doubt, they were going to reach the other side. All of them. Suddenly, he was flying free on his horse's back, ready to face the world. They had nothing to fear from the Alliance soldiers chasing them. They only had to keep moving.

Peering ahead, he spotted figures racing toward them from the direction of the Vanrian tower. Given the speed they were all traveling at, the distance between them was closing fast. The riders started as little black blobs in the dark, quickly resolving into seven individuals who were pushing their mounts as hard as he and his companions pushed theirs.

The Vanrian unit eased up on their horses, letting the animals slow. Kasiel dared a glance over his shoulder. The Alliance soldiers were pulling up and wheeling around to gallop in the other direction. He blew out a heavy exhale, relaxing into the saddle as they dropped to a weary trot before the two groups converged. That brief sense of elation faded away.

Two of the new arrivals called taunts after the retreating Alliance soldiers as they stopped their mounts.

"Ahninveth na sek," one rider greeted Jethan. "We've been hoping to see your unit for a while."

Jethan grinned at the man. "Good to see you, Ahndhomen Kastus. We've been away far too long." Jethan turned his mount to survey the group. "Anyone hurt?"

Kince was pulling at an arrow wedged in his shoulder armor. "More leather than flesh," he grumbled, "again."

Tath had dismounted and was helping Chander with an arrow embedded in his thigh. Their speed and the angle of the strike appeared to have kept it from sinking too deep.

"My horse has an arrow in his hip." Jethan swung off the animal. He looked up at Kasiel. "I know you kept him going. Thank you for that."

Kasiel flushed, grateful for the dark that hid it. He leaned down toward Jethan. "Something odd happened out there. I was certain we were going to lose someone. Then, for no apparent reason, that fear went away."

Jethan gestured to the man he called Kastus, who was steering his mount closer to them. "Kastus is an Enkindler. He can boost peoples' courage, make them feel braver and more optimistic. It's extremely useful on the battlefield and in other high-stress situations."

The knowledge that the man used mindcrafting on him gave Kasiel an uneasy twisting in his gut. It seemed like a relatively harmless form of mindcrafting, but being manipulated in any way didn't sit well. And yet, the man who had done it was smiling openly at them as if nothing out of the ordinary had occurred.

"I wanted you all to know you were almost home free." Kastus shifted his weight forward into something of a mounted bow. "You must be the young Lord Hahren Cavenos. It's an honor to meet you, my lord."

CHAPTER FOURTEEN

It took a little over an hour to tend injuries, then they were moving again, heading east and slightly north with an enclosed wagon driven by one of the watchtower soldiers. Kastus also accompanied them, riding outside to help Darro and Kince manage the horses for the first stretch while the others climbed inside the wagon to rest. They left Jethan's injured mount behind, letting the watchtower guards deal with its wound.

Tath wept herself to sleep in Merrin's embrace, devastated anew at returning to Vanris without Ahrin by her side. Merrin dozed off soon after, her arms still wrapped around the brokenhearted healer. Most of the others, Jethan included, also fell fast asleep as the wagon bumped along. Kasiel supposed that wasn't surprising. After months spent on high alert in enemy territory, they had completed their mission and were finally safe again. They were home.

He didn't share that sense of relief. His home in Fernwallow was a place he could never return to. A memory spoiled by the reality of how and why he had ended up there. That didn't mean he felt like he belonged here now. This land was foreign to him. The people here would expect things of him, as a mind-crafter and as the son of an important figure in their society, that he wasn't prepared for. If his current companions were typical, then this was a society full of highly trained and educated soldiers. What could an ignorant, sheltered youth from a backwater village offer them?

He glanced around at the others in the dim interior of the wagon. For a time, he had started feeling like he was becoming part of the group. Ahrin's death changed that. A few of those who pulled away after the incident appeared to be relaxing back to where they had been before, but it wasn't the same. Maybe they realized that the trade wasn't worth it. He couldn't heal and could barely fight. He knew next to nothing about their history or culture. He didn't even have proper ears. Of course, it was possible he was the one who couldn't move past it now. Did it matter? Other than Jethan, would he even see any of them again after they finished this? Or would they disappear from his life?

Kasiel got up and crept to the back of the wagon. He shifted the canvas aside, blinking at the bright light of day. A few of the horses tied behind the wagon lifted their heads, though most were too weary to register surprise at his sudden appearance. Spotting his horse among them, he climbed over the back and hopped down.

He was on the ground for about two strides when Darro, riding alongside the wagon, slowed his mount, dropping back parallel with Kasiel.

"You should stay inside. You'll want to be rested when we reach Etrion."

"I can't sleep," he countered. "I'd rather see the countryside if I'm going to be awake anyway."

Darro's expression hardened, and Kasiel recalled the look he had seen in the man's eyes when he killed the Alliance guard in the barn. Cold. Determined. Completely unmoved.

"No offense, Cavenos, but this mission isn't over until we present you to your father. I'd rather you remained safe in the wagon until then."

Kasiel wanted to argue, but he hesitated before Darro's hard stare.

"Don't worry, I'll watch out for him." Jethan hopped out of the wagon to join Kasiel. "Come on. We'll ride for a while. I can point out some of the local sights. Of which there really aren't many of out here," he added with a smirk, "but I'll try to make up something interesting."

Without stopping the procession, they pulled two horses from the line and mounted. Jethan took them to the opposite side of the wagon from where Darro and Kince were riding. Kastus was on this side, and he nodded a greeting to each of them, lowering his torso in a slight bow to Kasiel again.

Kasiel gave a nod in return, shifting uncomfortably in his saddle. How many people were going to offer him gestures of deference? He didn't like it. They all knew he hadn't earned it, and it reminded him of Ahrin's death and the priority they had put on his life as the son of Arhk Cavenos, Dhomvalen of Vanris, Beast of the Break.

He pushed those thoughts away. "Kastus addressed you as Ahninveth na sek. Is that a rank? Are you an officer?"

"The answers are yes and no. Darro and Kince are both inveths, second-level inveth in Darro's case. That would be the rough equivalent of a Pandrean Alliance captain. They would normally be the ranking officers in our unit. An ahninveth is an inveth with mind-crafter abilities. The na sek portion signifies that it is a temporary rank boost for a specific mission. It's a solid short-term promotion, considering I'm not quite two years out of basic combat training."

Kasiel nodded, trying not to dwell on whether he should have been in basic combat training until two years ago and what that lack would mean for him now.

"And the rank you gave Kastus?"

"Ahndhomen. A dhomen is the basic equivalent of an Alliance general, one rank above a fourth-level inveth—"

"And an ahndhomen is a mind-crafter of the same rank," Kasiel finished for him.

"Exactly, though mind-crafters technically outrank their non-mind-crafter counterparts." Jethan pointed north, abruptly changing the subject. "See those black crags out there?"

Kasiel pulled his thoughts back to their surroundings and looked in the specified direction. In the distance, a series of enormous, jagged black crags shot up high above the landscape, casting a vast shadow upon the gradual slopes leading up to them. "Hard to miss them."

"They stretch almost all the way to the eastern coast like that. They originally called the formation Vareyl's Gift after the woman whose expedition first reached the crags because the stone proved useful for construction and contains elements that we use in some of our alloys. It's more commonly called Vareyl's Warning now, however, because she also led the first expedition south of them that introduced us to the southern kingdoms we would eventually end up at war with. That black stone is everywhere around here, much of it below the dirt outside of Vareyl's Warning. There are forests and grasslands if you go a little further north, but down here, that black stone and plentiful clay deposits are our primary building materials, which is the reason the city looks like a black storm on the horizon," he said, pointing ahead of them now.

Peering forward, Kasiel realized the black blob he had passingly noticed on the horizon was developing the peaks and valleys of a city skyline like Andaro, only this appeared larger than the Sarket capital. Possibly much larger. His gut twisted at the thought.

By noon, the city on the horizon had grown considerably. Kastus left them, galloping ahead to herald their arrival, which increased the anxiety swelling in Kasiel at the idea of meeting his actual father.

The others cycled in and out of the wagon throughout the afternoon, everyone taking advantage of the opportunity to rest while they could. All except Jethan, who stayed with Kasiel. The possibility of being able to sleep became less and less likely the closer they got to the city with its immense black stone walls. Details like the aggressive diamond-shaped facades on the front of every tower and sharp peaks spearing up into the sky from taller buildings in the city grew more defined as they approached. The visible construction was all severe planes and angles, compounding the overall ominous appearance of the black city.

Kasiel's nerves danced. His mount tossed its head and pranced beneath him, reactive to his mood.

"What do you think of it?" Jethan asked when they were a couple of miles from the walls.

"It's… terrifying."

Wedro, riding nearby, barked a laugh. "It should be. That's what they designed it for. The city was in its early development when the war started. They already had to use the black stone for much of the construction here. The architects, aiming to discourage attacks, took a few tips from the fierce black crags of Vareyl's Warning and built intimidation into the very structures of the city and its walls."

"Etrion is the southern capital of Vanris," Jethan further explained. "The khevarin and her family intended to use our northern capital, Doran, as their primary residence. When war broke out, Khevarin Seylin declared that the palace in Etrion would be her primary residence so that she might be closer to her troops. That also contributed to the upscaling of the city and its defenses."

Kasiel scanned the arid landscape. "How is there enough water here to support a city that size?"

Jethan grinned. "There's a lot of water here. Can you guess where?"

He thought about it for a minute. It didn't seem possible in such a dry region, unless... "Underground?"

"Exactly. There are massive reservoirs deep underground here. More than enough to serve the population."

Kasiel contemplated the city in a more curious light now. "But how do you bring the water up?"

"You'd need an engineer to explain how it works, but I've seen the mechanisms. They're quite impressive. Maybe I'll take you down to see the workings once you're settled in."

Settled in? The words sent another flare of anxiety through him. His horse stopped, dropping its weight into its hindquarters, and reared up. He leaned into the rear, gripping with hands and legs that had grown stronger over the course of their journey. A month ago, he would have been on his ass in the dirt. He kicked the animal, driving it forward and back to the ground. When he had full control again, he noticed Jethan watching him, a hint of pride in his eyes.

"Well done, tehnaak."

His gaze lingered on the other youth for a few seconds. If not for him, this entire journey would have been a lot different. Jethan had kept him going and given him hope in his bleakest moments. "Will you be there when I meet him?"

A brief flicker of sympathy moved across Jethan's face that wasn't particularly comforting. "We'll all go before him to start, but I suspect your father will want to speak with you alone."

Kasiel drew a deep breath and let it slowly out. There was no escaping that coming encounter unless he made a run for it now, and as tempting as the idea was, it would never play out in his favor. "Will we at least have time to clean up?"

"Most likely not. An escort…" Jethan trailed off, directing Kasiel's attention to the city with a nod.

Looking toward the ever-growing walls, Kasiel spotted a cloud of dust rising outside the city, heading their way. "Our escort?"

Jethan nodded. "Yes. They'll take us directly to the palace." He moved closer to the wagon and smacked the side a few times. "Form up! We've got palace guards coming!"

A flurry of activity ensued as the group climbed out of the wagon, collected their horses, and mounted up. Once they were all on horseback, they moved out in front of the wagon and into formation with Kasiel and Jethan at the front. Darro and Kince flanked them on either side, staying a few strides back. The others lined up in their spirit sibling pairs behind them, except Tath, who rode alongside Merrin and Avris now that she no longer had a tehnaak of her own.

When the riders from the city reached them, they hailed Jethan and fell in around the group. There were ten guards plus Kastus in the lead, now on a fresh horse and wearing more formal-looking armor. One guard on each side held a purple and black banner with a creature that appeared cat-like and yet also vaguely reptilian, depicted in silver rearing up in the center. The guards wore armor of a much darker metal than he was familiar with. More of a metallic charcoal-gray color. The helmets that made it difficult to see their faces had the same rearing beast from the banners etched on the sides.

The gate was open when they reached it, towering over them on either side of the entrance. Ominous spikes forged of that same dark metal covered the front of the gate. One more detail to enhance the city's intimidating appearance. Once inside the walls, they moved across a large, open courtyard. The first buildings on either side looked like they might be military barracks for troops stationed on the walls. Beyond those, they continued along streets lined with smaller dwellings, all built of a mixture of pale clay and black stone. Everything tall enough to be seen over the walls was constructed of black stone.

Plenty of people moved about in the streets, especially as they continued deeper into an area full of shops. Several larger structures that appeared to be inns or taverns were mixed in amongst them. The people paused in their activities long enough to gaze curiously at the passing party. Observing them in return, Kasiel noticed a distinct absence of younger children and an abundance of both men and women carrying weapons and wearing light armor or uniforms displaying the heraldic colors of Vanris.

Were they all military?

In appearance, Kasiel could easily blend in with the folks watching them go by, but one vital difference made him yearn to find a hole somewhere and hide. Variations of the braids Jethan's unit wore were commonplace among the people there. A style choice that typically exposed at least one of their pointed ears. For the first time since leaving Fernwallow, he desperately missed the cowls he had worn in the village. All it would take was a light breeze to show them his disfigurement. The unsightly proof that he wasn't like them after all.

They continued through the city streets into a part of town filled with multistory houses along with several towering ornate structures made entirely of that black stone. The names on the signs in front of the buildings and shops were strange to him. Vanrian. The same language he heard being spoken all around them. Writing and sounds he couldn't begin to make sense of.

Jethan moved his mount closer as they passed a large, gated courtyard surrounded by elegant three and four-story buildings. "That's the Etrion Academy for Extended Education. There's a similar academy alongside the palace that specializes entirely in training mind-crafters," he said, speaking just loud enough for Kasiel to hear.

Was everyone here formally educated? He had assumed at least some folks would be like him, with humble origins that lacked the opportunity for a structured education. Now, looking at the city and people around him, that assumption struck him as dreadfully inaccurate.

Their journey brought them to another courtyard, this one far more ornate than the one near the main gates, complete with precisely even cobbles underfoot. A grand fountain in the center spouted water high in the air, letting it rain down into two levels of pools below. Past the fountain, sweeping stone stairs led up to the towering entrance of the palace.

The magnificent structure stretched out in a vast landscape of reaching spires extending from the varied rooftops of the sections. The exterior, constructed primarily of black stone, had hints of silver and that dark metal accenting it around windows, doors, and at the edges of roofs.

They dismounted, leaving the horses in the hands of a group of youths who emerged from what appeared to be a large stable to the left of the courtyard. They strode up to a front door that was easily three times as tall as Kasiel, arching up to a severe point at its pinnacle. Kastus and the guards escorted them through in the same formation they had ridden in, keeping a stiff posture and swift pace.

They proceeded down a long, wide entrance hall floored in gleaming white and purple stone that starkly contrasted the black everywhere else. The cleanliness of everything heightened his awareness of the grime from their travels that they carried in with them.

"The stone in this hall is a rare import from up north," Jethan whispered.

Decorative carpets, many with traces of the same distinctive purple from the banners worked into their patterns, lay under chairs in sitting alcoves or beneath tables holding vases full of flowers. The latter surprised Kasiel. Where did they grow such lush plants in the desert?

He didn't have time to absorb more before they took a sharp right turn and strode through a set of open double doors into a large circular room. The floor here was stone, though of a deep gray with patterns inset in it in that dark metal. The walls were polished black stone with Vanrian symbols carved into them. There were no tables with plants here, or chairs to sit on. Not even on the dais that curved out into the room, covering about a quarter of the floor space. A few other doors led from the room, two smaller and more discreet ones along the opposite edge, and a large double doorway entering from the back of the dais.

The group continued to the middle of the room behind Kastus. Jethan stopped at an inlaid circle that marked the center and knelt to the left of it, facing the dais. He gestured for Kasiel to do the same next to him. Kasiel tried to match his tehnaak's pose to the right of the circle while the rest of the unit sank to one knee behind them, still maintaining formation. The guards left them, all but two, heading back out with Kastus. The two who remained closed the entry doors and took positions inside them.

A moment of silence followed in which Kasiel noticed how clean and immaculately polished the floor was. It was an odd thing to focus on, but it was better than acknowledging the spiky ball of panic expanding in his chest.

The doors at the back of the dais opened and a woman in long purple and silver robes entered. She stepped to one side, waiting while three guards wearing black leather armor reinforced with dark metal plates came in and took positions inside those doors.

When the guards were in place, she announced, "High Lord Arhk Cavenos, Dhomvalen of Vanris, Right Hand of Khevarin Seylin Markanis."

Kasiel's breath caught, his throat constricting until he feared he might pass out from a lack of air. Given that everyone around him kept their heads bowed, he suspected he should do the same, but he couldn't. He had to find out who Arhk Cavenos was. He raised his head enough to see the man who entered.

Arhk was tall and slender, the sides of his long white-blond hair braided and tied loosely back, revealing perfectly pointed ears. He wore exquisitely tailored black clothes with subtle purple embroidery tastefully added upon the breast and around the buttonholes of a form-fitting jacket that draped to mid-calf in the back. Toggles on the jacket were made of that dark metal. The same material was used for an abundance of unusual trimming, precisely placed upon the jacket, boots, and gloves to give the outfit the suggestion of armor. The weight of those thin metal accent pieces combined with the unusual fabric gave a fluid-like motion to the jacket.

There was an elegance to his appearance and movement that somehow made him more intimidating. He strode over to them, making barely a sound in his knee-high boots. As he got closer, Kasiel noticed a series of small, stylized symbols tattooed in silver under his left eye, curving in a line that extended along his cheekbone to his hairline on that side. His eyes, gray-green like

Kasiel's only a few shades lighter, scanned them all with stern scrutiny, skimming over Kasiel with no trace of special interest.

"Ahninveth na sek Jethan Markanis." His voice was soft, and yet somehow commanded the attention of the room.

"Dhomvalen," Jethan returned instantly, keeping his head bowed.

Arhk said something in Vanrian, and Jethan answered in kind, his gaze shifting in Kasiel's direction as he did so. Arhk regarded Kasiel for a moment as if he were a fresh smear of dirt on a clean rug. His attention moved back to Jethan after a few seconds, and he spoke in Pandrean Common this time.

"You have completed your mission?"

The question brought forth a burst of irritation in Kasiel. He was right in front of the man. Their mission in the flesh, ready to be acknowledged by a father he had never seen before in his life, at least that he remembered. He clenched his hands at his sides and searched for a sense of calm.

"Yes, Dhomvalen," Jethan answered.

Arhk's eyes flickered to Kasiel for an instant and away again, too fast for him to catch any emotion in them. Then he looked at the rest of the group before dropping his gaze back to Jethan. "You lost a member of your unit. Tath's tehnaak, Healer Ahrin."

"Yes, Dhomvalen." Jethan's head sank a fraction lower, his shame in that moment almost palpable.

"This is, perhaps, a sign that you were not yet ready for such responsibility." The harsh edge in Arhk's tone pushed Jethan's head lower still.

"It wasn't his fault," Kasiel blurted. It was, given the sudden glacial look Arhk gave him and the way Jethan tensed alongside him, probably the wrong thing to do, but the words tumbled out before he could stop them.

Arhk's gaze cut into Kasiel as he addressed Jethan and the others. "I am grateful for what you have accomplished. I will ensure that your unit receives recognition for the success of this mission. You may all report to your commanding officers. They will handle the rest. I must speak with my son."

The unit rose, Jethan hesitating a moment as if he wanted to say something. Then he turned and led them from the room, leaving Kasiel alone with his father.

"You may *all* go," Arhk stated firmly, sending the remaining two guards hurrying out. The three at the back in black armor also stepped out at a nod from him. When they were gone, he gestured with one gloved hand for Kasiel to rise.

Kasiel hesitated a second, his gaze lingering on the sharp dark metal points that tipped the fingers of that black glove. He forced himself to stand, despite the potent fear that his legs might not hold him up. Standing at least showed him that his father wasn't more than a few inches taller than him, though something about the man's presence made a giant of him.

"There is more of your mother in your appearance than I expected," Arhk said softly, as if pondering this to himself. The slightest edge of sorrow tightened his voice. After a brief silence, he addressed Kasiel directly. "I appreciate that you have been able to bond with Jethan. We were uncertain how well a pairing would hold up after so many years apart. However, there is a place for defiance and a place to hold your tongue. I hope being raised in the remote reaches of the southern kingdoms has not made you too simple to learn the difference."

Anger swept up like a whirlwind in Kasiel, though he couldn't bring himself to speak in his own defense. Somehow, doing so would mean acknowledging a connection to the man currently casting well-spoken insults at him. Jethan's defense was another matter. "Jethan fully devoted himself to getting his unit home safe."

"The bare minimum expected of a good leader," Arhk countered calmly. "Why do you defend him when he failed to accomplish that? Because he is your tehnaak?"

"I defend him because he deserves it," Kasiel snapped, refusing to meet the eyes of this arrogant man who supposedly fathered him. "He brought me and all but one member of his unit back here after three months in enemy territory, and he's only seventeen."

Arhk arched one severe brow, a hint of disdain in his fine features. "As are you, as of a few days ago."

Kasiel's thoughts scattered for a second. It never occurred to him that the birthday he celebrated all his life might not be his actual birthday. He gave himself a mental shake, trying to focus on the moment. "And no one's asking me to lead dangerous missions."

Arhk's eyes narrowed. "Not yet, Hahren."

"Kasiel," he countered reflexively.

The anger that tightened Arhk's features sent a chill through Kasiel. It wasn't like him to argue. Why did he have to choose now to change that?

There was a threatening growl in Arhk's voice when he spoke. "You will not use the name *they* gave you in my presence ever again." He hesitated a second, darkness flashing in his eyes that made Kasiel's breath catch in his throat. Then he looked away. "Go clean yourself up."

With those words, Arhk spun and strode swiftly from the room, leaving through one of the doors he had come in and slamming it behind him. Kasiel stood there stunned, an intense ache blossoming in his chest, his ears ringing with the sound of the slamming door. Of all the scenarios he imagined, this was beyond the worst. He hadn't expected his father to embrace him or even get particularly emotional given his station, though he had dared fantasize about such an outcome once or twice. What he had tried to be prepared for was some awkwardness and distance. But this?

The pain in his chest made his vision blur and his throat constrict.

"Interesting."

Kasiel nearly jumped out of his skin. He stumbled a few steps to the side, turning to face the newcomer.

A woman stood there unlike any he had ever seen. She had hair the same white-blond as his father's, threaded through with delicate strands of silver, and eyes of a pale ice blue that shone like gemstones. She wore a long ivory gown with overlapping layers of sheer silver and pearlescent fabric that made it appear almost incandescent. An elegant, jeweled tiara of interwoven silver and dark metal rested on her pale brow, matched by a similar belt that hung loosely at her waist. A tattooed series of stylized silver symbols ran along the upper edge of each well-defined cheekbone, disappearing under her hairline.

Kasiel glanced past her at one of the side doors that now stood ajar. A woman in a simple purple and silver dress waited inside with her head bowed. Movement and a glint of metal in the shadows beyond suggested at least one guard standing watch. His gaze shifted back to the jeweled tiara, realization sinking in, and he dropped to one knee.

"My lady, um… your majesty," he blurted, hoping that was the right form of address. Why had he never asked Jethan and the others about etiquette?

"Stand. This is no formal audience." A faint smile curved her lips as if she had amused herself. "I suppose it is not an audience at all." Her gaze drifted to the door Arhk had vanished through as Kasiel rose unsteadily to his feet and looked the same direction. "This will not be easy for him. Though he always professed to believe that he would get you back someday, I suspect that, in his heart, he despaired of ever seeing you again the moment he learned you had been taken. You and your mother were his world. Losing you both changed him."

"He seems rather unimpressed with me now," Kasiel ventured cautiously, hoping she had insight to offer that would ease the agonizing sense of rejection.

"You are not Vanrian anymore." Her cutting look was sharper than a blade, slicing away what little pride he might have had in who he was. "Perhaps you can be again with some considerable effort."

Kasiel swallowed, trying to choke down the bitter pill she had given him, and averted his gaze. "Why did he even want me back then?"

"You will have to ask him that, Hahren."

When he looked up, her hard stare challenged him to correct her, making it obvious that she had witnessed that part of his encounter with his father. He clenched his teeth and held his tongue. Perhaps Arhk would be proud to see that he was already learning that part.

"For now, if you walk out the door you entered through, I suspect you will find that my nephew defied his orders and waited for you."

"Your nephew, Majesty?"

She drew in a soft breath and shook her head, making the light dance upon the ornate silver earrings she wore. "I see Jethan did not tell you. I will never understand the lengths to which he goes to pretend he is common." She gestured dismissively toward the door with one graceful hand, her long fingers tipped in pointed silver nails. "Go to him. He will help you find your way."

Something in her tone gave him the sense that she didn't mean that only in the immediate context. Eager to be away from the intensity of her presence, Kasiel attempted a hasty bow and hurried from the room.

When he stepped through the doors, Jethan was

indeed there, leaning against the opposite wall waiting for him. Whatever the other youth saw in Kasiel's expression as he emerged, he pushed quickly away from the wall and hurried over.

"Are you all right, Kas?" He put a hand on his arm to guide him away from the room.

Kasiel met his eyes. For the briefest of moments, he considered telling the other youth that he couldn't use that name anymore. Then he set his jaw and said nothing. His father and the khevarin both left him feeling like something less. Unworthy of this place. Unworthy of these people. Did they even know about his ears yet? If not, he suspected his value to them was going to drop that much further when they found out. He wanted to scream. He wanted to cry, too. Worst of all, he wanted to give up. There was no going back to the southern kingdoms for him, and there was nothing here for him. He was nothing.

Jethan's brows pinched, sorrow tugging down the corners of his mouth. "You don't need to answer that. I can see it in your eyes, tehnaak."

Before Kasiel could ask what exactly he saw, a man approached them wearing the silver and purple colors of Vanris. He offered a deep bow to Kasiel.

"If you will follow me, my lord, I can show you to your quarters."

A hint of frustration tightened Jethan's jaw. "I'll find you in the morning. Take advantage of the benefits of living in the palace. You've earned them." He gave Kasiel's forearm a squeeze. "You can do this, tehnaak."

Kasiel nodded in answer, not trusting himself to speak.

Jethan left, and the strange man turned away, gesturing for Kasiel to follow. He headed, to Kasiel's distress, deeper into the palace. The dark beauty of the halls they walked through felt stark and isolating. He stared at the man's back and did his best to ignore his surroundings and the people in them. When they finally stopped, after climbing some stairs and turning down an uncertain number of hallways, the man opened a door for him, bowing and gesturing for him to go inside. Kasiel had no idea how to find the entrance again from here, but that was a problem to confront after he got some rest.

The first room they entered had a sitting area with a large fireplace against the opposite wall. The room itself was half the size of his house back in Fernwallow. All the furniture—couches and chairs upholstered in soft purple and black fabric, the wood stained dark with tasteful silver accents—was devoid of sharp angles, creating a flow of gentle lines throughout the space. A carpet of swirling dark and light gray with sparing accents of white and black covered the floor. Unlike the portions of the palace he had seen so far, the walls here were a soft ivory with elegant dark wood wainscoting over the lower half. An open door at the back led into a similarly furnished bedroom that shared the pass-through fireplace from the sitting room. Pillows and a thick comforter that looked too luxurious to touch, let alone sleep in, covered the bed.

The man entered behind him. "These will be your quarters, my lord. There is water in the tub that should be about the right temperature for bathing by now, and you will find a few changes of clothing in the ward-robe. The fit may not be perfect. A tailor will be by in the morning to begin assembling a proper wardrobe for you. Is there anything else you need?"

Looking around at the extravagant space, the sense of not belonging here was almost too much to take. His stomach growled, turning his attention in a different direction. "Something to eat, if it's not too much trouble."

"Food is being prepared, my lord. It will be ready for you after you have bathed."

There was a firm suggestion in that last sentence.

At a distracted nod from Kasiel, the man hurried out. Finally alone, Kasiel wandered into the bedroom, pointedly not looking at the full-length mirror. Following the faint trace of aromatic steam in the air, he continued through another doorway into a smaller room with a large marble tub set against one wall. A window behind the tub looked out on a set of buildings that resembled the academy Jethan had pointed out earlier. That must be the mind-crafter academy. Less than an hour ago, that might have stirred curiosity in him. Now it stirred nothing.

Around the edges of the tub sat an array of bottles and implements that suggested a level of cleanliness he was confident he had never achieved in his life. It was daunting, but the idea of soaking his aching body in that hot water was enough to coax him out of his clothes and into the bath.

By the time he finished, the water had taken on a distinct brownish color. Lulled by the warmth, he was almost more interested in sleep now than food. He spent a moment inspecting the scar on his cheek in the full-length mirror outside the bathing room door, the reflection much clearer than in the small mirror he had in Fernwallow. The scar, perhaps an inch long, was small enough that it didn't alter his appearance significantly. Maybe it would give the illusion that he had more life experience than he did.

He had finished pulling on a pair of well-made black trousers and an ivory shirt that he discovered in the wardrobe when someone knocked on the door. When he opened it, a woman stood there holding a large platter upon which several covered dishes sat. It also held two goblets, a silver pitcher of what appeared to be water, and a decanter containing a deep red liquid.

"That must be heavy." He reached to take it from her.

Her eyes widened. "Oh, no, my lord. I'll carry it."

She moved forward, forcing him out of the way, and went to set the platter on the sitting-room table. Once there, she filled one goblet with water. As she began filling the second goblet with the red liquid, another figure appeared in the doorway.

Kasiel backed deeper into the room as Arhk walked in, a stifling sense of threat entering with him. Kasiel's instincts reacted to that uncertain danger, telling him to run. The woman by the table set down the decanter and sank to one knee, bowing her head. Kasiel moved to do the same, but something in the sharp look Arhk shot him stopped him.

The dhomvalen snapped a few words in Vanrian, the gruffness of anger giving a grating edge to his voice.

The woman hurried from the room, shutting the door behind her.

Kasiel searched his mind for what he had done wrong. Could it be something he said in his brief conversation with the khevarin? He hadn't been in Vanris long enough to do much that could be that offensive.

Arhk stepped over near the table, gazing at the contents for a moment in silence. Without looking at Kasiel, he said, "You are a Feral?"

That was an important question, mostly because it told Kasiel someone had provided his father with more information about their journey here, which also meant that whatever angered him may have occurred prior to his arrival in Etrion.

"Yes, Dhomvalen," he answered, struggling to keep his voice steady.

"How auspicious. We need more Ferals."

Kasiel wanted to ask what they needed them for, but a sinking feeling told him it was for the war. He let the question go unasked, preferring not to have that confirmed yet.

Arhk looked at him. Not precisely at him, but more at the side of his head. "Show me." Barely contained fury whispered through his voice like a coiled serpent, ready to strike.

A strange pressure filled the room. Something dropped heavily in Kasiel's chest. He hesitated, yearning for a way to escape the moment. Arhk's eyes narrowed and Kasiel forced his hand up, brushing his still-damp hair back from one ear.

Rage distorted Arhk's refined features. "Who did this?" he demanded, his voice deepening alarmingly.

An inhuman roar rose beneath the demand. The room darkened abruptly, as if someone had sucked all the light out. Black shapes with burning eyes bled from the walls, sweeping in from every corner, howling and screaming. Arhk's appearance changed with the room, his face stretching into a skeletal visage, with black voids where he should have eyes. A crown of spikes extended from his scalp, blood streaming down his face in rivulets from its base. Horrifying darkness moved within the bottomless hollows of his eyes.

Kasiel scrambled back, tripping over his own feet. He landed on his tailbone and continued to scoot away across the floor until he came up against a chair. Trapped, he threw a hand up in front of him to shield himself from Arhk's twisted countenance and the shrieking black figures diving at him through the darkness.

Then it stopped.

Kasiel lowered his arm, warily looking up at the man now standing over him. His heart raced so fast it felt as if it might burst from his chest.

Arhk, his appearance returned to normal, took a few deep breaths. He extended a black gloved hand in front of Kasiel in offering. As much as Kasiel didn't want to accept it, he deemed it safer to do so than to risk provoking more anger. The pointed metal tips of the glove's fingers pricked his skin as Arhk lifted him easily to his feet and immediately released him.

"My apologies. My Frightener ability has only..." He paused, and Kasiel got the sense that he was amending whatever he had been about to say. Changing what might have been the truth into something else. "That has never happened before."

Two things kept Kasiel from bolting for the door. The most obvious being that Arhk was in the way. The other, however, was more subtle. It was the faintest tremor of distress in Arhk's voice, as if what had occurred genuinely unsettled him.

Arhk's gaze flickered back to the side of Kasiel's head. "Who did that to you?" he asked more calmly this time, the tremor in his voice already gone.

"I don't remember." Kasiel heard the shaking in his own voice that his father would undoubtedly judge him poorly for. "I was five."

Arhk nodded at that and strode to the door. He paused with a hand on the lever. "You will meet your instructors tomorrow. They possess an expansive pool of knowledge amongst them. Do not waste it." He opened the door. "And learn your language."

With that, he stepped out. Kasiel sank to the floor in front of the chair and buried his head in his hands.

CHAPTER SIXTEEN

In spite of, or possibly because of, everything that had happened, Kasiel slept through the entire night. Nightmares plagued his dreams in which he tried repeatedly to get to Danica in the swamps near Fernwallow, only to have her dragged away by shadows before he could reach her. He woke with a sense of relief until he remembered where he was and how poorly his family reunion had gone.

The food they brought him after his bath the previous night had gone uneaten. His encounter with his father's Frightener ability effectively destroyed any appetite he had. He assumed that meal delivery was a onetime occurrence due to the unusual circumstances, but when he stepped out into the sitting room the next morning, that neglected meal was gone and a new platter laden with fruit, cheese, and thinly sliced meats had taken its place. He tried not to obsess over the fact that someone had been in the room while he slept. Maybe that was normal here.

The creamy, aromatic cheese redefined what he would have formerly considered delicious cheese, and the fruit presented him with an unexpected array of flavors, many of which he had never encountered before. The shavings of meat practically melted on his tongue. Along with those delights, a decanter of sweet wine and a silver pitcher of water were there to quench his thirst.

The selection struck him as unreasonably decadent, though he couldn't bring himself to object as he took another bite of something every time he passed near the table.

Before the sun finished rising on the black city, someone knocked on his door. The sound sent a spike of panic through him, dreading that it might be his father again. Though it turned out to be the tailor, the moment of fear left him jumpy and unsettled. The man went to work taking Kasiel's measurements, muttering to himself and making notes as he did so about Kasiel's hair color and length, eye color, and skin tone. He even made a few observations regarding the shape of his face, as if all these things would somehow inform the final product.

When Kasiel attempted to engage him in conversation, the man waved him off, saying he needed to keep his mind on his work. He was finishing the last of many awkward leg measurements when someone else knocked on the door. Kasiel startled so violently at the sound that the tailor almost fell over backwards.

The man looked at him as he might look at a strange and unpredictable animal. "Would you like me to get that for you, my lord?"

"Please." Kasiel took advantage of the few seconds while the tailor was answering the door to compose himself. His heart slowed back to something resembling normal when Jethan entered the room. A flash of irritation swept in on the heels of that relief. "Why didn't you warn me?"

Jethan shut the door, his brow furrowing. "About wha…?" His eyes widened. "Oh."

"Yes, oh," Kasiel snapped. Most of his anger wasn't really directed at the other youth, but it needed a target.

"My lord, we are finished. Unless you require anything else…"

"No. Thank you." Kasiel kept his tone civil long enough to dismiss the tailor while Jethan sauntered over to sample a few pieces of fruit and cheese from the table.

As soon as the door shut, he glanced at Kasiel. "Did you actually speak with my aunt?"

"Yes. A conversation I wasn't at all prepared for."

"I wasn't trying to keep secrets from you, tehnaak. I just don't want to be part of that life. Politics. Power. Court." He popped a bite of fruit into his mouth. "None of it interests me, and I don't like the way people treat me when they find out I'm related to the khevarin."

Kasiel cast a sour glance at him. "Is that an option, ignoring it all?"

Jethan walked over to him, searching his eyes. "What happened, Kas?"

Kasiel turned away. "You're not supposed to call me that anymore."

"Why not?"

"Because Dhomvalen Arhk doesn't want me using the name *they* gave me."

When Jethan didn't respond, Kasiel turned to see him over at the table again, picking up something else from the platter. He walked over and offered the wedge of black fruit to Kasiel. "Looks like you didn't try this. It's evalis fruit. We brought it with us from our former homeland. It's what we make the black mead out of."

"You brought a plant all that way so you could make mead?"

Jethan frowned at him. "Your tone tells me you really need to work on your priorities."

Kasiel looked away. "I don't want it."

Jethan held the piece up in front of him, his expression challenging him to a duel of patience. A duel Kasiel was confident he wouldn't win in his current state. He grabbed the wedge and shoved it in his mouth. The juices burst across his tongue, a sweeter version of the mead. It was delicious, though he wasn't in the mood to admit as much.

"Good, isn't it?" Jethan prompted.

"It's fine," Kasiel muttered.

"What name do *you* want me to use?"

"It doesn't matter. I don't want the dhomvalen Frightening the life out of my tehnaak because you called me by the wrong name." Kasiel strode to the sitting-room window, resting his hands on the sill. From this vantage, he could see part of the mind-crafter academy, if that's what it was. The black rooftops, made of some type of tile, gleamed ominously in the sunlight. "I can't stay here."

Jethan stepped up next to him, all traces of humor gone from his voice now. "What happened with your father, Kas?"

Kasiel's hands started shaking, and tears stung his eyes. He didn't want to cry. Crying not only fixed nothing, it also stopped up his nose and gave him a headache. Not to mention, it wasn't the way to make a great impression on his first day here. He refused to do it.

Jethan slid an arm around his shoulders and steered him to a chair. Once Kasiel sat, he shoved the table to the side and dragged another chair over to sit in front of him. Leaning forward, he rested his elbows on his knees, and looked Kasiel in the eyes.

"Talk to me. It's what I'm here for."

Kasiel closed his eyes for a second and drew a shaky breath. Then he told Jethan about the encounters with Arhk and the khevarin in the circular room. It was the later incident with his father in this very sitting room that he found most difficult to share. As he stumbled over his words, fighting the urge to downplay the event so it might sound less horrible, Jethan's eyes narrowed, the muscles in his jaw clenching. When Kasiel finished, Jethan got up and started pacing on the other side of the table.

"This isn't how this was supposed to go," he snapped.

"You can't do anything about it, Jeth. I'm just not Vanrian."

"Horseshit!" Jethan turned on him with a flash of rage in his eyes. "You never weren't Vanrian. I don't care where you were raised. You're not only Vanrian, you're a blasted Feral. I wonder how the dhomvalen would like it if you set your ability loose on him."

Kasiel choked out a bitter laugh. "Given my current skill level, he'd probably die laughing." To his surprise, the comment appeared to ignite a fire behind Jethan's eyes.

"I've got an idea. Get your boots on."

Minutes later, they were striding swiftly through the palace complex and out a side entrance. Jethan's fast pace gave Kasiel little chance to look around. He would have to rely on someone else to guide him to his rooms later, if he went back.

The side entrance opened onto an extensive garden enclosed entirely in a building made of black metal framing and clear glass. The structure itself was remarkable, but the array of lush plants, some laden with fruit and vegetables, others topped with clusters of bright flowers, was enough to send his eyes and nose into shock. Several plants he recognized, but many were unfamiliar, native to regions outside of his limited experience. Some perhaps brought over from the Vanrian homeland. Years spent managing the little garden in Fernwallow and searching for edible and medicinal plants in the wild inclined Kasiel to stop and investigate. But Jethan was on a mission.

They wound their way along several walkways until they came to a door in the far back corner of the structure. Jethan cast a conspiratorial grin over one shoulder and opened it, revealing a tunnel so dark it was hard to see more than a few feet into it after the brightness of the sunlit garden. He picked up a lantern from among a cluster of others set in an alcove inside the door. Using flint and steel from a small pile next to the lanterns, he lit it.

"You're going to love this."

Kasiel hesitated, staring down the long tunnel carved out of black stone. It appeared to slope distinctly downward. "I'm supposed to be meeting my instructors today."

"I know. Who do you think is supposed to take you to meet them? Don't worry. We have plenty of time."

Kasiel gave him a skeptical look.

Jethan laughed. "Come on. The walls don't bite." With that, he advanced down the passage.

Not wanting to be left alone in the dark, Kasiel hurried after him, trying not to read anything into the finality of the door behind them thumping shut. The tunnel extended far beyond the reach of Jethan's lantern.

"Where are we going?"

"Patience," was all the answer Jethan gave him.

Kasiel looked for patience. All he found was a blackness that reminded him of the gaping dark hollows that had taken the place of his father's eyes and the shadows that had stolen Danica away from him in his nightmares. He kept his attention on Jethan and the circle of light around them, fighting the suffocating press of remembered fear.

It was silly to think of Danica at all, given the distance that stood between them now. It wasn't only physical separation, either. This place was so different from anything he had ever known that it was hard to find a reference for the experiences he was having. The entire population of Fernwallow could live in the courtyard at the entrance of this obscenely large city. Could Jethan comprehend how strange all of this was to him?

As they walked, Kasiel, staring hard at the lantern, started smelling the desert. How odd that the dry, dusty heat had such a distinct aroma. That wasn't all he could smell, though. He caught the fragrance of plant life and the unexpected, crisp scent of water. Beneath all of that, he detected the musk of something else. Some kind of animal.

Faint hints of light glimmered in the dark ahead. Jethan's pace picked up, hurrying toward a door made of metal bars through which Kasiel could now see a hint of blue sky. When they reached the door, he saw a swath of packed down dirt between it and a towering fence of more metal bars about ten feet beyond. On the other side of those bars stretched a vast desert canyon, which they were currently at the bottom of. A variety of hardy plants dotted the landscape amidst formations of red dirt and stone.

He could hear running water. A waterfall, perhaps. There were other sounds, too. A few bird calls rang out, along with louder clicking noises and occasional distant screeches that sounded like something larger.

Jethan opened the door and stepped through, holding it for Kasiel to follow. He paused to blow out the lantern and set it beside the door. The iron bars Kasiel had assumed to be a mere fence formed a full wall, disappearing at the top into a rock overhang that sheltered the area from the sun.

"You little calloch," a woman's voice said behind them. "As soon as I heard you were back, I knew you wouldn't be able to resist sneaking down here."

Kasiel turned to see a young woman crouched on a rock above the exit. She had long, dark-blond hair, the sides pulled into two braids and bound in the back. Small, rust-colored symbols tattooed in a line down from the center of each pale red eye to above the corners of her mouth. She cocked her head at Kasiel in a manner that struck him as strangely animalistic before hopping down and stalking toward Jethan.

Jethan met her halfway. They gripped each other's arms at the elbow in a brief warrior's greeting that transformed into a fierce hug. Her stern expression melted before a wide smile.

"It's great to have you home." She stepped back, holding him at arm's length, and looked him over. "Still in one piece, it appears. You know, with you away, it's been months since I last got threatened with demotion or a night in the deeps."

Jethan considered her with mock seriousness. "That's awful. Whatever did you do for fun?"

She shook her head at him and turned to Kasiel. "And you must be his long-lost tehnaak. I assume they didn't teach you Vanrian down south." She extended a hand to him. "I'm Kenna."

"Good assumption," he answered, appreciating that she had included him in the conversation from the start.

When he accepted the offered hand, she jerked him into an embrace. The gesture startled him, but it was also unbelievably gratifying to receive such a warm welcome after everything that had happened. So much so that a touch of moisture came to his eyes, and he ducked his head for a second when she released him to regain his composure.

Jethan jumped in before the moment could become awkward. "Since you were missing for, well, twelve years," he explained to Kasiel, "I completed most of my education and training with Kenna and her tehnaak."

"Yes." Kenna bumped Jethan's shoulder firmly with her own, making him stagger sideways a step. "He's pretty much family, which means you're family too, Lord Hahren."

Kasiel swallowed back the urge to correct his name. "It's nice to meet you, Kenna." He couldn't stop his gaze from shifting to the expansive canyon habitat beyond the metal bars. A waterfall dropped out of the center of the nearest canyon wall, feeding a creek running along the bottom as far as he could see, which was a fraction of the vast space. "This is amazing."

She sauntered to the bars and peered through, a hint of pride in her smile. "It is, isn't it? This is one of the biggest and most successful kennels in Vanris."

He glanced at her in question. "Kennel?"

"That's what they call where they keep their hunting hounds in the southern kingdoms, isn't it?"

Kasiel shrugged.

"Well, this is where we keep our best *hounds*." She gave him a wink. "I'll assume, since Jeth snuck you down here, that you haven't seen the tethdraks yet?" When he shook his head, she turned and stared out into the canyon. "I'll see if I can get us one."

Jethan came up on his other side, a faint smirk curving his lips.

Kasiel watched Kenna for a few seconds, expecting her to do something more than stare into the distance before it dawned on him. "She's a Feral too?" he whispered.

"One of only two in Etrion," Jethan whispered back. "Well, three now."

"What's a tethdrak?"

Jethan hushed him, pointing into the canyon.

The beast that came loping around one of the larger rock formations was bigger than the werdyn cats that had nearly killed Jethan. It had the vague conformation of a hound, but its resemblance to any canine he had ever seen ended there. Varying shades of red and brown scaling covered the powerfully muscled limbs and torso. Spiked plates ran the length of its spine and down a thick tail that tapered down to a diamond-shaped plate at the end. Flared ridges on the backs of its legs looked a little like the fins of a fish. A similar fin-like membrane wrapped close around its neck, behind its jaw. It had two backswept horns extending from the top of a long triangular head. Massive jaws bristled with sharp teeth and curved claws dug runnels into the earth as it advanced.

When it noticed them, it slowed, lowering its stance like a predator on the hunt, its muscles bulging beneath the scaling. It emitted a series of clicks, followed by a quick screech that was almost painful this close.

Kasiel stepped back from the bars as it finished its approach, its wary gaze on him and Jethan. When it stopped, it extended its neck far enough that Kenna could reach through and place a hand on its snout. It barely had to lift its head to meet her eyes.

"Your hounds are… impressive," he managed, catching the hitch of fear in his own voice.

Kenna smiled affectionately at the beast before glancing over at him. "I know you're a Feral. Ahndhomen Adnar is supposed to be meeting with you later to begin assessment preparations."

Kasiel nodded absently. He watched the massive beast. What thoughts did it have? What ideas might he be able to give it? Could he compel it to move closer to him?

Without warning, the creature lunged in his direction, hissing and flaring out the fin-like frill around its neck. Kasiel jumped back, barely keeping his feet under him. The tethdrak growled again, then turned and loped away.

Kenna was grinning at him smugly. "Tethdraks aren't horses, Lord Hahren. You must earn their trust and learn how they think before you can get into their heads."

"That may be true," Jethan said, his eyes shining with enthusiasm, "but when his ability awakened, Kas stopped two full grown werdyn cats in their tracks, one of which nearly had its teeth in my throat."

Kenna eyed Kasiel with more interest now, her gaze boring into him as though she might somehow learn everything there was to know about him with a look. "Is that an exaggeration? How close exactly?"

"I was prone underneath it and bleeding." Jethan picked up a dramatic flourish in his voice as he spoke. "I could feel its whiskers brush my throat when it closed its mouth."

Kasiel shuddered at the memory. A heartbeat later.

Her eyebrows rose. "That's promising. Controlling something completely wild like that, without prior experience with the beasts, requires not only a powerful ability, but a strong natural empathy for the creatures. You…" She trailed off, her gaze shifting back to Jethan. "Did you call him Kas a second ago?"

"Kasiel is the name he grew up with."

Kasiel negated that with a shake of his head, hating what he was about to say. "The dhomvalen doesn't want me using it."

"I guess we best not use it when he's listening then," Jethan countered, his jaw tightening with fresh anger.

"It's fine, really. I don't want anyone getting in trouble on my behalf."

Kenna gave him a flat look. "Your expression says it isn't fine, Lord Kasiel." She stepped closer to Jethan, somehow looming over him despite being a few inches shorter. "I sense an ulterior motive to your bringing him down here."

Out in the habitat, the tethdrak had climbed up on a broad flat rock and reclined there watching them. Watching him specifically. He got the feeling he had offended the creature. Its calculating gaze was intimidating, especially with those strange, vertical pupils.

"Adnar is going to test him for a training companion, probably at the end of the week. I was thinking, if you gave him a chance to bond some with the juvenile tethdraks before the assessments, he could secure a more impressive training companion. That might help show the dhomvalen," Jethan said, glancing over at Kasiel before he continued, "show *everyone* that he is worthy of his place here."

Kenna glanced at Kasiel, a hint of sympathy in her regard. "Your father being a bit of a calloch, is he?" She didn't wait for an answer before facing Jethan again. "You know how much trouble I could get in for allowing him to interact with the tethdraks before his assessment? He's not supposed to have an advantage with any of the creatures going into the test. Back less than a day and you're already trying to get me demoted."

"Or thrown in the deeps." Jethan offered her a playful, scoundrelly smile that Kasiel hadn't seen from him before. It was disturbing how well it suited him.

After Jethan extracted a promise from Kenna to introduce Kasiel to the juvenile tethdraks the following morning, they spent the next several hours in the darkly elegant halls of the mind-crafter academy, meeting the instructors tasked with bringing Kasiel up to speed. An undertaking he would have considered impossible, given how many years of their education he had missed.

Each instructor they met with provided him with books he was to read through and somehow retain the contents of over the course of the week before they did assessments to determine what his official curriculum would need to cover. If he had anything going for him, it was that he could read and write well. Unfortunately, the individual instructors appeared oblivious to the reality that, taken together, the quantity of information he was supposed to get through in one week was enough to keep him busy for months. A problem further complicated by the fact that most of the books were written in Vanrian. Perhaps they simply didn't care.

He was ready to beg for mercy by the time Jethan informed him they only had two instructors left. The first was the combat trainer, Dhomen Farren, a tall, muscular man with a thick scar above one eye and red symbols tattooed up his neck to the base of his jaw in sharp, aggressive angles. He had the warm disposition of a brooding statue. After several humiliating rounds of sparring with two different weapons and his bare hands, Farren gave Kasiel a practice sword and three books about combat technique, then sent him off to nurse his fresh bruises.

"When will I get my sword and armor back?" Kasiel asked as he fastened the new sword belt around his waist to free his hands for carrying books.

Jethan gave him one of his dreaded sympathetic looks. "You might not. The Vanrian symbols your professor put on them are being examined. Sometime this evening, after we meet with Ahndhomen Adnar, they'll call you in for questioning about the experiments he was running."

Kasiel groaned as he took half of the stack of books. That sounded like a delightful way to wrap up the day. They wouldn't want him to have time to start on all this reading, after all. "Edmund didn't tell me much about what he was doing."

"Tell them everything you know. If they believe you're being honest with them, they're more likely to leave you alone about it after this."

Kasiel answered with a weary nod, following as Jethan started walking toward his final meeting. "Ahndhomen ranks above inveth and ahninveth, right?"

"Yes, and dhomen, technically."

"Ahndhomen Adnar is another Feral, like Kenna?"

Jethan nodded. "And you. We don't have a lot of Ferals in Etrion right now. There are some stationed along the border and in several cities north of Vareyl's Warning. We try to keep at least two Ferals managing each habitat in Vanris all the time. Adnar will do most of your instruction himself if he feels like your ability is strong enough to merit his attention. Otherwise, you might end up working with Kenna."

For the first time, Kasiel hoped his ability wasn't especially strong. Not that Kenna didn't have her intimidating side, but she had hugged him and welcomed him as family. After a day full of strangers who all gave him the impression they expected him to fail, it would be nice to work with someone who didn't seem to harbor an innate disappointment in him.

"Don't you have things you need to do other than walk around with me all day?"

"What could be better than this?" Jethan flashed him a smile.

"I'm serious. No more keeping secrets or being evasive."

A weight appeared to press down on the other youth's shoulders, and his smile faded. "You're my tehnaak, Kas. We should have trained together. Now that you're here, my progress is connected to yours and vice versa. We're a pairing. Pairings rise and fall together."

Frustration flared in Kasiel along with a crushing guilt. "You're going to be held back because of me?"

Jethan rallied as fast as he had slumped, standing straighter and summoning back his smile. "Don't look at it like that. I would go back to basic training in a heartbeat if that were the price for having my tehnaak here with me. Besides, this means you're going to get a lot of help, because I'm pretty strongly motivated to see you rise."

Kasiel tried to take comfort in that, but it did little to lift his spirits. How was he supposed to succeed with twelve years to catch up on? And his failures wouldn't be on only him now, they would fall on the back of the one person who had stood by him through everything. The one person who deserved far better. Jethan must have known this would happen before he led the mission south.

"Did you want to find me, knowing this would be

the outcome if you succeeded?"

Jethan stopped and spun around. "By the Break, Kas! Of course, I did. I begged to be given that mission. Most of my life I've lived as half of a broken whole. I'm complete now. That's worth any price." He held Kasiel's gaze for a few seconds, then turned and started walking again. "Come on. Adnar won't be kind if you're late."

Kasiel watched him for a moment. Jethan was complete now. He wished he could share that feeling. If only it were that simple.

Shaking his head, he jogged a few steps to catch up. Jethan led them to a fenced round pen alongside a stable near the back of the academy. The man waiting for them was easily as tall and unfriendly looking as Dhomen Farren, but there was a strange predatory wildness to his stance and the way his eyes tracked Kasiel as they approached. It reminded him of being watched by the tethdrak.

Jethan set the books he was carrying on a bench outside the ring before ducking through the fence. Kasiel followed his example.

"Ahndhomen Adnar," Jethan greeted, stopping in the center of the ring, and offering a slight bow.

"Ahndhomen Adnar." Kasiel imitated Jethan's greeting and bow.

Adnar flipped his long blond hair away from his face with a toss of his head and stalked toward them. He stopped in front of Kasiel, head tilting to the side as he regarded him. It wouldn't have surprised Kasiel in that moment if the man had sniffed him like an animal, but Adnar only frowned down at him.

"Lord Hahren Cavenos?"

"Yes, sir," Kasiel answered, anger rising in him at having to respond to that name for what felt like the hundredth time that day. The more exhausted he got, the harder it was to hide it.

Adnar's eyes narrowed as if he sensed that spark of anger. "What have you done with your ability so far?"

"I've controlled some horses," he answered.

"Individually or in groups?"

"Both, sir."

"And your awakening. You prevented a couple of werdyn cats from killing your tehnaak."

Was that an observation or a question? He went with the latter. "Yes, sir."

Adnar glanced at Jethan. "Step outside the ring, Lord Jethan," he ordered. Then he left them, heading through an open gate on one edge of the round pen and disappearing into the stable.

"You can do this, tehnaak." Jethan gave Kasiel a bump with his elbow before exiting to stand outside the fence near where they had left the books.

Kasiel waited, tension rising with each second that passed. An extremely long minute or two later, Adnar returned, leading a handsome black stallion. The animal tossed its head, snorting a few times as it pranced impatiently, pulling on the rope. At the entrance to the ring, Adnar unclasped the lead and sent the animal in, shutting the gate behind it. The stallion bolted, galloping across at such speed that Kasiel feared it would hit the fence on the far side. At the last second, it skidded to a stop and wheeled about. Then it took off, sprinting around the ring. It lunged in toward Kasiel at one point, making him jump back, then it resumed its circling.

"Calm him and bring him to the center of the ring. Get him to let you touch him," Adnar ordered.

Kasiel took a deep breath and focused on the animal, the powerful musculature, the gleaming coat, the whites of his eyes showing as he wheeled about again, running in the opposite direction now. He could sense fear. Anger. A lack of understanding. A kindred spirit, in some ways.

Reaching in with his thoughts, he brought himself to the stallion's attention again. The animal faced him and reared, ears flattening back against its skull. This one wasn't as easy as other horses he had worked with, but it still longed for the security of guidance.

Calm. Someone to take control. To comfort. Provide safety.

The stallion's feet struck the ground, and it snorted, stomping one foot a few times. Its sides heaved.

Calm. Safe.

Kasiel held out a hand and stepped closer. The stallion's ears flickered forward, back, then forward again. Kasiel continued to pass a sense of safety into the animal's mind with himself as the source. The stallion lowered its head, ears staying forward now, nose reaching out toward his hand.

Soft muzzle and palm made light contact. The stallion dropped its head more, its twitching tail settling, eyelids drooping, the whites no longer visible. Kasiel took another step, resting his hand on the animal's nose.

"Well done, Lord Hahren."

The name sent a pulse of rage blasting through Kasiel. The stallion reared, its front hooves barely missing his head. It wheeled about, ears flat against its skull, and bolted for the opposite fence. A cringing fear swept up in Kasiel as the animal leapt, its jump poorly calculated in its panic. One knee hit the fence, snapping the top rail. The animal landed off balance on the other side and stumbled forward, crashing to the ground.

Another presence broke through Kasiel's connection to the stallion, ejecting him from its mind violently enough that he fell back on his ass as if struck. Pain flared in his head, his vision going white for an instant. As the flash of white cleared, he saw Adnar crouching next to the now calm animal, examining a bleeding cut on one front leg.

Jethan gripped the fence rail on the other side so hard his knuckles were white, but he stayed outside the ring. He, at least, knew his place. Someone else emerged from the stable and clipped a lead on the stallion, taking it away after a brief whispered conversation with Adnar.

Kasiel stood, his head still pounding. "Will he be all right?" He cringed when Adnar's cutting gaze snapped around to him.

"No thanks to you," he growled, stalking over to Kasiel. "The most important rule of Feral mindcrafting is to leave your emotions out of it. Never allow your personal conflicts to influence your connection. You have the power to do incredible harm."

The man glared at him and Kasiel inclined his head, a flush of shame warming his cheeks. "I understand, sir."

"You had better." Adnar took a step back and stared at him for a few minutes, collecting his own anger before speaking again. "There is a book on that stool at the stable entrance. Take it and read it. That is your guidebook as a mind-crafter. When I see you tomorrow, I expect you to have left your personal issues at home."

And where was home, exactly? Kasiel bit the inside of his lip, fighting the frustration bubbling up in him. "Yes, sir."

"You're dismissed, Odrek."

Kasiel offered a bow, then strode to the fence, ducking out between the slats. Odrek, which he had thought an insult the first time an instructor used it, turned out to be the Vanrian word for recruit or trainee. Not an insult in itself, but the right tone certainly made it sound like one.

He grabbed the book off the stool, noting with a deeper sinking in his gut that this volume was also written in Vanrian. Only a few of the more basic texts appeared to have Pandrean Common translations to offer, which wasn't a tremendous surprise, given that they were in Vanris, but it presented a problem. He strode to where Jethan waited and snatched up the pile of books he had been carrying. So burdened, he stormed off in the direction they had come in, stopping again before he had gone more than ten feet.

Jethan trotted up beside him, holding the rest of the books. "Not sure which way to go?"

Kasiel answered with a curt nod.

"Follow me."

Jethan took the lead, guiding them out of the complex and to yet another palace entrance. In no time, they were back in Kasiel's rooms. He set his collection of books on the table and flopped on the couch. Jethan set his stack down as well before sinking into a chair. For a few minutes, they sat in silence, Kasiel staring at the piles while Jethan silently watched him. Kasiel sank deeper into the couch and let his head fall back, closing his eyes.

"This is hopeless," he grumbled. "Even if they were in Pandrean Common, I couldn't read them all by the end of the week, but most of these are in Vanrian."

"You are in Vanris," Jethan said unhelpfully.

Kasiel cast him a sour look. "How am I supposed to do this?"

"Well," Jethan began, resting one ankle on the opposite knee as he eyed the stacks, "you have two choices that I can see. You could request to have a Vanrian tutor assigned to help you translate them. Or you could ask your tehnaak, who can fill in the boring parts with witty asides and clever observations, to help you."

Kasiel leaned forward, grabbing the closest book, and chucked it at Jethan, who caught it with a grin.

He glanced at the cover. "Good choice."

Jethan had barely opened the book when an attendant knocked on the door. The time had come for Kasiel's questioning. With a dramatic sigh, he followed the attendant through the palace to an unexpectedly cozy little room. Shelves of books lined three of the walls and a warm fire blazed in a fireplace set in the far wall with a painting of what looked like a setting from the canyon habitat hung above it.

A dark wood table sat in the center, surrounded by cushioned chairs. He could imagine someone playing polite games of dice or cards there while enjoying a bottle of fine wine and discussing politics. A decanter of ruby liquid sat on the table now, with four filled goblets next to it. His armor, sword, and dagger were also on the table, their presence stealing some of the welcoming atmosphere from the scene.

To his surprise, Darro leaned in one corner of the room. He inclined his head to Kasiel as he entered, but said nothing, so Kasiel responded in kind. Kastus was also there. He stood up from his seat at the table along with an unfamiliar woman with honey-colored hair and striking blue eyes. She had a single braid on one side of her head that exposed a pointed ear decorated with several silver cuffs and earrings. A line of symbols in pale blue extended from the center of her forehead to halfway down the bridge of her nose, reducing in size so it tapered to a delicate point. More symbols ran down the sides of her neck, disappearing beneath the collar of her top.

"Lord Hahren Cavenos," Kastus greeted, forcing Kasiel to bite his tongue yet again. Eventually, he would get used to the name, wouldn't he? "You know Inveth Darro and I. This is Ahninveth Setera."

Another mind-crafter. That meant two of the three were mind-crafters and all were the equivalent or better of southern captains in rank.

"Please." Setera gestured to the chair opposite her and moved one goblet of wine in front of it. "Have a seat, Lord Hahren."

When Kasiel sat, Kastus and Setera did too, each taking a goblet of wine for themselves.

"Inveth Darro." Setera's tone held an unspoken command.

Darro, looking as out of place here as Kasiel felt, claimed a seat and some wine. He took an inelegant swig from the goblet that made Setera close her eyes for an instant and take a deep breath, her jaw tightening a fraction. Kasiel restrained a smile when Darro gave him a clandestine wink, the gesture making him feel a little less alone.

Setera set an open journal on the table and took a quill in hand, dabbing it into an inkwell beside her. "You were raised in the south?"

"A village called Fernwallow," Kasiel answered. One question down. An endless possibility of others to go.

"I know it's unlikely, given your age at the time, but do you recall anything from the night you were abducted?"

Kasiel shook his head.

She pressed her lips into a tight line and noted something in the journal. "The symbols on these items." She gestured to the armor and weapons. "They were put there by the man who raised you?"

Kasiel's chest tightened. Edmund had meant to kill him, and yet, he still felt like he would be betraying the professor if he told them anything. But, maybe it was all right. They were trying to understand, after all. It was their culture Edmund had been digging into. What harm could come of telling them the truth? Fernwallow was a long way from here.

Kasiel opened his mouth to respond, then shut it, casting a glance at Kastus. Was the man messing with his emotions?

Kastus returned his regard calmly, offering no insight.

"Yes," Kasiel finally answered.

"Do you know where he got them from? Why he used these particular symbols?"

The human skin jumped up in Kasiel's mind. The symbols on it had been the same as the ones etched inside the armor. He swallowed. "He had a… a skin with similar tattoos on it."

The temperature felt as if it dropped in the room. Kastus leaned over and whispered something to Setera. She nodded, staring at Kasiel. Barely suppressed anger flashed behind her eyes now.

"My guess is that he was trying to figure out how to awaken your ability. Did he run other experiments with you?"

Kasiel stared at his hands, struggling to resist the feelings of confidence and comfort he suspected weren't really his.

Setera leaned forward. "We have records of every tattoo our people receive in their lives. That specific arrangement of symbols belonged to Ahninveth Naren. She was a Charmer like your tehnaak, and a friend. She disappeared in a battle a little over a year ago."

The positive feelings faded, and something twisted in Kasiel's gut. He forced himself to meet her eyes. "Sometimes Edmund would ask for a few drops of my blood," he admitted.

Setera's jaw clenched as she made a note. "Tell us everything you can recall. Leave nothing out."

For the next few hours, Kasiel told them everything that struck him as relevant about his life with Edmund. He also gave every detail he could remember about the contents of Edmund's study and what he saw in the laboratory the day he ran away. When they finally let him leave, Darro accompanied him to the door. He placed a hand on Kasiel's shoulder.

"You did well," he said in a low voice. "Get some rest, danro."

Kasiel thought he heard a hint of affection in the other man's tone, though perhaps he was only tired and desperate enough for allies to imagine it. He inclined his head and stepped through the door, grateful to find an attendant waiting outside to show him back to his rooms.

When he reached his chambers, Jethan had the books arranged neatly on the table. He had also acquired paper, a quill, and ink. A fresh tray of food sat on the other end of the table, the aromas making Kasiel's mouth water.

Jethan looked up at him. "Is everything all right?"

Kasiel gave a weary nod. "Do you know Ahninveth Setera?"

Jethan cringed. "She was there?"

"Yes. Her and Kastus and Darro."

"Darro to give you a familiar face. Kastus to boost your confidence or take it away at precise moments. Setera to pull thoughts out of your head."

Kasiel's stomach turned. "She can read thoughts."

"She's what is called an Evoker. It's a relatively rare ability. She can only pull from what you're actively thinking about, but it's still a powerful ability. On the bright side, with her involved, there's a good chance they got everything they wanted, so they shouldn't be dragging you back in there."

"That's marginally comforting." Kasiel sank onto the couch.

Jethan switched the order of a few books on the table. "Can you take notes?"

"I've scribed for Edmund before."

"Excellent." He slid the paper, quill, and ink over in front of Kasiel. "Grab some food and we'll get to work."

CHAPTER EIGHTEEN

Morning arrived far too soon after another night plagued by bad dreams. Jethan had stayed late into the evening as they picked their way through much of the first book. Having his help proved valuable in several ways, since he knew the content well enough to focus Kasiel on what was important and summarize sections that were less so. Kasiel had a vague recollection of Jethan waking him up from where he had fallen asleep on the couch with a book in his lap and herding him off to his bed at some unfortunate hour.

When Kasiel stumbled out of bed in the morning, the meal they had shared while studying was gone and a new covered platter waited in its place. Apparently, this was a regular benefit of living in the palace. He almost missed waking up in the morning and making breakfast for Edmund and himself. A mundane task that brought comforting normalcy to his admittedly bland life in Fernwallow.

Jethan lay sound asleep on the couch, his mouth slightly open and one leg hanging off the side. He looked peaceful and yet somehow also like he could pop up and initiate some form of mischief at any second.

He gave his tehnaak a gentle shake. "When you chased me off the couch, I didn't realize that was because you wanted it."

Jethan sat up, rubbing his eyes and offering a groggy smile. "I skimmed through your notes after you went to bed to see if I could add anything useful."

The unexpected warmth of affection suffused Kasiel as he regarded his tousled spirit sibling. "The least I can do is make you breakfast, then." He grinned, lifting the top off the platter to reveal fresh fruits, meat, cheese, and a loaf of still-warm bread. "How did you sleep through them cleaning up last night's meal and bringing in an entirely new one?"

Jethan chuckled and reached for a slice of the bread. "The better question is, how did I sleep through the smell of this bread?" He took a bite and smiled.

There was soft butter and a sweet jam on the platter that Kasiel spread over a slice. He brought it to his lips and held it there, breathing in the aromas of the bread and jam. As he did so, he recognized the sweet smell. They made the jam from the evalis fruit they used for the black mead. He took a bite and closed his eyes. Warm bread, creamy butter, and sugary jam combined to create a more delightful single bite than anything he had eaten in his life. Had food ever tasted this fantastic before?

"See, not everything here is bad," Jethan said.

Kasiel opened his eyes to see his tehnaak dipping a chunk of bread directly into the jam. "You say that now, but what happens when I fail all these assessments and you're stuck going back to the beginning with me?"

Jethan's grin radiated confidence. "That won't happen."

Kasiel shook his head, unwilling to argue when so much fabulous food waited to be enjoyed.

A half hour later, Jethan escorted him back to the tunnel entrance in the corner of the enclosed garden. He opened the door and gestured to the selection of lanterns, watching while Kasiel lit one with flint and steel from the pile. That, at least, was something he was comfortable doing. What he wasn't comfortable with was the way Jethan stepped back out into the garden once the lantern was lit.

"Kenna's expecting you at the other end. When you're finished, head back here and out the front exit of the garden. I'll meet you there in an hour. I promised my ahndhomen that I would help a new Charmer with some basic exercises this morning."

Kasiel's chest tightened, but he forced himself to nod.

"Good luck, tehnaak." Jethan offered another encouraging smile before shutting the door between them.

Kasiel stared down the black tunnel. Nothing terrible had happened when he passed through it yesterday. The things that came out of the darkness were in his head, where Arhk had put them. There would be no shadows with burning eyes today. He wasn't going to let fear get in his way. With a deep breath, he held up the lantern in front of him and started walking.

For a few yards, everything was fine, but the moment he glanced over his shoulder where the light could barely penetrate the blackness behind him, shadows manifested at the edges of his vision. He increased his pace, his breathing speeding up along with the beating of his heart as the darkness gained form and began diving in at him. Howls and screams echoed in the enclosed space around him, filling the tunnel with their noise. A sudden sweat dampened his skin, and he broke into a sprint, racing down the passage.

When he reached the door at the end, he burst through, letting it clang shut behind him. He stumbled to the wall of bars and grabbed one, the lantern still hanging from his other hand. Pressing his head to the metal, he closed his eyes and swallowed against the dryness in his throat while he tried to calm his breathing.

"You know, we're supposed to be doing this in secret. You might try shutting the door a little more quietly."

Kasiel stepped away from the bars and faced Kenna, drawing in a deep, shaky breath. Her brows pinched together. She glanced from him to the tunnel and back again. He looked at the yawning black passage beyond that barred door. Nothing there but silent, empty darkness. Embarrassment heated his cheeks. He blew out the lantern and went to set it by the exit, giving himself an excuse to avoid her gaze.

"Is everything all right?"

He heard the soft crunch of her footsteps as she came up behind him. How was he supposed to face her? The son of the dhomvalen, afraid of the dark. It didn't matter that his father had caused this. What mattered was how it looked right now, in front of her.

"Kas," she said, her tone indulgently gentle, "why don't we go meet the tethdrak pups? Whatever's gone wrong, they'll make you forget about it. I promise."

He nodded in her direction, still dodging her gaze.

"This way." She struck out along a pathway to the right.

Kasiel followed in silence, glancing into the canyon to see if he could spot a tethdrak, but they were remarkably hard to find for such sizable beasts. The path led them to the east canyon wall. From there, it continued along the side, carved into the wall itself with the barrier of embedded bars still separating them from the rest of the habitat. At one point, they passed a gate with a heavy lock on it. The idea of going in there with those massive predators running loose sent a shiver through him.

"Kenna, is your tehnaak a mind-crafter too?" he asked, searching for anything else to occupy his thoughts.

She slowed her pace, falling back beside him in the narrow passage. "Therin? Yes. He's a Speaker."

Had Jethan told him about Speakers? Nothing came to mind. "What does a Speaker do?"

The corners of her mouth curved up. "Your ignorance is kind of charming."

Heat spread up his neck. "Do you have to call it ignorance?"

"Sorry." The way she cringed gave authenticity to her apology. "Poor choice of words. Perhaps inexperience would be more accurate. Speakers can speak into people's minds. As long as they're within a certain range of their subjects, they can communicate information to them. It's especially useful for coordinating troops in battle. Not so great when you're trying to flirt with a guy and your tehnaak is in the same room putting embarrassing thoughts in your head."

Kasiel managed a small chuckle at that, though her earlier words nagged at him. He hated feeling like an ignorant nobody from a tiny village in the middle of nowhere. Unfortunately, he was precisely that. "Do you think I'm stupid?"

Kenna made the moment more uncomfortable by stopping and facing him. He reluctantly turned to look at her too, painfully aware of how close the narrow corridor had placed them. Close enough that he noticed her eyes were mostly white, with a border of red around the iris that gave them their unusual color.

"Honestly, Kas, I barely know you, but no, you don't strike me as stupid or ignorant. You strike me as someone who grew up a lot differently than we did. If anything, I'm impressed by how well you're holding yourself together. All of this must be rather overwhelming."

Her serious regard made him want to take her at her word, but he still felt ignorant. He felt like a coward and a danro.

Her expression hardened. "Stop it," she snapped. "I can see you tearing yourself down. You need to let go of that. If I didn't think there was something worthwhile in you, I wouldn't be here risking my position to give you a chance."

He frowned at her. "How can you possibly know if I'm worth the risk after meeting me once?"

Something about her answering grin was unnervingly predatory. "Feral instincts. Spend enough time in the heads of beasts and you'll pick them up too. Come on." She continued along the path. "Let's see if we can bring out a little of the animal in you."

He fell back into step with her. They stopped a few minutes later next to a door embedded in the cliffside. Ducking through, she grabbed a thick gambeson from a table near the door and handed it out to him. Then she picked up a bowl full of chunks of raw meat and stepped back outside.

"Put that on. It'll help protect you from their claws and teeth while you're learning how to work with them."

It was too warm out for that much covering, but he didn't want his skin to look like the heavily scarred leather chest and arm pieces she was wearing, so he pulled the gambeson over his head. When he had it on, she nodded satisfaction and turned down the path once more.

"Self-confidence is important when working with tethdraks. They'll sense your doubt and use it against you," she warned. "Have you noticed yourself being drawn to animals?"

He wanted to say yes because he suspected that was the answer she was looking for, but it would be a lie. Lies had a way of spiraling out of control. "Not especially."

"Hm." She continued to a gate built into the bars and handed the bowl of meat to him. Then she pulled out a key and removed the lock, pushing the gate open.

"We're going in with them?"

"They fence this section off from the rest. We bring pregnant mothers in when they're about to give birth and keep them here until the young are big enough that the other adults are less likely to kill them." She took the bowl of meat back and stepped through, gesturing for him to follow. "Don't try to get in their heads. This is only an introduction."

They walked out from under the overhang into bright sunshine. Kenna closed the gate behind them, bolting it shut and double-checking it a few times. He supposed a tethdrak getting loose out where there were people could pose a serious risk. Then she stopped and stared farther into the enclosure, her focus changing.

While her attention was elsewhere, Kasiel took advantage of the moment to really look at her. She had pulled both sides of her hair into tight braids today, exposing her pointed ears. She wore two dark metal ear cuffs on the near side, one of which had a sharp little tooth dangling from it. Her features had an angularity to them that added severity to her appearance. In some ways, she looked as fierce as the creatures she cared for.

Her faint smile caught his attention, and he turned to see five smaller tethdraks, about knee-high at the shoulder, come loping up. They slowed when they saw him, hanging back to wait for the full-sized beast that strode up behind them. Their mother, Kasiel assumed, a twist of anxiety shooting through him at the idea of facing the massive female with no bars between them.

He started taking half a step back, but Kenna caught his arm, shaking her head at him when he glanced over at her.

The mother looked at Kenna with calm recognition. Then she turned to him, letting out a low growl punctuated with clicks that came from somewhere deep in her throat. Kenna casually handed him a piece of the meat and mimicked holding it up.

Confident that he would have one less appendage in a moment, Kasiel held the meat up on one palm before the beast. The tethdrak ignored it. Growling again, she stepped close enough to stretch over the offered morsel and flick her long tongue out in his face, smelling him. Her breath was warm, and not terribly unpleasant. She opened her jaws a fraction, giving him an intimate view of her mouthful of pointed teeth.

After a few seconds of inspection, she took a step back and picked the meat from his hand, swallowing it whole. Then she trotted off, going to lay in a shaded spot near the canyon wall.

Kasiel dared to breathe. He looked at Kenna and grinned.

She laughed. "Way to hold your ground, Lord Kasiel." She beckoned him over and handed him another chunk of meat. "Let's make some friends now."

Kenna had him toss morsels of raw meat to the juveniles until they ventured close enough to take them from his hand. He threw a few choice pieces to the watching mother, hoping to keep her appeased, but most went to the horde of enthusiastic young predators who rapidly lost their fear of him. Less than an hour later, Kenna had him sitting in the dirt with her while the tethdrak pups frolicked around them. Now and then, one would try to include him in their rambunctious wrestling sessions. Kenna showed him how to fend them off without hurting them or himself. About half the time, they mistook his efforts for him joining in the fun and got more excited, requiring her intervention.

When the large juveniles exhausted themselves, they piled into a heap in front of Kenna and Kasiel and fell asleep. One male, with darker scales around his eyes that ran up to the base of his horns, making it look as if he wore a mask, rolled up against Kasiel's legs and was soon snoring.

Kasiel couldn't stop grinning.

"There must be a lot of good in you, given how quickly they took to you."

"I'm flattered," he said, surprised at how true that was. He glanced over at the mother, still dozing in the shade. "They're almost big enough you could ride them."

"Almost." Kenna stroked the nose of one that had fallen asleep half in her lap. The tethdrak didn't stir. "They might be strong enough, too, but they aren't really built for a saddle, nor do they have the disposition for it. Not that the kanodraks do, but they're different."

These weren't the other mounts Jethan and Wedro mentioned, which meant that, somewhere here, they had more strange beasts. "I was told there were different mounts in the Vanrian stables. Those are the kanodraks, right?"

"Oh, we don't keep them in the stables. They'd eat the horses."

He glanced over at her, catching no hint of teasing in her expression. "You're serious?"

Kenna nodded. "Yes. If things continue to go this well, Adnar will probably introduce you to them at some point. Right now, however, you should probably get to your other studies."

They extracted themselves from the sleeping tethdraks, and she let them out through the gate. The one with the mask of dark scales around its eyes stood and followed, watching Kasiel until she finished locking the gate, then it trotted back and piled on with its siblings. Its gaze still followed him as he walked away, and Kasiel got the sense that the creature wanted him to stay.

CHAPTER NINETEEN

That day ended up being a road map for Kasiel's first week. After secret morning sessions with Kenna and the tethdraks, he went to daily lectures from each of his instructors. With Dhomen Farren, it was more of a daily beating. Training with Adnar went better after that first encounter, though the Feral ahndhomen was reluctant to trust him with anything especially challenging.

Given the option of doing his own thing or joining Kasiel for his training, Jethan chose to stay with him. His advanced education made him an invaluable asset for asking the right questions of the instructors. At the end of each day, they returned to Kasiel's rooms and Jethan helped him study, mixing it up with occasional combat practice. The latter probably should have been an outdoor pursuit, but they shoved the furniture against the walls and managed not to break anything that looked too valuable.

Jethan also pushed him to learn the Vanrian language as they studied by refusing to translate some words when he read out loud, forcing Kasiel to figure them out through context. As annoying as it was, Kasiel recognized the inevitable long-term benefits and only grumbled about it a little, mostly for the pleasure of bantering with his tehnaak.

He didn't see his father at all. Arhk appeared to have no interest in him now that he had him securely tucked away inside the city walls. Kasiel, on the other hand, thought of his father every night with his sleep plagued by nightmares and every morning as he struggled to walk through the tunnel, and not fondly. As far as he was concerned, he didn't care if he never saw the man's face again.

As the end of the week crept near, his assessments loomed like a towering wall he could see no way over. Jethan was far more optimistic. He insisted they were making substantial progress. Kasiel looked at what they still hadn't gotten through and couldn't share his confidence.

The morning before his assessments, he got a delivery of what the tailor told him was the first of several selections of clothing he would receive. This set consisted mostly of an array of attire meant for everyday use, including seven sets of expertly made trousers and shirts that fit him better than anything he had worn in his life up to now. It also included three jackets of varying lengths. His favorite was a charcoal-colored fitted jacket that hung to the back of his knees, accented with sparing hints of silver and dark metal. Even though it reminded him of his father's long black jacket, it was the most attractive piece of clothing he had ever owned. Still, it was too fine a garment for daily wear, so he donned a simpler, fitted tan jacket that hung to mid-hip when he headed to the canyon.

Kenna still made him leave the jacket outside the fence, insisting it was too nice to let a tethdrak pup drool on it. She didn't require him to wear the gambeson. He'd gotten competent enough at handling this group of juveniles now that he could keep them from climbing all over him, though she still wouldn't allow him to use his mindcraft on them.

His last morning to bond with the tethdraks before testing rushed by. After tempting them with morsels of fresh meat, he and Kenna sat amongst them while they played for a time. Kasiel rolled up his shirt sleeves to keep the masked tethdrak pup from tearing the fabric as it attempted to climb into his lap, despite being much too large and pointy to fit comfortably. Kenna cautioned him against letting the pup get away with it, but he found its desire to be close to him reassuring.

"I've never had so many clothes," he remarked, admiring the tight weave of the fabric as he finished rolling the second sleeve.

"You are the dhomvalen's son. Can't have you wearing the same thing two days in a row. The scandal." A hint of good-natured teasing sparkled in her eyes.

Fighting the temptation to use his ability, he finally got the tethdrak to settle with its head and front legs draped across his lap. "You're sure about this. I still shouldn't use my mindcraft on them?"

"Definitely not. Their response when you first touch their minds during the test needs to be genuine. If they don't react as expected, Adnar will know something's up. There are never any guarantees, but the familiarity you've built up should be enough to get at least one of them to yield to you with minimal effort."

"Won't he notice that they're already familiar with me?"

"I doubt it. In a strange environment without their mother, they'll be frightened and less trusting than they are here. In the time it takes for them to decide if they can still trust you in that new environment, you will have already passed or failed with them."

Passed *or* failed. At least it would be over quickly.

The masked tethdrak nipped playfully at his fingers. Given the size of its teeth, he found the behavior a little alarming even in play. He put a firm hand on top of its nose, applying enough pressure to move its head away. There was a sweet spot between the amount of pressure they would yield to and the amount they would resist. He was gradually getting the hang of it.

"What exactly will I need to do?"

"I'm still not telling you that, either." She gave him a chastising look. "Your reaction to the experience needs to be genuine, like theirs."

"Great." He glanced up at the sky, noticing how much the sun had moved since his arrival, then gently urged the tethdrak off his lap and got to his feet. "I better get going. This is my last chance to learn as much as I can before tomorrow."

Kenna stood with him. "You'll do fine, Kas."

She accompanied him to the gate. He waited, contemplating the young reptilian predators while she unlocked it. Once she opened it, he went through and waited again while she locked it after them. He followed along a few steps behind her as she led the way back. The position of the sun was such that the sunlight hit him as he strolled alongside the bars at the outer edge of the pathway. It felt good. If not for the terrifying horrors that tormented him each time he passed through the tunnel, his mornings in the canyon would be his favorite part of each day.

"I like the way the sunshine brings out so many varied shades of red in your hair. It's quite remarkable," Kenna stated, casting a brief glance over her shoulder at him.

Kasiel stared at her back, not sure how to respond to that. Was she flirting? Just being friendly? Why didn't he know the difference? After a few more strides in silence, she glanced over her shoulder again and smiled. Then she slowed, dropping alongside him in the narrow passage.

"Have you picked out the color and placement of your tattoos yet?"

"Tattoos?"

Kenna stopped and faced him, trapping them like she had the first day in that awkwardly narrow space together. "Yes. Everyone has tattoos. They tell people who and what we are. Mind-crafters also get rune tattoos that signify our abilities. Usually, they're given immediately after we go through our Trial. I imagine they'll do yours once you've completed your testing. I was thinking you might let your hair determine the color of your tattoos. Maybe about this shade here."

She reached toward his hair, and he reflexively caught her wrist in a firm grip.

Her eyes narrowed, a flash of anger making them appear redder. "Honestly, Kas, anyone paying attention to how your hair lays knows you're either southern born or your ears were cut. And if you were southern born, you wouldn't be walking around free within the walls of Etrion. It's an awful thing, and I'm sorry it happened to you, but you're only fooling yourself by trying to hide it."

His father's reaction to seeing his ears flashed through his mind. The distorted face looming over him with its haunted black hollows for eyes. The moment it entered his thoughts, voices started screaming in his head. He shoved her arm away, taking a few hasty steps back until he slammed up against the bars.

"Kas?"

He squeezed his eyes shut and fought the urge to cover his ears, knowing it wouldn't help. The images became clearer, the voices louder.

A hand touched his face, and he snapped his eyes open. The horrifying visage and voices retreated. Her red-tinted eyes were there before him, her brow furrowed with worry.

"Kas, what happened?"

"It's nothing. I need to go." He spun and hurried

away from her, heading back to the dreaded tunnel. To his relief, she didn't follow.

The rest of the day continued as usual, though his instructors focused on specific things that they considered most important. Kasiel tried to do the same, knowing anything they emphasized now was likely to come up in the tests tomorrow. Unfortunately, he couldn't get Kenna's words and his reaction to her mention of his ears out of his head. The incident with his father's Frightener ability had been terrifying, but why couldn't he get it out of his head? If anything, it caused him more grief with each passing day. Nightmares. Torturous visions in the tunnel. Now this moment of panic in broad daylight because someone dared to bring up his ears. There had to be a way to stop it.

When the day ended, they retreated to his rooms for one last study session. He found even that hard to focus on. Jethan repeatedly called his attention back until he finally gave up and sent him to bed, deciding that sleep might prove more valuable than drilling for a few more hours.

Kasiel spent the night tormented by nightmares in which Jethan and Kenna also appeared, being torn apart by wailing shadows alongside Danica. By morning, he felt shaky and exhausted, as if he had run a marathon rather than spending the night in bed. He managed, with help from his tehnaak, to get to the first portion of the assessment on time. Jethan had to leave him on his own from that point forward. He wouldn't see anyone other than his instructors again until the testing was complete.

Before parting ways, Jethan gave him an enthusiastic hug. "We've covered everything you need to know. You can do this, tehnaak."

Kasiel tried hard to appear confident, returning the hug briefly so Jethan wouldn't have time to notice the slight tremble in his hands. "Thanks, Jeth. For everything."

Jethan opened the door to the testing room. "I believe in you," he said in a low voice as Kasiel walked through with all the enthusiasm of a prisoner heading to execution.

They started with written testing. A trio of unfamiliar instructors asked questions about the different subjects, including everything from Vanrian history to combat theory and mindcrafting, taking notes while he answered them. None of them offered the slightest hint in their expressions of how he was doing. They gave him a few brief breaks to relieve himself and provided a noon meal, never allowing him to leave the supervised area. When they released him around mid-afternoon, his brain felt like a puddle of mush between his ears, and he still had no clue how he had performed. What he did know was that the next assessment was going to make mush of his body to match his brain.

Much to his relief, it wasn't Dhomen Farren who faced him across the combat ring when he arrived for that test. The dhomen stood off to one side to oversee and judge the mock battle. Kasiel's opponent was still faster and far more experienced. His practice with Jethan paid off a little, helping him land one decent strike against his opponent for every four or five he received before they finished. From there, his brain still mush and his body covered in drying sweat and bruises, he continued to his final evaluation.

The Feral test took place in a large building behind the round pen Adnar had used for his lessons. When he entered, he found himself inside an enormous cage that enclosed most of the open space in the center of the building, from floor to ceiling. Someone closed the door behind him, and he heard them sliding a bar into place outside. Not the most comforting experience.

There was an observation area to the right and left of the cage and a platform that went around the perimeter of the building between the wall and the cage one story up. At the back, a row of five smaller cages held different creatures. Four wolf-sized hounds, a cluster of critters that looked like large weasels, some reptilian beasts about half the size of the tethdrak pups, two juvenile cliff cats, and three of the young tethdraks, including the one with the mask. All the creatures paced restlessly, searching for a way out and riling each other up with their chorus of distressed calls.

He understood now why Kenna said he didn't need to worry about the tethdraks responding to him. They were so agitated they barely stopped moving long enough to focus on anything, him included.

Adnar watched from the viewing area to the right of the main cage. Two guards stood at the back in a narrow walkway behind the smaller cages alongside a series of levers.

"Odrek Hahren Cavenos, one of these creatures," Adnar swept an arm out to encompass the assortment of beasts as he spoke, "will become the primary companion you practice your mindcraft with. Which one depends on what you can control here today. All but the hounds are wild creatures. They've had limited contact with people, but no formal training. Some are more difficult to get control of than others. They are arranged from the least difficult," he said, pointing to the hounds with one hand, "to the most difficult." He pointed to the tethdraks with his other hand.

"Where you start is up to you, but you are not to touch their minds until they are out in the cage with you. If you do, I will use my ability to eject you from their heads. An experience you have some familiarity with."

Kasiel remembered the presence that had knocked

him off his feet with the stallion. He gave a sober nod.

"You can play it safe and start with the hounds. If you succeed there, you may move up and try the next, or stop if you feel you have reached the current limits of your ability. Or you can choose to start somewhere in the middle, if you are confident something there is within your ability. You could also choose to start with the most difficult if you are especially arrogant." Adnar's tone told him that would be a poor decision, regardless of whether Kasiel thought he could handle the tethdraks. "When you feel you have reached your limit, say as much and the test will end."

"And if I misjudge my ability, sir?"

A slight smirk twisted Adnar's lips. "Worry not, Lord Hahren. I will intervene before they eat you." Adnar gestured to the cages again. "Begin."

Kasiel regarded the beasts. He was tired, physically and mentally. It seemed almost cruel to end the day with this test, but then, maybe that was the point. Maybe they didn't want him working with a creature he could only control when he was at his best.

The hounds were the calmest. They would probably be no more challenging than horses. The weasel-like creatures or the smaller reptiles would be the wisest place to start. Yet, he had controlled wildcats before in a moment of panic and with no knowledge of what he was doing. He recalled the strange sensation of connecting with the werdyn cats as if it had just happened, his memory of it still so vivid he almost questioned its accuracy. Everything else aside, the incident proved he could handle them, and since Adnar had warned him off trying the tethdraks first, they were the next highest option.

He raised his hand to point at the cage with the cats. "The cliff cats."

Kasiel expected Adnar to question his choice, so it

caught him by surprise when a guard pulled that lever and the cage door swung open. One of the two blue and gray cats sprinted across the space, lunging up against the side of the cage where Kasiel had entered as if hoping to escape that way. The other cat followed it halfway, then skidded to a stop on the dirt floor and faced Kasiel. Its hackles went up, and it hissed.

Fear, desperation, and rage met the first tentative touch of his ability. The noise from the other animals compounded the emotions.

Before he could do much, the cat leapt at him. He threw himself to one side, surprised that he could still move that fast after his combat test. As he rolled up into a crouch, the cat skidded to a stop, spinning around to face him. He cast his ability toward the other cat, the one focused on escaping, and tried to refocus it on him, the human who had come in through that door. The human who could probably get back out the same way.

The cat by the exit stopped trying to get out and turned to face him, still cowering with its hackles up. He stayed crouched, aware that the closer of the two cats was growling and preparing to attack again. Quickly, he reached out to the threatening cat, urging its attention to its companion, showing it the other animal's hesitation. He continued to present himself as a path to freedom to the cat by the door. It only needed to trust him. The closer cat stayed poised, ready to attack, its mind filled with an overwhelming torrent of rage, but it held back as the first cat crept toward Kasiel, sniffing the air cautiously.

Freedom. Safety. Help.

The first cat began approaching with more confidence. Kasiel held one hand out and lowered his gaze to make himself less threatening while he continued to encourage it. He could feel curiosity rising in the second cat now, so he shared the ideas of freedom and safety over to it. A few minutes later, both cats stood next to him. They were still nervous, but they allowed him to touch them, looking to him for guidance now.

He felt a strange sensation then, like something nudging him away from the cats. He glanced over at Adnar, and the man nodded. With a touch of unease, he pulled back from them. An instant of panic sparked in their eyes, then they calmed and laid down, turning docile as Adnar took over and the two guards came to retrieve them.

When they were back in their cage, Kasiel returned to the middle of the large enclosure.

Adnar regarded him for a few seconds, as impossible to read as the other instructors had been. "There is only one step up from there. You did well with the cliff cats. Either of them would make an excellent training companion. Do you wish to stop?"

Kasiel took a deep breath and faced the last cage. "I'll continue."

The three tethdraks burst out when the cage door swung open. Unlike the cats, they stayed together, stopping as a unit before they were halfway across the dirt floor. Their eyes homed in on Kasiel, and not in the playful, curious way he had grown accustomed to. When he reached out to them, he realized he was no longer their friend. It was as if they didn't recognize him at all. Someone had taken them from their mother and put them in this place. He was the only one available to answer for those wrongs.

The tethdraks spread out, sinking into low hunting stances as they moved around him. They talked amongst themselves as they crept closer, coordinating with a series of deeper-than-usual clicking sounds and low growls. All the time he had spent with them now served as a reminder of their strength and the sharpness of their claws and teeth.

He reached out to them, seeking admission into their thoughts, but ran up against a staggering resistance. Their connection to each other gave them the comfort they yearned for, leaving no room for another protector.

Fortunately, having handled them some, he knew a few tricks about their anatomy. The masked tethdrak on his left lunged. Kasiel dropped low and grabbed the top of its muzzle, slipping his thumb into a gap in its mouth where the teeth didn't meet up precisely to get a solid grip. He rolled, taking the beast with him, and let go at the right moment to come up with it now standing between him and the other two.

His heart raced. At what point would Adnar intervene?

The other tethdraks were quick to adjust, swinging out wide around the masked one, trying again to surround him. The masked tethdrak gave off a hint of confusion and uncertainty now. Whether because Kasiel thwarted its attack or because the brief engagement triggered some recollection of their previous encounters, Kasiel wasn't sure, but it was a potential entry point. These were juveniles. They weren't mature hunters yet. They played to learn to hunt, and he knew their games.

Kasiel spread his touch into their minds, casting out the same playful energy he witnessed from them in the canyon. Joyful energy. Exuberance. Contentment.

The masked one hesitated. It rose slightly from its predatory stance. Kasiel made himself relax and sank to one knee, trying to focus his thoughts on those morning excursions, on the delight he got from them, the freedom he felt in the habitat. The masked one emitted a few clicks, higher in pitch now, closer to what he typically heard from them. Kasiel smiled, placing himself in its head as a companion, someone safe, a source of food and entertainment. He sent the same ideas and emotions out to the other two, aware that they were reacting to the change in the masked one's behavior.

Joyful relief swept through Kasiel as their stances relaxed and they inched closer, a swell of emotion that he shared across to them. The masked one came forward first and let him place a hand on its snout. The other two followed a few seconds after. Then he felt that mental nudge again and nodded to Adnar as he reluctantly released them. All three laid down instantly.

A sound from above caught Kasiel's attention. He looked up at the elevated platform as someone exited through a doorway up there. He thought he glimpsed the end of a long jacket and boots trimmed in dark metal accents disappearing through that door. It was probably too much to hope that his father cared enough to watch this.

He stood as they took the tethdraks to their cage, pride washing away some of his earlier exhaustion. Adnar entered the ring and strode over to him, something in his abrupt movement giving the impression that he wasn't as pleased as Kasiel had hoped he might be.

"Well done, Lord Hahren. You have passed at the highest level. We shall talk about what that means later. First, you're going to serve the next twelve hours in the deeps for cheating. Your accomplices started serving their time earlier today."

Four guards entered through the main door as Kasiel's stomach did a flip.

How had Adnar found out?

Kasiel considered trying to claim innocence, but he had cheated. He could try to argue that his inexperience with Vanrian culture made him a victim in this, but he had understood enough when Jethan and Kenna discussed familiarizing him with the young tethdraks to know better. Besides, if the two of them were facing punishment for this, could he do any less? He tried not to think too hard on what this might mean for his tenuous place in Vanris or his future as a Feral. Had he destroyed his chance to prove that he could belong here? For now, it was enough to dread what the next twelve hours would hold.

The stern manner of the guards discouraged questions, so he went with them quietly, accepting that this punishment was earned. Maybe the deeps wouldn't prove to be as ominous as it sounded. The route they took descended into corridors beneath the main level of the palace and to a much less welcoming section of the structure. It was darker down here, with periodic wall sconces to light the way along unpolished black stone halls, which Kasiel didn't find at all comforting.

They turned down a long corridor lined with barred cells, several of them occupied, and through a door at the end. To his surprise, it opened into a large circular tower with a patch of grass and flowers in the center, the fading light of late afternoon reaching down from the open top high above them. A statue in the center depicted a female Vanrian soldier holding a spear upright in front of her. She had her head bowed, forehead almost touching the haft of the spear, and eyes closed, sorrow forever etched in her features. Steel doors were set into the wall at intervals along a paved path that circled the perimeter of the space. It was to one of these doors that they took Kasiel, a sense of shame falling over him as they passed in front of the statue. One guard opened the door. Another unceremoniously pushed him through, and they shut it behind him, slamming a bolt home.

The second the door closed, blackness swallowed Kasiel. A cold sweat broke out across his skin. He stumbled back until he hit the solid barrier behind him, then turned and pounded on the door.

"No! You can't leave me here! I need light! Please!"

As he continued to shout, fists hitting the cold, unyielding steel, he could hear whispers in the darkness enveloping him. He yelled louder and punched the door harder, his hands protesting the abuse. The whispers escalated to wails and screams that quickly drowned out his own futile shouting.

He flinched away from the burning eyes of shadows sweeping in at the edges of his vision and continued to yell, slamming his fists against the metal until the warm wetness of blood coated his knuckles. His throat already felt raw, his voice cracking. No one was going to help.

He sank to the floor, pressing his back to the cold steel door, and curled his legs into his chest. Putting his hands over his ears and squeezing his eyes shut did nothing to stop the screams and wails. The shadows swarmed, mouths gaping open to reveal an even deeper, haunted blackness within as they dove at him through the dark. He could feel the chill of their touch now, when they brushed against his skin, the sharpness of their nails promising to tear him apart as their whispers said they had done to Danica. As they promised they were doing to Jethan and Kenna even now, locked away somewhere in their own darkness.

Then the screaming voices in his head started sounding familiar. People he cared about dying, torn apart by the shadows his real father had cursed him with.

What felt like an eternity later, the shadows quieted. He shuddered and blinked open his eyes to see that they had retreated far enough for him to see a starlit night sky shining overhead. Before he could look around, hands pushed him down, one shoving the side of his face into the mud. Someone grabbed his ear, pulling at it as if they meant to yank it off. They began cutting through cartilage to remove the pointed top, paying no heed to his screams. Kasiel tried to reach up to cover his ear, to protect it and stop the pain, but someone held his hands pinned at his sides. He could do nothing as they forced his head the other way and cut away part of that ear, too. They turned his head a few more times, trimming his ears down to the desired shape while his weakening cries rang out through the night.

The shadows moved in again, circling him and adding their wailing voices to his own. Mocking him. Blood soaked his hair, the pain of his wounds so all-consuming that he could barely register anything else now. A voice spoke into the darkness. Edmund's voice.

"Good enough. Bandage the wounds. We need to get moving."

•

A distant voice made its way through the fading chorus of screams and wails. A muffled voice. He found it hard to focus as he lay shivering in the cold, bloody hands throbbing.

"Kas, I'm so sorry."

He recognized that voice from somewhere.

"Keep talking. He's responding." A muffled woman's voice now. It also sounded vaguely familiar.

"Kas, it's Jethan."

Jethan was dead. The shadows had ripped him apart.

"Your tehnaak is not dead." The woman's voice again, her words striking a spark of hope in him. "There! I've got you now."

Light swept in, burning the shadows away and silencing the last of their noise. He snapped his eyes open. The first thing he saw was Ahninveth Setera's piercing, ice-blue eyes looking down at him. Not someone he ever expected to find leaning over him on his bed, and he was on his bed.

"Welcome back, Lord Hahren." She moved away, standing beside the bed. "Help get him reoriented, Lord Jethan. I'll be in the sitting room. I need a drink after that nightmare. Once the healer has dealt with his hands, I'll take care of the other problem."

As she walked through to the sitting room, Jethan stepped out of the corner and followed her, shutting and locking the door behind her. Then he went to the pass-through fireplace and slid a lever Kasiel hadn't noticed before. A panel sank down, cutting the fireplace off from the sitting room. There was a firm thump on the door.

"Lord Jethan, I want this door open," Setera demanded.

Jethan strode over to the door. "He's my tehnaak. You can give us a few minutes. Knock when the healer gets here."

There was no answer. Jethan went to the other side of the bed. Kasiel glanced down at his throbbing hands. The skin over his knuckles was split and bloodied, though it looked as though someone had rinsed the worst of it off. He didn't understand what had happened or why, but he had done this to himself. Gritting his teeth against the pain, he pushed up to a sitting position and slid back against the headboard of the bed.

Jethan ducked down to reach under the bed, coming up with a journal in one hand. He passed it to Kasiel, putting a finger to his lips as he did so. Then he pointed at the journal. Puzzled, Kasiel opened it to find a thin gray stick tucked inside. On the first page, it read: *Write everything you remember from when your father used his ability on you. Quickly. You'll understand later.* Below that, it read: *Kas, this is what the Evoker took from you.*

Kasiel picked up the odd stick and glanced at Jethan. The other youth nodded, gesturing to the journal again. His wounded knuckles protesting the movement, Kasiel started writing, more than a little surprised when the stick left rough, pale gray letters in its wake.

Jethan pulled off his boots and sat on the bed next to him. "I'm sorry this happened, Kas. I should have realized."

The genuine regret in Jethan's voice caught his attention. When he looked at him, the other youth gestured firmly to the journal, so he resumed writing. The encounter with his father was the last thing he wanted to think about right now. What he wanted was to know how he ended up here in his room. He remembered being locked in the cell and then…

Kasiel shuddered.

Jethan set a hand on his shoulder, giving it a reassuring squeeze.

"What should you have realized?" Kasiel asked, forcing himself to keep writing.

"When a Frightener uses their ability, there's a risk of it having a long-term effect. The stronger the Frightener's ability, the greater the risk. It's as if the experience gets trapped in the victim's mind. Over time, instead of fading, it keeps getting stronger. I didn't put it together until a short time ago." He lowered his voice a little. "Your reaction to the darkness in the tunnel or having someone bring up your ears."

Kasiel glanced at him again. "You spoke to—"

Jethan cut him off with a sharp shake of his head and gestured to the journal. When Kasiel resumed writing, he continued. "The moment I realized what was going on, I started trying to get you out of the deeps." He set his hands on his lap, staring down at them. "When they finally pulled you out, you wouldn't wake up."

Jethan's hands began shaking.

Barely suppressing another shudder at the memory, Kasiel placed a hand on his tehnaak's arm. "I'm all right."

Jethan's gaze went to his bloodied knuckles and his jaw muscles twitched. "Funny definition you have of all right."

Kasiel took his hand away and continued writing. He had barely finished his accounting of the incident when a knock came at the door. Jethan tucked the journal and odd stick beneath the bed before going to open it.

Setera stormed in, giving Jethan an irritated scowl as she stepped aside to let someone else enter. The man had red hair, lighter and longer than Kasiel's. He held a container of salve and some cloth bandages. At his request, Jethan brought a bowl of water and a towel from the bathroom. The man offered Kasiel a drink from the flask he carried to help with the pain, but Setera intervened, turning it away.

When the healer finished the unpleasant process of cleaning and wrapping Kasiel's hands, Setera escorted him out. She returned a few minutes later and sat on the edge of the bed next to Kasiel.

"Did Lord Jethan explain to you the problem you're facing?"

"Yes." Rage tightened Kasiel's voice. "My father scarred my mind with his ability."

Her lips pressed together in a tight line for a second before she continued. "There is one way to fix this. I need to extract the memory of that initial encounter from your mind. You will still recall the nightmares and waking terrors you have had since then. You may even still have a few for a while. They will lose their power, however, once the damaging incident is gone."

Panic burst through him at the idea of losing any part of his memories, followed immediately by anger at the thought that he would no longer know what his father had done to him. He now understood why Jethan had him write it down. It was all he could do to keep from casting a look of gratitude at his tehnaak.

"What about my father?" he asked.

"What about him?"

"Will they hold him accountable for what he's done?"

There might have been the slightest hint of pity in her eyes when she shook her head. "Your father is Dhomvalen of Vanris," she said, as if that made it all clear.

He supposed it did. His father was too important to be held accountable for this, even if the victim of his misdeed was his own son.

"What happens if we don't do this?" he asked.

"It gets worse. Eventually, we find you dead by your own hand to escape the horrors or locked so deep in your nightmares that I can't bring you back." She waited a few seconds. When Kasiel said nothing, she went on. "I need you to think about that encounter. Tell me about it. Recall it exactly as it occurred, in as much detail as you can. I will do my best to extract the incident and leave you with a sequence of memory that at least makes sense."

He gave her a hard stare. "Before we start this, did

you take any memories from me when you questioned me that day?"

"No, Lord Hahren. There was nothing to be gained by erasing those things from your mind."

Kasiel swallowed a bitter lump of anger and nodded. "Let's get this over with."

"Good. Try to maintain eye contact if you can. It's easier and more effective if you remain fully engaged with me." She took his hands, trying to avoid the fresh injuries.

Jethan sat quietly beside him, a comforting presence. Kasiel did as directed, recounting every disturbing detail of his father's visit and the horrifying display of his ability. It felt like only minutes later when she released his hands. Suddenly dizzy, he leaned his head back against the headboard and took a few deep breaths, waiting for the sensation to pass.

"Lord Hahren," Setera began, a change in her tone drawing his attention back to her. "Earlier, when I was trying to pull you out of your waking nightmares, the terror loop in your mind changed. You remembered having your ears cut."

The memory swept back in, and his stomach turned. It was all he could do not to reach for his ears. His ruined ears. Jethan's hand came to rest on his shoulder again.

"I don't know if it was a genuine memory."

Her expression softened to something more sympathetic. "Given what triggered it, I have a feeling it was. I couldn't quite get all of it through the chaos. Do you remember who was there?"

He hadn't seen any of them, but he had heard their voices. Edmund. Edmund had been there. He hadn't found Kasiel with his ears already cut, like he always claimed. He had watched them do it to him. Had approved of it.

Kasiel clenched his jaw, struggling with a wrenching

pain in his chest.

Apparently satisfied with whatever she had gleaned from his thoughts, Setera gave his arm a squeeze before she stood up. "Get some rest. I think you'll find that a little easier, going forward." Her gaze shifted to Jethan. "Can I speak with you a moment in the sitting room?"

"Be right back, tehnaak." Jethan followed her out.

Kasiel rested his head back again, a few tears escaping from the corners of his eyes when he squeezed them shut. Edmund had lied to him from the beginning. About everything. Did the man ever care at all, or had Kasiel only been a test subject to study?

The bed shifted a few minutes later when Jethan sat beside him again and slid an arm around his shoulders. He leaned against the other youth and let the tears creep forth for a time. When they finally ran themselves out, he extracted himself and sat up straight. Jethan reached under the bed and pulled up the journal. He opened it to a page in the back and read the writing there before nodding to himself and closing it.

"You spoke to Kenna?" Kasiel asked.

"We got taken to the deeps less than an hour after your testing started, so we were getting out a few hours after you got thrown in," Jethan explained. "She was worried about how you reacted when she brought up your ears the other morning, so she mentioned it to me as we were leaving. She also said that you seemed to fear going through the tunnel each day. It's rare for a Frightener to use their ability on one of our own people, so it didn't occur to me at first. After talking to her, it all clicked. I realized then that the deeps was the worst place for you to end up. I had to explain the situation to Adnar before I could get them to let you out." Jethan eyed him curiously. "Do you remember what happened the night Arhk asked you about your ears?"

"Of course," Kasiel answered.

"Tell me."

"He asked me to show him my ears, then…" A dizzy spell forced him to pause. He took a deep breath to clear his head before continuing. "Then… he asked who did it, and I told him I couldn't remember. He left."

Jethan opened the journal and handed it to him. Kasiel read the entry. A strange, disconnected sensation made him dizzy again. Setera really had taken his memory of the incident away. Here it was, detailed out in front of him in his own hand, and it was like reading a story made up by someone else. Anger heated his chest. He clenched his jaw, fighting the urge to rip the pages from the book.

Jethan, perhaps sensing that urge, took the journal from him and set it aside. "She also extracted my memories of you talking to me about it. Fortunately, I had a feeling that might happen when Adnar sent for her, so I wrote it down too. I also told Kenna about it, but I didn't tell Adnar or Setera that she knows, so what your father did to you isn't going to disappear."

"But couldn't Setera read your mind and find all those things out?"

"Her ability has limits. You need to be actively thinking about something for her to get it. Even then, if she's looking for something specific, there's a chance she'll miss anything else."

"But why…?" He started clenching his hands into fists until the pain stopped him. That only made him angrier. "I understand her doing it to help me, but why take your memory of it? Is she protecting my father?"

"I would assume so," Jethan answered, sounding much less upset than Kasiel felt it merited. "We aren't nearly as important to the khevarin—to Vanris—as he is. We can't make him pay for it, but we don't have to let him start over with a clean slate. If he wants your trust now, he's going to have to earn it."

Recognizing that Jethan was right, Kasiel did his best to push aside the rage, opening the door for another concern. "What does all this mean for my testing?"

Jethan lowered his gaze, turning away from Kasiel. "I don't know, tehnaak. I'm sorry. This is my fault."

"Don't try to carry all the blame. We rise and fall together, remember? I would never have made it this far without you."

"That's probably true." Jethan managed a shadow of his teasing smile as he got up from the bed. The expression didn't last. "You wouldn't be in this trouble without me, Kas."

Kasiel scowled at him, a hint of frustration creeping through his weariness. "This may be hard to believe, but I'm not a complete idiot. It was obvious from Kenna's reaction that what you were suggesting could get us into trouble. I just wanted to succeed at something. To prove to myself that I wasn't as worthless as my father thinks I am. But I didn't believe I could pull it off on my own."

Jethan looked away again, his jaw clenching. "*I* should have believed in you enough for both of us, tehnaak. I should have been the one helping you find the confidence to succeed, not dragging you down a path that might hurt your future." He didn't give Kasiel time to respond to that. "There are a few hours of dark left. You should get some rest. They'll most likely summon you before the end of the day to present your results."

Kasiel groaned at the realization that it was already the next day. After a long day of testing and turmoil, he had yet to really sleep at all. Facing his examiners in his current state sounded as appealing as another nightmare. "Will you be there?"

Jethan nodded. "They call pairings in together for things like this."

Kasiel exhaled a little of his tension. "That's something."

"Isn't it?" Jethan muttered. He stopped in the doorway to the sitting room and blew out the sconce next to the door. When he glanced back, the way he refused to meet Kasiel's eyes told him all he needed to know about the weight of the guilt the youth carried out with him. "Goodnight, tehnaak."

Kasiel didn't want to watch Jethan leave this way. He wanted him to know that it didn't matter if his scheme had gotten them in trouble or if he had doubted Kasiel's ability to control the tethdraks. The important thing was that he had been at his side for every step of this journey, regardless of the challenges. When he tried to think of a way to put all that into words, his mind went blank. He was simply too exhausted. All he managed was a somewhat defeated goodnight.

CHAPTER TWENTY ONE

Kasiel woke to the sound of someone knocking on the wall outside the doorway into his bedroom. The smell of fresh baked bread wafted in from the sitting room, countering his lingering exhaustion and the throbbing in his hands. He hadn't eaten after his testing, a fact his stomach was more than happy to remind him of now.

He sat up, groggily eyeing the doorway. "Who is it?"

"Excuse us, Lord Hahren," a woman's voice answered. "We were asked to prepare a bath for you, so you might have the chance to clean up before the tailor arrives."

The tailor? Again? He pulled back the covers and got up, wearing only the bandages on his hands and a pair of soft sleeping trousers he had changed into after Jethan left. "Please, go ahead."

Two women entered, carrying a heavy container full of water between them. The younger of the two, bringing up the back, looked in his direction and blushed. He glanced at the long mirror in the corner near the bathing room, a little surprised to see that he wasn't the skinny, soft youth he thought of himself as anymore. Since leaving Fernwallow, he had filled out some and started developing actual lean muscle. Was that what made her blush, or was it simply the fact that he barely had any clothes on?

He watched them lug the container into the bathing room. For once, he was too tired and hungry to offer help. His injured hands would make it more difficult anyhow. Besides, he knew from prior attempts that they would refuse him. Instead, he wandered out to the sitting room and dug into the food waiting there.

By the time he had eaten his fill, the attendants were gone, and the bath was ready. His split knuckles made the hot, scented water less pleasant than it might have been otherwise, so he made quick work of cleaning up and getting out. Fresh wraps and a container of salve sat by the basin in the bathing room. It was awkward trying to wrap his own hands, but he did his best, tucking the end of the wraps in against his palms and hoping they would stay in place.

The tailor arrived as he was emerging in a clean pair of comfortable sleeping trousers. The man carried in a set of fitted black trousers with elegant purple embroidery down the outside seams, a similarly embroidered black vest, an ivory shirt, and a hip-length jacket that matched the ensemble.

Another man entered behind him and bowed. "Lord Hahren, we must prepare you for your appearance before the testing panel."

Kasiel frowned at the tray an attendant carried in with a selection of brushes, combs, and other mysterious tools on it. "How prepared do I need to be?"

The man looked him over with a thin-lipped smile and gestured to the tailor.

They got him dressed in the outfit first. While the tailor moved about checking the fit, the other man went to work. He plucked Kasiel's brows, trimmed the ends of his hair, and brushed something through it to give it more shine and smoothness. He abandoned his effort to braid up one side of Kasiel's hair after a firm objection from him and pivoted to two small decorative braids on one side that didn't expose that ear.

Maybe Kenna was right. Maybe anyone here could see that his ears were cut from the way his hair hung over them. That didn't mean he wanted to put his disfigurement on display.

Before leaving him, the groomer, as Kasiel had dubbed the man in his head, redid Kasiel's bandages, making them both more secure and less unsightly. The tailor assured him that his summons would come within the hour before also ducking out the door.

Kasiel considered his reflection in the full-length mirror again. The person gazing back didn't look like him, at least not as he envisioned himself. His hair, parted to the left and with a new subtle shine to it, hung straight down a little past his shoulders now. In the sunlight that came through the windows, he could see the varying shades of red in it that Kenna had mentioned. His pale, gray-green eyes unfortunately reminded him of his father. What about his mother? Had he perhaps gotten his red hair from her?

The scar on his cheek was clearly visible with his hair parted this way. Was that intentional? He couldn't imagine the groomer hadn't noticed it.

He didn't like the cut of the jacket. After a moment, he pulled it off and changed into the charcoal-colored jacket that reminded him of Arhk's black one. It was precisely fitted and hung longer in the back, dipping to behind his knees. The material was the same as his father's, with that fluid-like movement to it. It had similar dark metal accents weighing it down strategically and giving the suggestion of armor to the garment. It also made him look taller somehow, and perhaps a little more imposing. An image he was certain he had never pulled off before. If they were about to knock him down to size for his performance in the testing and his cheating, it might help to wear a garment that made him feel more significant going in.

When Jethan arrived a short time later, he stopped inside the doorway and gave Kasiel a brief once over.

"You wear nobility well." His observant gaze flickered to the jacket that matched Kasiel's outfit lying discarded on the back of a chair, and he grinned. "With a touch of defiance. I like it."

Even with his quick show of good humor, there was a hint of reservation in Jethan's manner. The guilt he wore under his fine clothes still weighed on him. They would have to address that later. For now, Kasiel noted his attire, attractive dark brown trousers, an ivory shirt, and a mid-thigh length jacket the same color as the trousers, accented in black and deep green. He gave a nod of appreciation.

"You don't look so bad yourself, tehnaak." His gaze caught on the tattoos showing above Jethan's collar and Kenna's comment returned to him. "We need to talk about tattoos. Where to put them. What color to make them."

"Ah, yes. Probably should have had that conversation days ago," Jethan answered, his brow furrowing.

A young female attendant stepped into the doorway Jethan had left open and cleared her throat softly. When they faced her, she said, "Perhaps my lords could discuss these things along the way." Her eyes met Kasiel's, her mouth opening slightly as if she might say more, then she closed it and lowered her gaze.

"What is it?" Kasiel asked, walking toward her.

"It's not my place," she answered, though her gaze returned to his face, unspoken words dancing behind pale, lavender eyes.

"Pretend it is," he countered, captivated by those eyes.

She brushed a strand of silvery-white hair away from her face, her brows pinching together as she considered him. "It appears as though your life has already partially answered the question of placement." She took a step closer and brought one hand up, stopping a few inches shy of touching the scar on his cheek. Then she lowered her arm to her side.

"Interesting observation." Jethan gestured for her to lead the way, eyeing Kasiel's scar as they followed her out. "Since you're offering your opinions, do you have any regarding what color he should go with?"

"Kenna suggested a red to complement my hair," Kasiel said.

The woman stopped and turned, her intense gaze focusing on his hair. He watched her, intrigued. She reached out, and he had to fight the urge to grab her hand the way he had Kenna's. That reaction had upset Kenna more than the knowledge that his ears were cut. Perhaps there was a lesson to be learned there.

Taking a little of his hair, she separated the strands by rubbing it between her thumb and fingers. He startled when she unceremoniously plucked a strand.

Jethan barked a laugh.

"This color, I think." She held the strand of hair out to him.

Kasiel chuckled, accepting the offering. "What's your name?"

"Nerith," she answered. She turned and resumed walking. "Come. You shouldn't be late."

Kasiel wound the strand of hair into a little loop and tucked it in a pocket as they followed her. Nerith kept a quick pace, leading them to one of several still unfamiliar parts of the palace. Kasiel attempted to draw her into their conversation a few times along the way, but she only smiled politely and increased her speed. Eventually, she stopped outside a set of double doors. The guards in front opened them, and she stepped to one side, gesturing for them to enter.

Kasiel bit back the urge to ask her if she might be around later. He wasn't sure why he even considered it. The notion came unbidden, and he kept it suitably imprisoned in his head. Instead, he forced himself to step into the room, grateful to have Jethan at his side.

This chamber looked a lot like the round one where he had first met his father. Only a long table stretched across the dais here, its shape following the curve of the platform. His instructors and the three examiners who had conducted the oral part of the exam sat behind it. At the far end of the table, beside Dhomen Farren, sat Ahndhomen Adnar with a full-grown tethdrak resting on the floor next to him. The creature's head stuck up above the table, even laying down as it was. Its scales were a darker red color, like the mask on the pup Kasiel had grown fond of. It was the first time he had seen one of the beasts outside of an enclosure. Even though he suspected Adnar's control of it was more than adequate, seeing it resting there with no visible restraints was unnerving.

The first instructor stood, gesturing to the dark metal circle inlaid in the center of the room. Kasiel went to stand to one side of the circle, sinking to a knee when Jethan did so next to him. The instructor came around in front of the table and looked down at them from the dais. The corners of her mouth curved in the faintest hint of a smile.

"Lord Hahren Cavenos, for the oral portion of your test, I speak for all of us," she said, sweeping a hand back to take in the instructors and examiners, excluding Farren and Adnar, "when I say we were pleasantly surprised by the level of dedication and effort demonstrated by your pairing in your quick mastery of the materials assigned to you."

Kasiel's breath caught for a second. That wasn't at all what he expected. He fought to hold back a delighted grin that would undermine the composure he was trying to maintain. At the edge of his vision, he noticed the slightest twitch at the corner of Jethan's mouth as he held back his own smile.

"You still have much to learn to reach the level of education of your peers, but this foundation, and your tehnaak, will serve you well as you proceed. You will join the academy at a third-year level with additional supplementary courses to bring you up to speed." Her gaze lingered on Jethan for a second before she continued. "We understand this will be a step back for you, Lord Jethan, but the advantage you gain in having learned these things already will allow you to better assist your tehnaak. You have already shown considerable devotion to Lord Hahren, so we assume this will not be a problem."

"I am honored to stand with my tehnaak," Jethan answered, his lack of hesitation sending a surge of affection through Kasiel.

"Very well." She looked toward the opposite end of the table as she returned to her seat. "I pass them to you, Dhomen Farren."

Farren stood, allowing the tethdrak plenty of space as he came around. The sharp lines of his tattoos and the deep red color amplified his intimidating presence. That was something to keep in mind, as Kasiel considered the tattoos they would give him. Never in his life had he thought of permanently marking his skin in such a way. Now, with how well the first portion of the testing went, a spark of excitement ignited in him at the idea.

"While there was nothing surprising or impressive in your combat performance, Lord Hahren," Farren stated in his blunt way, "it was evident that your pairing put forth a reasonable effort to prepare you. It was also apparent that you have the potential to be a capable fighter given proper instruction. For the next few months, you will train with your tehnaak and the inren you faced in testing. When you have mastered the fundamental skills, I will take over your training myself."

Not a glowing review, but still better than he had expected. Kasiel allowed himself a small exhalation of relief.

Without another word, Farren returned to his seat, offering a gruff nod to Adnar as he strode past.

There was a disconcerting similarity to the way Adnar and his tethdrak moved when they rose together and stalked around in front of the table. Kasiel's chest tightened. This was when it would all go wrong. Adnar didn't strike him as the forgiving type. He would expose their misdeeds and destroy everything they had accomplished, and they would deserve it.

The tethdrak came off the dais and lowered its head, flicking its tongue out to smell Kasiel. It growled deep in its throat, emitting a few sharp clicking sounds that made him flinch in surprise. Then it hopped back up and circled around Adnar to sit at his side, its head nearly level with his shoulder.

"Lord Hahren," Adnar rested a hand on the tethdrak's shoulder as he spoke, "coming from someone recently introduced to Vanris and her ways, your bold choice to begin testing with the cliff cats was unexpected. Not only did you bring them under control quickly, you demonstrated an impressive ability to anticipate their attacks, a skill you appear to lack when facing a human opponent."

Kasiel's shoulders tightened with irritation at the tacked on critical observation, but he had earned worse from Adnar, so he kept his expression neutral.

"I saw the same ability in your test with the

tethdraks. You anticipated the attack and moved with it, avoiding injury to yourself and the beast. As with the cliff cats, when you took control, it was not with force and domination, but through an understanding of their fears and motivations. It has been a long time since I have seen a Feral with so much empathy for their subjects. You have earned your choice of the juvenile tethdraks as a companion. You will come to the habitat tomorrow afternoon to make your selection. I will continue to oversee most of your training myself."

Adnar and the tethdrak returned to the table. Kasiel stared at the floor, waiting for more. Waiting to have his cheating exposed, but Adnar said nothing else.

The instructor who had spoken first rose and the rest of those at the table stood with her this time. "You may rise, Lord Hahren and Lord Jethan." When they had both done so, she continued. "You have accomplished much in your short time as a pairing. Lord Hahren, we have determined that you will, on this day, receive your ke'hanoath, assuming there are no objections."

In a moment of silence, the eyes of the instructors shifted toward the side of the room. Kasiel turned his head enough to see Arhk in his periphery, standing near a door there. Fury overpowered a fleeting glimmer of pride as he recalled everything that had happened in the night. The horrifying experience in the deeps. Setera extracting his memories.

His hands started curling into fists, sudden pain intensifying his rage. If Arhk objected...

No one spoke.

"Congratulations, Lord Hahren Cavenos. You become a true Vanrian this day. After your ke'hanoath is complete, you are free to go celebrate your accomplishments."

He barely caught himself before correcting his name. The longing to defy his father was powerful enough he nearly destroyed a moment of victory for it. The door at the side of the room clicked shut. Arhk had departed. There was no one here he wanted to defy now.

Kasiel drew a deep, calming breath and bowed to the table of instructors. He let instinct guide his words. "I've been lucky to work with each of you over the last week. It will be an honor to continue doing so. I won't betray the confidence you put in me today."

He caught the slightest nod of approval from Adnar before turning with Jethan to exit the room. Not approval from his father, but from the man whose trust he *had* betrayed. The man who could have exposed his cheating and denied him this victory, but who, for whatever reason, had chosen not to.

The moment the doors closed behind them, Jethan caught him in a fierce hug.

"You did it, Kas! You're amazing!" He stepped away then, regret apparent in his avoidant gaze. "I really never should have doubted you."

"*We* did it," Kasiel corrected him.

Before Jethan could put a voice to the disagreement building in his eyes, Nerith rejoined them. "My lords, they asked me to escort you to the palace Heartsmith."

"The what?" Somehow, a Heartsmith didn't sound like a positive thing. He liked his heart exactly as it was.

Jethan's serious regard broke upon a laugh he couldn't hold back. "Don't look so alarmed. It's where the tattoos are done."

Nerith placed a hand over her mouth, covering her own bright laughter. "Follow me, my lords."

Kasiel and Jethan hurried after her.

"You don't have to keep calling me 'my lord'," Kasiel said.

Nerith was silent, though an amused smile curved her lips.

Jethan arched a brow at him in question.

Kasiel shrugged. "I can't recall exactly, but wasn't there something in all those books about the ke'ha..." He trailed off, looking hopefully at Jethan.

"Ke'hanoath," Nerith offered. "It's your identity. Who you are in your heart, as well as who you are as a Vanrian. It begins when you are a child, when they tattoo the symbols of your tehnaak and your family on the back of your head. For you, as a mind-crafter, another part of your ke'hanoath normally would have been added when you went through the Trial. You'll receive the runes of your craft, along with a story that is unique to you." She glanced over at him, her gaze lingering on the scar on his cheek for a moment before she faced forward again. "Because you are a soldier in Etrion, you will also have a small version of the symbols of your family and your tehnaak done on the inside of one wrist and one ankle, in case you die in battle and there are difficulties identifying the body."

Her last words caused a sinking sensation in the pit of his stomach. "I was feeling much more positive about today until you said that."

Nerith stopped before a door and looked up at him, her lavender eyes sparkling with amusement. "We're here. Do you still have that strand of hair, or would you like me to pluck another one, my lord?" Her gaze shifted to his hair as if seeking a second victim.

Kasiel held a hand up between them. "No. I still have it."

She gestured to the door.

"I, um... Thank you."

Jethan snickered behind Kasiel as he yanked open the door and stepped through to hide the warmth rising in his cheeks.

They entered a round, domed chamber about half the size of the room they had just left. Several stone tables were arranged around a circular platform in the center of the chamber. They looked like sacrificial altars to Kasiel, with gutters carved into the floor beside each one, leading to drain holes. Skylights in the domed ceiling let in bright daylight with an abundance of sconces and candelabras chasing away any lingering shadows along the walls.

A heavyset older man strode confidently across the room to greet them. "Lords Hahren Cavenos and Jethan Markanis, I have been awaiting you."

As he approached, Kasiel noticed his eyes were milky white. Even the pupils. He glanced at Jethan, unsettled, but trying not to be rude by pointing out the issue.

"All Heartsmiths are blind," Jethan stated, as if that were an adequate explanation.

"Your story has changed, young Jethan," the man said, his milky eyes staring through them.

"It has, Heartsmith Ganok." Jethan inclined his head politely as if the man might somehow see the gesture.

A woman entered the room and came to stand to one side of Ganok, her head bowed in patient waiting.

"Have you chosen your color, Lord Hahren?" Ganok asked.

Kasiel pulled the strand of hair from his pocket. "Can you use this as a color sample?"

Ganok gestured to the woman next to him. "Take this sample and blend the color for Lord Hahren. While you are there, please also blend a small batch for Lord Jethan in his color. We must add to his ke'hanoath today as well."

The woman took the strand of hair and bowed to Ganok before disappearing into a side room. Ganok gestured to two tables that had padding laid over them. Once they had each seated themselves on one, the Heartsmith removed a flask from his belt. He poured a greenish liquid into three tiny cups.

"Drink." He held one out to Kasiel.

Kasiel hesitated.

"It helps the Heartsmith find your story. It's nothing harmful," Jethan assured him.

Kasiel accepted the cup and downed the bitter liquid. Jethan accepted a cup from the Heartsmith and did the same. When he gave it back to Ganok, the Heartsmith drank from the third cup. Then he returned the flask to his belt and sat on a stool next to a table full of tools. The woman reemerged carrying two stone bowls, one containing a reddish liquid that was a match for the strand of hair he had given her. The other held a darker green, the same color as Jethan's existing tattoos.

"First, we place the markings of your family and your tehnaak's family on your wrist and ankle. By the time those are complete, your spirit will be ready to speak to me."

Ganok picked up a sharp, hollow piece of wood and dipped it in the ink. Using a small hammer, he began tapping it into the skin above Kasiel's ankle. While not excruciating, it was sufficiently painful to make him wince in surprise at the first hit.

"With all the remarkable painkillers you have here, why is it that this has to hurt so much?" He grimaced as Ganok continued working with no apparent concern for his discomfort.

Jethan shrugged. "Pain is part of the ritual. Relax, tehnaak. Let the experience guide you."

Kasiel lay back on the table, gritting his teeth, and stared up at the skylight.

What was he doing? Here he was in an unfamiliar country full of strange people and customs, letting a blind man tattoo permanent symbols into his skin. Although, this should have been his home all along. He would have been part of this from the beginning if Edmund hadn't taken him. What had the khevarin said? Perhaps he could be Vanrian again? This was a step along that path, but the first week had gone by so fast, he hadn't had time to figure out if this was who he wanted to be.

As he stared at the skylight, the pain gradually became a distant buzzing in his mind. His thoughts drifted, wandering over snippets of his childhood with Edmund, his peaceful life in Fernwallow, growing up with Danica, the mercenaries, meeting Jethan, the harrowing journey that brought him here, and everything that had happened since his arrival.

"Ah, I see you now, young Kasiel." Ganok's voice echoed oddly in his head. "You are starting to share your story."

Several hours later, Jethan led them out through the city streets. Over the past week, Kasiel had remained within the closed circuit between the palace, the tunnel to the canyon habitat, and the mind-crafter academy. This was his first time venturing out into the rest of the city since their arrival. He felt conspicuous still wearing his finer clothes, especially given that the fresh tattoo, covered in a thin layer of salve, forced him to leave the collar of his shirt hanging open.

A series of symbols and runes in deep coppery-red created a chain that hung around his neck. He didn't recall suggesting the placement, but it worked somehow. The elongated symbol at the base, where a pendant would hang on an actual chain, looked almost like a blade. Ganok had explained that it represented his severance from his birth home in Vanris, with the symbols that linked it to the rest on either side representing his return and reconnection to that home.

"You're sure I shouldn't go change first?" he asked for the fourth time.

Jethan winked at him. "Are you kidding? The ladies won't be able to take their eyes off that strong, freshly tattooed chest."

Kasiel spun on the ball of one foot and started walking back toward the palace.

Laughing, Jethan grabbed his arm and turned him around. "You're fine, tehnaak. Look at this place. There's no dress code here unless you're on duty. And it's not like you don't have an obvious reason for wearing the shirt that way right now. Come on. Live a little. You've earned it." He kept hold of Kasiel's arm, guiding him along.

Jethan wasn't wrong. People around them, at least those not in military uniforms, wore everything from tattered common garb to the occasional outfit almost as fine as what the two of them were wearing. The jacket made him the most uncomfortable because it so resembled the one the prominent Dhomvalen Arhk Cavenos often wore. No one else he saw in the streets had anything like it.

And he did get attention, his appearance ultimately drawing less of it than his company did. Jethan was the khevarin's nephew, so it made sense that much of the city would recognize him. Many people greeted him along the way, most hailing him as Lord Jethan while they gave Kasiel curious or suspicious looks. Jethan returned the greetings in a distracted manner that discouraged anyone from trying to engage him further, an approach Kasiel appreciated.

Kasiel reached up to touch the one symbol that was separated from the rest, tattooed on his cheek. The longest line stretched above the scar along his cheekbone, sweeping gradually down to a point at the end. The other lines that made up the symbol had similar styling, tapering to sharp points that gave the coppery-red markings an aggressive quality in the manner of Farren's tattoos, yet somehow also provided a touch of elegance. Ganok said the symbol represented the indomitable strength of their spirit pairing that had persevered through so many challenges and would continue to do so as long as they remembered to honor it. Jethan now had a similar symbol added to the set climbing the side of his neck, though his was deep green and had softer edges to match the rest of his tattoos.

Kasiel flinched in surprise when Jethan slapped his arm.

"Don't mess with it."

Kasiel dropped his hand to his side. "It just feels so obvious. Like I won't ever be able to go unnoticed in a crowd again."

"When did you ever go unnoticed in a crowd before?" Jethan asked. "I mean, there weren't really enough people in Fernwallow to make a crowd, were there?"

Kasiel narrowed his eyes at him in mock anger. "As soon as my hands heal—"

"You'll need a lot more combat training before that threat worries me," Jethan interrupted, stepping briefly behind Kasiel as he spoke to get out of the path of a man too busy talking to his companion to watch where he was going. His companion shrugged apologetically, his gaze lingering on Kasiel a little too long.

"At least I have a goal to work toward now."

Jethan stopped him outside a building with wide double doors of black wood that had panels of polished black stone down either side and no windows. The black stone framing the door had a column of Vanrian symbols embedded in it using that dark metal they were so fond of. The name of the establishment, Kasiel assumed, though he couldn't hope to read it any more than he could read the symbols and runes tattooed on his flesh. He only knew what they said because Ganok told him.

"What does it say?"

"The Twisted Vine," Jethan answered absently, doing a quick scan of the area as if looking for someone. "Wait here. I'm going to make sure they have room for us."

He winked at Kasiel and disappeared through the door before he could ask him exactly how much room they needed for the two of them. Left alone outside, he turned to watch the people walking past, becoming aware, as he listened to them speaking in Vanrian, of how sheltered he had been over the last week. Not one person passing by said a word in Pandrean Common. And why would they? This was Vanris. They would use their native tongue here. He caught one or two words he had learned, but he was a long way from understanding full sentences.

"Look at that."

Kasiel turned, surprised to hear someone speaking Pandrean Common after the observations he had just made. Three younger men emerged from The Twisted Vine and strolled toward him, sneering at him with open disdain.

"The renegade son shows his face," the one in the lead remarked. "I can't believe they let him out unsupervised."

A dark anger swept through Kasiel. His hands started curling into fists until the stiffness and pain in his knuckles stopped them. That discomfort reminded him he was at a disadvantage not only because of his injuries but also because he was alone and hadn't grown up learning how to fight like the people here had.

"What's this?" One man moved closer and reached toward the fresh tattoo on his cheek.

Kasiel jerked away, taking a quick step back. He cast a glance at the door, hoping Jethan might reappear.

"They're even letting him pretend to be one of us." The man drew back his hand, curling his lip in disgust.

The third said something in Vanrian and all three laughed. Kasiel recognized the word for a southerner. The rest was beyond him, though he was confident it wasn't anything complimentary. Their humor vanished a moment later when someone stepped up past Kasiel and punched the man who had spoken in the jaw, sending him sprawling. Darro rushed in, placing himself between the three men and Kince, who had done the punching.

"That's enough. You three get out of here," Darro snapped, putting a hand on Kince's chest to warn him off.

The first man advanced a step, then his gaze caught upon an insignia on Darro's jacket, and he lifted his hands, backing away. The other one helped their fallen companion to his feet, casting a look full of loathing at Kasiel before they departed.

Wedro put an arm around Kasiel's shoulders. "Out of the palace one day, and you're already causing a commotion. I knew I liked you."

Darro shoved Kince toward the door. He glanced at Kasiel. "Come on, danro." He beckoned him with a wave before following Kince.

Wedro steered Kasiel after them into the crowded interior of what turned out to be a tavern. A rich black wood made up the tables, bar, and exposed rafters, but the abundance of lighting and the laughter of patrons warmed the spacious interior. Skylights in the ceiling, akin to those in the Heartsmith's chamber, added to the bright, uplifting atmosphere. Paintings, weapons, and heraldry hung upon the walls. The paintings he found fascinating in that many of them depicted landscapes in which volcanoes played a prominent role. Images from the original Vanrian homeland.

Jethan was finishing helping a server clear off a long table in the back. He grinned as they all filed in, gesturing for Kasiel to take a seat near the middle of one bench set against the wall. The rest took places around the table. All of them. Chander was there with Wedro. Avris, Merrin, and Tath came in together a few seconds later and claimed seats at the table.

Avris pointed at Kasiel, making a little v motion with her finger as she leaned on the table to indicate his tattoo chain. "I like this. Vanris looks good on you, country boy."

Kasiel breathed a laugh, a touch of heat rising in his cheeks. Dodging her attention, he looked at Kince. "What did that guy outside say?"

"He called you an earless southerner," Darro answered.

"Calloch," Kince growled under his breath.

"And you came to my defense?" Kasiel tried not to sound too shocked.

Kince's attention focused on him with unsettling intensity. "The moment you made the choice to ride away with us rather than go back to the people and places that were familiar to you, you became part of our unit. That unit became our tehsheyn, our spirit family, out there. You also saved Jethan and helped us with your mindcraft when you could. If you ever need anything—help with training, a night at the tavern, someone to punch a calloch for you—don't hesitate to reach out to one of us."

Kasiel glanced at the others, surprised to see nods all around, even from Tath.

The server slid a tray full of mugs of Vanrian Black Mead into the center of the table and Jethan started handing them around. "Now that we've got the sentimental crap out of the way, let's crack a stone to the newly confirmed Vanrian in our midst!"

They all grabbed their mugs and lifted them, shouting, "To Kasiel!"

Kasiel raised his mug self-consciously and took a drink. The unit was his family, his tehsheyn. He liked that idea. Even as low as his expectations had been, the blood family he found here turned out to be a disappointment. This, however, was a family he could appreciate. They weren't without their tensions, but what family was? That they would accept him as part of their group even after losing Ahrin told him this was the kind of family he wanted.

He leaned closer to Jethan. "What *is* a calloch?"

Wedro, ever the subtle one, let out a guffaw where he was sitting on Kasiel's other side.

Jethan leaned forward to point at Wedro. "That's a pretty good example."

A few others who were paying attention laughed, and Wedro gave them all a sour look. "That's family for you. We'll see what happens next time one of you needs my help." He raised his mug and took a long drink.

Chander leaned on the table, giving Kasiel a conspiratorial wink. "Truth is, not one of us has ever seen, or smelled, calloch for real. Back in our original homeland, there were these nasty little monkeys that lived in a particular area of the rainforest. Great place to find some of the best herbs for healing and brewing. But if the monkeys saw someone entering their territory, the little bastards would excrete a rank musk into their dung piles and roll it into balls. When the intruder got in range, they would get bombarded with them. Those reeking dung balls were called callochs. It probably won't surprise you to learn that we didn't bring any of those monkeys with us. No one alive now has ever seen them or smelled that musk, but the little bastards earned a slice of immortality with their dung."

He took a drink and Wedro piped up. "Now you know a calloch is an especially rank ball of monkey dung. Feel bad for laughing when Jeth called me that now, don't you?"

Kasiel cracked a crooked smile. "Not especially."

"Oh!" Wedro rocked back exaggeratedly on the bench and placed a hand over his chest. "You've wounded me to the heart, you have." He leaned in and winked at Kasiel. "Guess I won't be doing you any favors either."

Kasiel only smiled. He noticed some of the other patrons in the tavern watching them. A few appeared more curious, but several regarded them, or rather, him specifically, with suspicious or disdainful looks.

Merrin followed the direction of his gaze and leaned across the table toward him. "I'm afraid you'll have to deal with that for a while. Some people are content to be happy that the dhomvalen got this son back. But many don't like that someone raised in the south has moved into the palace and is now being allowed to integrate with our society."

Darro nodded agreement, lowering his voice. "Some are jealous of the privilege and status you stepped into. They don't feel you've earned it. Others are afraid that, after twelve years, you might be loyal to the southern kingdoms. They think giving you access to our city, palace, and customs could compromise our secrets and our safety."

Kasiel glanced around the room, observing those dark looks. Could he blame them? They had plenty of valid reasons to be suspicious of him.

"Do any of you feel that way?"

Avris smiled, the hint of affection in her gaze a balm to his sudden discomfort. "No, we know you're a simple country boy beneath all those sexy tattoos."

"Avris!" Merrin smacked her tehnaak on the arm.

"By the Break, Avris," Darro grumbled, "do you have to go there?"

Next to Kasiel, Jethan had a hand over his mouth, which did nothing to hide the fact that he was snorting with laughter.

Avris grinned. "Come on, who wasn't thinking it?"

To Kasiel's embarrassment, Chander was the only one who raised a hand.

Darro and Kince both shrugged.

"I mean, she's right," Wedro added unhelpfully. "It looks like Vanris had a splendid time getting its ink into you."

Kasiel took a long drink of his mead, attempting to hide what he suspected was a very country boy blush while laughter blossomed around the table.

A few small groups remained at the tavern when they finally left. Kince and Darro accompanied Jethan and Kasiel back to the palace entrance. They said it was merely for a chance to keep visiting, but Kasiel suspected it had more to do with the hostile looks he had received throughout the evening. Regardless, since he was a little off kilter from a few too many mugs of mead, he appreciated the extra company.

Eventually, he and Jethan stumbled back into Kasiel's room. He hung his jacket, gracelessly tugged off his boots, and flopped on the bed upside down, setting his feet up on the ornate headboard. Jethan sat on the other side, leaning against the headboard in a more traditional fashion.

"Don't you have your own rooms?" Kasiel asked.

"Is that your not-very-polite way of telling me to leave?" Jethan arched a brow at him.

Kasiel chuckled. "No. It's just that half the time you sleep on my couch. I can't imagine it's more comfortable than your bed."

"Well, since I've spent the last week studying with you until some ridiculous hour most nights, it's often been easier to sleep here. Also," he paused, making a show of looking around the room, "I think your rooms might be a little nicer than mine."

"I doubt that."

"Actually, no, I really think they are." He stood up. "However, if I'm going to stumble off to my own rooms tonight, I best get moving. I'm likely to take a few wrong turns the way the halls are spinning right now."

Kasiel gave him a sideways look. "You can stay."

"Nah, I've got things to take care of in the morning. I suspect dragging you out of bed as early as I need to get up would put undue strain on our pairing. Remember what Ganok said about honoring it and all?"

"True." Kasiel sat up and watched Jethan meander in a not-so-straight line to the sitting room entrance. "Jeth?"

The other youth stopped and looked back, bracing himself against the doorway. "Yes."

"How do I get an audience with my father?"

Jethan's brow crinkled. "You know, I've never had to get an audience with my parents."

"Where are your parents?" Kasiel asked, realizing the only part of Jethan's family he had met or heard his tehnaak even mention was the khevarin.

"They're in Doran, the northern capital. That's where I grew up. I'll have to take you there to meet them someday. They weren't happy with your father when he granted my request to lead if they sent a team south to find you." He put out a hand to lean against the doorframe, chuckling when he nearly missed. "Regarding your question, I wouldn't expect you to have to put in a formal request considering, but I honestly don't know. I'll see what I can find out tomorrow, that is, if you're sure you *want* an audience with him."

Kasiel nodded. "I think so."

"All right. Sleep well, tehnaak. Don't mess with those sexy tattoos." Jethan winked and blew out the sconce by the door.

Kasiel threw a pillow in his direction, hitting the wall as Jethan ducked out the doorway laughing.

ood morning, Lord Hahren."

The familiar feminine voice snapped Kasiel awake. He held his breath for a moment, hoping he had dreamed it. Then he opened his eyes and looked toward the sitting room. Nerith leaned in the doorway wearing a purple attendant's dress, accented in silver and black. She reached down to pick the pillow he had thrown at Jethan up off the floor. He closed his eyes and turned into his pillow to muffle a groan. Why was she here?

"You probably shouldn't have slept in those clothes." A hint of laughter brightened her voice.

He opened his eyes, watching her fluff the pillow and walk around to place it on the other side of the bed. "Why are you here?"

She flashed him an indignant look, though he caught the slight upward twitch at the corner of her mouth. "Why, Lord Hahren, I've brought you your breakfast. I would have expected you to be a bit more appreciative."

He cast a glance and the midmorning sun glaring in through the window. "Isn't it a little late for the usual breakfast delivery?" He got up and peered down at the rumpled clothing he had fallen asleep in.

"It would be, but I received a message from your tehnaak around dawn this morning asking that you not be disturbed too early. He also asked that I help you figure out how to get in to meet with your father." She headed him off when he moved to walk around the bed and tilted her head to one side, gazing up at him.

Kasiel regarded her warily in return.

"The color was a good choice."

Oh yes, that was why his face hurt, and he had a stinging ring of pain running around his neck and down his sternum. He lifted his fingers toward his cheek, and her hand came up too, poised to smack his.

She gave him a warning look. "Don't mess with it."

Kasiel scowled at her. "You're as bad as Jethan."

A hint of pleasure lit her answering smile. "Good. There's some salve in the bathing room you can put on the tattoos. Don't mix it up with the one for your knuckles."

Kasiel glanced down. The bandage had come off one hand, revealing his wounds. "Thanks." He fought the urge to hide his injured hands behind him.

"It looks like you lost a battle with a steel door."

He narrowed his eyes at her. "That's uncannily accurate."

Nerith held up her hands in a gesture of innocence. "I promise I'm not keeping tabs on you, Lord Hahren." She turned and strode for the door as she spoke, forcing him to follow. "I did a little inquiring this morning. If you wish it, I can get you in to meet with the dhomvalen in an hour. That should be sufficient time to wash away the smell of mead, maybe put on something less wrinkled, and still have time to eat."

His stomach turned at the thought of seeing his father. A foolish idea conceived by a markedly less sober version of himself. Then again, who knew when he would get another opportunity? "Thank you. I'll be ready." He followed her out into the sitting room, trying to come up with an excuse to keep her there a few seconds longer. His gaze lit upon the breakfast platter.

"Are you hungry?"

She stopped and faced him, lips pressing together briefly as she fought to hold in the laughter sparkling in her eyes. "Are you... offering to share your breakfast with me? Might it not be inappropriate for me to abandon my duties to dine alone with you in your rooms?"

Kasiel shifted his feet, wishing he could disappear. "Sorry. Never mind."

"My lord." She inclined her head and opened the door. "I'll be back within the hour."

He blew out a heavy breath when the door clicked shut behind her. What was it about her that made him feel like a bumbling idiot? He suspected Jethan had caught on to that fact. Why else would he have sent his message to Nerith specifically? He wasn't sure whether to thank his tehnaak or hit him for it when he saw him next.

Kasiel piled cheese and sliced meat on a fresh chunk of bread and wandered toward the bathroom to get cleaned up. When Nerith returned, he wore an ivory shirt with the laces undone to avoid the fabric rubbing on the tattoo, black trousers, and a short, fitted jacket made of material suitable for his pending visit to the canyon habitat. Having an audience with his father right before going to see Adnar for another encounter fraught with tension was feeling increasingly like a poor choice, but he couldn't see a way out of it now. His father must be expecting him at this point.

Nerith looked him over once, her slender brows rising. "This is a casual audience, I presume?"

"He is my father," Kasiel answered, not doing the best job of hiding his irritation with the man as he stepped out of his rooms with her.

"And the dhomvalen of Vanris," she countered.

"He'll get over it."

Nerith started walking, her expression guarded.

Kasiel fell into step beside her. "You think I'm not showing proper respect for him?"

"I think that's between you and him," she answered cautiously.

He had hoped to strike up a conversation with her and learn who she was when she wasn't escorting people around the palace, but the uneasy exchange left him at a loss for something to say.

He didn't remember his last conversation with his father in its entirety, not since the Evoker extracted it, but he had read his journal entry several times. Having the memory of the encounter removed had stopped his nightmares, but it also distanced him from his anger with Arhk for using his Frightener ability on him. The resentment wasn't a feeling he enjoyed, but his father deserved it. And, while he didn't recall the actual incident anymore, reading about it in the journal and remembering the grief it caused him in the days that followed was enough to build up an acute apprehension as they walked along.

What if something like that happened again? Were there greater risks in having memories extracted multiple times? What if the Frightener ability had cumulative effects?

"We're here, my lord."

The coil of anxiety in Kasiel's chest tightened when she stopped, making it harder to draw a breath. He hesitated, staring at the door. Why had it been such a brief walk from his rooms? If this section of the palace was all private living areas, did that mean these were his father's personal chambers? The idea of facing him in the comfort of his own space didn't make this easier. For whatever reason, it also sparked more resentment before he even stepped through the door.

"You don't need to call me 'my lord'," he said, aware that he was trying to delay the encounter with his father as much as prolong his time with her.

"It's my place, my lord." She glanced at the door. "You should probably knock."

"Maybe we can talk more about that later." He straightened his jacket and took a deep breath, trying to ignore the fact that he had indirectly suggested they should meet up another time.

Nerith offered a slight bow and retreated several steps as he knocked.

"Enter." It was Arhk's soft, yet eerily powerful voice that beckoned him in.

Kasiel made himself open the door and strode through with a show of confidence that was entirely forced. He closed the door behind him, not especially surprised to find himself in a sitting room about twice the size of the one in his chambers. Arched windows lined the far wall, looking out over a different section of the academy. The set of ornate double doors to the rear of the space likely led to his bedroom.

Arhk stood in the center of the room, one hand resting on the back of the couch. He wasn't wearing his long jacket, but he didn't need it. The power of his presence lost nothing without it, and the rest of what he wore made him look ready to either meet with the khevarin or strike terror into his foes on a battlefield. That one outfit could inspire both impressions said remarkable things for his tailor.

Kasiel bowed, aware of his father's pale eyed gaze skimming over his tattoos as he straightened. "Dhomvalen," he greeted stiffly.

"At least you look somewhat Vanrian now." Arhk's tone was insultingly dismissive. "I wondered if you would have the courage to seek me out."

Kasiel's anger rose far too quickly. He shouldn't have come here. "I wondered if you would have the decency to come apologize. I guess we both have our answers."

Arhk regarded him in stone-faced silence.

The man's apparent disinterest stoked Kasiel's rage, clouding his thoughts. He latched on to a question he had intended to ask at some point, though the plan had been to approach it in a far more circumspect manner than he was now. "Why did you even send the mission to retrieve me if you didn't want me here?"

"Had you grown up here, Hahren," Arhk began. Kasiel's jaw tensed and Arhk's eyes narrowed as if he noticed that hint of stifled defiance. "Then you would know we never willingly leave a mind-crafter, awakened or otherwise, in enemy hands to be experimented upon or possibly turned against us. We had little choice once we realized the Vanrian rumored to be living in the far south might be you."

Kasiel's blood pounded in his ears, making it hard to think. "That's it? You didn't care about getting your son back?"

Arhk wandered to the window on the far side of the sitting room. He clasped his hands behind his low back. His tone changed when he spoke again, edged with a hint of something that could have been regret, though Kasiel was wary of reading too much into it.

"When I lost control of my ability the other night, I told you it had never happened before. That was not entirely true. It has happened one other time. On the night I learned that my wife and son were gone, I lost control. Only, on that occasion, there were more people around to suffer for it. Having you here..." he paused, the ache of loss in his voice nearly enough to break through Kasiel's resentment for a moment. Arhk glanced over a shoulder at him. "Every time I see you, it returns me to that night. I will recognize you as my son and ensure that your needs are met. Beyond that, I think it is best if we avoid one another, unless the situation demands otherwise."

The brief flicker of sympathy for his father burned away with those last words. Kasiel took a few steps farther into the room, anger pulsing through him. "With all the learning and changing I have to do to fit in here, I would have thought that keeping control of your ability to avoid breaking your own son was a fairly small ask." He spun and strode to the door.

Arhk's frustratingly calm voice stopped him. "I sent that mission because I wanted my wife and son back. But I cannot have my wife back, and you are not my son. You are a young man someone else raised."

"If you don't see me as your son," Kasiel snapped, "then I wouldn't expect you to care if I choose not to use his name." He reached for the door handle, the tears that stung his eyes fueling his anger. It wasn't fair that a man who cared nothing for him had the power to make him feel so worthless.

"You would be wrong." Warning added a sharp edge to Arhk's tone.

Kasiel started opening the door, then hesitated again, a burst of longing making him linger in the bitter emptiness of the space between them. He stared at the lever as if it could somehow save him from the hollow growing inside. "What was her name?" he asked softly.

The stifling silence lingered. When Kasiel was about to give up and leave, Arhk answered him.

"Ellaris. Your mother's name was Ellaris."

The weight of her name landed heavily on his shoulders. A crushing sensation in his chest made each breath hurt. Why? He didn't even remember her. Or maybe that was why. That his own mother's name—a beautiful name—should sound like the name of a stranger to him.

Kasiel walked out, easing the door shut behind him, his rage submerged beneath heartache. He strode back to his rooms as fast as he could walk, barely suppressing the urge to run there. Once inside, he shut the door and slumped against it, sinking to the floor. Tears streamed silently down his cheeks. He balled his hands into fists, welcoming the pain in his knuckles. His mother's name played back in his mind repeatedly, spoken in a voice burdened with loss and longing. The voice of a man who had loved deeply once and appeared incapable of doing so again.

The tears stung as they ran over the fresh lines of the tattoo on his cheek. His Vanrian tattoo. A laugh broke free at the absurdity of the whole mess.

There was a soft knock on the door.

Kasiel wiped away the tears and got to his feet. When he opened the door, Nerith stood there, looking worriedly up at him.

"It sounded as if you were laughing… or crying, my lord."

"Can't I do both?"

Discomfort made his tone defensive, though it apparently didn't discourage her. She reached up and brushed the remnant of a tear from his cheek with her thumb.

Kasiel drew back, avoiding her sympathetic gaze. "Did you need something?"

"Jethan also asked me to escort you to the canyon habitat. He said you might not know the way to the main entrance."

Kasiel breathed a mirthless laugh. "He might be right. How much did he put in that message?"

A gentle warmth lit her eyes. "It was more of a short novel. You are his tehnaak. It's clear that he cares deeply for you." She shifted, trying to look him in the eyes. "Do you need a few more minutes?"

He shook his head. "A few minutes won't fix this."

She stepped back, giving him space to come out, and led him away from his rooms again. When they exited the palace, walking along the outside of the enclosed garden, Kasiel could breathe more freely. It was as if Arhk's presence in the palace suffocated him. The desire to get to know Nerith better reemerged, offering a welcome distraction.

"How long have you worked in the palace?"

A trace of her smile returned. "I've had some kind of work here since I turned fifteen, so a couple of years. Working in the palace pays well while I train to become a healer, and it's usually easy enough work."

"Escorting the dejected son of the dhomvalen around doesn't seem too difficult." He forced a teasing smile.

"Sometimes the work is even pleasant." She cast a quick glance his way, her cheeks reddening. "My tehnaak was at The Twisted Vine last night. She said you were there too, and that your friends called you Kasiel. Is that the name you prefer to go by?"

He couldn't escape a sense of sinking dread at the thought of what other things her tehnaak might have observed, but it was too late to do much about that now. They hadn't been excessively rambunctious. At least, he hoped they hadn't.

"It is, but my father doesn't want me using it." A hint of anger tightened his voice.

A few delicate lines furrowed her brow. "He wants you to use the name they gave you at birth?"

"Yes, but it doesn't feel like my name. Of course, now that I know the people who gave me the name Kasiel lied to me all my life and were the ones who cut my ears, perhaps I shouldn't feel so attached to that name, either."

"I'm sorry." She placed a hand on his arm. "I imagine this is all incredibly difficult. But you now have your ke'hanoath written upon your skin. No matter what name people call you by, they can't take that identity away from you."

Kasiel glanced over at her, wishing she would leave her hand there. She didn't though, and he fought the urge to reach after it. Instead, he looked ahead at the enormous building they appeared to be heading toward, its entrance guarded by two fierce tethdrak statues. When they reached the statutes, Nerith stopped and gazed down at her clasped hands.

"I should get back."

"Thank you, Nerith, for everything." He watched her, hoping she would look up and see in his expression how sincere his gratitude was, but she kept her eyes down.

"Kasiel?"

His heart sped up a little when she spoke his name in that tentative voice. "Yes?"

"I'm leaving for a couple of weeks to attend the passing ceremony of my tehnaak's father up north. When I get back, if you'd be interested, I could help you with your Vanrian. I'm sure it's frustrating not knowing what people around you are saying." She looked up at him, a flush rising in her cheeks. "Of course, you probably have plenty of help from Jethan and..." She trailed off when he smiled.

"I'd like that very much."

Her lavender eyes lit up. "All right. Um... Oh! Go inside here." She pointed to the door between the statues. "There's a lift that descends to the bottom of the canyon at the back. Ahndhomen Adnar should be waiting for you. I'll see you in two weeks, my lord."

Unsure what else to say, he blurted, "You don't have to call me 'my lord'."

She flashed a quick smile at him and hurried off. As he stood there watching her disappear, he wished those two weeks were already over.

And wondered what a lift was.

With a sigh, he turned and strode between the stone tethdraks into the building.

CHAPTER TWENTY FOUR

Entering the building banished all other thoughts from Kasiel's mind. Directly in front of him, in the center of a large open room with towering ceilings, was a statue of something he had only seen as an emblem on the banners and armor of Vanris. It appeared to be more feline than reptile now that he saw it in greater detail, like a massive cat with a scaled hide instead of fur. It had what initially looked like plate armor along its spine, with chain mail draping down over its shoulders and haunches. The rider wore similar armor. Judging from the size of the creature compared to the person on its back, it was larger than the average horse.

It was hard to tell from the sculpture which details were part of the beast, and which were armor. Did it have natural bone plating along its neck and down to its tail like a tethdrak, or was that all added armor embellishment? The stone creature stood with its jaws opened in a roar that gave an excellent view of the pointed teeth, of which the top two in the front stretched down below its lower jaw. Kasiel could imagine its roar in his mind. The teeth and claws alone were terrifying, but the athletic musculature beneath that smooth scaled hide warned of brutal strength and speed as well.

Kasiel wandered closer, his attention locked on the statue, until a guard moved into his path. The woman was as well-armed and armored as any palace guard, which surprised him a little, since he would have expected a place like this, so deep in the city, to be relatively safe. Unless she wasn't only guarding from threats getting in.

"Halt."

Kasiel stopped. "I'm—"

"Lord Hahren Cavenos," she finished for him, her gaze skimming over his tattoos as if she were reading a book. "Our new Feral."

"I'll take him from here." Kenna came striding out of a side room. "Thank you," she added, effectively dismissing the woman, who shrugged and returned to her post along the wall. Kenna gave him a tentative hug, wary of his healing tattoos. "I'm glad you survived the deeps unharmed."

He held up his bandaged hands. "Mostly."

"Mostly is better than not at all." She leaned to one side, eyeing the tattoo on his cheek. "I see I was right about the color. It looks great on you."

Kasiel refrained from mentioning that she wasn't the only one who had suggested that color. It felt as if receiving the tattoos not only granted him an identity, but somehow made him significantly more interesting, at least to other Vanrians. It was disconcerting. Almost as if they hadn't seen him at all until now.

He gestured to the statue. "What is that?"

"A kanodrak."

"So, that's a depiction of an actual living creature?"

Kenna laughed. "Yes, danro, that's an actual creature. If you're talented enough, you might even ride one someday. Etrion is one of very few cities in Vanris that has some."

She struck off toward the rear of the building, gesturing for him to join her. As they moved around the kanodrak statue, he noticed a ten-foot-high section of the back wall, stretching across the entire length of the room, opened to a viewing platform looking out over the canyon.

"Incredible," he breathed, following her through the open wall and out onto the platform. The canyon stretched before him, its magnificent, layered walls reaching as far as he could see. In the distance below, he spotted a group of tethdraks lounging in the sun. "How many tethdraks are there here?"

"Fifty-three adults right now."

"How do you keep them all fed?"

Kenna set her hands on the railing next to him and looked down at the beasts. "It's difficult. We bring in a lot of antelope and other prey from further north where it's easier to maintain large herds. It's important to give them live prey as often as we can. They get aggressive with each other if they don't get the opportunity to hunt enough, and we want them to keep those hunting skills honed for when we take them into battle."

"And the kanodraks?"

"We have seven here right now. They're harder to maintain. There's a larger group in Doran."

Kasiel tried to imagine seven of those beasts and shuddered. It was no wonder they didn't keep them with the horses. "How do you keep the tethdraks and kanodraks from going after Vanrian horses and soldiers in the field?"

"That's part of the Feral's job. You'll learn all about that soon enough."

Mechanical noises to their left drew his attention to a fenced off area where a piece of the platform appeared to be missing. Around it stood a steel framework laden with an array of odd parts, many of which were now moving. When he glanced at Kenna in question, she leaned over the rail and pointed down to the left. Kasiel leaned out as well, spotting that missing piece of platform rising in the center of a steel framework that extended all the way to the canyon floor. A person was standing on it.

"That's the lift?"

"Mm-hmm. We'll ride that down as soon as it gets up here. Adnar was meeting with one of the second rank inveths heading out into the Break tomorrow. They want a Feral to go with the unit."

Something twisted in Kasiel's gut. With everything else going on, he had forgotten that they were so close to the Crimson Break, where active conflict might occur at any time. In Fernwallow, it had been too far away to think about.

"Is there fighting near here now?"

Kenna nodded. "To the southwest, in the Break. There have been escalating hostilities in that area since we brought you here. Apparently, the Pandrean Alliance doesn't appreciate that we sent a strike team all the way south and extracted someone under their noses."

So much trouble for one person, though his father's words suggested that a mind-crafter in enemy hands wasn't something to be taken lightly. If Jethan and the others hadn't come, he would have remained in the custody of mercenaries who were intent on torturing him near to death. He would never know what waited for him after that, but he had a feeling it wouldn't have been pleasant.

"How bad is the fighting?"

She gave him a long, unreadable look, then faced back out over the canyon. "Don't worry about it. You have other things that require your attention."

He drew a breath and exhaled, letting go of the brief flash of irritation. She was right. It wasn't as if he could do anything about it. "Will Ahndhomen Adnar go?"

"He can't. He's the only one in the city right now who can work with the kanodraks."

Kasiel faced her. "Does that mean they'll send you?"

Kenna nodded. "Yes. If anyone goes, it'll be me. I specialize in working with cliff cats. I've been helping with the tethdraks because we don't have enough Ferals here to manage everything. If Adnar feels like you can handle some of my work, he'll send me."

"I think this is the first time I've genuinely wanted to be found incompetent."

Kenna smiled at him before turning to watch the lift finish its ascent. "I appreciate the concern, Kas, but I want to see you succeed. Besides, it's an honor to fight for Vanris. It's what we train for all our lives."

Kasiel said nothing. It wasn't a sentiment he understood. At least not yet. Maybe, someday, he would feel that kind of devotion to a place, but he couldn't imagine it now, especially after speaking with his father.

The officer who stepped off the lift inclined her head briefly to Kenna before striding toward the exit. Kenna returned the nod. Then she walked over and opened a gate next to the platform. She gestured for him to go through. With his nerves dancing, Kasiel stepped across the two-inch gap of open air onto the platform, the slightest give under his feet making his heart jump into his throat.

Apparently noticing his alarm, Kenna said, "Don't worry. If I wanted you dead, I'd find a less public way to do it."

Kasiel arched a brow at her as she joined him on the platform, struggling not to react when it shifted under her added weight. "Not really the most reassuring thing you've ever said."

A glimmer of humor lit her eyes as she pulled the lever that set the contraption in motion. She came to stand next to him while he forced himself not to hold his breath.

"Keep your eyes on the view, Kas. You'll come to

love this."

Dragging his gaze from the drop below them, Kasiel looked out over the canyon. Sunlight reflected off a pale clay layer in the canyon wall that rested on a thicker layer of redder earth that absorbed the light. It resulted in a sunset effect where the colors joined. The plant life here, especially close to the stream, was far lusher than that outside the canyon, making it something of an oasis in the arid region.

He could see the group of resting tethdraks in the distance, basking in the sun, their reddish-brown scales helping them become part of the surrounding land-scape.

"If they aren't native, how is it that the tethdraks blend in so well?"

"The color of their scales can shift, allowing them to better match the environment they're in."

"That's…" He paused, considering how useful that could be in combat situations, providing one was on their side. "That's both terrifying and amazing."

"Since they'll be working for you, I'd recommend focusing on the amazing part."

Somehow, that did nothing to lessen the terrifying aspect of it.

As they neared the bottom, he spotted Adnar stand-ing within the fenced off area. The tethdrak he had the day before was with him on this side of the bars. Separated into a small enclosure on the opposite side of the fence, the three juvenile tethdraks that had been at Kasiel's testing wrestled with each other.

The platform settled on the bottom gently despite a few nerve-wracking clangs as it connected with the base of the framework. Kasiel was happy to step off it, though Adnar's unreadable gaze made him a little less eager to proceed. Still, hesitation wasn't going to win the man over. Donning a mantle of false confidence, he forged ahead alongside Kenna.

As soon as they stopped before Adnar, both inclining their heads respectfully, the Feral ahndhomen addressed Kenna. "See to your cats, Ahninveth. Your troop marches at dawn."

"Yes, Ahndhomen." Kenna lowered her head a fraction farther. Without looking at Kasiel, she turned and strode away, disappearing through a doorway in the cliff face.

Kasiel watched her go, wishing he could do or say something to ensure her safety. She had never even mentioned that she was an officer. Discovering that now was a reminder of how much he still had to learn about these people.

"Omren Hahren, you and I have other business to focus on."

Adnar's hard tone caught his attention as something of a warning, but Kasiel also noticed that he had given him the title for a common troop rather than a trainee. How much should he read into that? He didn't think he had learned enough to step out of trainee status yet, but maybe things worked differently when the soldier in question was a mind-crafter.

"Yes, Ahndhomen." He fought the urge to shift his feet or clench his hands. This wasn't the time to let his soaring anxiety show itself. "May I ask a question, sir?"

Adnar inclined his head. "You may."

"Why grant me the tethdrak if you know I cheated?"

Adnar gestured toward the far corner. His tethdrak trotted over there and laid down, leaving Kasiel to wonder if the beast was that attuned to his physical cues or if there had been a mental command as well.

"Several reasons," Adnar began. "The first being that your cheating only gained you the partial advantage of familiarity from your side. Because I knew you had been working with them, I blocked the memory of the last week from their minds for the duration of your test, making you a stranger as far as they were concerned. Also, because you started with the cats, you demonstrated an ability to work with challenging and unfamiliar creatures."

He strode toward the enclosure, gesturing for Kasiel to accompany him. The moment they neared the bars, the masked tethdrak pup faced them, ignoring one of its siblings as it tried to tackle him. A slight smile touched Kasiel's lips. The knee-high reptilian pup snapped at the other beast, driving it off, then loped over to the edge of the cage. Kasiel stepped closer and put his hand through, letting the creature press its naturally armored snout into his palm. A broader smile forced itself across his features as the tethdrak emitted a few of the soft clicks he had learned to associate with happiness.

"Omren," Adnar snapped.

Kasiel jerked his hand back and turned to face the ahndhomen. The tethdrak sat next to him on the other side of the bars, also facing Adnar.

Adnar looked from him to the young beast. "This is the primary reason I am not holding you back. I watched you out there with the young tethdraks several times when you came to visit. It became apparent rather quickly that this one had already chosen you. The empathy you have for them won you the loyalty of this beast before you ever touched its mind. That kind of empathy is the most vital skill a Feral can have, and one of the rarest. It is also necessary if you are ever going to work with the kanodraks. To punish you by denying this would have been counterproductive."

The tethdrak's hard nose touched his hand through the bars, and pride surged through Kasiel. He wasn't ready to let the subject go, though. "So, you allowed us to continue our cheating and then threw us in the deeps for it."

Adnar gave him a hard look. "If I had not been somewhat complicit in letting your behavior continue, your punishment would have been far worse. Vanris needs skilled Ferals, Omren Hahren. We also need disciplined ones. I advise you not to test the rules going forward. I will not be so generous again."

Kasiel inclined his head. "Understood, sir."

"Good. This tethdrak is now your responsibility. We will work on training and control here at first. Once I feel you are both ready, you will start taking excursions around the city with it. There are to be no incidents on these excursions. You must always maintain full control of the tethdrak outside of this space. I will also need help with Kenna gone. That presents us an opportunity to advance your group control faster than planned. You will oversee the juveniles and will practice with them every time you check in on them. This also means learning to handle their mother, though she should be receptive to you by now. I will manage the other adults until I feel you are ready. Then I will have you help with them and begin learning to control them. Do you understand?"

Kasiel wasn't sure he was ready for all of this, but he answered with the confidence he knew Adnar was looking for. "Yes, sir!"

"Good. Get your tethdrak out of the enclosure and we will get started." Adnar tossed him the key to the gate.

A thrill of excitement swept through him as he caught the key and slid it into the lock. On the other side, receptive to his mood, the masked tethdrak leapt up, bouncing his front feet against the bars. That they barely moved made Kasiel wonder how deep in the ground they were driven. The incident also served as a warning. Before opening the gate, he reached out to the juvenile, seeking admission to the creature's mind with a sense of comfort and belonging. The speed with which it welcomed him in supported Adnar's claim that the tethdrak had already bonded with him.

Unlocking the gate, he opened it and brought the masked tethdrak out, encouraging calm and control. Though he could feel the creature's barely contained excitement through their connection, it yielded to his influence, waiting while he locked the gate again and turned to Adnar. With a touch of persuasion and patience, he got it to come sit by his side facing the Feral ahndhomen.

To Kasiel's considerable surprise, a proud smile curved Adnar's lips.

CHAPTER TWENTY FIVE

By the end of his second week in Vanris, Kasiel had already fallen into a new routine. Mornings he got up extra early to check on the juvenile tethdraks and visit with the masked one he had named Sylaryth, which roughly translated to "shadow mask" in Pandrean Common. Afterward, he attended lessons until early afternoon, usually with Jethan unless his tehnaak had other duties to attend to. If Jethan didn't make it to the lessons, he rarely missed combat practice, where Kasiel found himself ganged up on two-to-one much of the time. If he failed to figure out the various techniques on his own the first few times, Jethan would patiently guide him through the forms until he got them. They also trained him in unarmed combat on Farren's orders, given how many people disliked him being in Vanris.

Late afternoons, he spent working primarily with Sylaryth, though he would slip in practice with the mother and other juvenile tethdraks when he went to collect him or return him to the enclosure. For the first two days, Adnar refused to let Jethan join them in the canyon when Kasiel worked with Sylaryth. Once he proved he had adequate control of the beast, the ahndhomen removed that restriction, allowing Jethan to come watch and using him to test Kasiel's ability on more than one occasion.

At the start of the third week, Adnar sent him out into the city with Sylaryth. It felt too ambitious to Kasiel. Wandering amongst so many people with a deadly beast at his side that had already grown several more inches was unnerving, though he learned to appreciate the tethdrak's presence the first time someone gave him a disdainful look and Sylaryth growled in response, sending them hurrying on their way.

Nerith didn't return at the end of the third week. When Kasiel asked another attendant, they told him that her tehnaak had extended the visit with her family. They expected her back toward the end of the month. Kasiel waited hopefully for her return and Kenna's. In the interim, he invested himself in classes, training, and building his bond with Sylaryth. Free time, he spent with Jethan, who added more Vanrian words in their conversations daily, scaling the difficulty alongside Kasiel's formal lessons. When they met up with the rest of the unit that had brought him to Vanris, the others now joined the process, making a game of trying to trip him up. A game he often lost to their considerable amusement, especially given how similar some Vanrian words, such as the ones for mug and tryst, sounded to the untrained ear. A fact that led to an awkward moment with one of the servers in the tavern.

Ignoring the lurking awareness of his father and the knowledge that, not far away, fighting continued between Vanris and the southern kingdoms, he almost believed there might be hope for making this his home. Of course, he still didn't dare wander the city without Jethan, and often Sylaryth, along for a reason. The suspicious and resentful looks continued, but it was easier to ignore them with his tehnaak and the tethdrak at his side.

Toward the middle of the fourth week, Wedro, Chander, and Tath got subbed in for downed members of a unit on the active front, which meant the mood at their week's end get-together was likely to be more subdued. For the first time, Kasiel took Sylaryth to the tavern with him at Adnar's urging. Given the risks, he would be extremely careful about how much he drank. He didn't trust himself to control the tethdrak if he got even a little drunk.

They gathered at what had become their usual table in the rear. Kasiel sat with his back toward the room. Not his favorite position, considering how many people resented his presence in the city, but it was easier to make space for Sylaryth alongside the open bench than up against the wall. At least, with the tethdrak there, he was confident no one would try messing with him. The tables closest to them at that end remained conspicuously empty throughout the evening.

Sylaryth was restless in the enclosed area with so many people around. Most of the first hour, Kasiel had to touch the tethdrak's mind every few minutes to keep him calm. He tried to avoid taking full control and forcing the beast to relax. If Sylaryth got there on his own with the aid of occasional comforting touches, he would adapt more easily to such situations going forward.

Kasiel was sipping from the mead he had been nursing since their arrival when Jethan, sitting across from him, met his eyes and gestured toward the entrance with a jerk of his head. Kasiel turned, spotting Nerith at the same moment she caught sight of him. Her smile caused a fluttering in his stomach. The red-headed woman next to her noticed them as well and took Nerith by the shoulders, steering her in their direction.

At Jethan's prompting, Avris and Merrin got up and moved around to the other side of the table, making room on the bench. Kasiel stood as Nerith and her friend, her tehnaak, he suspected, walked up. Sylaryth rose too, and both women stopped in their tracks when the tethdrak took a step toward them. Kasiel set a hand on the beast's shoulder. There was a slight bend to his elbow now when he did so. Sylaryth was growing fast.

"Don't worry. He won't hurt you."

The red-headed woman met his eyes over Nerith's shoulder. "If your tethdrak eats my tehnaak, I will chop you into a million pieces."

Nerith smacked the hand still resting on her shoulder. "Behave." She met his eyes, taking a step to the side, and gestured to the redhead. "This is my tehnaak, Leysa."

"A pleasure." He inclined his head to the other woman before turning his attention to the tethdrak. "This is my companion, Sylaryth."

Nerith started reaching a hand toward the tethdrak, then retracted it, seeming to think better of it.

Kasiel stepped forward and held his hand out, palm down. "Like this."

Sylaryth moved his nose under Kasiel's hand and pushed it up into his palm. Still eyeing the beast warily, Nerith eased her hand out. Sylaryth moved to smell it, flicking out his tongue. He emitted a few curious clicks, the frill around his neck vibrating. Kasiel answered with a sense of reassurance and fondness. After a few seconds, the tethdrak brought his nose under Nerith's hand and touched it.

"Oh."

Her breathy gasp of surprise and delight thrilled Kasiel. She was standing close enough that he could smell lavender on her along with some of the flowers the healers used in their salves and elixirs. A thoroughly pleasant mixture. He probably smelled like mead and tethdrak. Instantly self-conscious, he took a step back to offer her a seat at the table, only to find his companions smirking at him.

"Now that you've introduced your best friend there,

perhaps you'd care to introduce the ladies to some of the soldiers who saved your emaciated ass from mercenaries down south," Kince said. He raised his mug to take a swig, eyeing Kasiel expectantly over the top of it.

"Nerith, Leysa, this is part of the group that brought me to Etrion." He pointed to each as he named them. "That's Avris, Merrin, Darro, and the one with no manners is Kince."

"Hold on, Kas." Avris gave him a pout as if to suggest he had hurt her feelings. "I haven't got any manners either."

"It's true," Darro agreed, grunting when Avris kicked him under the table.

Kasiel rolled his eyes at them, holding back a laugh. "And of course, my tehnaak, Jethan, who you've already had the pleasure of meeting," he added with a glance at Nerith.

"Sit." Darro gestured to the bench beside Kasiel. "We'll regale you with some exciting and perhaps embarrassing tales of our favorite country boy."

Kasiel waited to sit until Nerith and Leysa had done so, guiding Sylaryth to settle alongside him. "Could we perhaps not do that? I'm sure there are more interesting things to talk about."

Nerith gave him a playful smile that set his pulse racing. "Oh no, I think I'd like to hear those tales."

Jethan leaned his elbows on the table and grinned at Kasiel. "Wouldn't you just? Where shall we begin?"

As the evening wore on, Kasiel found an unexpected ally in Sylaryth. The more embarrassed he got from his friends' teasing, the more restless the tethdrak became, forcing them to exhibit a modicum of self-control. Eventually, they took pity on him and switched to other subjects. Leysa spoke for a time about their journey north and the passing of her father. Though the hint of unshed tears in her eyes during the conversation suggested considerable sorrow, the passing ceremony sounded more like a festival to Kasiel than a funeral. Another cultural difference he would have to find out more about. Different was becoming normal for his life, however, so he focused on listening and learning.

Leysa excused herself after that, claiming a need to be up early. At her encouragement, Nerith stayed a while longer. Kasiel found himself content to watch her smile and laugh as she engaged with the people who had become his family—his tehsheyn—in Vanris.

Eventually, she also got up to excuse herself. "I've got to be up early tomorrow, too. I probably should have left when Leysa did."

Kasiel and Sylaryth stood with her. After she said her farewells and turned to walk away, Kasiel followed, stopping her with a hand on her elbow.

"I can escort you home if you like."

Nerith gave him a lovely, indulgent smile. "I was navigating Vanrian streets alone almost before I could walk. I'm sure I can handle it. Besides, I imagine you need to take Sylaryth to the enclosure before you head home."

Home. Perhaps this was becoming home after all.

Kasiel's hand slid, seemingly of its own free will, down her arm. He was a little surprised with it ended up nestled in her hand.

"You're sure?"

Their eyes met, and he thought she might change her mind. Then she averted her gaze, her cheeks flushed. "I'll see you in the morning, Lord Kasiel." She gave his hand a gentle squeeze before slipping away.

When he returned to the table, Kince leaned close to Jethan and said, "You know how those country boys are. Today it's a little hand-holding, tomorrow it's five kids and a farm."

Kasiel rolled his eyes and settled in to polish off his

drink as the others laughed. When he finished, he and Jethan struck out for the habitat to drop Sylaryth off. The tethdrak bounded along beside them through the quiet nighttime streets, full of energy after lying in the tavern for so long. Despite his exuberance, he remained within Kasiel's control, responding immediately to his signals even without a mind touch.

"I've never asked. Is there anyone here you're interested in?" Kasiel's thoughts wandered back to those beautiful lavender eyes as he spoke.

"Is that what that dreamy look is about?" Jethan teased. "Are you interested in someone? I hadn't noticed."

"Funny."

Jethan's expression sobered, and he kicked a pebble from his path. "I was, actually. But about a month before the mission to find you departed, her parents both died in a battle along the southern border of the Break. She didn't want to stay here after that. Her tehnaak's family is up north, so she and her tehnaak went to live with them."

"I'm sorry." Sylaryth pressed into his other hand as he watched his tehnaak. "Do you think you'll see her again?"

Jethan shrugged in an unconvincing show of disinterest. "Honestly, Vanris is a big place. There are a lot of other people to choose from, especially up north. I don't expect her to wait around for me to show up."

"I would, I mean, if you were my type."

Jethan chuckled and kicked another pebble, this time in Kasiel's direction. It went under his feet and Sylaryth pounced on it.

"Nice reflexes," Jethan commented. "I'm pretty sure that pebble is dead."

"Yes." Kasiel glanced down at the beast by his side. "He's a little scary sometimes."

When he finally made it back to his rooms, Kasiel climbed straight into bed, eager for tomorrow. Perhaps Nerith would be free later in the day. Obviously, she was working part of it, or she wouldn't have said she would see him in the morning. Or would she? Was it impossible to imagine that she might want to spend time with him? After all, she had taken his hand when he slipped it into hers.

Or maybe she did that because she didn't want to embarrass him in front of his friends.

He stared at the ceiling, holding her face in his mind until he started drifting off. Her pale skin turned dark, her silvery hair becoming long black braids.

Dani.

Did Danica know what her father and Edmund had done to him? He couldn't bring himself to believe so. She might have been the only one in Fernwallow who genuinely cared for him.

Had Garrick helped hold him down as a child to cut his ears? Maybe those rough blacksmith hands had done the cutting.

Kasiel shuddered, fighting the urge to put his hands over his ears as the newly unlocked memory swept in. Edmund's voice echoed in his head, approving of the mutilation they had inflicted on a child not quite five years old. What had Edmund done with the blood samples he collected over the years? The symbols, runes, and skin from dead Vanrians all had some purpose. What was he trying to do? Awaken Kasiel's ability? If so, to what end? What had he hoped to learn?

•

Kasiel startled awake at the sound of someone moving in the sitting area. A hint of early morning sunlight crept in through the window coverings. Dreams of life in Fernwallow left him momentarily disoriented until he recalled who he hoped to find in his sitting room this morning.

That fluttering sensation in his stomach returned. He hurried out of bed, then stood there uncertainly. It couldn't be appropriate to walk out wearing his sleeping trousers and nothing else. Yet, he would have to walk by the open doorway to the sitting area to retrieve any other clothes from his wardrobe. He kept meaning to leave a dressing robe on the chair near his bed, but he still wasn't used to the idea of people entering his rooms while he was away or asleep. Palace life was peculiar that way. How far he had come from his simple village existence.

Steeling himself, he walked to the doorway and peeked out. The butterflies in his stomach evaporated when he saw one of the male attendants arranging breakfast on the table. He stepped out, no longer concerned with what he was wearing.

The attendant offered a slight bow. "Good morning, Lord Hahren."

"Good morning. I… ah…" How did he ask about her without making his interest apparent? Did it matter? "I thought Nerith had returned from her trip."

The way the man averted his gaze caused a twisting in Kasiel's gut.

"She has, my lord. I'm afraid she's in the care of the healers."

A jolt of alarm worsened the twisting sensation. The room tilted around him as if he'd had too much to drink. "The healers. Why?"

"She was attacked last night. Not violated, as I understand, but beaten badly."

The room was shrinking in on him now. "Because of me," he whispered. Perhaps it was arrogant to default to that, but the thought carried a heavy weight of certainty with it.

"What was that, my lord?"

"Nothing. Thank you." He grabbed the door jamb to steady himself and turned into the bedroom. Pausing a moment, he glanced back over his shoulder. "Why tell me she wasn't violated? That kind of information should be private, shouldn't it?"

"Apologies, my lord." A nervous tremor entered the attendant's voice now. "There were rumors you had taken an interest in her. I thought..." He trailed off, averting his gaze.

It happened because of him, and this man expected him to be put off if they had sexually violated her. Red closed in around the edges of his vision. "Get out."

"Of course, my lord."

As the door to his room clicked shut, Kasiel swallowed back a rush of bile and yanked on some clothes.

The healers had a three-story building at the edge of the palace district. They dedicated part of one floor to processing the plants necessary for making the many elixirs and salves that they used for healing. The building stayed well-guarded for that reason. Vanris knew how much of an advantage their healing preparations gave them in tending the wounded. They weren't about to let those secrets fall into the wrong hands.

Even after Kasiel showed the tattoo on his wrist that marked him as the son of Dhomvalen Arhk Cavenos, the guards hesitated to let him in. Ultimately, leaning into his unwanted lineage gave him the leverage he needed to get through the door. Once inside, a woman in one of the gray and purple uniforms that made healers easy to spot within those walls approached him.

"Do you need aid, or are you here to see someone?"

He didn't know Nerith's family name. Did that matter? "I'm looking for a young woman who was brought in last night. Her name's Nerith."

The woman's expression hardened, suspicion narrowing her eyes. She nodded curtly. "Follow me."

She led him down a few hallways to a room with two guards standing outside. One of them held a hand up to stop them and came forward. Kasiel took a quick step back from the finger the healer pointed at him.

"This man was asking after that poor girl." The disgust in her tone made it clear she considered him a suspect.

The guard eyed Kasiel for a moment, his gaze sinking to the tattoos that showed at the edge of his collar. "He's not one of her attackers." His lip raised in a silent sneer. "He's the reason they attacked her."

The look the healer gave him then was even more hateful. "Well, he's your problem now." She stormed off.

Kasiel forced himself to step forward. "Can I see her?"

The guard looked at his fellow, who took a deep breath, regarding Kasiel as if he were the lowest of creatures. He finally nodded. "Don't upset her. If she tells you anything about what happened, you will share that information with me before you leave here."

"Of course."

The guard nodded again and opened the door.

Kasiel hurried through and stopped inside, his heart dropping into his gut.

Nerith had a delicate build, but she looked incredibly fragile lying in the bed within. One eye had dark bruising and swelling around it, and her lower lip was split. A bandage covered one cheek. The same cheek he had his scar on. There was bruising around her throat as if someone had tried to choke her. The blankets hid any further injuries.

She opened her eyes when the door clicked shut behind him, the swollen one barely a slit. When she saw him, she closed her eyes again and a few tears spilled out, running down into her hair. Kasiel hurried over to sit in a chair next to the bed. He carefully brushed away a tear on that side.

"I guess I should have let you walk me home," she said, her voice rough, as if talking took effort.

"I'm so sorry. This is my fault."

Her eyes opened again. The pain in them made his chest ache. "Unless you volunteered to be abducted as a child, I don't think it really is."

His guilt ignored the comment. "Who did this?"

"I didn't see their faces. There were three of them. They wore hoods with fabric across the front to hide everything but their eyes." Her gaze flickered to his scar, now framed within the tattoo on that cheek. "They cut my face like yours." More tears broke free. "They said traitors should match."

Hatred welled up in Kasiel like nothing he had ever felt before, not even for Edmund. The room blurred around him, his vision going dark at the edges. He fought it, trying to stay focused on her.

"Can I do anything for you?"

"Please leave, Kas."

"Nerith."

"No." She gave the smallest shake of her head. "I can't do this. I'm not strong enough to fall in love with you."

He struggled to speak past a lump in his throat. "Is that what you were doing?"

She turned her head away and squeezed her eyes shut again. "Please. Just go."

Kasiel got up and walked to the door, his heart hurting for something he might have had, if he were someone else. Anyone else. When he opened the door, he saw Jethan standing across the hall. His tehnaak glanced past him at Nerith, and fury twisted his features. Kasiel walked out, letting the guard shut the door behind him. The one he had spoken to before going in beckoned him over.

"Did she tell you anything?" the man demanded.

"She said she couldn't see their faces," he answered.

The guard exhaled heavily. "No then. You should leave."

Kasiel met his eyes. It didn't matter if Nerith wanted nothing to do with him now. This was still because of him. A fire started burning in his chest. One that might consume him if he couldn't appease its hunger. "You don't approve of my being in Etrion, do you?"

"Not really. I think there were more efficient ways to eliminate the risk you posed to Vanris if you awakened."

He didn't need to elaborate. His unspoken words and the disgust in his regard were enough to fill in what he left out. Jethan stepped up beside Kasiel, hands curling into fists, but Kasiel put a hand on his arm to stay him.

"But you don't approve of what they did to her either, do you?"

The man's expression darkened. "No. She's innocent. There's no excuse for this."

"Then let me help you find who did it."

"It's not your place, danro. Leave it to the guards and go find someone else's life to ruin."

The words stung. Kasiel spun and strode away, afraid he might do something he would regret if he lingered. Jethan kept pace, not speaking until they were outside the building.

"What are you thinking?" he asked as they moved away from the guards stationed out front.

"How did you know to find me here?" Kasiel asked.

"An attendant came and got me when he saw you leaving the palace. He told me what happened."

Kasiel narrowed his eyes at his tehnaak. "Are you paying the attendants off, because they sure do help you out a lot?"

"Maybe they find me *charming*." Something in his tone said that his choice of words was very intentional.

"You're using your ability on them?"

Jethan shrugged. "Not always. Sometimes they really do want to help. Now tell me what you're thinking, Kas, because I can tell you're not going to let this go."

"I'm thinking I know how to draw out whoever did this."

"Give them a shot at the person they really want?"

He glanced at his tehnaak. "Exactly. We're going to need more help, though."

CHAPTER TWENTY SIX

Has it occurred to you that, if they were willing to do that to Nerith merely for taking a liking to you, they're probably more than willing to kill you." Merrin paced the room as she spoke, more animated than Kasiel had ever seen her.

They were sitting in Darro and Kince's dining area. The two other inveths they shared the house with were currently out on the front lines, which provided their group a private place to plan.

"Why should that change anything?" Kasiel slapped a hand down on the table, earning himself everyone's attention. "If that's true, it will be just as true tomorrow and the next day as it is today. If someone doesn't stop them now, they're going to find me alone eventually. But if I'm the one who stops them, then maybe other like-minded callochs will think twice before trying something like this, and maybe I can keep more people I care about from getting hurt."

"Murder is illegal, you know." Avris put her feet up on the table. "They can't expect to kill the son of the dhomvalen and get away with it."

Merrin glanced at her tehnaak, negating the comment with a shake of her head. "I have a feeling they don't care. They accused Nerith of being a traitor because she took an interest in Kas. Whoever they are, they believe he's loyal to the south. If they've convinced themselves they're protecting their homeland, my guess is that they're willing to risk the consequences."

"Kince and I are officers," Darro said, reaching over to push Avris's feet off the table. "If we're going to get involved in this, Kas, you need to swear that you won't revenge kill anyone. We catch them and turn them over to the guards. No killing unless you have no other choice."

Kasiel met his eyes. "Then you think it could work."

Darro nodded. "They wanted to draw you out with this. They'll be watching for it. Hoping you're young and impulsive enough to do something rash."

Jethan, who had been leaning in the corner looking pensive, stepped forward. "Kince, you've worked with the guards before. They'll increase guard presence after what happened with Nerith. Can you draw us up a route that might not be heavily watched?"

"I should be able to come up with something. I'll make sure it trends toward the healer's building. You know," he added, glancing at Kasiel, "just in case."

"Thanks for the vote of confidence." Kasiel tried to sound flippant, to hide the chill of his own doubts creeping up his spine.

Kince shrugged. "You don't have half the training these guys are going to have." He flipped the dagger he was holding in the air, letting it come down and embed itself in the table with a final-sounding *thunk*.

Jethan grabbed the dagger and leaned on the table, pointing it at each of them as he spoke. "There's one thing I need from all of you. I need you to help me make sure my tehnaak comes out of this in one piece."

Kince snatched the dagger back from him. "Your tehnaak, your problem." He eyed Kasiel critically as he sheathed the weapon. "Though we are growing fond of our little country boy. We'll keep him breathing for you."

"And you." Jethan gave Kasiel a stern look. "You need to promise me two things. The first is that you won't let your tethdrak eat me. The second, which will have a bearing on the first, is that you won't take any excessive risks. You die, Syl will make a snack out of me. You know I'm right."

Kasiel met his eyes. He could feel Sylaryth even now, with the tethdrak out in the canyon a fair way away from where they were talking. Was that normal? The more time he spent with the beast, the more constant his awareness of him became from ever-increasing distances. It left a persistent sense of wildness in his head now, like the lingering aftertaste of a complex wine. Was this why Kenna and Adnar always had that slightly predatory bearing?

"Syl will be fine. Keep him close enough to where I am to move in quickly. Until then, I'll make sure he stays with you, so if anyone spots him, they don't think there's a loose tethdrak in the city." He scanned the table. "You all know what you're doing? No one makes a move until I call Syl in."

There were nods all around.

Darro leaned forward, giving him a hard stare. "No revenge killings."

It was a promise Kasiel didn't want to make, but he knew Darro was right. If they were going to risk doing this without the support of the city guard, he needed to ensure things didn't get too messy. "No revenge killings."

"Good." Darro stood, and the rest of them followed suit. "Remember, we'll see them if they go after you, but you won't. Hopefully, they'll want to gloat over their victory before they try to kill you. But there's a chance they'll go straight for the kill. Be ready for anything."

Kasiel nodded, calling up Nerith's bruised and bandaged face in his mind to bolster his resolve. "An hour after dark then."

They all agreed.

For the next two nights, increased patrols in the vicinity of The Twisted Vine made it impossible to put their plan into action. Kince, leveraging his connections with the city guards, learned that they would spread their search out away from the tavern starting on the third night.

By the time evening rolled around on that day, Kasiel was as ready as he was going to be. He found his thoughts wandering to simpler times spent organizing Edmund's study or searching for ingredients in the woods. His reality not that many months ago, and already that felt like a life he had dreamed up. Another place. Another version of himself. He would never have intentionally confronted the mercenaries in Fernwallow, and yet, here he was, preparing to draw out unknown and obviously violent adversaries, using himself as bait.

He made a point of taking Sylaryth out for a few hours, then returned him to the habitat by evening, hoping Nerith's attackers might be watching. After dark, he snuck through the tunnel he had used for his clandestine meetings with Kenna the week before his testing and brought the tethdrak back out that way. They met up with Jethan in the enclosed garden. He gave Kasiel a dagger to wear in place of his own, insisting it was lucky and would help keep him safe.

Kasiel sent Sylaryth with Jethan, using his ability to convince the beast to do so, though he could feel through their connection that the tethdrak disliked the arrangement. Jethan would keep to the dark side alleys close to where Kasiel intended to pass through after a stop by The Twisted Vine.

It wasn't their group's usual night to meet up, but Avris and Merrin were there. He stayed for a drink with them, making a point of scanning the other patrons as if searching for suspicious behavior. Before long, he excused himself, telling the two women he wasn't in the right mood to hang out after what happened to Nerith. He wanted his targets to believe he was out looking for revenge.

The two women walked out with him, saying they were meeting Kince and Darro at another tavern, on the off chance anyone was close enough to overhear. When they asked him to join them, he turned them down.

"I need time to think things through."

Avris gave him a sympathetic look that didn't appear at all forced. "I get it. Take care of yourself, Kas."

He caught the slightest hint of command in her last words and inclined his head. "I'll try."

They parted ways. The two women would cut back around the block and begin carefully following him, watching for anyone else doing the same. Darro and Kince were somewhere along his route already, hidden and waiting. As soon as their targets showed themselves, the two would go find the nearest guards. Kasiel sensed Sylaryth close by. Unexpectedly, there was an awareness of Jethan through his connection to the tethdrak that made it easier to keep the beast oriented on his tehnaak for now.

Kasiel kept his ears tuned for the sounds of pursuit, his eyes constantly searching for motion in the darkness. Needles of fear pricked his skin, trying to pick apart his mask of confidence. He knew how to fight now better than he ever had, but Darro was right. The people after him would have grown up training for combat. This was a military city. If you lived here, you were either a soldier or someone who supported them.

The dark city streets felt different tonight, and not only because he was diverging from his usual routes to avoid patrols. He never traveled alone in the city, for the very reason he was doing it now. Plenty of people disliked him being here. He was an outsider raised in the southern kingdoms. A danro who had twelve years to build up loyalty to the enemy and a mere few months to do the same in Vanris.

He wasn't loyal to the Pandrean Alliance, though. He never really had been. Being the only one who had to hide what he was in a tiny village full of people all looking to escape from the outside world didn't inspire a deep devotion. Once, he would have considered himself loyal to Edmund, but the man who raised him effectively destroyed that when he started talking about killing him to keep him out of the hands of the Alliance and Vanris.

His thoughts latched onto that suddenly. Why? What was Edmund doing that he didn't even want mercenaries sent by the Pandrean Alliance getting their hands on him? Was it because he didn't want Kasiel ending up in Vanris, or could he have been trying to hide his experiments from the Alliance? To what end? The answers to those questions were hundreds of miles away.

Kasiel turned down an alley and came out into an empty square behind a blacksmith's shop that had closed for the night. A man dressed all in black with a black hood pulled over his head emerged from the shadows ahead of him. He stopped several feet back, out of range of any melee weapons Kasiel might be carrying.

"I had a feeling you'd be angry enough after we roughed up your girl to come looking for revenge. Proof you really are just a stupid southerner." He spoke in Pandrean Common, apparently wanting to be sure Kasiel understood his taunts.

"You're right about one thing. I am angry." Kasiel fought to keep his voice steady while he held back the increasingly agitated tethdrak. "I had a feeling you might be enough of an arrogant ass to be out here hunting again already."

Nerith had said there were three of them, but Kasiel didn't know where the others might be yet. He needed to keep this one busy long enough to draw them out before calling for help. If they didn't get all three tonight, the others would be that much harder to catch.

"You little calloch. You may have the khevarin and your father fooled, but we know what you are. We'll send you back across the border to your allies in pieces." The man took hold of a piece of black fabric at his neck and pulled it over the lower half of his face.

A flare of panic from Sylaryth gave Kasiel a heartbeat of warning before someone lunged at him from behind. He jumped to one side and spun, mostly avoiding the blade. Pain flashed along his side as the man's dagger cut a deep gash below his ribs. He felt the heat and wetness of his blood streaming from the wound. A surge of protective fury crashed over him from Sylaryth. The distraction of the pain made it more difficult to keep the tethdrak back.

The man who cut him, also dressed all in black with a hood and partially covered face like Nerith had described, had his dagger up and was ready to move again. Wary of being attacked from another direction, Kasiel backed up closer to the building. Eliminating the possibility of a second rear attack.

He pressed a hand to the wound and glared at the first man, who was moving around in front of him again. "I guess you aren't interested in a fair fight."

"You don't deserve a fair fight, traitor." The man sank into a fighting stance.

In his periphery, Kasiel could see someone else coming up on his other side now. All three were out in the open, exactly where he wanted them. Though the warmth spreading down his side and soaking into the hip of his trousers made him feel much less in control of the situation. Pain made it a struggle to focus on the threats around him and on his tethdrak. The strike might not have resulted in the lethal hit they were hoping for, but it was still a substantial wound. Sylaryth, desperate to come to his defense, fought his control, and was close to winning.

"Remember those words," Kasiel said through gritted teeth. "I'm not the enemy of Vanris you want me to be, but I am your enemy now."

His focus wavered. Suddenly, he was looking at himself from the outside. He stood slightly hunched over his wound, fighting the pain. Three men blocked all directions of escape, the two on the sides inching closer with their blades drawn. Everything was a hint brighter than it had been a moment ago. The colors, such as that of the red blood on his white shirt, were shockingly vivid.

The man on the left lunged in.

Kasiel was abruptly looking out through his own eyes again. He faced his attacker, hopping back and to the side, narrowly evading the first two quick strikes while trying not to end up on the blades of the men now on his right and behind him. His opponent's eyes gleamed with malicious pleasure, but Kasiel had his rhythm now. On the third swipe, he caught the man's wrist, diverting the weapon away. Knowing the other two would take advantage of the moment, he pulled in his backup. A chilling shriek blasted through the night. Sylaryth rushed out of the darkness, lunging past on his right between him and the man he had spoken with. A shout and the thud of impact was enough to tell him the man who had cut him was no longer a threat, though he tried to maintain enough control of the beast to keep him from killing anyone.

The man he was grappling with swept out with one leg, knocking Kasiel's feet out from under him. He kept hold of the man's wrist as he fell and kicked out, hitting the side of his knee, and taking him down, too. Impact with the ground sent a fresh blast of pain through his wound. The man he was fighting lost his knife but caught himself on his knees. He swung with his free hand, landing a solid blow to Kasiel's jaw that dazed him for an instant.

Shaking his head to clear it, Kasiel rolled into the man to dodge a second punch. He brought up his knee, connecting a direct hit to his groin. It was dirty fighting, but Jethan had put no little effort into teaching him that sometimes that was how you survived. Kasiel grabbed Jethan's lucky dagger and pressed it against the man's throat. With the sudden change in advantage and the snarling tethdrak close by, the man stopped fighting and held up his hands. Kasiel pushed harder, breathing fast, his blood pounding in his ears. Nerith's wounded face filled his vision. A trickle of red ran from beneath the blade's edge. He wanted to cut. Wanted it desperately.

But he had never killed someone with his own hands, and he had made a promise to Darro.

Sylaryth stood over one man lying on the ground a few feet away. His foot pressed on the whimpering man's chest, claws piercing through clothing and flesh. He growled, his snout lowering to the man's face, ready to finish off his prey. Because of the tenuous control Kasiel still had over him, he waited. The man Kasiel had been speaking with stood a few feet away, Jethan behind him holding a dagger to his throat.

The crunching of feet in the gritty streets heralded more people hurrying into the square. Merrin grabbed the man leaning over Kasiel and yanked him up, removing the temptation to end him. Avris stepped in and helped Kasiel to his feet.

As planned, Kince and Darro arrived with several city guards. Kasiel slumped back against the building, one hand pressed to his side, watching the guards take custody of the two men from Merrin and Jethan.

Another guard, this one with the insignia of an inveth on his armor, eyed Sylaryth warily. He glanced at Kasiel. "Inveth Darro said these are the men who attacked that young woman the other night. Is that correct?"

"We had nothing to do with that," the one who had spoken to Kasiel declared, glaring at him.

"Sure, you didn't." The inveth yanked the man's face covering and hood off, nodding for his companion to do the same with the other. He held up the fabric. "This isn't suspicious at all."

Kasiel looked at the one still pinned under Sylaryth, finding strength in his hatred. "I know you attacked Nerith. I recommend confessing. Sylaryth hates liars."

"We had nothing to do with it," the man echoed his companion, though his voice trembled.

Sweat beaded on his forehead as he stared up into the tethdrak's jaws. It wasn't going to take much to break him. At a mental direction from Kasiel, Sylaryth growled, a strand of drool dripping onto the man's cheek, and flexed his claws, digging them deeper into the man's chest.

"Yes! We attacked her," he blurted. "Please, get it off me."

One of the other two shouted out in protest and the guard holding him twisted his arm behind his back, silencing him.

The guard inveth nodded to Kasiel. "Call off your tethdrak."

Kasiel directed Sylaryth to his side, allowing the guards to pick the third man up.

The inveth turned to Kasiel, offering a respectful nod. "We haven't had a new Feral in the city in a while. I don't know how anyone else is going to feel about what you did tonight, but you have my gratitude,

Lord Hahren. I had hoped to bring these men to justice quickly. You should have warned us beforehand of your plan, but there's little point arguing about that now." He gestured to Jethan. "Lord Jethan, I would recommend taking your tehnaak to the healers. We can take care of these three from here."

Kasiel grimaced as Jethan moved alongside him to help him step away from the building. "We need to take Syl back."

Jethan glanced at the blood dripping between Kasiel's fingers, then turned to Avris and Merrin. "See if you can find Ahndhomen Adnar and bring him to the healer's building. Tell him we need him to take Kas… Hahren's tethdrak back to the habitat."

The two hurried off, accepting his orders without hesitation.

Darro approached them, eyeing Kasiel with a furrowed brow. "Kince is going to assist the guards. He'll make sure these callochs end up where they belong. I'll run ahead and let the healers know you're coming." He turned and started jogging in that direction.

"Hey!" They looked up to see Kince pulling off his jacket and shirt. He tossed the shirt to Jethan and slipped the jacket back on. "Use that to put pressure on the wound. Can't have him bleeding out on you."

"Thanks, Kince." Jethan folded the shirt and handed it to Kasiel. "Press this over the wound. You can use me for support while we walk if you need to." He waited until Kasiel had the shirt in place. "You know, I was talking to you too when I told everyone to help make sure you got out of this in one piece."

"Maybe you should have been a little clearer on that," Kasiel said, managing a brief, pained laugh as he and Jethan began walking. Every step was agony, and his hands were shaking with the realization of exactly how close he had come to getting himself killed. Without

Sylaryth's warning, it might have been a lethal wound.

He passed gratitude to the tethdrak clinging close on his other side, emitting a series of low, worried clicks.

"Well, you didn't get killed," Jethan said, casting a glance at Kasiel's side, "but you came a lot closer than I care for. Since there are undoubtedly others who feel the way these three do, I think we should invest more time in your combat skills once you're healed up."

"Great… idea," Kasiel managed around a gasp when his foot came down hard on a low spot in the street.

"Only a few more blocks, Kas. I'd carry you, but I don't think it would hurt any less."

Kasiel forced himself onward, trying hard to keep part of his attention on Sylaryth. The folded shirt was warm and wet under his hand. The tethdrak's claws dug runnels in the street as he grew more distressed. "What was I thinking?"

Jethan's look then held an abundance of affection. "That others have controlled your life for long enough. The danro we rescued from those mercenaries would never have confronted these bastards the way you did back there. I can't say it was the best thought-out plan, but you accomplished what you set out to do. Nerith's assailants are in custody and when word gets out about how you hid Sylaryth's presence from them, anyone else will think twice before they assume you're vulnerable."

"I can't believe you all went along with it."

"What Kince said before is true, Kas. You're my tehnaak. I'll always stand with you, but we all went through a great deal to get you here. We wouldn't have succeeded if you hadn't thrown your lot in with us when it mattered."

"Well…" A burst of fresh pain shot through his side, taking his breath away. When he could speak again, he said, "At least I don't have to act foolish by myself anymore."

Jethan's laugh somehow eased the pain for a few seconds, letting him catch his breath. When they reached the healer's building, the male healer who had tended Kasiel's hands after his incident in the deeps was standing by the door with Darro. They took Kasiel to a room where two more healers waited. Once he was out of his shirt, they laid him on his side to examine the steadily bleeding cut. One of the other healers held a flask out to Kasiel, but the man pushed it away.

"We can't put him out with his tethdrak here." He gave Kasiel an apologetic look. "We need to get this cleaned and closed, but I'm afraid you'll have to be awake for it."

Darro stepped forward. "Ahndhomen Adnar's been summoned to take the tethdrak. He should be here soon."

"Good. Let us know when he's arrived, but given this," he held up Kince's blood-soaked shirt, "I don't think we should wait." He looked at Jethan, who knelt alongside the bed next to Kasiel. "You're his tehnaak?"

Jethan nodded.

"You can stay. Anyone else who isn't a healer needs to leave."

Jethan took Kasiel's hand as the others cleared the room. "Hold on as tight as you need to."

"I will." Kasiel was dizzy and tired. He closed his eyes and Jethan gave his hand a painful squeeze.

"Remember your tethdrak. We don't want him eating the healers."

"We definitely don't," the healer confirmed with a nervous chuckle. "All right, I'm going to clean this, and it's going to hurt. I need you to stay still and focus on your companion. Let him know I'm trying to help you and let me know if you start feeling like you might pass out."

"Got it," Kasiel answered.

One of the other healers gave him a piece of hardened leather to bite down on. Then there was nothing but pain and a desperate battle to keep Sylaryth from coming to his defense. The frantic clicks from the beast as he stood there, muscles tensed to lunge, did nothing to ease the stress in the room. Jethan grimaced as Kasiel crushed his hand in a death grip, but he didn't complain.

They had already started stitching when Adnar arrived. Kasiel was aware of being gently nudged out of Sylaryth's mind. Then the tethdrak was gone, and a nurse gave him some foul-tasting elixir. After that, he was aware of nothing else.

Kasiel woke in an unfamiliar room from the one they had put him to sleep in. He didn't recall being moved. The ache in his swollen jaw was a tickle compared to the sharp pain in his side. Jethan, asleep in a chair next to the bed, startled awake when the door to the room opened.

"Good, you're awake." The healer who entered wasn't one of those who had helped him last night. She sat on the edge of the bed and held a small container out to Jethan, who groaned as he stretched his shoulders and neck. "I had a feeling you'd regret your sleeping choices when you woke up, Lord Jethan, so I brought you a little something to help. Rub this on the tight muscles and it should loosen them up again."

Jethan gazed at the container groggily for a second, his eyes lighting as he caught up with what she had said and accepted it. "Thank you."

"As for you, Lord Hahren, I need you to roll onto your side and let me look at that wound."

Kasiel did as directed. When she reached to pull the sheet down, he grabbed it, realizing someone had removed his bloodied trousers.

The healer exhaled and gave him a long-suffering look. "You have nothing I haven't seen a thousand times in this place, but if it makes you feel better, I'll let you adjust the sheet so that you may ensure your privacy. I only need full access to your wound."

Jethan chuckled, earning a sour look from Kasiel. He had cracked open the container and was rubbing its contents into the side of his neck. "How's Nerith?"

Kasiel's stomach twisted unpleasantly, but he tried to hide that reaction while he arranged the sheet to expose the stitched and bandaged cut. The healer removed the bandages and leaned closer, inspecting the wound with a critical eye.

"This might hurt a little," she warned before she went to work cleaning the wound and wiping a thin layer of salve over the stitches.

Kasiel clenched his teeth, hissing through them a few times. What madness had infected him to make him think last night was a good idea?

"Nerith is improving. We may let her leave in a day or two if she's stable. Someone told her the three men who attacked her were in custody. She appeared to sleep more soundly after hearing that."

Oh, yes. That was why he thought it was a good idea. Knowing their actions had already brought Nerith some peace made the pain worth it.

The healer carefully applied a fresh bandage over Kasiel's wound. When she finished, she sat for a moment, gazing at the covered cut. "Some guards are calling for all of you to be punished for taking this into your own hands." She pressed down a stubborn corner of the bandage. "I don't think I'm alone, however, in wanting to thank you for what you did. Nerith won't be the only one who sleeps better knowing those callochs are going to pay for this."

"Does Nerith know who caught them?" Jethan asked.

The healer met Kasiel's eyes. Her solemn regard made him wonder how much she knew of his brief and broken relationship with Nerith.

"No. We're supposed to keep the details quiet until they address the complaints of the guards." She took a deep breath and stood, her more candid demeanor vanishing before a polite bedside smile. "You can leave today if you wish. No strenuous activity until the stitches are out, but if you keep it clean and reapply that salve three times a day, it should heal quickly. The healers in the palace will check in on you."

"Thank you." Kasiel struggled to find a smile for her. Somehow, having her gratitude made him wish he could have done something before Nerith got hurt. It was a foolish notion, since he couldn't have known what was coming, but emotions were often irrational things.

"Can we pay her a visit?" Jethan asked.

"No," Kasiel said before the healer could answer. He avoided his tehnaak's gaze, meeting the healer's eyes instead.

The healer gave him a sad smile and a nod before she left the room.

Jethan turned to him, brows pinched together. "I thought you did this mostly for her. Why don't you want to see her?"

"I did. For her and anyone else I might want to spend time around without having to fear for their safety." Kasiel slid his legs out of the bed and sat up. It was awkward trying to do so without putting strain on the stitches, but the pain made him more than willing to puzzle it out.

Jethan grabbed a stack of folded garments off a corner table and set it on the bed next to him. "I had some clean clothes brought for you."

"Thanks."

"You didn't answer the question. Why don't you want to see her?"

Kasiel began the painful process of pulling on his

trousers. "You've got it backwards. She doesn't want to see me."

"Did she say that?"

"Yes." His throat tightened when he said it. He swallowed and reached across the city with his mind, searching out the welcoming presence of Sylaryth. The tethdrak gave off a sense of contentment with his siblings and mother nearby. Hopeful excitement greeted Kasiel's light touch.

Kasiel closed his eyes and looked out upon the canyon through strange eyes that saw color in ways he could never have imagined it. A sunrise full of gold, pink, and violet. The scales of the other tethdraks defined in shades of warm reds and browns. Everything richer. More complex. Heart-wrenchingly beautiful.

"Kas?"

He pulled back and opened his eyes to find his tehnaak staring at him, brows still pinched together in concern.

"Are you all right?"

Kasiel answered with a faint smile, considering his tehnaak. If he could trust anyone, it was the person sitting in front of him now. "I can see through Syl's eyes. It happened last night by accident, but I did it again just now. Is that a normal Feral thing?"

"You're being serious?"

Kasiel nodded.

"I don't honestly know. Ferals aren't my specialty, but it sounds extraordinary."

"It is." Kasiel finished pulling his shirt on as a knock came at the door.

Jethan went to answer it while he tugged on his boots. The salve the healer had put on the wound eased the pain, which was a relief, but it also meant he would have to be more mindful of not overdoing it.

Jethan stepped back as he opened the door, revealing

the four guards waiting outside.

"Lord Jethan. Lord Kasiel." The lead guard inclined his head to each of them. "We're here to escort you two to the palace. There is an inquiry in progress into last night's events."

Kasiel got to his feet, meeting the guard's eyes. He had done no wrong. Not as far as he was concerned. And neither had his companions. "Lead the way."

Getting to the palace took longer than it normally would have. The wound in his side was fresh and painful enough that it restricted any attempt at a brisk pace. Along the way, the lead guard informed them that the three men had undergone interrogation overnight. The guards involved, along with Darro, Kince, Avris, and Merrin, were called in before dawn that morning. Jethan and Kasiel were the last ones being brought in because of Kasiel's injury.

The guards escorted them to the same chamber where Kasiel had received his testing results. When they arrived, the group of guards they had met in the night were entering the room, and the two he had encountered when he went to visit Nerith at the healer's building were leaving. Darro, Kince, Avris, and Merrin stood outside the door.

Avris stepped up to meet them. "We've already been questioned. They—"

"No talking," a guard standing by the door in palace livery snapped.

Avris rolled her eyes as they all went to sit on two benches in the hall in restless silence. The guards from last night left a short time later, though their inveth didn't go with them.

"Lord Hahren Cavenos and Lord Jethan Markanis, you may enter now. The rest of you may go in with them." The attendant's gesture encompassed Darro, Kince, Avris, and Merrin. "You will remain toward the back."

A weighty silence filled the room as they went inside. The dhomen who oversaw the city guards sat at the table on the dais with Ahninveth Setera and Adnar, who had his tethdrak at his side. Surprise and unease soared in Kasiel when he saw his father standing behind Khevarin Seylin Markanis in front of the curved table. Arhk's black attire contrasted Seylin's shimmering, pale dress, providing the perfect balance of ethereal beauty and elegant darkness between them.

An attendant guided Kasiel and Jethan to the center below where Khevarin Seylin stood on the dais. Their companions were directed to stand several feet behind them. They all knelt with their heads bowed.

"You may rise." The khevarin's voice was bolder and more commanding than Kasiel remembered from his one brief encounter with her. Though, as she had pointed out at that time, it hadn't been a formal audience.

Kasiel's wound protested the movement, but Jethan, anticipating the problem, stepped in to support him up. When they were standing, the khevarin looked at the guard inveth from last night, who stood to one side of the room.

"Inveth Tarik, if we understand everything we have been told correctly, Lord Hahren Cavenos and his companions took it upon themselves to find the men who attacked one of my palace attendants, a young healer in training. This, despite a warning from the guards to leave it in their hands. Yes?"

"Yes, Majesty." Tarik answered.

She looked at Kasiel, her icy gaze offering no insight into her opinions on the matter. "Lord Hahren, why did you feel entitled to take this matter into your own hands?"

He met her eyes, unsure whether that was the proper thing to do. "I didn't feel entitled, Majesty, I felt responsible. The men in question hurt Nerith to get to me. It was my responsibility to see that they faced punishment for their actions and to make sure they didn't hurt anyone else."

"By using yourself as bait to draw them out?"

Kasiel inclined his head. "Yes, Majesty."

"You had your companions and your tethdrak hidden nearby to help you apprehend these men once they took the bait. Is that correct?" She strolled along part of the curved table as she spoke, letting her pointed fingernails whisper across the polished wood.

"Yes, Majesty."

The khevarin glanced at Adnar. Whatever message passed in the silent look she cast at the Feral Ahndhomen, his answering expression revealed nothing.

She turned back to Kasiel. "Why did you believe these men were trying to get you?"

Kasiel could feel his father's eyes on him. Apparently, this was one of those situations where they could not avoid one another. He hoped it made Arhk desperately uncomfortable. "As I'm sure you are aware, Majesty, there are those in the city who question my loyalties, and dislike that I'm allowed to move about openly within the city and palace."

Walking to the edge of the dais, she gazed down at him with her cold blue eyes. "And where do your loyalties lie?"

His nerves sang to life. He didn't dare lie with Setera there. "With my tehnaak and my companions, Majesty."

"Your companions? By whom you mean the four behind you?" She gestured toward the others, her metallic fingernails shimmering in the light from several sconces and an elegant chandelier overhead.

He nodded.

"These companions are the ones who brought you here from the south, though a few appear to be missing."

"Three of us are on the front lines right now,

Majesty," Darro offered.

Her gaze flickered to him, her impeccable posture adding height to her delicate figure. "Thank you, Inveth Darro." She was silent a moment, her gaze skimming thoughtfully over them. "These people you choose to give your loyalty to appear Vanrian to us." She glanced at the dhomen of the guard. "You may inform your guards that we are not concerned about Lord Hahren's loyalties. In fact, we are rather impressed by his initiative, courage, and dedication to those he cares for, as well as the devotion they have shown him in return. The Feral mastery he demonstrated with his tethdrak, after barely a month working together, also deserves recognition."

Kasiel stared intently at a sconce at the back of the room. After their first encounter, the last thing he had expected was for the khevarin to be speaking his praises, especially now, but he would do everything in his power not to mess it up. The best way to accomplish that, in his estimation, was to avoid opening his mouth unless she directly addressed him.

"Dhomvalen Arhk and Ahninveth Setera have already secured confessions from the three men involved in this crime. After reviewing those confessions and questioning the guards and your companions, we see little value in questioning you further. You all acted without the proper authority. That merits some form of discipline." Her eyes flashed with a sudden intensity. "However, we will not tolerate the senseless abuse of our people. You enabled the capture of these men before they could harm anyone else, and without giving in to the temptation to mete out your own justice along the way. For that, you deserve commendation."

Her gaze raked over the six of them.

"For your circumvention of authority, all of you will devote half of one free day each week for the next two months to assisting the guards with various duties under

Inveth Tarik's supervision. For your service to the people of this city, the Heartsmith is being asked to add a special symbol of our recognition to your ke'hanoaths."

She turned away from them, her gaze falling on Arhk. No one in the room moved. A strange tension formed between the khevarin and the dhomvalen when their eyes locked. It stifled the air in the chamber, slowly making it heavy and suffocating. Sweat broke out on the back of Kasiel's neck. Then she faced them again. The moment the eye contact ended, the air in the room reverted to normal and the tension eased.

"For you, Lord Hahren Cavenos, we recommend accelerating your advancement. We will leave the implementation of that recommendation in Ahndhomen Adnar's hands. You are all dismissed."

Within seconds of her last words, a group of palace guards escorted the khevarin, Arhk, and Setera through a door at the rear of the room. The dhomen of the city guard joined Inveth Tarik, who offered a nod to Kasiel before departing with his commanding officer. Kasiel returned the gesture, then faced his companions only to see Adnar and his tethdrak stalking over.

Jethan glanced from Adnar to Kasiel. "We'll meet you out in the hall when you're done here."

Kasiel nodded, making himself stay where he was while they departed, even though something in the predatory way Adnar and the tethdrak approached made him yearn to follow them. In minutes, they were the only three in the room. The dark tethdrak emitted a few deep clicks and a soft rumble that wasn't quite a growl. The beast sat next to Adnar, who looked Kasiel dead in the eyes.

"You Break-blasted calloch!"

Kasiel caught himself before he could step back from the verbal assault and the fury that burned in Adnar's eyes.

"Do you know what could have happened if that wound you took had been lethal, as I imagine they intended it to be? You put yourself, your tethdrak, and everyone else there in danger. Your tethdrak is not a toy or a pet. It is a weapon. Even as a juvenile, that creature can take down several grown men in a matter of seconds."

A flush of defensive anger surged up in Kasiel. "I know he's dangerous. That's why I had him there. But he's more than a weapon. He's a protector and a companion. That's why empathy is so important. I learned that from you."

Adnar shifted his weight back, staring down his nose at Kasiel, his lips set in a hard line.

"Sir," Kasiel added as his initial burst of anger faded.

"You're right." Adnar's calmer tone said his rage had also burned down some. "Sylaryth is more than a weapon. And you are more than a man. You are a Feral. Vanris needs you. I admire your desire to protect the people you care about, but I am your ahndhomen. You will speak to me before you use your tethdrak for anything like this again. I am the only one here right now who can handle the problem if things go wrong. I am also well-equipped to make sure they do not go wrong."

Kasiel lowered his gaze, a despised flare of shame warming his cheeks. "Yes, sir."

"No other mind-crafter works quite the way Ferals do, and no one else understands the complications and risks of working with these creatures. We cannot afford to undermine our position."

"I'm sorry, sir. I should have come to you first." He gave his words a second to settle in before continuing. "I wanted to ask about something that happened while I was out there with Sylaryth last night."

Adnar stared at him a moment, as if he were considering adding more to his lecture. Then he set a hand on his tethdrak's shoulder and gave a gruff nod. "Ask."

"When those men had me surrounded, I glimpsed myself through Sylaryth's eyes. Is that normal?"

Adnar's expression was stone, but the tethdrak stood, emitting a series of higher pitched, agitated clicks. The ahndhomen gestured for the beast to sit, and it did, but its tail continued to twitch restlessly. "You are certain."

"Yes. It was unintentional last night, but I tried it again this morning and could see the sunrise in the canyon and the other tethdraks through his eyes."

Adnar was silent for several seconds, thoughts churning behind his furrowed brow. Finally, he said, "You cannot continue combat training until those stitches are out. I will inform Dhomen Farren that you will work extra hours with the tethdraks until you can resume your training with him. I want you to work with the adults more. Take Sylaryth into the enclosure with you. You are to keep the others from getting aggressive with him. Focus on controlling them in groups over the next week."

"Yes, sir. But about seeing through his eyes."

"It is rare. Keep practicing it. Make it second nature." Adnar gestured toward the door. "Go. Meet with your companions. I have work to do."

"Yes, sir." Kasiel inclined his head, then strode from the room slower than he wanted to, given the restriction of his wound. When he stepped out into the hall, his five companions closed in around him.

Kince put an arm over his shoulders. "You lucky little calloch. I thought we were in for it."

Kasiel looked at them all, surprised by their smiles. "You're not upset about losing the free days?"

"Half a free day a week for two months is a slap on the hand," Jethan said, practically bouncing in place. "We get the recognition of Khevarin Seylin added to our ke'hanoath forever. For anyone to see."

"Wedro, Chander, and Tath are going to be so jealous." Avris smirked. "Where shall we put it?"

"Somewhere visible," Darro said, striking out toward the Heartsmith. The rest of them fell in with him. "Back of the hand, maybe. I'd say cheek, but we don't want to mess with our danro's perfectly arranged asymmetry."

"Can't have that." Kince gave Kasiel a wink and a firm pat on the shoulder as he took his arm away.

"I like the back of the hand. Nice and visible when playing dice or cards." Merrin mimed holding a hand of cards up in front of her. "A little intimidation tactic."

Jethan moved closer to Kasiel as they walked, keeping his voice low. "Did everything go all right with Adnar?"

"He wasn't happy about my using Syl, especially without talking to him first, but I think he's decided not to turn me into tethdrak food yet."

Jethan breathed a laugh. "And the other thing?" He gestured discreetly toward his eyes.

"He said it's rare, and that I should keep practicing it. Then he sent me away, claiming he had work to do."

"Not especially helpful."

Kasiel shook his head, his thoughts wandering back to the moment after he had asked about seeing through Sylaryth's eyes. Particularly, Adnar's tethdrak's reaction. Adnar showed nothing on the outside, but tethdraks responded to their companion's emotions. He had been working with Sylaryth long enough to notice that. The Feral ahndhomen was holding something back.

CHAPTER TWENTY EIGHT

The canyon landscape swept past as Sylaryth sprinted along. Kasiel soared on the high of that speed and the beauty of the altered spectrum of colors he could see through the tethdrak's eyes. They leapt over the stream and darted through a group of five adults basking in the warm sun. All five snapped their heads up, two of them lunging to their feet with growls. Sylaryth kept running.

Kasiel swept his awareness out, latching on to the five adults and easing into their minds, encouraging them to run with the juvenile. Not to give chase, but to rejoice in the simple pleasure of stretching their powerful limbs. He grinned to himself as they bounded up and joined Sylaryth, only one of the five offering any resistance. That one, a large alpha male, gave into his coaxing once the others had left him standing there alone, the inclination to stay with the pack working in Kasiel's favor.

He shared the joy he experienced riding along in Sylaryth's mind with them. The surge of bright emotion infected the group. Peering through his tethdrak's eyes, he watched as one of the other beasts leapt over a rock, kicking into the air as it landed like a bucking horse. High clicks and excited screeches came from a few of the others.

The group sprinted past another lone tethdrak resting on a tall rock formation. Kasiel extended his awareness, gently pushing through a brief resistance and drawing the beast in with the others. A second alpha male. Aggression flashed briefly between the two alphas that Kasiel hastily subdued. It would impress Adnar that he had brought the two together without incident.

Dropping back behind his own eyes, he left a portion of his awareness split among the approaching beasts. A faint tremor shook the ground as the big predators galloped into view. Kasiel slowed them and eased them to a stop about five feet from where he and Adnar stood. He had them lay down there in a line, allowing Sylaryth to come the rest of the way forward to sit by his side. A couple more months of growth had the young tethdrak's shoulder now up to a little above Kasiel's hip.

It wasn't until the beasts had all settled that he recognized the darker of the two males as Adnar's companion. A flash of panic tightened his chest, and he cast a worried glance at his ahndhomen.

"I swear, I did not mean to take control of your tethdrak, sir."

Adnar shocked Kasiel with a deep laugh. "I've never been kicked out of a tethdrak's head so effortlessly. My own companion." He chuckled. "Well done, Omren Hahren. Very well done."

Breathing a sigh of relief, Kasiel absently held out a hand in front of Sylaryth and the masked tethdrak pressed his head into it. Sylaryth's sides heaved with the effort of his long run, but he was calm now. Somewhere over the last couple of months, that had become normal. When Sylaryth was with him, the tethdrak settled with no need for additional manipulation from Kasiel. That was especially impressive today, considering how keyed up he was himself. It was week's end, and they had finally finished giving half of a free day a week to the city guard. Several troops had also come in from the Break early that morning, which meant some of their absent companions might have returned.

"That's enough for now. Release them. I have something else I'd like to try with you today."

Kasiel sent the adult tethdraks out into the canyon, moving the two alphas far away from each other before releasing his influence over them. When he finished, he pulled his awareness back in and nodded to Adnar, setting a hand on Sylaryth's shoulder.

The ahndhomen turned away. "Follow me."

Adnar led him out of the enclosure and into a wide passage carved through the west wall of the canyon. It was large enough for Sylaryth to continue along by his side. The long dimly lit tunnel took him back to his first days coming to the canyon to meet in supposed secret with Kenna. Shadows didn't sweep in at him now, though. For all that he sometimes resented Setera for taking away the memory of what his father did to him, he appreciated that the incident no longer haunted him. Unfortunately, unsettling dreams were still a problem, but for other reasons now. Since remembering the night his ears were cut, he had nightmares about it regularly.

Perhaps Setera could do something about that too, though he wasn't sure he wanted her to. Even with the khevarin's symbol of recognition on the back of his hand, he was still an earless southerner to many of the people here. That was Edmund's fault, and he would not let the Evoker remove that. Edmund lied to him from the beginning. Kasiel refused to let go of the hollow ache of betrayal that accompanied thoughts of the man who had raised him. The rage. No one would ever take that from him.

A few low, worried clicks from Sylaryth pulled Kasiel back to the present. The dark temper that came with his thoughts faded. He had a new family now with Jethan and the others—his tehsheyn—and a most unexpected companion.

He passed reassurance across to the tethdrak, pleased with how fast the beast relaxed again.

The passage took them to another canyon that split off at a different angle. Like the canyon the tethdraks resided in, this one had an overhung area in the front barred off from the rest. Adnar turned to him, his gaze lingering on Sylaryth.

"There's an alcove there." He pointed toward the far back corner. "Send Sylaryth into it and make sure he stays."

Kasiel did as ordered, urging the tethdrak into the alcove with gentle persuasion. It was getting easier to convince the beasts to do what he wanted. Though he could force them now with minimal effort, he tried not to impose his will on them. Finesse and encouragement didn't get the fastest results, but a gentler approach created trust. That trust led to a stronger connection that made them more willing to do what he asked without the need for force. With Sylaryth, the strength of the bond they had developed made it so that coaxing the tethdrak to do what he wanted with a light touch was almost effortless now. Sylaryth was eager to please him. He hoped to get to that point with the others in time.

Once Sylaryth was out of sight, Adnar focused his attention on the enclosure. At least a minute passed with Kasiel waiting and watching, before the reason they were here came loping up from a deeper spot in the canyon with long, ground-consuming strides. Having seen a kanodrak depicted in stone did nothing to prepare him for how magnificent and terrifying the beast was in the flesh.

A gray and silver, smooth-scaled hide covered the vaguely feline body. Natural plates of bone armor started at its rounded muzzle and continued along to the base of its neck like a rigid mane. Claws extended from its massive cat-like paws as it moved, ripping gouges in the soil. The bone armor over its head wrapped down in front of its eyes and curved over its nose. Two oversized upper canines extended below its lower jaw. Its eyes, when it turned his way and hissed, were a milky white that reminded him of the Heartsmith.

He fought the urge to take a step back from the bars between them. The kanodrak was at least a foot taller at the shoulder than any horse he had ever seen. Powerful muscles rippled beneath its thick hide.

"Can it see?" he asked, his voice hushed with instinctive reverence.

"Yes. Though not exactly in the way we do." Adnar's voice was low and heavy with respect for the deadly creature before them. "Step closer to the bars, Omren. Let it smell you. Reach out to its mind, but don't try to force your way in. Just be present."

Those instructions sounded like terrible ideas, but he would trust his ahndhomen. The man knew these beasts better than anyone else here. He stepped closer to the bars, and the kanodrak sank into a threatening posture, slowly advancing until it was near enough that he could feel its breath on him as it sniffed at him. He swallowed hard.

"Stand your ground," Adnar said in a low voice.

With those strange eyes now staring him in the face, Kasiel reached out warily to touch the creature's mind. He met a wall of resistance and stopped there. The kanodrak raised its head and let out an ear-splitting roar. Kasiel jumped, his heart suddenly racing, but he did as Adnar directed and stood his ground. The beast lowered its head and sniffed at him again, then it turned and trotted off as if it had grown bored with them.

Kasiel blew out the breath he was holding. His muscles trembled. When he looked at Adnar, it surprised him to see a proud smile lighting the ahndhomen's typically stern features.

"One day, Omren Hahren," he said with certainty, "you will ride one of those."

Kasiel wasn't so sure, but a part of him reveled in the thought.

"For now, you are free to join your companions."

"Thank you, sir." He spun toward the exit, charged with nervous energy, and called Sylaryth to him.

When he reached the top of the lift, he was still processing the encounter. How confident Adnar was that he would ride one. How pleased the ahndhomen was with him for what he would have considered an unimpressive performance when faced with the kanodrak. Though, if all that was required was to stand his ground, he had managed that much.

"Kas!"

Kasiel's attention snapped up as Kenna vaulted over the low gate that closed off the lift. He dropped one hand parallel to the ground, signaling Sylaryth to lie down, and caught her with his other arm as she enfolded him in a fierce embrace, sending him staggering back a few steps. The lift platform wobbled alarmingly beneath them, bouncing his heart into his throat. Despite that, he grinned like a fool.

"You're back." He reached out with a mental touch to be sure Sylaryth was calm, then wrapped both arms around her to return the hug.

Jethan leaned on the gate, his grin a match for Kasiel's own. "I ran into her on my way here to collect you."

Kenna released him and bounced back, setting the platform wobbling again. She reached out and squeezed his upper arm, giving Jethan a wide-eyed look. "Wow. Did you feel this? Someone's been busy with combat training."

Kasiel averted his gaze when she looked at him again, not sure whether to bask in the praise or try to hide his flush behind his hair. He gestured to the gate. "Can we continue this reunion off the platform hanging precariously over the canyon?"

Jethan and Kenna both laughed, though his tehnaak was kind enough to open the gate as he did so. Kasiel stepped off with Sylaryth at his heels. Kenna stayed where she was.

"Actually, I need to report to Adnar, but Jeth said you're all meeting at The Twisted Vine in a bit and I can come crash the party if I want."

Kasiel nodded. "You absolutely should."

"I will." She hit the lever as Jethan closed the gate. "See you both there."

They leaned on the fence together for a moment, watching the platform descend.

"You smell like tethdrak."

"Thanks." Kasiel bumped his shoulder into Jethan's. "I'm confident I can blame that on Sylaryth."

"I didn't say it was bad. Some ladies might like that husky predator musk."

Kasiel rolled his eyes and stepped away from the gate. "You're impossible. Let's go."

They strode through the city together, Sylaryth catching attention as he always did, especially as he continued to grow larger. People here were all aware of the tethdraks, but they still didn't see the beasts up close all that often. The downside of that was that everyone knew who Kasiel was and could recognize him on sight now, even when he didn't have his tethdrak along.

"Adnar took me to see the kanodraks today."

"Lucky calloch!" Jethan's sudden wide-eyed excitement caught him by surprise. "Was it amazing?"

He walked at an angle for a few strides, eyeing his tehnaak. "Haven't you seen one?"

"No. There isn't a viewing platform over their enclosure like there is for the tethdraks. With Adnar being the only one here who can control them right now, they don't really get brought out." Jethan was quiet for a few strides, then he bounced up on the balls of his feet in a quick hop-step. "By the Break, Kas! He must really think you have potential if he took you in there. My tehnaak, a kanodrak rider. That's something I never expected when I met your half-starved ass."

"Let's not get ahead of ourselves. It's only been a matter of months since I got here. I'm not even fluent in the language yet. I don't think I'll be galloping around the countryside on a kanodrak anytime soon." Kasiel absently dropped a hand to Sylaryth's shoulder when the tethdrak jealously bumped him from the other side. "Easy, Syl, you can't be the center of attention all the time."

"Yes, and if we have to fight for your attention, I'm pretty sure I'll be on the losing end of that battle." Jethan gave the tethdrak a sideways smirk. "You know, Kas, you may not have the language down yet, but you went from country boy to lord and moved into the palace the day you arrived. You haven't been taking things slow."

Kasiel breathed a laugh and shook his head. Jethan was right though. Things had changed for him at a dizzying speed. He sometimes wished they would slow down a little.

When they entered The Twisted Vine, their group at the back table stood. Kasiel gestured for Sylaryth to lie down again when Wedro and Chander, returned from the front, strode over to greet him and Jethan with exuberant hugs.

"Nice tethdrak." Chander eyed Sylaryth with a mix of admiration and wariness.

"Already strutting around town with a deadly beast at your side, danro? I'd say you're doing a fine job learning how to be Vanrian." Wedro, sporting a freshly stitched cut down the side of his neck, took Kasiel's hand, turning it so Chander could see the khevarin's tattoo. He arched a brow at them. "And what about this? You all couldn't have waited until we got back to do this?"

Jethan slapped Wedro on the shoulder. "Maybe we can talk Khevarin Seylin into some honorary tattoos for you two and..." he trailed off.

Kasiel caught his tehnaak's hesitation, glancing around the group. "Where's Tath?"

"Haven't seen her since the fighting a few nights ago." Chander shifted his feet as if the subject made him uneasy. "We were told they still needed healers, so they kept her there."

"They sent the rest of you back, though. Has the fighting stopped?" Kasiel asked, trying to get a read on the other man's sudden discomfort.

"It has slowed." Wedro turned, leading them to the table. "Apparently, the Pandrean Alliance requested a cease in hostilities for some sort of negotiation. Anything more than that is above our rank, I'm afraid."

Kasiel caught the eye of the barkeep, Nok, and gave him a nod of greeting. The man raised the mug he was filling in response, a broad grin cracking his features. The tethdrak—a respected symbol of their homeland that supposedly brought good fortune—was apparently excellent for business. No matter how any of them felt about Kasiel, Sylaryth was always welcome.

Kasiel took the seat at the end of the bench, leaving space for the tethdrak to lie on the floor beside him. The group sitting at the next table over shifted toward the opposite end of their benches. Revered creature or not, he was still a lethal predator. Kasiel smirked to himself and set his hand on the beast's head between his backswept horns.

The Twisted Vine was one of several taverns in the

city. It being week's end, most of them, this one included, were more crowded than usual. Kasiel was learning to appreciate the camaraderie that formed amongst
these people who shared a common experience as soldiers in Etrion, especially now that, intentionally or not,
he was one of them. He still hadn't gotten used to being
around this many people at once, though. Most groups
within the tavern crowded in on each other, eking out
whatever space they could find with their friends. The
best way to ensure your party had room to move was
apparently to bring a deadly beast with you.

Darro was sharing the tale of how they had earned
the khevarin's favor when Sylaryth emitted a couple of
wary clicks next to him and looked toward the entrance.
After a few months of working with him, that was more
than enough to catch Kasiel's attention. He followed the
tethdrak's gaze, watching curiously as the door opened.

Ahndhomen Adnar stepped into the tavern, his
massive tethdrak filling the doorway behind him. The
noise level dropped instantly, dwindling to silence as
more people took notice. Those standing in his path
hastily found alternative places to plant their feet.

Adnar didn't come any farther into the building. He
scanned the room until his gaze came to rest on Kasiel.
"Ahninveth Hahren Cavenos, come with me."

Kasiel and Sylaryth stood.

Behind him, Wedro asked in a low voice, "When did
he get promoted?"

Kasiel wanted to know the same thing, but this
didn't seem like the right place to question his ahndhomen. He leaned close to Jethan. "I'll let you know
what's going on as soon as I find out."

"I'll pay for the drinks," Jethan said, giving his arm
a squeeze that offered both support and encouragement.

Kasiel gave him a sideways glance. "I know. It was
your turn anyway."

He strode across the room. People shifted out of the way to allow him extra space for his tethdrak. Everyone's eyes were on him. Anyone unhappy with his presence in Vanris must have loved hearing him addressed as an ahninveth, the equivalent of a captain in the south. Not only a captain, but a mind-crafter captain, which technically ranked him above a normal inveth. That couldn't be right. Adnar must have given him the title in error.

The minute he reached Adnar, the ahndhomen turned and strode out, heading swiftly away from the tavern. Kasiel had to jog a few steps to catch up.

"Have I been promoted, sir?" he asked the moment they were clear of the small crowd out front.

"I need you to be an officer to take you where we're going. Besides, the khevarin gave me a directive to accelerate your advancement after your ill-advised heroics a couple of months ago. Consider yourself accelerated."

Kasiel pondered that. He wanted to be excited about the advancement, but he was more alarmed that it came so unexpectedly, and at this precise moment. Wherever Adnar was taking him, he hoped he would have a better idea of how to feel about it after they got there.

Kasiel jogged a few steps to keep up again, getting a flash of excitement from Sylaryth as the beast bounded alongside him. Adnar's tethdrak growled at the juvenile. Kasiel turned his focus to calming his own nerves so his tethdrak wouldn't stay riled and anger the other beast.

"Where are we going, sir?"

"First, we're visiting your rooms so you can get cleaned up. You can worry about the next stop after that."

CHAPTER TWENTY NINE

Twenty minutes later, they strode through the halls of the palace again with Kasiel cleaned up and dressed in some of his finer attire. His long dark metal-accented jacket rippled behind him as he extended his stride to keep pace with Adnar. The two tethdraks moved along on either side of them so that they took up most of the wide hallway between the four of them. The few people they encountered along the way stepped into doorways or crossed halls to let them pass. Did Adnar enjoy the feeling of power that came with that immediate deference? He could see how it had potential to become somewhat intoxicating.

Adnar had given him some insight into where they were going while he changed, but he still felt like he was about to enter a bear's den unarmed.

They stopped before a set of double doors and the guards outside inclined their heads to Adnar, one of them taking a reflexive step back from his tethdrak. Adnar knocked on the door. It opened a crack. Whoever waited on the inside greeted him and opened it the rest of the way.

Kasiel and Sylaryth followed the ahndhomen and his tethdrak into a long room. Detailed maps lined the walls in between shelves of well-worn books. Single doors left the room from two other sides. A long table occupied the center, laden with more maps, a pile of weapons, a few scrolls, and three large stoneglass bottles of black mead, two of them already open.

Six people stood around the table, two of them dhomens and three inveths according to the insignias on their uniforms. Kasiel recognized only his father, who stood near the head of the table, eyes narrowing when his gaze fixed upon him.

"Ahndhomen Adnar, what is Omren Hahren doing here?"

Kasiel's respect for Adnar increased exponentially when the ahndhomen didn't miss a stride before Arhk's fierce gaze.

He gestured for Kasiel to approach the table with him. "The first subject we need to discuss concerns Ahninveth Hahren, perhaps more than anyone else in this room. It is appropriate that he be made aware of the situation and given a voice in its resolution."

Arhk's lip curled into a slight sneer. "Ahninveth?"

Kasiel inclined his head a fraction, not breaking eye contact with his father as he did so, despite the quiver of dread in his gut. "Yes, Dhomvalen."

Arhk held his gaze, eyes narrowing more, and Kasiel got the feeling he was about to be kicked out of the room. He set his hand on the table, making the gesture appear casual, but it had the desired effect. Arhk's gaze flickered down to the khevarin's symbol tattooed on the back of that hand. His nostrils flared a little as he drew in a deep breath.

"Very well, Ahninveth Hahren may stay."

The scornful emphasis he put on the title made it clear he wasn't pleased with the situation, but if Adnar saw fit to ignore that, Kasiel decided he would as well.

"If I may, Dhomvalen," a woman on the opposite side of the table inclined her head to Arhk respectfully as she spoke. She was one of the two dhomens in the room. A scar ran from above her eyebrow down to her jawline on the right side of her face. It cut through part of her ke'hanoath made up of a series of symbols curving beneath that eye. Braids worked into her long red hair on both sides pulled it away from fine pointed ears adorned with delicate dark metal cuffs and a few small spikes.

Arhk looked at her, releasing Kasiel from the pressure of his gaze. "Proceed, Dhomen Nevias."

"The Alliance has requested a meeting to negotiate a cease of current hostilities in the central region of the Crimson Break. Casualties on both sides have been unfortunately high in the latest battles. They captured two of our healers in the last encounter—"

"Tath," Kasiel blurted.

Even before she spoke, her solemn gaze told him he was right. "Healer Tath was one of those taken. Before negotiating this cease of hostilities and the release of prisoners, they wish to address the strike mission we sent to retrieve Lord Hahren Cavenos. They claim it violated the Boundaries Treaty we signed with them seven years ago."

"Which it did." That came from an inveth on Kasiel's side of the table.

"Which it did," she conceded.

"If someone on their side had not abducted him as a child, that violation would not have been necessary," Arhk stated flatly.

It was odd to have them discussing Kasiel's life as if he weren't in the room. He held his tongue for now and listened, watching the flickering shadows from the few wall sconces. Did those shadows make him appear fiercer the way they did his father, Nevias, and Adnar? Or did they only make him look uncertain, like the others in the room?

Sylaryth shifted next to him. He set a hand on the

tethdrak's shoulder, taking comfort from his presence as much as giving it.

"Be that as it may," Nevias resumed, "they state that, because he lived there for twelve years, he was a citizen and should be returned to the family that raised him."

A sudden stifling pressure filled the room as rage flared in Arhk's eyes. The same pressure Kasiel had felt the day the khevarin passed judgement on him and his companions for their part in catching Nerith's assailants. It was his father's ability that did that.

Adnar spoke before Arhk could. "Even if we believed that, we would never hand over a mind-crafter to them."

"They appear convinced that he is here against his will and, given the choice, would return to the south," Nevias said.

"Why would they make such an assumption?" the other dhomen asked.

"Edmund," Kasiel stated with certainty. All eyes turned to him, and he had to stifle the urge to shrink back from that attention. "The man who raised me, Edmund Danovan. He must be advising them in some capacity."

"The man who cut your ears?" Arhk's voice was soft and menacing.

A pulse of pressure moved through the room, and Kasiel drew in a slow breath to steady his nerves. Did one ever get used to talking to Arhk when his ire was up?

"He was there, yes," Kasiel answered, focusing on the corner of a map behind his father.

"Whatever the reason," Nevias said, pulling their attention back to her, "if we intend to advance negotiations, our delegation will need to convince them that Ahninveth Hahren wants to stay in Vanris. If we aren't careful, the Boundaries Treaty could collapse, and we could end up losing our healers. We need to keep that from happening while making it clear that our new Feral isn't going anywhere."

The idea that struck Kasiel then felt reckless, but he tossed it out anyhow. "Let me go with the delegation. I can tell them myself that I have no desire to return to the south. They can't expect you to force me to go back if I don't wish to."

Arhk slammed a hand down on the table. "Absolutely not!"

Kasiel flinched at the vehemence in his father's voice, but some others were regarding him thoughtfully now.

"It's not a terrible idea," Nevias said.

"We'd be risking a Feral, tehnaak," Adnar countered.

His words jolted Kasiel. Nevias was Adnar's tehnaak? She wasn't a mind-crafter. He could see how they might make a good pairing, though. The dhomen might not be a Feral, but she had a dangerous, predatory bearing to her.

"In established neutral territory." The barest hint of a smile on Nevias's hardened features suggested she was warming to the idea. "The neutrality of the Hall at Katovan has not been violated by either side since it was declared neutral. We take Lord Hahren with us, with plenty of protection, and only bring him into the negotiations if necessary, in which case he barely has to do more than show himself. His answer is written upon his skin. If we end up not needing to bring him in, he gets a brief excursion into the Break. No harm done."

"I said no," Arhk stated firmly.

Kasiel met his father's gaze this time. "Respectfully, Dhomvalen, I think I should go."

"You're outranked." Arhk's tone made it apparent he felt the conversation was over.

"Dhomvalen," Adnar began, his voice deferential

yet firm, "Nevias and Hahren may have a point."

Arhk's irritated gaze flickered to Kasiel as if he had spoken. He forced himself not to react in any visible way by drawing on Sylaryth's calm, the tethdrak content to be at his side.

"We can claim that he wants to be here until the Break turns green," Adnar went on, "but they have no reason to take our word for it. However, if they hear it from his own lips, they will have to accept that it's true. That should open the door for us to suggest different terms, at which point we can remove him from the negotiations to a safer position. This could be the only way to avoid a deadlock."

The entire time Adnar was speaking, Kasiel remained the unfortunate recipient of Arhk's searing gaze. The room and his eyes darkened.

Kasiel forced himself to hold that stare, hating that his father believed he could intimidate him out of doing this. He touched on Sylaryth's mind, letting the tethdrak feel a little of the anger and defiance he yearned to show his father. Sylaryth stood and growled at Arhk.

"Control your beast," Arhk demanded.

The slightest hint of a smirk turned Kasiel's lips. "I am."

Arhk's reaction was the opposite of what Kasiel expected. The darkness in his eyes and the room retreated. One corner of his mouth curved up ever so slightly. "So be it. Ahninveth Hahren will go to Katovan to declare his own desire to remain in Vanris. I expect the two of you," he said, pausing for emphasis as he picked out Adnar and then Nevias with his piercing gaze, "to ensure that he is well-prepared and protected." He faced Kasiel again, his expression more thoughtful now. "The rest of what we need to discuss does not concern you, Ahninveth."

Adnar shared a quick look with Nevias that Kasiel

would have said was one of victory. Then the Feral ahndhomen turned to Kasiel.

"Thank you for your time, Ahninveth Hahren. The delegation will depart in three days. Dhomen Nevias and I will call on you tomorrow to begin preparations."

"I'll be ready, sir." He answered, offering Adnar a bow.

Relief washed over Kasiel at the prospect of leaving the tension-filled room. He inclined his head to each of the others, deliberately acknowledging his father with a slight bow, regardless of how much he wanted to snub the man. Without requiring any visible or verbal command, Sylaryth rose and went to the exit with him. The guard inclined his head and opened the door, stepping back from the tethdrak as they passed through. As soon as he was clear of the room, Kasiel focused on breathing, trying to slow his heartbeat and ease the nervous vibration running through him.

Had he just talked his way into a political negotiation in the Break? Why? What experience did he have with such affairs? And why did he feel like he had somehow gained ground with his father?

•

Three days of preparation, interrupted by a brief ceremony to make his promotion official, sped by too fast. The delegation that struck out for the Hall at Katovan on the morning of the fourth day consisted primarily of soldiers. Dhomen Nevias was the officer in command of the mission, leading a few other high-ranking officers, all of whom brought their own units of soldiers. Because mind-crafters made the Pandrean Alliance negotiators uncomfortable, Kasiel was one of two in the entire group. The other was Jethan, who earned his place there simply by being Kasiel's tehnaak.

Darro and Kince also rode with them, assigned to Kasiel both as protection and advisors, given how new he was to his rank and being a soldier.

Sylaryth also accompanied them. The tethdrak's presence gave Kasiel ample opportunities to practice using his ability on the horses, who grew nervous around the large predator. It had been a while since he worked in the head of a prey animal. Their thoughts felt unfocused. Chaotic compared to the intense focus of a predator's mind. Even so, by a few hours into the journey, he had grown used to keeping himself keyed to the state of the mounts traveling nearest the tethdrak. Dhomen Nevias took notice of his efforts, expressing a gruff appreciation at the end of that first day that reminded him of Adnar.

The Hall at Katovan was close to a three-day ride from Etrion at a reasonable pace. Kasiel's role would be simple. Nevias expected the Alliance to lead with the subject of Vanris's strike mission into their territory and the dispute over where he belonged. They would call him in if, and only if, the Alliance leaders were unwilling to accept that he was where he should be now. He got the impression that she expected the southern negotiators to be stubborn about it. They had a point to make, even though both sides knew the Alliance would never have handed over a mind-crafter if Vanris had attempted to negotiate for his return instead of simply taking him.

The Hall itself was a small keep that backed up against the side of a plateau at the edge of the razed town of Katovan. The main building was maintained by a nonviolent faction of Havaad worshipers from the south who lived there year-round and provided food and services for visiting dignitaries during rare gatherings like this one. A few hollowed-out shops and houses or lonely remains of walls still stood amidst the crumbled ruins of the rest of the town, now partly covered in sandy reddish dust.

Before the Crimson Break became a desolate war zone, Katovan had been on the northeastern corner of the kingdom of Sarket. They constructed the buildings there of red stone and clay with the curved architecture popular in that part of the kingdom. Even the two towers on the front corners of the Hall had rounded crenelations at the top. The walls still bore black scars from Pandrean Alliance firebombs, memories of the battles that had destroyed the rest of the town.

They arrived at the ruined city on the third morning, most of the delegation wearing their hoods up. A precaution to prevent anyone on the opposing side from recognizing Kasiel or his companions as they approached.

A heavily armed contingent of Alliance soldiers moved around a camp on the far southern side of the ruins. In numbers, the group appeared comparable to their own. Their camp had a few large tents, undoubtedly reserved for important personages, and several canopies attached to the remains of walls provided shelter from the sun. It was hot in the daytime, though a chill came on after dark, and the bright sunlight could burn the skin and weary the eyes.

The Vanrian company struck camp on the north side, arranging themselves so that the Hall itself hid a substantial portion of their camp from view of the Alliance soldiers. Nevias directed Kasiel and his companions to stay out of sight as much as possible for the time being given his unique status as a subject of contention between the two sides.

Dhomen Nevias and the other delegates went inside with an accompaniment of guards after advising him and his companions to eat and rest while they had the time to do so.

About thirty minutes later, with the camp largely

set up, Kasiel, Jethan, Kince, and Darro ate in relative silence, hungry from a hard ride to cover the last ten miles to Katovan. Nevias had wanted to arrive as early as possible to get discussions underway. Once they had sated their hunger, the others appeared to relax a little, a state Kasiel couldn't achieve for himself. He scuffed his foot along the ground, listening to the grating of gritty sand over the solidly packed soil. Beside him, Sylaryth flexed and extended his claws, effortlessly digging runnels in the nearly rock-hard dirt.

"Nervous?"

Kasiel met Jethan's eyes. "I don't think nervous covers it."

Darro gave him a crooked grin, chewing a piece of dried meat as he spoke. "You've developed a knack for appearing confident even when you're about to shit yourself. I think you'll be fine, sir."

Kasiel scowled at him. "Don't call me that. I may outrank you on a technicality, but you earned your positions, and you know what you're doing."

Kince barked a laugh. "Less often than you might think." He winked and added, "sir."

Kasiel chucked a piece of bread at him. It bounced off his chest and hit the ground. Kince picked it up and popped it into his mouth.

Kasiel eyed his tehnaak. "Why haven't they promoted you? You led that unit south."

"Charmers and Speakers rarely become officers. In battle, they need Speakers in subordinate roles, and no one trusts Charmers enough to grant them any authority." He added the last with a crooked grin.

Far behind Kince and Darro, one of Nevias's subordinates emerged from a door in the side of the Hall, her gaze settling on Kasiel. Sylaryth's tail swished back and forth in agitation, churning up a plume of dust as Kasiel's food turned to stone in his stomach. He set aside what he hadn't eaten yet and watched as the woman approached them.

"Ahninveth Hahren, it's time to get you ready."

He was thankful, as he got up and his companions stood with him, that he at least didn't have to go in alone.

Kasiel restlessly paced the length of the small room they waited in, despite Jethan's periodic attempts to get him to settle. Sylaryth, who had attempted to walk with him for a time, now lay next to his tehnaak, head resting on his clawed feet, eyes tracking Kasiel back and forth across the room.

They had dressed Kasiel in sleek black trousers and an ivory shirt with a few sparing purple and silver accents on it. The colors of Vanris. The tailor designed the shirt precisely to lay open toward the top so his chain of tattoos, his ke'hanoath, would show. It had been a last-minute commission created specifically for this moment. He wore the long charcoal jacket with its dark metal accents and similarly detailed black boots. They had put a few braids in his hair that, after his vehement arguments against it, did not expose his cut ears. The parting of his hair and the braids worked together to ensure that the tattoo on his cheek was plainly visible.

"Aren't you tired of moving yet?" Kince asked from where he reclined on a long bench tucked into one corner.

Kasiel made an abrupt spin to pace back the other way and shook his head. He didn't trust himself to speak.

"Well, you're making me tired." Kince leaned his head against the wall and closed his eyes.

"Give him a break. It's not…" Jethan trailed off when the inner door that led to the meeting room opened.

Kasiel stopped pacing and Sylaryth hopped to his feet, coming to stand at his side.

The woman who had brought them here walked in. "It's time. Do you remember everything Dhomen Nevias told you?"

Kasiel nodded.

"They may ask questions or press certain points. Don't let them get to you."

Kasiel opted for another silent nod.

Jethan walked up to him, taking a moment to straighten the collar of Kasiel's jacket and adjust his shirt around his tattoos the way a mother might. "I know you're all grown up now, but I want you looking your best when you go out into the world."

Kasiel breathed a soft laugh. "Thanks, Jeth."

The woman smiled at them for a second, then her expression turned solemn again. "You three will enter with him but stay at the back of the room. Keep an eye on things and be ready to act if there's any trouble."

When she had a nod from each of his companions, she met Kasiel's eyes. "You can take Sylaryth as far as the edge of the table on the Vanrian side. You continue alone from there. Let's go, Ahninveth Hahren."

Kasiel followed her through the door with Sylaryth, resisting the urge to look back and make sure the others were coming. He knew they would, he just yearned for the extra comfort of visual confirmation. Instead, he faced ahead, hearing himself introduced as Ahninveth Hahren Cavenos when he stepped into the large, square room.

The interior of the meeting hall was decorated in soft shades of tan and cream. Calming colors that failed to do anything for him in that moment. A series of long tables were set out in a horseshoe shape on three sides around an open center space. Highly polished, and age-worn, the tables appeared to be carved from a pale wood cut in sections too large to be from any of the gnarled, stunted trees that were native to the region. On the side nearest the door he had entered through sat the four members of the Vanrian delegation with their guards lined up along the wall about ten feet behind them. On the opposite side, facing them, sat the six Pandrean Alliance delegates, two in the green and silver of the kingdom of Sarket, two in the tan and blue of Delaphine, and two in the black and gray of Fallend. The guards along the wall behind them wore Pandrean Alliance red and gold.

A solitary man sat at the head of the table wearing simple brown robes with no insignia or colors proclaiming an affiliation. A facilitator, according to what Nevias and Darro had both told him about how these things worked. Dark hair, olive skin, and rounded ears were enough to declare his southern lineage. Despite that, his role was to act as a neutral mediator to keep discussions on track or make certain decisions about how the council itself was proceeding. A Vanrian officer sat to his right, there to assist in case of disputes.

Repeating Nevias's instructions in his head, Kasiel strode out to the edge of the table. Despite his dread that this would, for some unfathomable reason, be the moment the tethdrak stopped listening to him, Sylaryth sat instantly beside him. With a thought, he directed his companion to remain there and continued halfway up the center of the horseshoe alone, keeping his eyes on the facilitator. Murmurs rose among the Alliance delegates as he took his place between the two sides. He inclined his head to the facilitator, feeling exposed without the tethdrak or his tehnaak beside him.

The facilitator offered a nod, casting a brief look

toward the Alliance delegates. "Ahninveth Hahren Cavenos, are you prepared to answer the questions of the Pandrean Alliance delegation in order to settle the dispute over your recent relocation?"

"I am, sir." Could they see how his heart was racing? Did they have any idea at all how desperately he wanted to run from the room as he stood there, schooling his features to appear calm and collected? He hoped Darro was right about his ability to look confident.

The facilitator nodded to the Alliance delegation. "You may proceed with your questions."

Kasiel had expected this, based on the coaching he got from Nevias and Darro. He turned to face the Alliance delegates. Sylaryth became a nervous presence in his mind, unhappy at being separated from him.

One delegate from Sarket, a gray-haired man with a nose that appeared to have been broken more than once, cleared his throat a few times prior to speaking. His gaze flickered from the tethdrak at the corner to the chain of tattoos around Kasiel's neck, then lingered on the tattoo on his face before finally meeting his eyes. "Kasiel Danovan—"

"Hahren Cavenos," Dhomen Nevias interrupted.

As fast as that, Kasiel found himself stuck in an awkward position. If he went with his inclination to say "Kasiel Cavenos," then his preference for the name Edmund had given him might skew their perception of the situation. Still, he refused to use Hahren. No matter who had given it to him at his birth, it wasn't the name he answered to now, at least not by choice. After a second's hesitation with all eyes on him, a solution occurred to him.

"Ahninveth Cavenos, if you would."

Unlike Vanris, the Pandrean Alliance kingdoms gave military title followed by surname as the preferred form of address. This way, he could appear respectful of their customs and conveniently avoid using either of the given first names.

The delegate pressed his lips together in an irritated line, but he inclined his head after a moment. "Of course. Ahninveth Cavenos, you were raised in Fallend in a small village called Fernwallow. Is this true?"

"For twelve years. Yes." Nevias told him to keep his answers clear, factual, and uncomplicated. She also said it might be helpful to add certain details when appropriate. How he was supposed to figure out what details and when it was appropriate to include them, he didn't know. All he could do was try to trust his instincts.

"From the age of five until mercenaries took you away earlier this year."

Was there value to pointing out that he had run away before the mercenaries caught him? For now, anger raised by the memory of how those three had treated him took priority. "Mercenaries wearing the insignia of the Pandrean Alliance. Mercenaries who attempted to control me through physical abuse and starvation."

One of the dark-skinned men from Delaphine averted his gaze, taking a sudden interest in a scroll sitting on the table in front of him.

The one questioning him forged ahead. "Then a strike team from Vanris attacked those mercenaries in Alliance territory, killing them and taking you as their prisoner."

"No," Kasiel stated firmly. "I was never their prisoner."

The delegate's eyes narrowed. "You're suggesting that they would have let you return home had you wished it?"

He hesitated. It would be a lie to say yes. If he had tried to leave, they would have had to come after him. He understood that now. Even with his ability not awakened, they couldn't have left a mind-crafter alive in the south had he refused to go with them. "Not necessarily. I'm saying that they unbound me, tended my wounds, fed me, and gave me a horse to ride. They even returned my weapons to me. They treated more like a member of their group than a prisoner."

The corners of the delegate's mouth twitched up a fraction. "But they would not have let you go?"

It was a dangerous line of questioning, but Kasiel had his directions. With no way to seek guidance from the Vanrian delegation behind him, he would simply continue to follow the truth. "No. Had I attempted to leave, I believe they would have had to stop me. However, since I chose to remain with them, that's speculation on my part."

"And do you not consider yourself a prisoner in Etrion?"

"No." He reached a mental touch out to Sylaryth for comfort, getting a flicker of happiness from the beast in response to the contact. "I'm Vanrian. Etrion is where I belong."

The delegate frowned at that and adjusted a pile of papers sitting in front of him. "Are you saying you do not wish to return to your home and family in Fernwallow?"

Family indeed. "I'm saying, given a choice, I choose to stay in Etrion."

The delegates leaned together, speaking in hushed voices amongst themselves. They seemed as taken aback by his responses as they had been by his appearance. It was apparent that this wasn't what Edmund had led them to expect.

"This is foolishness!"

The sound of Edmund's voice threw the entire room off-kilter for Kasiel. He looked up to see the professor entering through one of the many doors behind the Alliance delegation. Hatred, loathing, and a desperate, unexpected surge of heartache made his head spin. This man raised him, taught him to read and write, instructed him on how to brew teas for enjoyment and for medicinal purposes, showed him how to identify beneficial plants in the wild. Used him. Lied to him.

Sylaryth got to his feet at the end of the table, growling low in his throat, eyes locked on the source of Kasiel's distress. He heard chairs scraping the floor as the Vanrian delegates stood behind him.

The delegate who had been questioning him turned in his seat to face Edmund. "Professor Danovan, you have not been called upon yet."

"What is the meaning of this?" Nevias demanded.

The facilitator also stood now. "Please. Everyone calm down and return to your seats. Professor Edmund Danovan's presence is as relevant to this discussion as Ahninveth Cavenos's. All sides must be considered. The girl, however, cannot be in here."

Edmund glanced back at the door he had entered through. Kasiel followed his gaze to where Danica now stood in the doorway in a light blue dress with modest white trimming. Not a remarkable outfit if he ignored that she had always hated dresses. She stared at Kasiel, her features drawn with sorrow and a hint of fearful uncertainty. He longed to reassure her, but that was something he could never do for her again. Not given who he was and the choices he had made.

"Apologies, my lord." Edmund inclined his head to the facilitator. "Danica, my dear, please go wait with your father."

After a moment of hesitation, she tore her gaze from Kasiel and ducked back through the door, slamming it hard enough that the noise echoed across the meeting room.

Danica. He stared at the closed door, an ache spreading in his chest.

"I take it you had something you wished to add to the current line of questioning, Professor?" the facilitator prompted.

Edmund strode up to the table and placed his hands on the back of an empty chair next to the Alliance delegates. He regarded Kasiel, his brow furrowed, his lips pulling down in a deepening frown. "I raised this young man, my lords, and it is clear to me from looking at him that he has changed significantly in the months since I last saw him. Changed, I would allege, to an unprecedented degree. This raises considerable concerns in me. When the Vanrians took him, young Kasiel was in a highly vulnerable, highly suggestible state. How can we trust that anything he is telling us is true, given that he has spent these months in the hands of people who can manipulate the mind?"

"The professor has a point," one of the Delaphinian delegates was too eager to add.

They were no longer speaking to Kasiel, but what they were saying about him raised alarms in his head. Edmund was using Vanrian mindcrafting as an excuse to cast doubt on the validity of every word he spoke, trying to take away his voice in the discussion.

A bright white fury exploded behind his eyes. "You manipulative calloch!"

Sylaryth snarled and shifted into a hunting posture. He emitted a series of high-pitched clicks that sent the Alliance delegates pushing away from the table in alarm. Even Edmund took a few wary steps back, his calculating gaze shifting from Kasiel to the beast who had advanced a few steps toward the center.

"I would never do anything to harm you, Kasiel. Whatever you think I've done, you must believe me when I say it is not real." Edmund's calm, pitying tone was fuel for the fury building up inside Kasiel. "Ask yourself why I would want to hurt the child I raised as my own son. My only child. This isn't who you are. You're a good lad, Kasiel."

The familiar phrase was a blade twisting in his chest, the pain made worse by the realization that part of him still longed to believe Edmund's words. "You used me! You lied to me!"

Sylaryth sank weight into his hindquarters as if he meant to charge, and Edmund took another wary step back, a hint of genuine fear rising in his eyes now.

Jethan was suddenly at Kasiel's side, placing a hand on his arm. "Kas." The physical contact and his low, urgent tone drew Kasiel's attention to him. "You need to calm Sylaryth down."

"Get him out of here," Nevias ordered.

Not allowing himself to look at Edmund again, Kasiel nodded to Jethan and drew Sylaryth along with him as his tehnaak led them back to the room they had waited in. Darro and Kince let them pass through the door, then fell in line to follow them inside.

They had barely finished closing the door behind them when a tentative voice said, "My lord?"

They turned, hands going to their weapons. Sylaryth snarled. All color drained from the face of the serving woman waiting in a corner of the room and she dropped the tray she was holding. The mugs of water on the tray upended as it hit the tiles. The woman bolted out through a side door, a piece of paper fluttering to the floor in her wake.

Kince snatched the paper up before the water could soak through it. After wiping it dry on his leg, he unfolded and skimmed it then gave it to Kasiel without a word. It read: *There is a mostly intact building at the northwestern corner of the keep, near your camp. If you are able, meet me there tonight, an hour after dark. Dani.*

Kasiel held it for Jethan to read over his shoulder, then handed it to Darro.

Darro looked it over and gave it back. "I want to go on the record as having said that I think this is a bad idea."

Darro had said exactly that outside of Andaro, making Jethan's response easy to predict.

"Noted." Jethan met Kasiel's eyes. "I can probably get a few select guards to look the other way."

Kince gave a derisive snort. "There's no probably about it. It's not like we don't all know you're a Charmer, Jeth."

Kasiel could only nod. Fury still pulsed through him, forcing him to put extra effort into calming Sylaryth. The tethdrak was too well-tuned to his temper and ready to protect him from whatever threat had upset him.

Deep down, Kasiel agreed with Darro. Meeting Danica, assuming this note really was from her, was a terrible idea. He still intended to do it. He took a few breaths, trying and failing to find a sense of balance within himself.

"Thank you, tehnaak." He led the way from the building through the side door. If they wanted him back in the negotiations at some point, they could come get him.

CHAPTER THIRTY ONE

Kasiel sat on the ground in one corner of a canopied area, his back pressed against the lone surviving wall of a destroyed building. Sylaryth rested alongside him, most of his body stretched out under the bright sunshine, his heavy head laying in the shade across Kasiel's thighs. They had been like that for a few hours now. The feeling had gone away in Kasiel's ass a short time ago with the tethdrak's heavy head pressing down on his legs. The possibility that it might never come back had occurred to him more than once.

Kince and Darro sat on the other side of the shelter playing a game of dice, a slab of stone they had dragged over serving as a table. They remained close enough to respond if Kasiel needed them, yet far enough away to give him the privacy he had asked for when they came out here.

While he was running mental circles around the jumbled emotions from everything that happened in the meeting, Jethan had sat in on several rounds of dice, then dropped out to go in search of something to eat. He returned now, carrying two wide trenchers of a remarkable smelling stew with a loaf of bread balanced across them, and four mugs haphazardly tucked under his arms. He set one trencher on the slab of stone between Kince and Darro, along with half the bread and two mugs.

"You'll have to share. I only had two hands." He pulled a stoneglass bottle from somewhere in his jacket, waiting while Kince and Darro uncorked it and filled their mugs.

"You know, Jeth, you're all right sometimes," Darro said.

Jethan wrinkled his nose at Darro and snatched the bottle from him. "Was that a 'thank you, Jethan, you're the best' I heard? I'm going to pretend it was," he said as he walked away, coming to sit next to Kasiel. He set out the remaining food and mugs between them.

Sylaryth's head shifted closer to the food. He darted out his tongue to smell it, a soft, fast clicking rising from somewhere deep in his throat.

Jethan chuckled. "Optimistic, aren't you, Syl." He leaned a little closer to Kasiel, lowering his voice. "How are you doing, tehnaak?"

Kasiel closed his eyes and shook his head, still wanting for some sense of equilibrium. Of certainty. When he opened them again, Jethan was pouring them each a drink, waiting patiently for him to answer when he was ready.

Kasiel ran his hands through his hair, fingertips brushing against the scars that topped his ears. "Even after everything that's happened, there was a part of me that wanted Edmund to be right. So much has changed. At every turn, there's some new challenge to overcome. So much still to learn to be on par with the average person my age in Vanris. Sometimes I really do wish I could have my simple life back."

Jethan sat back and offered him a sympathetic smile. "You know, Kas, you are allowed to miss what you had. You may realize now that it wasn't the peaceful, perfect life you thought it was, but that doesn't mean every happy moment you had there is no longer valid. Those moments were real. There's nothing at all wrong with you if you remember that peace and happiness fondly and even long for it sometimes."

Kasiel's eyes started stinging, so he lowered his gaze, staring into the mug of Vanrian Black Mead Jethan had poured for him. "If it weren't for you, tehnaak, I might doubt my entire reality right now, but somehow you always make me feel like I can make it through moments like this."

Jethan's smile broadened. "That's why I'm here, to keep you going so you can be here to do the same for me."

Kasiel lifted his mug, making himself look at Jethan. If anyone wouldn't judge him for the shine of unshed tears in his eyes, Jethan was the one. He genuinely believed that. "Here's to getting each other through the dark times."

Jethan raised his mug. "And celebrating the good times together."

They clicked their mugs, and both took a drink. When Kasiel lowered his, he caught sight of Darro watching them, a hint of approval softening the man's typically austere expression before he turned back to the current round of dice.

"I shouldn't meet her tonight," Kasiel said, dipping a hunk of bread into the stew to soak up some gravy.

Jethan arched a brow at him. "Probably not."

Kasiel paused, the piece of bread almost to his lips. "Then why are you going to help me do it?"

"Well, the letter offered a meeting place close to our camp, so the greater risk falls on her. All we need to do is shout, and we've got all our guards there in a heartbeat. You'll also have Sylaryth and the three of us close by to make sure you're safe."

Kasiel ate the bread and licked a bit of gravy off his fingers, then gave Jethan a searching look. "That tells me why you think it isn't too dangerous. It doesn't tell me why you're enabling it."

Jethan stared out toward the Hall as he took another drink of his mead. "I don't know. I guess I feel like it might help you bring some closure to that part of your life. After all," he said, smirking at the tethdrak, who was intently watching every bite of bread or stew that approached their lips, "Syl really hates sharing you with all these people from your past."

"Oh, Syl does, huh?" Kasiel chuckled and handed the tethdrak a chunk of meat, somehow managing not to lose any of his fingers in the process.

Jethan winked and dug into the stew.

As evening descended upon the ruined town, the delegates and guards emerged from the Hall and retired to their camps. Nevias called Kasiel and his companions to the tent that was set up for the four delegates. When they entered, she was pacing as restlessly as Kasiel had been in the room earlier that day. Intense irritation charged the air within that modest space.

She stopped moving and faced him. "Ahninveth Hahren, I apologize for what happened in there. We were not made aware that the man who raised you was going to attend these proceedings."

"It's not your fault." He pushed aside a brief flare of irrational anger that needed someone to blame. "I apologize for losing my temper. There are several things I would have liked the opportunity to confront him with had I kept my head about me."

Her brows lifted. "I'm certain there are. I'm afraid we made little to no progress on any front today. Our healers are here at least. They allowed me to visit them briefly. They're being held under heavy guard in a room at the back of the Hall. However, given that we clearly don't intend to hand you over, the Alliance delegation has become a lot more resistant to our attempts to negotiate for their return. They want reparations for our violation of the Boundaries Treaty first."

She took a deep breath, hands coming to rest on her hips. Her gaze settled on Sylaryth. "They had to have known we weren't going to let them have you before we came. I'm curious what game they're playing, but that doesn't concern you. We may have to call you back in tomorrow, though I'll try to avoid it." She rubbed at her temples.

An uneasy chill tightened Kasiel's shoulders. What game were they playing? And why bring Edmund into this if they knew Vanris wouldn't give up a mind-crafter, no matter the circumstances?

"For now, don't wander out of the camp. The tent between this one and the cliff is open for your group. We don't want you out where anyone can see you overnight. Just a little extra precaution." Her gaze turned inward for a moment, a hint of a fond smile curving her lips. "Adnar would never forgive me if something happened to you."

"Thank you, Dhomen Nevias." Kasiel said after a brief silence in which he had half-expected one of his companions to say something. Were they letting him take the lead with her because of the circumstances, or because he technically outranked them all now? A concept that he was going to have a hard time adjusting to. "We'll go get settled."

After she dismissed them, they did exactly that, moving into the designated tent. They kicked back to crack a stone together while they waited for it to be time for his rendezvous with Danica. In a moment of over-exuberance, Sylaryth started sprinting around the tent. Unable to execute a sharp enough turn in the limited space, he plowed through the fabric at the back, creating a second entrance there. Kasiel hadn't expressly encouraged the tethdrak's behavior, though he might not have discouraged it either. A guard got added outside the unplanned doorway, but that would be easy enough for Jethan to deal with.

When it was time, Jethan stepped out through their custom rear exit and spoke to the guard for a few minutes. When he was done, the guard walked several feet away and stood staring out into the darkness. He didn't look back when they all slipped through the opening.

They crept along the side of the Hall, sticking to deeper shadows. The building Danica had chosen was close enough that they wouldn't have to worry about getting past many guards. The only other one who presented a problem Jethan easily chatted up and diverted, convincing him there was no reason to watch the area they were sneaking past.

When they reached the hollowed-out building, Darro peaked through one window. After a few seconds, he nodded to Kasiel and went to stand watch at the far corner. Kince took up position at the opposite corner. Jethan stayed with him to the door.

"I'll be right here. If you get even the slightest feeling that something's off, call me."

Kasiel placed a hand on Sylaryth's shoulder. "Thank you. I'll have Syl too. If there's danger, he'll probably be the first to let us know."

Jethan nodded, his unusually sober expression making it apparent that the situation set him on edge. "Just be careful."

Kasiel gave Jethan's shoulder a quick squeeze. "I will, tehnaak."

Drawing a deep breath and forcing himself to stand tall, Kasiel walked inside. Danica stood at the back of the main room. She had traded the dress for simple brown trousers and a tan shirt. Her dark skin and hair turned her into a shadow in the moonlight that shone through where large portions of the roof had collapsed.

She had been leaning against the wall, anxiously picking at her fingernails when he entered. Now she straightened. A hopeful, nervous smile teased at the corners of her mouth as she walked partway across the room.

"Kas, I didn't know if you'd…" she trailed off, taking several steps back when Sylaryth followed him in.

"Don't worry," Kasiel said, directing the tethdrak to settle near the door with a subtle gesture, "he won't hurt you." He took a few more strides forward, stopping when she retreated another step, this time from him. The reaction was a cut to his heart. "I won't hurt you either, Dani. I would never hurt you."

"I'm sorry." She met his eyes, holding his gaze for a long moment. Then she tentatively approached him again. "It's just, you've changed so much. So fast."

She stopped less than a foot from him, narrowing her eyes in the dim light from the moonlit sky above. One of her hands reached toward him, stopping to hang in the air between them. Suddenly he was the one afraid to move, to do anything that might startle her and cause her to retreat again. After a second of uncertain silence, her hand resumed its path. She traced part of the chain of his ke'hanoath with one fingertip. His pulse jumped, and he had to focus to keep his breathing even.

Had she always been this beautiful? This bold?

"It's not only physical." She reached up, touching his jaw to turn his head, so she might get a better look at the symbol on his cheek around the scar there. "I mean, I kind of like the physical changes. The way you filled out. Even your tattoos. It all looks unexpectedly attractive on you." She swallowed, her gaze moving down to where his shirt hung open again. "It's just that, working the forge meant I was always the stronger one. I don't think that's so true now." She breathed a nervous laugh. "But you're more confident, too. Stronger in a way that's not physical."

Kasiel drew a breath, trying hard to think past the nearness of her, the smell of her, the feel of her fingers briefly touching his skin. "Why did Edmund bring you here?"

"I thought I was here because my father believed in me. Because he and Edmund thought I could help them help you. Now, I'm not so sure." Her voice caught, and a tear slid down one cheek. She brusquely brushed it away, but another took its place. "I think maybe they see me as a tool to manipulate you. I followed Edmund into that room today because he told me to. He had to have already known I wasn't supposed to be in there. I think he wanted to make sure you saw me."

Kasiel reached up and brushed away a tear. The moment Nerith had done the same for him flashed through his mind. He swallowed against a seizing pain in his throat.

"How did you get out of the camp?"

She shook her head, a hint of anger in the tightening around her eyes. "I'm not important here, Kas. No one's watching me. They're too busy with their scheming."

The hurt in her voice tugged at him, but he could do nothing for her. They belonged to different worlds now. "I'm so sorry."

He moved to draw his hand back, but she caught it, sliding hers into it and twining her fingers through his. "Come home. I don't want to go back to Fernwallow without you."

"You have to. I don't belong there. I never did. Besides, even if Edmund wasn't a problem, I can't hide what I am anymore."

"Kas, I lo—"

He stopped her with a finger to her lips. "Don't."

She took that hand too and stepped into the space between them, leaning in to press her lips to his. For a second, he considered moving back and ending it before it really started. He knew that was the smart thing to do, but his body didn't care. The touch of her soft lips against his set him on fire, sweeping through every nerve with a sensation that made him feel indomitably alive. He pressed into the kiss, freeing one of his hands from hers and moving it around the back of her neck to encourage her closer.

Her lips parted. An invitation he accepted, sliding his tongue between them, joining with her as he had never done with anyone. She brought a hand up into his hair, pressing her lean, muscular body against him, quickly becoming the center of every heated thought racing through his mind. He moved his other hand, the one still holding hers, around her waist to press her in tighter.

Her thumb brushed his ear, sliding over part of the scar, and their reality crashed in on him. Kasiel ended the kiss, breathing hard as he released her and took a step back. His pulse was racing. He looked away, staring into a dark corner as he tried to regain control of the chaos in his head.

"Kas?" Her breathless voice had a tremor of uncertainty to it.

There was a soft knock by the door. He turned partially toward it as Jethan leaned in, speaking in Vanrian. "Sorry, tehnaak, but we can't stay here much longer."

Kasiel's jaw clenched in frustration. He made himself nod and answered in Vanrian, hoping it would remind Danica—remind him—how uncrossable the distance that lay between them really was. "I'll be right there."

When he looked back at her, she glanced away, clasping her hands in front of her self-consciously.

"That young man, he was there that night in the woods, wasn't he? I remember how you put yourself between him and the crossbow. Such a brave thing to do. So selfless."

He took a step closer to her again. "I wouldn't have made it this far without him. He's…" he hesitated. There wasn't time to explain the bond he and his tehnaak shared. "He's like a brother." An inadequate analogy, but it would have to do.

"I'm glad you have someone like that to look out for you." Something in her tone said that she envied him. That she wanted a comparable person in her life.

He reached out and brushed the backs of his fingers lightly over her cheek. Her skin was soft and warm. The contact recalled the sensation of her mouth against his, tentative and desperate at once. Heat flushed through him. He drew in a deep breath, struggling to keep his thoughts on track.

"I have to go."

She caught his hand in hers again and pressed her cheek against it. "I know." She met his eyes, then placed a light kiss on his lips before releasing him and retreating a step. "Be careful, Kas. I heard my father and Edmund talking this evening. They never expected to get you back. There's something else they're hoping to accomplish here."

An uneasy chill swept up his spine, chasing away the heat that had come with her nearness. "Thank you for the warning. Don't let them get you hurt."

It was an inadequate way to say goodbye, but he couldn't think of anything better. Sensing his intent, Sylaryth came to his side and Danica backed up. He set a hand on the beast, pulling strength from his presence to make it a little less difficult to turn around and leave. When he passed through the doorway, Jethan and the other two fell in with him, letting him have his silence as they made their way to the tent. Once there, he went straight to his bedroll and lay down. As soon as he closed his eyes, he was back with Danica, lips touching, bodies pressed together. It wasn't enough, but the memory was all he was going to get.

He said in his head then what he couldn't say out loud.

I love you too, Dani.

CHAPTER THIRTY TWO

The next morning, Kince, Darro, and Jethan stayed unexpectedly quiet about Kasiel's nocturnal encounter. Perhaps they sensed the rawness of the wound. He spent some of the morning trying to get into the heads of various mounts along the horse lines, seeing the world through their eyes in brief flashes. It worked, but it was different with them. More of a hostile takeover than the welcomed companionship he got with Sylaryth. He didn't keep it up for long for that reason and because of the way they saw the world. They lacked the spectrum of color that the tethdraks, or even humans, had. The way they could see on both sides of their head independently also left him feeling slightly ill after a while.

From there, he moved on to watching his companions out of Sylaryth's eyes for a time, until around midmorning when the tethdrak suddenly turned toward the Hall. He spotted Nevias stalking in their direction, her hair and armor picking up new colors through Sylaryth's vision. Pulling back behind his own eyes, he got up and drew the tethdrak to sit at his side.

Jethan came up on his other side. "She doesn't look happy. Do you think someone saw us last night?"

Kasiel shook his head. "No. This is something else."

When she reached them, she gestured for them to gather close. "Be ready to leave quickly. I've got some of our soldiers pulling together and preparing what they can without drawing attention."

"Has something happened?" Darro asked.

"I believe something may happen. The Alliance is stalling, and I don't think it's in our best interest to stick around and find out why. If something doesn't change soon, we're abandoning negotiations and heading home. Stay alert and don't wander." She started turning away.

"Wait." Kasiel met her eyes when she faced them again, dreading the answer before even asking his question. "What about our healers?"

Her hands tightened to fists briefly. She drew a heavy breath and let it out, giving the slightest shake of her head. "There's not much we can do. We'll lose too many people if we try to take them back by force, and we'd be breaking the neutral territory agreement here. I can't risk that over a bad feeling."

"If they're planning something, aren't they already breaking that agreement," Jethan snapped, an edge of desperation in his voice.

Tath.

"I'm sorry. We don't know what they're up to. Maybe nothing—"

"No," Kasiel interrupted, "they have something planned."

Nevias eyed him shrewdly. "I'm curious why you sound so certain of that, but we don't have time to discuss it now. Unless there's a dramatic change in tone in the next round of discussions, we're leaving here without our healers. I can't risk the delegation, and I absolutely can't risk you. Make sure you're ready."

They watched her walk away in silence, then Kasiel turned to the sky, searching.

"Kas, what—"

Kasiel was aware of Jethan cutting Darro off with a shake of his head. His tehnaak had already figured out what he was doing. After a few seconds, he spotted what he was looking for. A large raptor, probably a sandhawk, circled in the distance, watching for movement below that might signal a meal. Kasiel reached out to it, closing his eyes, and seeking entry into its mind. It happened so fast it felt like he stumbled into place behind the raptor's eyes.

The spectrum of color that greeted him was comparable to what he could see through Sylaryth's eyes, but the elevated vantage point and the soaring motion along with the expanded field of vision made him instantly nauseous. A hand closed on his shoulder, steadying him as he swallowed back a rush of bile and took control of the creature. He didn't like forcing it, but the situation called for urgency.

He turned to the ruins of Katovan first, spotting the Hall and the canopy they were standing under to orient himself. Then he swept out wide, searching the horizon.

"Which direction would an Alliance threat most likely come from?" he asked, struggling to hold his place behind the bird's eyes while maintaining enough of an awareness of his physical self to speak. A distant thrill of delight sparked in him when he succeeded.

"The nearest Alliance base is to the south and slightly east," Darro answered, "but they could bring in troops faster from the active front to the west of here."

Kasiel turned the raptor back toward the Hall, re-orienting himself again to figure out which direction would be west. Then he circled around that way. It didn't take long to spot what he was looking for. His gut twisted into an unpleasant collection of knots as he watched a large company of riders approaching from that direction. They weren't moving fast, perhaps to avoid creating a dust cloud that would warn the Vanrian contingent they were coming.

He continued soaring toward them for a few minutes.

Trying to calculate numbers at this distance was difficult. They were far enough away that picking out individual riders was next to impossible, even with the sandhawk's exceptional vision. A rough estimate of the company's size would have to be sufficient.

As he swept back around, something else caught his attention. A smaller group of riders coming from the north. They were closer and moving faster, traveling along the floor of a narrow canyon that would keep them hidden for a while yet. Still, the plume of dust rising behind their horses would become visible from Katovan before too long.

Kasiel returned to himself. The sudden transition from the raptor was disorienting enough that he had to bend over and brace his hands on his legs to stay upright. He focused on breathing for several seconds until the powerful urge to vomit passed.

Jethan squeezed his shoulder. "You all right?"

He gave a careful nod. "Yes. I've just never tried that with a bird before."

"Tried what?" An edge of suspicion deepened Kince's voice.

"He can see through the eyes of the creatures he connects with," Jethan answered for him, giving Kasiel a few more seconds to recover.

"Of course, because simply being a coveted Feral wasn't good enough. You had to be some Break-blasted prodigy," Kince grumbled.

"Hey, at least he's our Break-blasted prodigy," Darro countered. "What did you see, Kas?"

Kasiel straightened. "There's a company riding this way from the west. Moving slow like they're trying to avoid notice. Maybe eighty to a hundred strong. That's something of a wild guess, though. They're still too far off to get a good count."

"How far is too far?" Jethan asked.

Kasiel grimaced. The sandhawk's vision was so different from his own. It was hard to give a reliable estimate. "If I were to venture a guess, I'd say less than an hour. Maybe thirty to forty minutes out if they don't speed up significantly."

"So, the Alliance delegation is stalling for a reason. They may hope to get their hands on some higher pro-file prisoners." Darro's expression soured. "That's not a lot of time. We should—"

"Hold on," Kasiel interrupted. "I also saw a smaller group coming down from the north. They're moving fast along the floor of a canyon, heading this way."

A flicker of excitement lit Jethan's eyes. "Vanrian?"

"I think so."

Darro blew out a heavy breath. "Well, we unfortu-nately don't have enough information to know if we can count on them to rescue our healers."

As if sharing one mind, they all looked toward the Hall.

"What do you think?" Kince asked.

"I think it's risky," Jethan answered.

Kasiel didn't have to ask what they were talking about. He knew them well enough now to be on the same track. "She's part of our tehsheyn. I'm already leav-ing Danica behind. I don't intend to leave Tath, too."

Darro was fiddling with the hilt of his sword as if ea-ger to draw it. "Kince and I have been delegation guards here before. I say we enter the Hall through the side door. Nevias was talking to us a few minutes ago. Any-one who sees us heading over there will assume you've been called in to the negotiations again. Once we're inside, I can slip into the meeting room and pull one of our guards aside to tell them what you saw. They'll make an opportunity to warn Nevias, so our company knows what's coming.

"There's a hallway and a series of rooms that go up

the far side of the building to the back, where they're holding our healers. After I leave the warning, we can cut through the room we used yesterday to get over there. Most of our troops are out here or guarding the delegates in the meeting room, but the Alliance will have guards in that hallway and several in the back chamber where they're holding our healers. We won't get all the way in and back out without a fight."

Kince was nodding, his expression growing hard as he fiddled with the hilt of one of the several daggers he wore. His gaze settled on Kasiel. "Are you sure you want to do this, Kas?"

"You *are* the biggest target here," Jethan added. "You could sit this one out."

Kasiel shook his head. Maybe it was frustration at having to leave Danica behind again. Maybe it was how much he cared for this group of friends, including Tath. Whatever compelled him now, he had no desire to play it safe. "I'm coming. We can't expect anyone else here to go against Nevias's orders and help us. With four of us and Sylaryth, our odds aren't that bad." He touched the tethdrak, getting a mental shudder of anticipation from the beast. "One thing, though. Before we go in there, assuming we're going to make it back out, I want your word that you'll all say it was my idea if we get called in for acting without proper authorization again."

Jethan shook his head, but Kince and Darro nodded.

"You are the ranking officer," Darro stated with a smirk.

"And you're a Feral." Kince slapped a hand on his shoulder. "No matter how angry they get, you'll still be their favorite."

Kasiel gave Jethan a hard look.

"Blast it!" Jethan kicked at the ground, raising a cloud of dust. "I don't like the idea of making you pay for a decision we made together."

"We don't have a lot of time, tehnaak." He kept his tone firm while trying to let his affection for Jethan show through in his regard. "Please, give me your word. For Tath."

"Shit! Fine. You have my word. Let's get this done."

"Thank you." Kasiel turned, catching a quick nod from Kince and Darro, then started toward the Hall, Sylaryth keeping close beside him.

No one questioned them on their way to the side entrance, but the Vanrian guard stationed outside the door eyed them sternly. "Ahninveth Hahren, you should already know you can't bring your weapons inside."

Jethan shifted forward as if he meant to intervene, but Kasiel tried first. "Of course. We weren't expecting to get called in today. We'll drop them all in the room."

The guard's brows pinched together, considering his suggestion. Then he shook his head. "Maybe you should leave them with me."

Jethan stepped closer, getting the man to look at him. "Come on. You know you can trust us."

After a second of hesitation, the guard's expression relaxed. "Of course, Lord Jethan. Go on in." He moved to the side, opening the door for them.

Once they were in the room, Darro discarded his weapons on a bench. "Wait here a minute. I'll tell one of the inner guards what you saw so they can find an opportunity to alert Nevias."

Darro ducked through the door into the meeting hall. Less than a minute passed before he slipped back into the room and collected his weapons. "All right, it's up to Nevias to decide how to handle the approaching company. We've got our own mission to complete. This place isn't that complicated. We need to sneak past the entry guards, but they'll be posted toward the front of the main entrance, facing out. If we're quick and quiet, we should be able to cross at the back of the entrance without drawing attention."

Kasiel inclined his head along with the others, all of them responding immediately to the need for silence.

Darro nodded. "Good. Stay close. There's a room like this on the far side. It has an entrance to the hall going up that side and another one that leads into the series of rooms along the hall. I'm hoping it will be empty like this one, but we won't know until we get in there, so be ready."

Darro took point, setting a hand on the door lever at the far side of the room. He stood there for a moment, listening, then eased the lever down and pushed the door open. They slipped through in single file, pacing silently across the wide entrance area. Two guards stood at the front of the entrance hall a good forty feet away, one in a Vanrian uniform and the other in Alliance garb. As Darro had suggested, both were facing the open archway that led into the entry, pointedly not engaging with one another, something that worked to their group's advantage.

Darro barely hesitated at the other door, straightening, and stepping boldly into the room beyond as if he belonged there. That room was as empty as the one they had come in through, likely with a guard posted outside. Two doors at the back led deeper into the Hall. Darro walked to the second one and stood watching as they filed in and eased the door to the entry closed behind them.

"I think we have a better chance of not raising alarms if we cut up through the side rooms rather than the hallway," he whispered. "Any objections?"

"No." Jethan moved up next to him. "Let me go first. If there's only one or two guards, I might be able to Charm them before they make too much noise." He handed Darro his sword and dagger. "Stay out of sight."

Kasiel's chest tightened at the thought of his tehnaak

going in alone without weapons. But he had the perfect ability to subdue a solitary guard without violence.

They all moved out to the sides where no one would see them through the doorway. Jethan listened for a second, then he proceeded as Darro had at the previous door, opening it, and stepping into the next room as if he had every right to be there.

"Halt." The metallic whisper of someone drawing a sword accompanied the voice.

Kasiel reached for his sword, but Darro held a hand up to stop him.

"Oh, excuse me," Jethan sounded genuinely apologetic. "I was told there was a washroom in here somewhere, but this is clearly not it."

"Get out of here, you Vanrian pig," the Alliance guard growled.

"No need for insults, friend. You know, you really look like you could use a break. Why don't you find a quiet spot to relax?"

Something about Jethan's voice at that moment came across as incredibly soothing. So much so that Kasiel almost wanted to sit down and take a break himself.

They heard the sword sliding back in its sheath. A door opened and closed somewhere else in the room.

Jethan ducked his head through the doorway. "All clear."

They moved into the room. A rectangular table surrounded by chairs and benches occupied the center, and a long sideboard stood against one wall. A couple of cabinets were situated against another wall, piles of plates and bowls of various sizes stacked on the open upper shelves.

Kince moved up beside Jethan, a hint of a smirk turning his lips. "You laid that on so heavy we could feel it in the next room. The guy's going to be taking a break for a week."

Jethan grinned. "Fine with me."

Sylaryth flicked his tongue out to sniff the air and Kasiel followed his cue, catching the faint hints of something cooking from the next room. "Kitchen perhaps?"

Darro nodded. "There may be serving staff working in there." He met Jethan's eyes. "You want to try again?"

"Sure."

Sylaryth growled softly, a few low warning clicks rising from deep in his throat.

"No," Kasiel objected. "There's more than just serving staff in there."

Darro glanced at the tethdrak. "Handy, isn't he? All right then. We need a different approach. Everyone back against the walls again."

Darro and Kince stood on either side of the door. Darro directed Jethan to stand behind him and Kasiel to go behind Kince. The two in front locked eyes. Kince drew his dagger. Darro opened the door a crack, staying behind it.

"Someone there?"

Again, the sound of a sword being drawn. The point of a blade bumped the door further open, and an Alliance soldier advanced warily into the room, leading with his weapon. He had barely cleared the doorway when Kince grabbed him and yanked him through, driving his dagger into the gap between helmet and chest armor. Before he had finished taking the man out, Darro and Jethan were through the door. Kasiel hurried after them, avoiding looking at the dying soldier as Kince eased the man to the floor to keep him from making noise when he landed.

Inside the room, which turned out to be a modest kitchen, a serving woman sat on the floor in one corner, her eyes shut tight. Jethan knelt before her, his hand over her mouth.

"I don't want to hurt you," Jethan insisted. "Please, look at me for a minute."

She mumbled a protest and tears squeezed out of the corners of her eyes.

Ignoring them, Darro hurried to another door in the room, this one leading into the hallway, and pressed an ear to it.

"I only want to verify where the prisoners are." Jethan cast a frustrated look at Kasiel as she continued to keep her eyes closed, not giving him an opportunity to fully engage her.

Gut twisting with guilt, Kasiel sent Sylaryth to hover next to her. The tethdrak growled and her eyes popped open. She let out a scream, muffled by Jethan's hand, and tried to press herself deeper into the corner.

"I can make sure he doesn't hurt you," Jethan said.

The woman's eyes shifted to him.

"That's right. You're going to be fine now, aren't you?" Jethan's voice picked up that powerful soothing quality again, bringing a sense of calm over the entire room.

The woman slowly nodded.

"You know where the prisoners are, don't you?"

She nodded again, the fear in her eyes beginning to fade.

"Why don't you tell me? Then you can go take a little rest." Jethan cautiously lifted his hand from her mouth.

"They're in the last room, across the hall." She sounded almost drowsy.

"Excellent." Jethan smiled at her, and she smiled tremulously back, her eyes not wavering from his. "Are there guards in the hall?"

"Only two, guarding the door at the end." She sniffled, but the shaky smile remained.

"And how many are in the room?"

"Seven, I... I think. I'm sorry. They keep changing it, so that might be wrong."

Jethan took her hands and stood, lifting her to her feet with him. She didn't even look at Sylaryth. Her eyes stayed glued to his. "That's fantastic. Now, why don't you go into the next room, sit at the table, and lay your head down for a little nap? You've earned it, right?"

She nodded, full-on smiling now. "I have."

Jethan wrapped an arm around her shoulders to turn her, then gave her a gentle push toward the room they had come from. She walked through the door, stepping over the legs of the dead guard without looking down, and sat at the table. She rested her head on her hands, and her eyes slipped closed.

A shiver coursed through Kasiel. He looked at his tehnaak. "That was rather disturbing."

"Honestly, I agree, but it was effective. Thanks for the assist with Syl."

Kasiel turned to Kince and Darro, his nerves too fired up for him to accept gratitude with any grace.

"Well done," Darro said. "From this point, there should be two more rooms on this side of the hall. There's another hallway that runs behind the primary meeting room branching off on the other side, then the room the healers are being held in. If we enter the hall here, we can probably—hopefully—get to the two guards before they have time to raise much of an alarm, especially if you lead with Sylaryth. He'll be faster than anyone of us, and the surprise factor might be enough to throw them off."

Kasiel placed a hand on the tethdrak's shoulder to hide the tremble in it. Darro was asking him to use Sylaryth to kill someone. He had seen how fast the beast could take a person down when they went after Nerith's attackers. He had also noticed how effortlessly those claws sank through clothing and flesh. If he were being honest, he had even wanted to let him kill that man. But he hadn't. He hadn't played an active part in killing anyone. The armored soldier kicked by the horse outside Andaro might have died, but Kasiel would never know for certain, and he preferred it that way.

"Kas?"

He glanced at Jethan. Using Sylaryth would increase their chances of rescuing the healers and surviving this. It would help him keep his tehnaak alive. In the end, that was what mattered most.

He met Darro's eyes and nodded, moving closer to the door with the tethdrak.

"Out and to the left," Darro said. "No hesitation."

Kasiel nodded again. "No hesitation."

It was becoming second nature to slip into Sylaryth's mind and look out through his eyes. Kasiel encouraged the tethdrak into position and stepped back to make room for Kince and Darro behind him. He would send Sylaryth, who could move faster, after the farthest guard. They would follow and try to take out the nearest one before that guard could call for help.

Kasiel's heart was pounding, and not in a pleasant way. Trying to rescue Tath and the other healer was the right thing to do. They had no way to know if the riders coming from the north really were Vanrian and, if so, what their purpose was. Did that group know about the approaching Alliance force? If they did, were they trying to warn the delegation and get them out of here before it was too late, or might they be planning to put up a fight? It didn't seem like a large enough group to engage in combat with a company that size.

Regardless, the likelihood that Tath and the other healer might get left behind was too great. That was where the internal debate ended. He wasn't going to let them lose Tath. They lost Ahrin because of him. That was already too high a price to pay. Tath was part of their tehsheyn. His true family.

Kasiel drew on his anger. Anger with Edmund and Garrick for making him live a lie. For stealing him from his birth home, killing his mother, and cutting his ears. Anger with Arhk for putting people at risk to bring him back just so he could cast him aside. Anger with the Alliance for stalling to keep them here until more troops could arrive. He took it all and shared it with Sylaryth.

The tethdrak growled, a series of ominous deep clicks accompanying the sound. Darro and Kince both glanced down at the beast, then back at Kasiel, who gave an absent nod, his attention invested in the tethdrak.

Darro opened the door.

Sylaryth bolted through. Even not yet fully grown as he was, he was a massive, powerful beast. His claws dug gouges in the stone floor as he burst into the hallway. With his huge, lunging strides, he was at the opposite side of the hall in less than a second. Kasiel could see the two guards backpedaling toward the door behind them, surprise and terror contorting their features. Then Sylaryth was on them. He leapt for the second guard, but with a swipe of his claws, ripped open the face and throat of the first one as he flew past. His jaws closed on the face of the second guard, crushing bones, and Kasiel withdrew from him, struggling not to throw up.

Darro and Kince slowed as they neared the door, staring at the instantaneous carnage Sylaryth had wrought. The tethdrak faced them, blood dripping from his jaws as he stood over his kills.

Jethan grabbed Kasiel's arm and pulled him down the hallway to the others.

"Everything all right out there?" a voice called from inside the room with the prisoners.

Darro's jaw tensed, and he grabbed the door handle, shoving it open. It hit a guard who had been approaching on the other side, sending him staggering back. Kasiel swallowed his nausea and forced himself to reconnect with Sylaryth, doing his best not to look at the dead men as he sent the tethdrak through after his companions. He could join the fray with his sword, but Sylaryth had already shown that he could do considerably more damage with far less effort. Kasiel wasn't confident he could fight while controlling the beast, so he stayed where he was, letting the tethdrak be his weapon.

Through Sylaryth's eyes, he took a quick inventory. Rather than the seven guards they expected, there were nine in the room. The woman had told them the numbers changed periodically. The Alliance might have increased the watch, knowing how high the stakes were if someone spotted their approaching company too soon. Unfortunately, that meant the odds for their small team were suddenly less attractive, even with the tethdrak.

His companions were engaged in combat already. At the far end of the room, the Alliance had Tath and the other healer, an older man, chained to brackets in the wall. Three of the guards were close to them, one of whom drew his sword and grabbed the male healer. Whether he intended to kill the man or use him to bargain with didn't matter. The guards near the two prisoners were now the biggest threat.

Sylaryth sprinted across the room. He lunged for the guard, hitting him hard enough that both guard and healer went sprawling on the stone floor. The tethdrak tore the guard's throat out and spun. Another of the guards was charging at him, sword raised. He leapt to one side and twisted, reaching out to rip the man's calf open with his claws. The man cried out as he fell forward, hitting the floor with bone-cracking force next to his dead comrade.

Kasiel's stomach turned, and he fought to hold his link. Then two sets of hands grabbed him from behind. They covered his mouth and twisted his arms behind him, dragging him away from the battle. His visual connection with Sylaryth broke. Another man, dressed more like a mercenary than an Alliance guard, went past him into the room carrying a long spear. He smirked and shut the door, closing off Kasiel's view of the fight. Kasiel struggled to break free as they pulled him into a room across the hall. Another man wearing mismatched mercenary armor slammed that door and threw the bolt.

His companions were up against eight opponents now, and Sylaryth would undoubtedly abandon them to come after him. If that weren't bad enough, he suspected the man with the spear had gone in specifically to take down the tethdrak.

Kasiel dove back in, reestablishing his visual connection with Sylaryth, who was heading for the exit as predicted, leaving the crippled guard alive behind him. Kasiel spun the tethdrak around in time to see that guard crawl to the male healer where he still lay stunned from his impact with the floor and drive a sword into his chest.

Tath would be next.

He forced the tethdrak back after the guards by the healers. With a swipe of his deadly claws, he partially decapitated the crippled guard. Then he turned on the third one. The man backpedaled, his eyes popping wide. There wasn't time for mercy. Sylaryth lunged, tearing through the man's leather armor and into his chest.

In the other room, Kasiel struggled to break free of his captors while keeping most of his attention tuned to the battle through Sylaryth. His efforts were ineffective. As fit as he had gotten, his captors were still stronger and had the advantage. Something struck the back of his legs hard. He fell forward, knees hitting the stone floor with a burst of pain. One man holding him knelt a leg across his calves, pinning him down. That man wrapped one arm firmly around Kasiel's chest and twisted his right arm up behind him with the other. The man on his left cut through several straps on Kasiel's armor with startling efficiency, removing the pauldron and bracer on that arm, and leaving the chest piece hanging loose. Then he knelt and put one thickly muscled arm around Kasiel's neck. His other hand grabbed Kasiel's wrist in a vice-like grip, pulling his left arm down alongside him, and pressed a knee into his elbow to force the arm straight.

Though his own situation was turning desperate, Kasiel continued to hold his focus on the tethdrak. The guards in the back of the other room were dead now, and Darro had struck down one of the two he was fighting. That left six more. Jethan fought near the entrance, cornered by two guards. The man with the spear was running at Sylaryth. Jethan let out a shout, bright blood turning his sleeve red from a cut in his arm near the elbow. Sylaryth charged, ducking under a thrust from the spear to come to his aid.

Someone in the room with Kasiel started speaking. "The Alliance wants the boy alive."

"We should give him to them. We don't have time for this."

Kasiel didn't recognize the first speaker's voice, but the second caught his attention. It was Garrick, Danica's father, speaking close to his left ear. He was the one who had Kasiel by the throat and was holding his arm out.

"They don't understand how dangerous a Feral with the strength of his bloodline could be. Fools." That was Edmund, standing over him. For a split second, Kasiel saw both the back of the guard fighting Jethan as Sylaryth leapt upon him and the man who raised him staring down at him. The effect was dizzying. "If you insist on handing him over to them, so be it, but I need something from him first. I might not get another chance once the council has control of him."

Pain pulled Kasiel fully into the tethdrak. The man with the spear had caught him with a strike to the hip as he was biting through the spine of the guard he had taken down. The spear tip cut in below the natural armor on his back, but he twisted away with a snarl, narrowly avoiding a debilitating wound. That pain amplified the tethdrak's fury.

Kasiel was distantly aware of Edmund kneeling in front of his physical self and using a dagger to cut open the arm of his shirt. An ominous development, but he was too busy elsewhere right now, and the way they had him held, he couldn't stop them anyhow.

Sylaryth turned, squaring off with the spearman.

"Hold him there. That's perfect." Edmund's voice echoed strangely amidst the sounds of fighting around Sylaryth.

This time, the pain was Kasiel's. He cried out, most of his awareness snapping back into his own body. Edmund had cut a precise line in the front of his arm, opening a vein from the elbow down a couple inches along his forearm. The professor pushed the mouth of a flask up against the wound, capturing the blood that poured forth.

"I am sorry, lad. It's a shame that things worked out this way."

Kasiel spat in the professor's face. It wasn't helpful at all, but it was mildly satisfying.

Edmund's face reddened. He glared at Garrick. "Hold him still!"

Garrick removed his arm from around Kasiel's neck and grabbed his jaw, turning his head to keep him from doing it again. The blacksmith's rough fingers dug into Kasiel's skin.

"We don't have time for this," Garrick said again, his voice a low growl in Kasiel's ear.

Kasiel closed his eyes—it was the only way he could hold his focus now—and watched through Sylaryth's vision as the tethdrak moved in on the man with the spear, searching for an opening. He drove him back with a lunge, but the man wielded his weapon expertly, keeping the beast away. A cry rang out to his left. Since it didn't sound like one of his companions, he kept Sylaryth's attention on the immediate threat.

Pain made it increasingly harder for Kasiel to maintain his connection with the tethdrak. Not only from the cut on his arm, but from being forced upright by the man holding him with his lower legs crushed against the floor. His blood filled the flask and Edmund pulled out a second one, sealing the first and handing it to a mercenary standing behind him. Kasiel imagined the flask as an hourglass of sorts. When Edmund had what he wanted, his time would be up.

He clung desperately to his connection to Sylaryth. If he could use the tethdrak to free up the others, they might have time to return the favor, but the beast was still trying to get past the spear. Kasiel and Sylaryth growled together in frustration. A dagger flew from somewhere on the tethdrak's left, sinking deep into the man's throat. The spearman stopped moving, his eyes going wide. He toppled to the ground, his weapon hitting the stone floor with a final *clang*.

"Jeth, where's Kasiel?" Kince shouted.

The guards were all down. Darro was already at the back of the room, searching bodies for the keys to free Tath.

Jethan's eyes met Sylaryth's, panic rising in them. "I don't fucking know. Where is he, Syl?"

Sylaryth bolted toward the door.

Kasiel slipped into himself, losing his visual link with the tethdrak. He could still sense him, but even that connection was fading. Edmund corked the second flask and handed it up to the mercenary. Blood continued to stream unchecked down Kasiel's arm, now pooling on the floor.

"Take those out and put them in my packs."

"Yes, sir." The mercenary disappeared through a hidden doorway that opened in the back of the room.

A servant's passage. Kasiel smirked, his thoughts drifting. He had read about those in some of Edmund's books. They didn't have them in Vanris. Not that he had seen.

Another mercenary ducked into the room past the one that was leaving. "The Bane is in Katovan, Professor."

"We've no choice now. We'll never get away from Kasiel's father if we try to take him with us, and we can't let Vanris have him back." Edmund glanced at the mercenary. "Go make sure Danica's mounted and ready to depart." He picked up the dagger he had used to cut Kasiel's arm as the man hurried out. Pushing Kasiel's damaged armor aside, he pressed along his ribs to the left of his sternum, then poised the blade to drive between them. A hint of genuine sorrow moistened his eyes. "I never meant for all of this to end so violently."

His words strengthened Kasiel's desire to lash out at him. With Garrick still gripping his jaw, he couldn't even put voice to the venomous loathing uncoiling in his gut. He was going to die here.

One hand on the hilt, the other palm atop the pommel, Edmund tensed to shove the blade home. The door burst off its hinges and flew past them. Something slammed into them from the left. The point of the dagger pierced Kasiel's flesh, cutting to the side instead of stabbing in as the impact pushed him. Sylaryth snarled as he dragged Garrick off Kasiel.

The other man holding Kasiel let go, setting him free. Kasiel grabbed the dagger from Edmund, and half-lunged, half-fell forward, catching himself on one numb foot as he rammed the blade into the professor's chest.

It was difficult shoving the weapon in. Harder than he expected it to be. Although, having never stabbed anyone before, he had nothing to compare the experience with. He was also lightheaded and shaky. He let go of the hilt, leaving the blade in Edmund's chest, and swung his elbow up, cracking the professor in the jaw with it. The man went limp, collapsing to the floor unconscious.

Kasiel fell over him, catching himself with his uninjured arm. Blood still streamed from the other one. He slumped to the side, landing on his hip. The position provided him an opportunity to look around. Jethan was wiping blood off his dagger on the jacket of the mercenary who had helped hold Kasiel. A few feet away, Sylaryth stood over Garrick, most of the back of the blacksmith's neck torn out.

There was a horrid twisting sensation in his chest.

I'm sorry, Dani.

Jethan came to help him up. "By the Break, Kas, you're bleeding all over."

"I noticed. Let's get out of here?"

Jethan cast a dark look at Edmund. "Bastard," he muttered.

When they stepped into the hall, Darro and Kince met them. Kince had a makeshift bandage around one thigh, a bright stripe of blood seeping through it. Darro appeared uninjured. Tath was with them, also mostly unharmed if somewhat haggard looking. She glanced at Kasiel's arm and sucked in a sharp breath.

"We need to stop that bleeding now."

Darro led them to the kitchen, and Tath made a pressure bandage for his arm with clean dishtowels. She ordered him to hold it bent up above his chest. With that done, she made a snug wrap for his ribs where the blade had cut him and another for the wound Jethan had taken to his arm. In a matter of minutes, they were on their way out of the building. The doors to the meeting room from the hall stood open, the large chamber empty now. To save time, they cut across it, Sylaryth pressing close enough to Kasiel that it made walking awkward. The tethdrak's cut was in a spot they couldn't easily wrap, but the bleeding had at least slowed.

They were halfway to the exit, hindered by injuries, when it started getting darker and a familiar pressure began building. Kasiel recalled what the one mercenary had said.

"The Bane is in Katovan, Professor."

"My father's here."

"And apparently really pissed off," Kince added.

"But how can he alter the physical world like this?" Kasiel asked. He stumbled as he finished speaking and Jethan caught him, wincing at the strain on his own injury. "Sorry, tehnaak." He moved Sylaryth to the other side.

Taking the hint, Jethan switched places with the tethdrak, so his uninjured side was to Kasiel, staying close enough to offer support if needed.

"He can't change the physical world." Darro threw open the door of the room that would lead them out, checking to be sure it was empty. "But he can alter how our minds perceive it. It's like earlier when we could feel some of Jethan's soothing. He wasn't trying to influence us. He was putting enough into Charming the guard and that woman that we got some overflow. In your father's case, it overflows a lot, especially when he's angry. Probably because he's that powerful."

They could hear some fighting outside as they entered the room. Darro looked them over and grimaced.

"I can still fight," Jethan said.

Tath took a step forward. "I can fight too."

Darro glanced from one to the other, appearing less than impressed. "We keep Kas and Kince in the back. Can Syl still fight?" He met Kasiel's eyes.

Kasiel shifted his awareness into the tethdrak. The discomfort of their wounds was a distraction, but a sense of anticipation charged the beast, like an intense vibration that moved across the link. Adrenaline from battle—from drawing blood—still rushed through him. Kasiel did his best not to remember the carnage his companion had created.

"He's hurt, but he can still help."

Darro cracked the door and peeked out before pulling it the rest of the way open. That eerie, oppressive darkness blanketed the area, blocking out much of the sunlight. The light that seeped through hit the reddish dirt, giving a rust-colored glow to the fog of darkness. At least, that was what Kasiel saw. Did the others see it the same?

They struck out across the Vanrian camp. One of the abandoned tents was on fire, adding an orange cast to the surrounding area. Two figures fought off to the right at the edge of their visible range. As they advanced, a second group locked in combat came into view. Kasiel instantly recognized his father as one of the three, his white-blond hair hanging below the edge of his black helmet, the brightest thing in the darkness. The dark metal and black leather armor he wore bore a striking resemblance to his palace finery, only here the color blended with the unnatural darkness, making it difficult to track his movements. He wielded a dark metal blade that was equally hard to follow in the low light.

While Arhk fought the two soldiers in front of him, a mounted Alliance soldier charged out of the darkness behind him, battle-axe raised. Kasiel took control of the man's horse, panicking the beast and making it rear. Before its hooves hit the ground again, he had Sylaryth there. The tethdrak leapt on the horse's back, taking down mount and rider together.

Arhk's sword sliced through the neck of one opponent. He twisted under an attack from the other and drove his blade through the back of the man's armor. The two Alliance soldiers were still falling when Arhk turned. He glanced at the downed horse and rider behind him, Sylaryth standing over them. His gaze moved to their group, picking Kasiel out. Removing his helmet, he inclined his head in what might have been a gesture of gratitude and strode over to them as if he were walking along a hall in the palace. He scanned their group, his gaze pausing for an instant on each of their various injuries as he came to a stop before them. Then he shook the blood off his blade and sheathed the weapon.

The other Vanrian soldier, a woman wearing armor similar to Arhk's, finished dispatching her opponent and approached, halting a few feet back from the dhomvalen. A man and another woman dressed in the same armor stepped out of the darkness, stopping alongside the first woman.

"There should be horses nearby, if you would, Ahninveth Hahren." Arhk's voice remained unnervingly calm.

"Yes, Dhomvalen." Kasiel reached out into the darkness, easily finding the waiting animals. It was a simple thing to get in their heads and call them in, even as unsteady as he was right then. He could hear more horses approaching from another direction. A lot more. And they were moving fast.

"We arrived in time to extract our delegation before the Alliance company could attack. It helped that they had your warning and were prepared to depart." Arhk's gaze lit upon Kasiel with a flicker of approval. "We would be well away from this place if you four had not disappeared." His tone, unexpectedly, held no hint of anger or accusation. His attention lingered on Tath for a moment, shifting away when their horses emerged from the darkness. There were enough for eight riders. No one had planned mounts for the healers.

Arhk swung up on an impressive black stallion wearing black and dark metal gear that perfectly matched his rider's attire. The animal tossed his head and snorted. Kasiel barely resisted the temptation to make it rear. The idea made him giddy. A sign, he suspected, that he was ready to be done for the day. The other three mounted as well.

Darro and Tath helped the rest of them get on the horses. After giving Kince a long pensive look, Tath climbed up behind Kasiel, declaring that he was the most likely to need healing along the way. Her statement earned Kasiel another scrutinizing look from his father that he somehow met with a steady gaze.

Sylaryth came to stand beside their horse and Kasiel swept a sense of calm out among the animals to make sure they wouldn't spook at the tethdrak's presence.

"Dhomen Nevias said the man who raised you is here." Arhk didn't look at Kasiel this time, a hint of anger showed in the tightening around his eyes.

"He was," Jethan answered, sparing Kasiel the need to explain. "Ka... Hahren killed him."

The sound of pounding hooves was growing louder.

Arhk's expression didn't change. He turned to one of the female soldiers. "Lead them to the delegation."

"Yes, Dhomvalen."

A flash of alarm swept through Kasiel. "Wait!"

Arhk looked at him, one brow arched in question.

"Aren't you coming with us... Dhomvalen?" Kasiel nearly forgot the title. His thoughts were growing fuzzy.

"I'll catch up." Black spread across Arhk's eyes as he turned away. He donned his helmet and charged into the darkness toward the approaching riders, the other two soldiers following.

CHAPTER THIRTY FOUR

Arhk and his two soldiers rejoined them in the night. Kasiel didn't know when they arrived. His father was just there when he woke up, dusty and tired looking, but otherwise unharmed. They had put Kasiel and several others to sleep to tend their injuries once they were far enough away from Katovan to risk stopping. There were several others injured outside of those in their small group that had rescued Tath. Fighting had apparently broken out as soon as Nevias announced that the Vanrian delegation was leaving. The Alliance, their stalling tactics having failed them, attempted to use force to keep them there long enough for the approaching company to move in.

Fortunately, Arhk's unit arrived first. A Vanrian scout posted near the western front had spotted the Alliance company when it split off from their main force to head east. The scout had made a run for Etrion to report the suspicious movement. Upon receiving the information, Arhk pulled a small unit together, sacrificing numbers for speed, to try reaching Katovan ahead of the Alliance company to evacuate the delegation.

Had Kasiel not been there to see it, he wouldn't have believed his father had galloped off into the darkness to face a company of around one hundred riders with only two soldiers watching his back and returned unscathed.

It was a hard reality to get his head around. His father. The Beast of the Break. One of the most powerful mind-crafters in Vanris. No wonder the khevarin kept Arhk close.

Along the ride back to Etrion, memories of their rescue mission haunted Kasiel. The carnage Sylaryth was capable of placed greater weight on what it meant to be a Feral. The encounter with Edmund and Garrick tormented him, as well. He had stabbed his father, or rather, the man who had played that paternal role for much of his life. And Sylaryth had killed Danica's father. The people that connected him to his childhood in Fernwallow were dead or, in Danica's case, separated by events neither of them could have predicted. He wanted it to feel liberating, but it didn't.

He could recall the resistance of the dagger as distinctly as if he had just that second shoved it into Edmund's chest. It was still too hard to reconcile who Edmund turned out to be with the man Kasiel had grown up with. It left him feeling fragmented and full of sorrow. Maybe he would feel differently in time.

"The Alliance wants the boy alive."

Those were Garrick's words to Edmund. But why? What had the Alliance planned to do with him? Use him as leverage against his father, perhaps? Whatever it was, Edmund had been willing to take the chance to collect Kasiel's blood before handing him over. But the professor still thought killing him was the better option when he found out that Arhk had arrived at Katovan. Not that it mattered anymore. Edmund wouldn't be doing anything with those flasks of blood now.

No one confronted them about their unsanctioned rescue mission. Dhomen Nevias checked a few times to make certain they were all faring well but said little to them otherwise. The rest of the journey, she rode near the front alongside Arhk, though the two didn't appear to talk much. Once they were within a few hours of Etrion, Arhk and his three black-armored soldiers galloped ahead. The rest of the company under Nevias's command traveled at a slower speed to accommodate the injured.

They entered the city a little after dark, most of the regular soldiers breaking off at the barracks or splitting away to go visit the healers for ongoing injury care. Nevias led Kasiel's group and the other delegates to the palace. Once there, palace guards escorted them, rather slowly given the wound in Kince's thigh, to the increasingly familiar room with its curved table set upon the curved dais.

Aside from the door guards, the room was empty. Seconds after they entered, the double doors at the back opened. In the room beyond, Kasiel got a glimpse of several officers gathered around a long table. Khevarin Seylin emerged from that room and came to stand on the dais with Arhk at her side in a fresh set of clothes, the dust from the road washed away. He looked as if he had never left. Adnar walked out and stopped to wait near the edge of the long table.

Dhomen Nevias signaled the rest of the party to stop as she continued forward to kneel in the center of the room. The khevarin's gaze skimmed over all of them before she acknowledged Nevias.

"Rise, Dhomen Nevias. You may step aside a moment while we address Ahninveth Hahren and his unit."

Looking as puzzled as Kasiel felt, Nevias stood and moved to one side. Setting a hand on Sylaryth, Kasiel went forward with Jethan, Kince, and Darro. Tath joined them, though it was unclear if Khevarin Seylin considered her part of his "unit." When they moved to kneel, the khevarin gestured for them to remain standing with an abrupt lifting motion of one hand.

"As some..." She looked over them again and her

delicate brows pinched together. "As *most* of you appear to be injured, we shall skip such formalities. We merely wish to express our appreciation to you, Ahninveth Hahren, for the warning you provided regarding the approaching Alliance company and for the success of your mission."

Kasiel hesitated a moment. Had he heard her correctly? Perhaps the intense pain in his ribs and arm were messing with his head. "Our mission, Majesty?"

Her lips pressed together for an instant, and she cast a glance at Arhk, waiting until he offered a subtle nod before answering. "Yes. The mission to rescue our healers, as ordered by Dhomvalen Arhk Cavenos in Katovan."

It was all Kasiel could do not to stare at his father or turn to Jethan to ask if he had heard her right. He deepened his connection to Sylaryth, seeking balance in the tethdrak's surge of affection. Then he noticed the twitching at the edge of Jethan's mouth out of the corner of his eye. His tehnaak was fighting hard to hold back a grin. Kasiel had apparently heard her right.

He inclined his head. "It was our honor to serve, Majesty." He gave himself a mental pat on the back for keeping his voice steady.

"We will expect reports from each of you regarding the events in Katovan, but we have important matters to discuss with our delegates. For now, you may rest or call upon the healers if you need them, which you certainly appear to. Ahninveth Hahren, Ahndhomen Adnar has offered to escort your tethdrak to a recovery pen where its injuries can be properly tended so that you might focus on recovering from your own wounds."

Kasiel felt the gentle nudge against his link to Sylaryth. It was hard to let go after several days spent intimately connected to the tethdrak. The idea of being without him was almost daunting. He forced himself to relinquish control, getting resistance from Sylaryth until he passed a sense of calm reassurance through to him. The tethdrak strode over to Adnar and began following him from the room, a slight hitch in his step from the hip wound. Even with Adnar in control, Sylaryth stopped in the doorway to glance back at Kasiel before reluctantly leaving.

"Your unit is dismissed." Khevarin Seylin's cool regard hid whatever her feelings were about the odd situation. "Though we would ask you to join us in the war room, Healer Tath. You may have additional insight into the Alliance's betrayal of our neutral territory agreement in Katovan."

Paying little mind to their audience, Tath gave each of them a tearful hug, being careful of their various injuries. "I'll be checking on all of you tomorrow, except you, Darro. You're fine."

Darro winked at her. "I always knew you thought so."

The way Tath colored at that made Kasiel wonder if there might be something developing between the two. Now, however, it was time to leave, judging from Khevarin Seylin's arched brow as she watched their less than prompt departure. The four of them offered bows to the khevarin and walked, or limped, in Kince's case, from the room together.

As soon as they were outside, Kasiel glanced around at them. "Can my father do that?"

Darro shrugged. "I've never heard of anyone ordering a mission after it was complete, but apparently the dhomvalen has that power."

"The better question might be, why would he do that? He could be protecting his son from punishment for acting without orders." Kince grunted a few times as he spoke, grimacing with every other step. "He's your father, Kas." He looked at Kasiel as if expecting enlightenment.

"That helps a lot less than you might think," Kasiel said, focused on minimizing his movements to avoid causing himself unnecessary pain.

Jethan nudged Kasiel's arm with his elbow. "I think someone wants to talk to you." He gestured to one side of the hall with a tilt of his head.

Nerith stood watching them from the entrance to one of many sitting alcoves along the way, her hands clenched in front of her. When she saw him notice her, she moved as if to take a step toward them, then drew her foot back, looking uncertain.

Kince moved closer to Kasiel, wincing when he put weight on the injured leg. He grinned at Jethan and whispered, "If he kisses her, let me know how it compares to that kiss in the building in Katovan." He waved a hand in front of his face as if fanning himself.

Blood rushed to Kasiel's cheeks. "What?"

Darro smirked, offering his tehnaak a supporting arm. "It was impressive. Really. It surprised me that either of you could stand up after that."

"You callochs." Jethan threw a jesting kick after them as Darro helped Kince limp away, both laughing.

Mortified, Kasiel looked at his tehnaak. "Did you all see that?"

Jethan averted his gaze, trying and failing to control his grin. "There were a lot of windows in that building, and a distinct lack of shutters."

"Fabulous." Embarrassment gave way before a twist of regret as the image of Danica's father lying dead swept to the surface.

Something of his distress must have shown in his features, because Jethan's expression turned serious and he set a hand on Kasiel's shoulder, giving it a gentle squeeze. "If you aren't up for talking to her right now, I can make an excuse for you. You've gone through a lot.

She'll understand if you need time to recover."

"No. I'll talk to her. Would you mind seeing if we can get some food sent to my chambers, assuming you don't object to hanging out there for a bit?"

"Not at all. I was thinking of sleeping on your couch again." Jethan cracked a scoundrel smile. "Good luck." He strode away, turning back to give a quick wink before he vanished down another hallway.

Drawing a deep breath, Kasiel gave himself a mental kick to get moving and started toward Nerith. The shaky smile she offered him drew him onward. When he reached her, she took several steps back, beckoning him into the relative privacy of the alcove with one hand. The scar on her cheek was in the same place as his, though hers was smaller and cleaner, given the better care it had received. When he stopped in front of her, he stared stupidly into those lovely lavender eyes, his mind going blank.

She glanced at the heavy bandage on his arm that forced him to keep his sleeve rolled up and the bulge of the other one around his ribs, then met his eyes. "I heard things went badly in Katovan. I was worried." She swallowed, searching his face for something, though he wasn't sure what. If he knew, he would happily give it to her. "I told you I wasn't strong enough to fall in love with you, but I'm not sure I'm strong enough to stay away, either."

Her words broke through the silence in his head. He smiled, brushing a lock of hair behind one of her perfectly delicate, pointed ears. "I think you're a lot stronger than you believe you are."

A smile broke across her lips, bringing light into her eyes. She came up on the balls of her feet. He leaned in and met her lips in a gentle kiss. A flash of Danica slipped into his mind, but she was in his past now. Perhaps this was his future.

Nerith lingered a few seconds after the kiss, her lips almost touching his, their breath mingling, then she sank back. He slid a hand down her arm to her hand, twining his fingers through hers. The way her eyes sparkled with pleasure as her warm fingers curled in on his hand made him want to kiss her again, but there would be time for such things.

"Care to join Jethan and I for something to eat?"

"He won't mind?"

He considered his tehnaak and shook his head. "No. I don't think so."

They started walking together. He reached out with his ability, finding an instant welcome from Sylaryth. The tethdrak was already in part of the canyon, fenced off from the others where he could heal without being harassed. He was lying on a slab of stone that still radiated warmth from the sun, drifting on the edge of sleep. Kasiel drew away from him, letting him rest, and brushed his thumb lightly along the smooth back of Nerith's hand.

Her gaze sank to the wrap on his arm. "Are you sure this is a good idea? Shouldn't you be recovering?"

"I'm all right." If he were being honest, he didn't feel great, not physically nor emotionally, but things were looking up. "Besides, whether you're there or not, Jethan and I will probably be up for a while. Your company would be welcome."

When they entered Kasiel's chambers, Jethan was sitting in a chair with a healer re-bandaging his arm. A array of food sat out on the table. More than enough for all of them. The three goblets made it apparent that was no accident.

Kasiel gave his tehnaak a quick look of gratitude.

The healer, the same one who had tended the cut in his side the night they lured out Nerith's attackers, stood and bowed to him. "Lord Hahren." His gaze shifted to

Nerith after noting their twined hands. "Healer Nerith."

"Not a full healer yet, Iatan." She extracted her hand and gestured to the couch. "I assume he's here for you, my lord." Her stern look told Kasiel she expected him to sit and accept the man's ministrations.

He sat on the couch as Nerith took a place in the other empty chair, leaving room for Iatan to sit next to him. Nerith gasped when the man removed the bandage from Kasiel's arm. After he checked the stitched cut and applied healing salve and a new covering to it, he had Kasiel remove his shirt so he could tend to the other wound.

"You're gathering quite the collection of scars, Lord Hahren," Iatan remarked, glancing down at the lower scar.

"Yes. A habit I'm hoping to break," Kasiel answered with a wry grin.

When that bandage over his ribs came off, Nerith sucked in a sharp breath, her brows pinching together. "By the Break, Kas, I thought you said you were all right. Neither of those injuries qualifies you as all right."

Jethan smiled at him, an expression full of open affection. "Did he tell you he got those injuries because he was so busy trying to protect the rest of us that he couldn't save himself?"

Nerith's gaze softened as she regarded Kasiel. "No, he didn't."

"I believe saving myself was outside of my control." Kasiel clenched his teeth, trying not to flinch as Iatan spread the salve across the wound. He didn't want to prove Nerith right.

"I can finish that." Nerith shooed Iatan out of the way and took his spot next to Kasiel on the couch.

The healer passed her the rest of the wound coverings and collected his things. "You're in expert hands, Lord Hahren."

"Thank you, Healer Iatan." Kasiel didn't look away from Nerith as she repositioned the dressing, her fingers lighting fires in him as they brushed his skin.

Jethan stood. "I need to grab something from my room. I'll be back in a few minutes."

Iatan and Jethan left them. Nerith glanced up, meeting his eyes as she leaned in to wrap the bandage around his back. He brought his hand up, cupping her jaw, his fingers slipping into her silvery hair. As though sharing his thoughts, she moved closer, her mouth pressing against his in a melding of desires stronger than either of them. Her lips parted, and he could feel them curve in a smile as her tongue lightly teased his lower lip. Kasiel opened his mouth, letting the kiss deepen into something more passionate. His thoughts scattered before a molten flood of longing, and he pulled her closer.

Sudden pain in his side forced a sharp inhale. Nerith moved away, grinning guiltily, and pushed him back with her palm on his chest, her fingers covering the symbol that made the pendant of the tattoo chain.

She winced apologetically. "Sorry."

"If there was ever something you didn't need to apologize for, I'm pretty sure that was it." Even with the pain, he yearned to try again.

"We can revisit that conversation when you've had time to heal." She ducked her head, focusing on bandaging the wound. The way she smiled to herself as she worked, her cheeks now lightly flushed, made the discomfort worth it.

Jethan came back a few minutes later carrying a bottle of Vanrian Black Mead. He held it up as he entered the room. "Care to crack a stone with me?" He glanced at each of them and grinned. "Unless you need more time alone, that is."

"I think we're good for the moment." Nerith gave Kasiel a wink and got up to return to the other chair.

He caught her hand. "You can stay here with me, if you'd like to."

She nodded and sank back on the couch next to him, curling her legs up onto the seat. Kasiel left for a moment, going to find a shirt he could wear that was loose enough to put on over the bandages. Being half-naked with Nerith that close was far too distracting. When he returned, Jethan had poured the mead, and they each lifted their mugs.

"To surviving the second fall of Katovan," Jethan said.

"Barely," Kasiel added before he took a drink.

It was a sobering thought, though. Not so long ago, he wouldn't have been in a position to even know about such things. Now, as a Feral in Etrion, the situation between Vanris and the Pandrean Alliance affected him significantly, and, in this case, he had taken part in the shaping of those events. The Alliance's failed attempt to strike at the delegation and get their hands on valuable prisoners would increase tensions between the warring sides. That meant more battles would break out. Potentially a lot more. Battles he and his tehsheyn might have to fight in.

He was a soldier of Vanris now. His tehnaak was here. Sylaryth was here. His new family and Nerith were all here. Even his blood father was here, for what that was worth. Living his sheltered life in Fernwallow, he never would have dreamed of becoming a part of such things. That had been Edmund's intention from the start, to keep him hidden away and under control. But here he was, despite Edmund's efforts.

Nerith picked up a juicy slice of evalis fruit, breathing a laugh as she avoided his attempt to take it from her hand, and placed it at his lips. He grinned and opened his mouth, biting into the middle with his lips apart so that the juice sprayed them both. Giggling, she grabbed a linen and wiped it away. Jethan put his feet up on the table and proceeded to regale her with the tale of their "mission" in Katovan, starting with how Kasiel had used the sandhawk to spot the approaching Alliance company and Arhk's unit. It sounded impressive the way he told it. Maybe it was.

Kasiel watched them, a slow smile spreading across his lips. This was where he belonged. No matter what challenges tomorrow held, he would not have to face them alone.

THE END

ACKNOWLEDGEMENTS

If you've been in my life while I was working on this series, you know how completely it pulled me in. Kasiel's story has been an extraordinary adventure for me as well as an escape from difficult things. I am grateful to him and his companions for the joy they brought me while I shared their story on these pages. There are also many people who deserve my appreciation, so I will try to capture them all here.

To Linda, who was my first reader as always and provided so much support and valuable feedback throughout the process. I can't imagine doing this without you.

To Kai, who took the brunt of dealing with my constant distraction and obsessive need to write at all hours of all days, and still allowed me to read the book to him out loud. Thank you for your patience.

As always, my best friends and beta readers, Rick and Ann, who somehow continue to stand by me regardless of where my crazy goes. You are now, and always will be, my tehsheyn.

To my additional beta readers, Todd and Jordan, your feedback was invaluable. You are greatly appreciated.

As always, I want to acknowledge the fantastic team who helped me put together the finished book. Robert Crescenzio, my incredibly talented cover artist whose vision helps bring these books to life on the covers. Alexander Lockwood, my fantastic editor, fellow author, and now friend. Brian Short, my amazing formatter, whom I would also like to thank for your excellent company on many coffeeshop writing days. I love working with you all.

To my other friends and family, know that I love you and value your place in my life even if I don't call you out specifically here.

Last, but certainly not least, to my readers. To me, books are a collaborative effort between the author and their readers. Without you, this world would only ever come to life in my head. I hope you enjoy experiencing it as much as I did and will continue along the journey as the rest of this series releases into the world.

AUTHOR BIO

Nikki started writing her first novel at the age of 11, which she still has tucked in a briefcase in her home office. She lives in the magnificent Pacific Northwest with her wondrous cat-god. She feeds her imagination by sitting on the ocean in her kayak gazing out across the never-ending water or hanging from a rope in a cave, embraced by darkness and the sound of dripping water. She finds peace through practicing iaido or shooting her longbow.

•

Thank you for taking time to read this novel. Please leave a review if you enjoyed it.

•

For more about me and my work visit me at
http://elysiumpalace.com.

OTHER NOVELS by NIKKI McCORMACK

CLOCKWORK ENTERPRISES
The Girl and the Clockwork Cat
The Girl and the Clockwork Conspiracy
The Girl and the Clockwork Crossfire

FORBIDDEN THINGS
Dissident
Exile
Apostate

ELYSIUM'S FALL
Dark Hope of the Dragons
Dark Savior of the Dragons

STANDALONE WORK
Golden Eyes
The Keeper

SILVERBLOOD RAVEN
A Path of Blood and Amber
A Path of Secrets and Dreams
A Path of Storms and Reckonings

BLOOD OF VANRIS

Muscle rippled beneath the kanodrak's silver-gray scaled hide, her long claws digging into the stone under her feet like it was clay. The lashing of her tail warned of her irritation. Her milky white eyes watched him while he watched her in turn, his gaze drifting to the elongated upper canines that dipped be-low her lower jaw. She was a massive beast, at least a foot taller at the shoulder than the average horse. Kasiel, by comparison, felt rather unimpressive standing before her, his mind tentatively reaching out to hers in search of some connection. In fact, he couldn't remember when he had last felt as insignificant as he did now, facing that magnificent predator. Perhaps back when he was not quite five years old and Edmund, the man who would raise him as a son, had his partners pin Kasiel in the mud so they could cut off the tops of his ears.

A sweat broke out across his forehead as he tried to stop the surge of dark rage that memory brought up, but he wasn't fast enough. The kanodrak snarled and rejected Kasiel's mental presence with sufficient force that he staggered back a step. The beast lashed out with one paw, too swift for him to react, and swept his legs out from under him. Kasiel hit the ground, curling around the flare of pain in his still-healing chest. The stitches were long gone, but the area over his heart where Edmund's dagger sliced into his chest remained sensitive.

The vaguely feline beast lowered her armored head, the tips of those extended front fangs almost brushing Kasiel's face. Her milky white eyes stared at the side of his head as she sniffed at him. Then she snorted, depositing a spray of mucus on his cheek, and loped away.

Kasiel stayed on the ground, waiting for the searing pain in his chest to ease. Once he managed to catch his breath, he wiped his cheek off with one sleeve and sat up. Adnar stood watching him from outside the bars that walled the front of the canyon off from the habitat where the kanodraks resided. He tossed his head, throwing his long blond hair back from his face, the corners of his mouth pulling down.

Kasiel heaved a sigh and climbed to his feet. "That didn't go so well."

"Did she have her claws retracted when she struck you?" Adnar asked.

"Obviously. I still have all my parts." Kasiel struggled to keep the bitterness from his tone. Judging from the way Adnar's eyes narrowed, he failed.

"Then it could have gone much worse." Adnar unlocked the gate and held it open for him. "You need to focus."

"Maybe it's not me. Maybe she's the problem," Kasiel snapped.

Adnar's fist tightened on the bars. He slammed the gate behind Kasiel with a solid clang and slapped the lock into place. "Do you want to know how I know you're wrong?"

Kasiel drew a breath, trying to leash the poor temper that nagged him at every turn lately. "How?"

"Because a kanodrak is never wrong." Adnar double-checked the lock, then faced him. "If you are still having this much pain, perhaps you should not be working with the kanodraks yet."

Frustration burst like a white light behind Kasiel's eyes. "I'm fine. It's healing more every day. I can do this."

Adnar stalked up to him, glowering down at him with his head cocked to one side in an animalistic way. The ahndhomen wasn't that much taller than Kasiel, but his muscular bulk and the intimidating way he moved, like a predator about to strike, made him seem bigger.

"You're right, Ahninveth Hahren. It isn't your injury that's the problem. It's your head. You need to be one hundred percent focused on this, and you're not even close."

Hatred for his Vanrian name piled on top of his frustration. "I don't care! I have to learn this!"

Adnar didn't react at all to his outburst, and Kasiel suddenly felt like an idiot. He reached out to the next canyon over with his mind and found Sylaryth, his tethdrak, basking in the last of the late afternoon sunshine. The large reptile responded instantly, welcoming his presence with a glimmer of excitement. Kasiel slipped into his head and looked out through his eyes, seeing several more of the beasts lounging in the sun nearby. He soaked in the tethdrak's contentment for a second before drawing back to himself.

"Apologies, Ahndhomen. It's not the kanodrak," he admitted. "I almost died in Katovan because I couldn't balance my awareness between myself and Sylaryth. Worse, Syl nearly abandoned the others when I got taken. They might have all died if I hadn't succeeded in turning him back. I just need to get better at controlling my ability so something like that doesn't happen again."

The aggression in Adnar's stance faded, and he gave a slow nod. "This is something you will struggle with as a Feral. Only through practice can you perfect being in their head and yours at the same time. Particularly in your case. The ability to see through their eyes, while it does open more options to you, also puts you at greater risk. It is one thing to split your attention between more than one mind. Another entirely to see through their eyes and yours at the same time. Balancing that will be difficult."

Kasiel peered out into the habitat. The kanodrak was drinking from a stream that flowed along the floor of the canyon. As if aware of his scrutiny, she lifted her head and looked back at him. Her heavy tail swished once, and she flexed her long claws into the ground, then she trotted off deeper into the canyon.

"How do *you* do it, sir?" He asked, turning his attention back to Adnar.

Adnar's face could have been chiseled from stone for all the emotion it showed. "I cannot see through their eyes." He turned and strode toward one of several doors embedded in the west canyon wall. "We will work with the tethdraks tomorrow, Ahninveth."

Kasiel stared after him, at a loss for words.

Adnar, the powerful Feral, the only one in Etrion who could handle the kanodraks, couldn't see through the eyes of his beasts. Adnar told him the gift was rare when Kasiel first mentioned seeing through Sylaryth's eyes, but Adnar was a fourth-level ahndhomen. A mind-crafter of the highest rank under the Dhomvalen, who answered only to the ruler of Vanris. It never occurred to him that he might be capable of something Adnar couldn't do.

Kasiel walked along the tunnel that took him between the two canyons, rubbing at the long scar across the left side of his ribs. It hurt to push on it, but the scar tissue would limit his mobility if he didn't loosen it up. Edmund had intended the injury to be fatal. It would have been if Sylaryth hadn't burst through the door at that moment. The tethdrak's timely arrival had saved his life.

In the other canyon, Kasiel took the key and let himself in to the tethdrak habitat. Sylaryth came bounding up before he had finished closing the gate. Nearly full-grown now, the tethdrak's back reached up to about mid-ribcage on Kasiel. The dusty red scaling over his body had darkened as he matured. The darker mask pattern that ran around his eyes and up to his horns was a deep maroon now. His massive claws dug runnels in the hard ground when he skidded to a halt, stopping a few inches shy of slamming into Kasiel, who made no effort to get out of the way. He trusted Sylaryth.

The powerful beast angled his nose toward the ground, his backswept horns pointing to the sky. Kasiel placed his palm against the heavy armor plating on the tethdrak's forehead and Sylaryth pressed into it with a surprising gentleness. A series of contented clicks emerged from somewhere in his throat and a vibration moved through the closed frill around his neck. In response to his mental touch, Kasiel received a flood of affection from the beast and a weary smile curved his lips.

Overhead, the sky was picking up a hint of orange with the approach of sunset. He sent a quick thought to Sylaryth, showing him where he wanted to go. They turned together toward a large, flat formation of red rock that rose about ten feet above the canyon floor not far from the entrance. The tethdrak bolted ahead, lunging up the sloped backside of the formation to stand at the top. He flared the frill around his neck and called out with a high-pitched shriek, declaring the spot as theirs. Then he leapt off the other side and came bounding back to Kasiel, dancing from foot to foot with impatience.

Kasiel chuckled and broke into an easy jog, trying not to jar his sore spots too much as he indulged the tethdrak. They climbed up together this time and Kasiel sat at the edge, secure on the gritty sandstone as he dangled his legs off the side. Sylaryth lay down beside him, resting his uncomfortably heavy angular head across Kasiel's thighs. It was a discomfort he was content to endure for the bond they shared.

A few minutes had passed when Sylaryth's head jerked up again, and he turned to look back the way they had come. Kasiel slipped in behind his eyes, watching in the intense array of colors the tethdrak could see as Kenna and Jethan paused outside the gate, talking for a moment. Then Kenna let Jethan in and locked it after him. Splitting his vision, Kasiel tried to watch his tehnaak, his spirit sibling, approaching through Sylaryth's eyes while also tracking the slowly changing sunset through his own. The effect was nauseating.

"Kenna promised you wouldn't let the tethdraks eat me," Jethan said, joining them on top of the rock.

Sylaryth returned his head to Kasiel's lap as Jethan sat on Kasiel's other side. The orange was spreading across the sky, a hint of pink bathing the clouds at their edges. The horizon itself shone a bright, searing yellow that was hard to look at. Layers of soil that formed the towering canyon walls began to glow a bloody gold.

"We'll see how it goes. Is she joining us?"

Jethan reacted with a look of mock offense. "We'll see how it goes?"

Kasiel fought a smile, though he suspected the twitch at the corner of his mouth gave him away.

"Calloch." Jethan bumped his shoulder, earning a half-hearted snarl from Sylaryth for the disturbance. "She's not. I asked her to do a quick favor for me. How did training go with the kanodrak?"

Irritation flared in Kasiel and Sylaryth tensed in response. Aware of how sensitive the tethdrak was to his moods, he tried to quell the emotion. "Not great. Adnar wants me to go back to working with the tethdraks tomorrow. He says I'm not focused enough."

Jethan picked up a pebble and tossed it off the side of the formation. He gazed out, the brilliant sunset reflecting in his eyes as its colors gradually climbed the glowing walls. "He's right, Kas. I've noticed it too. You haven't been yourself since Katovan."

The muscles through Kasiel's jaw and shoulders tightened as he stared hard into the canyon, clinging to his silence like a shield.

"You can talk to me about whatever's bothering you, you know."

The irritation flared again and Sylaryth lifted his head, claws digging into the rock. "I don't want..." he started to raise his voice, then stopped himself. This was Jethan. No one deserved his temper less than his tehnaak did. "I'm sorry." Sylaryth's feet relaxed, his claws leaving behind gouges the stone. "I'm just... I haven't been sleeping much."

Jethan was quiet until the tethdrak settled his head down on Kasiel's thighs again. Then he said, "Is it because of what happened with Edmund?"

Kasiel clenched his teeth and nodded. "Sometimes. I have nightmares where I stab him again like I did in that room. Only in my dreams, he grabs my hand that's holding the dagger in his chest and won't let go. He starts crying, telling me how he wishes things could have been different. I can't pull away, even though I know I'm going to bleed to death from the wounds he inflicted. Then I see bottles of my blood sitting on the table, fifteen or twenty of them, and I realize I'm already dead, I just haven't fallen over yet because he's holding onto me. The absurd thing is, I still feel guilty in the dream for stabbing him."

When Jethan opened his mouth to speak, Kasiel held up a finger to stop him. He slipped back behind the tethdrak's eyes to see the sunset in that more brilliant array of colors, letting it distract him as he continued. "That's not all. There are also the nightmares with Danica. She's crying and screaming at me for killing her father. Her face is mangled, torn open by the claws of a tethdrak." He set a hand on Sylaryth's shoulder. "My tethdrak. There's blood dripping from her jaw. I can see her teeth and tongue moving through the jagged rips in the side of her face, but she won't let me help her because I killed her father."

Jethan let out a low whistle. "By the Break, Kas, it's no wonder you can't sleep or focus."

Kasiel swallowed against the tightening in his throat. The searing light had climbed almost to the top of the canyon walls now, casting a red glow into the spreading darkness below. "I killed them, Jeth. I killed the man who raised me and the father of the girl I loved."

A sharp edge entered Jethan's tone when he spoke. "Technically, Syl killed Garrick, and you know why. Because they were killing you. They deserved it."

"Dani didn't deserve to lose her father. Her mother died of a sickness that got into her lungs when Dani was seven. She didn't have anyone else."

"Maybe that's true, but you didn't deserve to be kidnapped and have your ears cut as a child, either. They lied to you your whole life and used you for experiments. I know Edmund was the only father you knew growing up, but you've got to let him go. You have a tehsheyn now. A chosen family that won't use you or lie to you. Let us in."

Kasiel glanced over at his tehnaak, fighting the wave of nausea that came with trying to hold on to that split vision. "I know you're right, but I'd never killed anyone with my own hands before that. Starting with the man who raised me..." He retreated fully behind his own eyes to stare down at his palms.

Jethan shifted closer and put an arm around his shoulders. "Hang in there. It will get easier in time. Until then, you've got me, and you've got that big bastard." He gestured to Sylaryth with his free hand and the tethdrak lifted his head to snort at him.

Kasiel chuckled softly, the brief humor not quite penetrating the melancholy that hung over him.

Sylaryth stood suddenly, staring at him expectantly.

Jethan looked at the beast, then at Kasiel. "I take it you're ready to head in?"

Kasiel nodded. Sylaryth was always the first to catch on to his desires and intent, sometimes before he was aware of those things himself. They stood, and he paused long enough to place a hand to the tethdrak's forehead before heading out through the gate with his tehnaak.

"Have you come up with any theories as to why Edmund wanted your blood bad enough to risk dying for it?" Jethan asked while he waited for Kasiel to lock the gate behind them.

"No comforting ones, but I don't suppose it matters now. Unless you think he could have survived." Kasiel's chest seized at the thought. That fear had also haunted his dreams and sabotaged his tenuous focus of late.

Jethan shrugged, his gaze moving up to where the last hints of sunset were turning a dark purple on the horizon. "It isn't impossible. It would depend on how deep the wound was and how fast help arrived, if it ever did."

"That isn't going to help with my nightmares," Kasiel muttered dryly.

Jethan waved his comment away. "I've got an idea for that. Let's get some food and I'll tell you all about it."

"All right. I'll try anything at this point."

They strolled to the palace in comfortable silence.

A private smile curved Jethan's lips now and then when he peered out into the evening streets. Kasiel considered asking about it, but he didn't feel like chatting. Perhaps that was selfish. His tehnaak was clearly pleased with something. Maybe after they had eaten, he would find the energy to be more social.

When they arrived at Kasiel's private chambers in the palace, Jethan stopped outside the door. "I almost forgot. I need to grab something from my room. I'll be right back."

The mischief in his grin captured Kasiel's curiosity at last, but he trotted off down the hall too fast for questioning. Kasiel vowed to give it the attention it deserved when his tehnaak returned. He walked into the large sitting room outside his bedroom, where a covered tray waited on the table. Whatever delectable dishes lay hidden within smelled fantastic. He closed the door and started in that direction, halting mid-step when someone knocked. Puzzled, he turned and opened it. A slow smile crept across his lips.

Nerith stood there, one side of her silvery hair pulled up in a braid that showed off a pointed ear with several decorative cuffs and earrings upon it. Her lavender eyes glinted with delight as she smiled at him. Then she put her arms around his neck and kissed him as she advanced into the room, moving him back. He slid one arm around her waist, pushing the door shut behind her with the other, and kissed her in return, frustration and sorrow slipping away as she opened her soft lips to him.

After a moment, he drew back and met those captivating eyes. He had yet to see anyone else in Etrion with eyes quite that color. "I thought you were working late with the healers again tonight."

She stepped back against the door, her arms sliding away until her hands rested on his shoulders. "Someone convinced me that a night off might be good for me, especially with the right company."

He chuckled, recalling the mischief in his tehnaak's eyes and that pleased little smile. "Someone being Jeth."

She grinned.

"He's not coming back tonight, is he?"

Nerith shook her head, tapping him lightly on the nose with one finger. "Nope. You're all mine tonight."

They migrated to the couch and ate together while Kasiel asked about her last several days of training as a healer. Soon, she would undergo testing to see if she was ready to advance to the status of full healer. It was easy enough, given her nervous excitement around the coming assessments, to keep her talking about that. It allowed him to avoid burdening her with the things that troubled him. Twice she tried to redirect the conversation to him, but he found ways to flip it back quickly. He didn't want to dwell on the dark places his mind had been stuck in of late. Better by far to let her dominate his thoughts for a few hours.

When they finished eating, they lingered on the couch, sipping mead for a time. Nerith traced the coppery-red symbol tattooed around the scar on his right cheek with one finger. She had a similar scar on her cheek now, given to her by a trio of men who didn't approve of Kasiel's presence in Vanris. Those three loitered in prison cells now, however, while she sat here with him, warm and safe.

Her head came to rest on his shoulder. She ran her finger along one side of the chain of symbols and runes tattooed around his neck, the final symbol hanging like a pendant on his breastbone. Letting his head fall back on the couch, he closed his eyes, getting lost in the feel of her touch on his skin. Her hand sank from there down to the scar across the left side of his chest, finding it through the light fabric of his shirt.

"Want me to rub this?"

He cracked one eye open to look at her. "Not really."

Whenever she suspected he wasn't rubbing it enough, she was quick to step in, and she was merciless. Even with the threat of that torture, he wished they had more time to spend together. The extensive hours she dedicated to working in the healer's building to prove to her instructors that she was ready to graduate left little time for them. It wouldn't be much longer, though. When she passed her tests, as he was confident she would, they would have more time for moments like this.

Nerith breathed a laugh. "Oh, so fragile."

"I'll have you know I was raised to be quite fragile," he answered, lightly tickling her side with the hand wrapped around her waist.

She squirmed, grabbing his wrist, and kissed his shoulder. "Then the man who raised you failed miserably."

He opened his eyes, regarding her thoughtfully as a flame of uncertainty ignited in his chest. "Are you tired?"

"Mm-hmm."

"Want me to walk you home?" That wasn't at all what he longed to do with her, but they were both tired and distracted. She deserved his full attention if they took their relationship farther. Not to mention, having never gotten beyond kissing someone, he worried he might make a fool of himself trying.

Nerith shook her head and stood, pulling on his hand to draw him up with her. She led him into the bedroom and sat him on the bed as insecurity and longing waged war in his body. Slowly, she lifted his shirt off, pausing a moment to admire him, something he suspected she wouldn't have enjoyed as much before all the combat training beat the spindly teenager out of him. She removed her shoes while he pulled off his boots, then went to his wardrobe and got out a pair of soft sleeping trousers and one of his longer shirts. The former, she tossed to him. The latter, she took into the bathing room. She returned a few minutes later, giving him just enough time to change into the trousers, wearing his shirt in place of her clothes. It hung almost to her knees.

Kasiel watched her walk around the bed and climb under the covers, hoping the hunger she sparked in him didn't show through too much. Apprehension lost power before his desire to touch her in so many ways, but her drowsy smile said tonight was not that night. He could be content just having her close. Taking a deep breath to calm his heart and the yearning smoldering at his core, he slipped into the bed next to her. Nerith moved over against his side and rested her head on his chest. Kasiel wrapped his arm around her and placed a kiss on her forehead. Then he settled back and closed his eyes, waiting for his racing pulse to slow so he could sleep.

Coming soon...